O nce a year, ~~~~~~ the first snowstorm, they opened the front doors wide and dragged in a big pine tree from outside. The same people who scolded him when he came in with muddy paws ignored bugs and dirt and sap and set the tree right smack in the middle of the living room carpet. They hung round, shiny objects from the branches and strung twinkling lights from top to bottom. Then, when that was all done, they placed boxes underneath the lowest branches. Everyone who came to visit gathered around the tree to give each other presents that weren't half as much fun as catnip or a ball of yarn. All things considered, it was a most puzzling time of the year.

—from "Home for the Holidays" by Barbara Bretton

THE
CHRISTMAS
C A T

Julie Beard   Jo Beverley
Barbara Bretton
Lynn Kurland

BERKLEY BOOKS, NEW YORK

THE CHRISTMAS CAT

A Berkley Book/ published by arrangement with
the authors

PRINTING HISTORY
Berkley edition / November 1996

The Putnam Berkley World Wide Web site address is
http://www.berkley.com/berkley

ISBN: 0-425-15542-0

BERKLEY®
Berkley Books are published by The Berkley Publishing Group
200 Madison Avenue, New York, New York 10016.
BERKLEY and the "B" design
are trademarks belonging to Berkley Publishing Corporation.

PRINTED IN THE UNITED STATES OF AMERICA

10 9 8 7 6 5 4 3 2 1

Contents

My True Love Gave to Me

Julie Beard

Chapter One

"Have yourself a merry little Christmas," Anne Clancy sang to herself, humming along with Johnny Mathis.

She clutched the pewter unicorn dangling from her neck with one hand and turned up the volume on her CD player with the other. The sad, sweet melody swelled through her cottage.

She circled her bulging Scotch Pine Christmas tree, grabbed an iron poker, and jabbed the orange embers sizzling in the fireplace. Satisfied that all was in order, she turned back to the picture window for the hundredth time that day and sighed, staring at the swirling snowstorm.

Anne could not appreciate the veritable Currier and Ives white Christmas scene that nature was dumping onto her wooded Wisconsin landscape. She was too busy scanning the horizon, searching for a black furball, a mewing cinder in a sea of white. But there was no sign of her precious black cat, and realizing it had been a week since she'd last seen the feisty feline, a surge of sadness threatened to ruin Anne's Christmas Eve.

"Damn it, Niner, where are you?" she muttered tensely, remembering with affection the peculiar way he would shut one green eye in a human-like wink.

She swiped hot tears from the corners of her eyes and swallowed a quivering breath. Niner was gone. She simply had to face it. Her beautiful black cat had run away and would probably never come back.

Heaving a sigh, Anne headed toward the kitchen for a little Christmas cheer. She glanced at her reflection in the hallway mirror, grimaced at the tangled spray of her long, reddish-gold hair, and tugged at her bangs. Her eyes were puffy, and she hoped her neighbor wouldn't drop by and see that she had been crying. Mrs. Jensen worried over her like a mother hen.

"I *will* have a good Christmas Eve," Anne pronounced, pulling open the refrigerator door with force and plucking out an unopened carton of eggnog. "I will, I will, I will. I will be happy and cheerful and grateful for all my blessings. Even if I *am* all alone."

Buoyed by her affirmation, Anne poured herself a cup of the sweet drink and nestled in an overstuffed chair before the flickering fire. She pulled her legs up under her hips and smoothed out the pleated folds of the floor-length green and red Christmas gown her mother used to wear. Just because Anne was alone was no reason to schlep around in jeans over the holiday. As soon as she was comfortable in the chair, the doorbell rang.

"Naturally," she muttered, rising reluctantly.

"Anne, are you there?" Mrs. Jensen's muted voice piped through the front door, followed by a knock.

"On my way!" Anne responded. She slipped her stockinged feet into her leather slippers and padded to the door.

"Anne, I was hoping you'd go away for Christmas, dear," Mrs. Jensen said even before Anne had swung the door fully open. "You shouldn't be alone."

That's what her mother would have said, Anne realized, and blinked with a surge of longing. Her mother had passed away a year ago last Sunday.

"Have you been crying?" Mrs. Jensen queried.

"No, not really." She brushed her fingertips beneath her eyelashes, searching for any telltale tears. "I was cutting an onion."

Her gray-haired neighbor narrowed her bright eyes skeptically, and Anne's resolve wilted.

"Oh, why pretend? I am so upset about Niner running away that I can't think straight. You'd better step inside before you freeze to death."

"I won't be but a minute." Mrs. Jensen stomped her

snow boots on the welcome mat. "You should have flown east to visit your college friend, just to get your mind off your troubles."

"I couldn't. Not as long as Niner is out there, alone somewhere. If he came back and I was gone, I'd never forgive myself. On the other hand, if he does come back, I swear I'll kill him for being so damned adventurous! I was going to give notice this month to the guy who owns the house and move to Milwaukee in January, so I can get on with my life. Now that Mom is gone, no since sticking around here. But I don't want to go until I'm sure Niner is . . . well, I want to be sure he's not coming back."

At the age of twenty-seven, Anne was ready for some adventure. She'd often thought she should take a page out of her cat's life. She'd named him Niner because he was such a daredevil, she'd been certain he'd use up every one of his nine lives. In fact, Niner had had eight distinct brushes with death. The last one was just six months ago, when he'd nearly been run over by a car on the road in front of Anne's cottage. Too bad his proverbial ninth life had apparently gone to waste.

"Well, dear, let's not worry about the future tonight. It's Christmas Eve. I came over for two reasons. First, I wanted to thank you for sending the postcard. It was lovely."

"You liked it?" Anne smiled. She was an unabashed sponge for praise and always perked up when someone complimented her artwork.

"Your best ever."

"Which one did I send you? I can't remember. I painted twelve this year."

"Well, it had a man on the front with a nest on his head. He looked like a sexy Father Christmas."

"That was the Lord of Misrule. Isn't he handsome? As far as I'm concerned, you could put the Lord of Misrule on a Wanted poster for my own personal 'Mr. Right.' I found him in a history book. I based him on a drawing by an anonymous medieval artist."

Anne led Mrs. Jensen to the art table, where Anne had laid out her twelve original paintings. They comprised a series of scenes that she'd produced for Personal Mementos, the greeting card manufacturer in Milwaukee that Anne worked for as a freelance artist. Each scene represented one of the twelve days of Christmas. Anne'd had copies made for her own limited edition, which she sent to friends and prospective clients.

"You see, Mrs. Jensen, the first card depicts a lord and lady lighting the Yule log. That happens on Christmas Eve, which is the eve of the first day of Christmas. The next card is the one you received. He's the Lord of Misrule. Often the Lord of the castle would hire someone to act as the Lord of Misrule, to oversee the holiday festivities, sort of like a medieval emcee, I guess. I hope I'm not boring you. I just love talking about medieval history. I find it so fascinating."

"Not at all, dear. Please, go on."

With great enthusiasm, Anne explained the other scenes—the hunting of the wild boar, the wassail bowl, the exchanging of gifts.

"No partridge in a pear tree?" Mrs. Jensen asked.

"No, but I did think of that song when I was doing my research. The last card, of course, is Twelfth Night, which is January 6th, or Epiphany. That was the time when the Wise Men presented their gifts to baby Jesus. Look, do you see the pots of incense and myrrh in the foreground? I also showed a wild celebration in the background, since Twelfth Night was frequently a time for mischievous and raucous parties in Merry Olde England."

Mrs. Jensen peered up at her over bifocals with warm brown eyes. "You're such a bright girl, Anne. I'm so glad my son invited his friend."

The cozy spell Anne had worked herself into while discussing history slowly dissipated. "What did you say?"

"I said my son has invited a friend from Milwaukee to join us tonight for Christmas Eve dinner. I want you to meet him. He loves history, too."

Anne let out a slow breath through her thinned lips. Mrs. Jensen was always trying to play the matchmaker. Anne couldn't really decline the invitation. But she was in no mood for the polite chitchat required of two people scoping each other out for possible romance. Sad to say, Anne would rather spend the evening gazing at her painting of the Lord of Misrule. Now there was a man! He was dark and handsome, but he also clearly had a devilish sense of humor. Just the kind of man Anne would want to marry, *if* she ever decided to try wedded bliss again.

She'd been married for all of six months during college, until David's parents had discovered that their only son had eloped. They'd insisted on an annulment, and David, never one for sticking to his guns, had knuckled under the pressure. Anne would never forgive him for that, though she later realized she was glad she wouldn't have to spend the rest of her life with a man who didn't have the strength of character to stand up for her. She'd vowed then that if she ever married again, she would marry a strong man. Someone who would fight for his marriage. Or, to put it in a medieval context, someone who would fight for his lady's honor.

"Do you want to talk about it, dear?"

Anne shook herself from her reverie, only to realize Mrs. Jensen had been scrutinizing her with a worried frown, apparently for some time.

"Do I want to talk about what?"

"The funeral. That's what you were daydreaming about, wasn't it?"

"No, I— Actually, I haven't thought about Annabelle's death all day. I don't have any regrets about missing the funeral. Even though she was my namesake, I didn't really know her that well. She lived in New York. We just talked now and then on the phone. If I'm upset at all, it's because she was Mom's best friend. Somehow, losing Annabelle was like losing my last living connection with Mom. But more than sad, I'm a little spooked that Mom and her best friend both died on the same day exactly one year apart. December seventeenth. A week ago."

Mrs. Jensen frowned again. "The seventeenth? Isn't that the day Niner ran away?"

Anne bit her lower lip, calculating. "You're right. Wow, now I'm *really* spooked." The fine hair on her nape rose to attention. She shrugged, feigning a light heart, and retrieved her cup of eggnog from the end table near the fire. "Can I get you something to drink?"

"No, I've got to get back to the house and put the turkey in the oven. But you must come over later. Say, around six? And if that nice young man gets lost, point him down the road to our house."

"Will do. Thanks, Mrs. Jensen. And Merry Christmas." Anne gave her a peck on the cheek.

"Merry Christmas to you, too, dear. See you later."

Anne watched through the picture window to make sure Mrs. Jensen made it to her two-story farmhouse across the snow-covered field separating their properties. Then she sank into her chair by the fire and dreamily gazed into the blazing yellow flames. Scenes from her postcards danced in her head like sugarplums, and she wondered, what if?

What if she were a medieval Lady who had just ignited the Yule log, marking the beginning of the joyous holiday season in her magnificent castle? And what if there were a handsome lord who held her hand as she lit the fire, his touch igniting a blaze of passion inside her? A man who could satisfy the longing she sensed was sleeping deep within her. A lord who adored her and defended her with every ounce of his being.

But then "what ifs" paled in the harsh light of reality. How would she deal without commodes and central heating? Every day would be a struggle. Life then was often short and brutal. Yet she was certain it was also vibrant. No one wasted time filled with angst about the future, because no one was certain that there would be a future. People then lived as fully as possible. With the specter of death so near, life must have been very exciting.

Another knock on the door sharply ended Anne's fantasy. She sighed and stirred again from her comfy chair. It was probably dear Mrs. Jensen. Or so she thought, until she swung the door open and found no one. She was certain she'd heard a knock. Anne poked her head out the door.

"Mrs. Jensen? Mrs. Jensen?"

Anne wrapped her arms around herself and stepped into the frantic swirl of snow just far enough to peek around the corner of her house. In the fifteen minutes since her neighbor's departure, the blizzard had turned into a virtual whiteout. She couldn't see an arm's length ahead of herself.

"Lord, I'll be socked in by morning," she said worriedly. "Well, whatever Mrs. Jensen wanted obviously hadn't been that important."

Anne headed for the door, brushing a dusting of snow from her shoulders. She glanced at the empty mailbox by the door, then halted abruptly.

It wasn't empty.

There was a piece of mail sticking out of the black box. *It can't be real mail,* she thought. This was Sunday and there was no postal delivery.

"Must be a note from Mrs. Jensen." *One of these days,* Anne thought, *I'm going to have to stop talking to myself.* She'd obviously lived too long alone in the country.

She picked up the note and realized it was one of her postcards, apparently returned. Maybe a wrong address. She flipped the Christmas scene over. When she saw the New York zip code, goose bumps raced up her arms.

"Mrs. Annabelle Donahue," Anne whispered, reading her own handwriting. This was the card she had sent to Annabelle, unaware that her mother's friend had just died. How macabre! For obvious reasons, the post office had sent the card back. But how had it arrived on a Sunday?

"Curiouser and curiouser, as Alice would say." Anne shivered, not entirely from the cold, and scooted into the house. A sharp wind rose, pushing at the door. She leaned against it until the latch clicked, and she was left alone with Johnny Mathis. *"Faithful friends who are dear to us gather near to us once more."*

Anne turned the card over again and gazed at the quaint scene. This was card #11. The wassailing procession. The cozy painting depicted a merry group of lords and ladies, bundled in cloaks against the cold. They were traipsing through a village, going door to door, offering a cup of spiced ale from their wassail bowl, shouting "Wassail!" which meant "Be Whole!" Anne had painted them at a doorway, laughing. She liked the merriment she'd captured in their eyes. She'd spent a lot of time on costume research, from their ornate broaches right down to their pointy shoes. She particularly liked the—

"Cat! What the—?" Anne's hands tightened around the frayed edges of the card. Her heart lurched into high gear. Her eyes felt like they were popping out of her head.

"A cat?" she shrieked again, scowling at the postcard. She bounded into the living room and thrust the card under the intense beam of light from her gooseneck lamp. "My God, there *is* a cat."

Confusion ripped through her brain at such high speed that her head ached, and she rubbed her temples. "This is impossible."

In the narrow beam of light, Anne saw a black cat coiling, with arched back, around the legs of one of the ladies. There could be no mistaking the drawing. It was Niner. Someone had painted *her cat* on this postcard and had returned it. Had hand-delivered it just moments ago, she realized. Unless, of course, it had materialized out of thin air. Had someone stolen Niner? A catnapping? The idea was preposterous.

Anne rushed back to the door and flung it open. A bitter gust of wind whooshed into the house. For once, she didn't give a damn about the heating bill. She wanted to find the jerk who was playing this cruel practical joke.

Then she heard a bell. A faint tinkle, tinkle. This time the goose bumps sprang up all over her body, for it was Niner's bell. The bell he wore around his collar.

"He's come back," she whispered excitedly.

Anne reached for the coat stand and grabbed the first object her hand touched—a heavy cape she'd bought at the medieval fair in southern Wisconsin last summer. She threw it over her shoulders, pulled the hood over her head, and dashed into her front yard.

"Niner! Come here, boy. Ni-ner!" her voice sang. She kept calling, worried her kitty would never hear her against the wail of the muffled wind. She had to rely on sound, for she could see nothing through the onslaught of snow. Dusk was at hand, and the dull gray sky was slowly fading to a dusty black.

She stopped and listened. It was still there, the faint tinkle of a bell. It came from the other side of the road. She trudged her way through snowdrifts and up a slight embankment until she stood in the middle of the country road.

"Niner!" she shouted, her throat raw. She coughed and took a deep breath. Cold pricked her burning lungs. She listened, and heard a new sound. The crunch of snow. That peculiar sound that could be made by one thing alone—a car tire. Anne's heart lurched into her throat. She swung around just in time to see two headlights glowing through snowflakes. She tried to leap off the road, but her feet started to slide out from under her.

I'm going to die, she thought calmly. It was her last cogent thought before the car struck her. It was a glancing blow. Nevertheless, she flew down the slippery embankment, and as she lost consciousness, white snow turned to black.

Chapter Two

"God's wounds! Are you hurt?"

The voice was deep. Rich. Masculine. And comforting. Anne felt a strong and callused palm warm her forehead. Then two fingers touched the racing pulse in her neck.

"Still alive. By Beelzebub, 'tis a stroke of good fortune."

"Oooh," she groaned in response. Mustering all her strength, she forced open her eyes, only to discover a sparkling blue pair looming over her, blinking with concern.

"By all the Saints in Heaven, maiden, are you well?" the stranger asked urgently. "You were nearly killed."

"I'm fine," she demurred. Actually, her head felt as if it were splitting open. She must have hit a rock when the car had knocked her off the road. But there was no blood. And no searing pain. Just a sense of confusion. Who was this handsome man?

She found herself focusing on the dazzling specks of gold in his irises. "Are you wearing colored contact lenses?"

"Contact what?" the stranger repeated with a frown.

"Contact lenses. Your eyes are too beautiful to be real."

"By the Rood, I think you've lost your wits, gentle lady. You must have suffered quite a blow."

Anne shook her head. "No, I always ask impertinent questions. Forgive me. I should be more discreet with strangers."

She tried to rise from her bed of matted snow, but her head began to pound in earnest and she sank back. "Help me, please."

The unbelievably gorgeous stranger slipped an iron hand under her neck and another beneath the small of her back and lifted her to a sitting position.

"There you are, lady."

"Thank you, mister."

She smiled.

He didn't.

"Nay, please call me Robert."

"It was just a joke, Robert." She rubbed her hands over her eyes, finally regaining a semblance of clarity, as well as her sense of humor. "The last person who called me 'lady' was a cab driver upset over the amount of his tip."

Robert's frown deepened. "Cab driver?"

"Yeah, you know, in New York. A rude cabbie. I was there peddling my artwork. I'm an artist. I do greeting cards. I guess Mrs. Jensen didn't mention it."

His fine velvet brown brows curled together as if in a question mark. Then he shook his head soberly and pressed the back of his hand against her forehead, checking her temperature. "I fear you need rest, maiden. You seem to be somewhat . . . out of sorts."

Struck by his gentleness, she looked fully into his face for the first time, and what she saw took her breath away.

His cerulean eyes were just one part of the perfect puzzle. There were many other fine pieces: his forehead, strong and finely carved; his nose, aquiline, with only a small, intriguing ridge marring an otherwise perfect descending line; his cheeks, high and nicked with a few scars; his chin, firm and square; and his lips, molded sensuously like the silky folds of a rose petal, only infinitely more masculine.

"What did you . . . what did you say your name was?" she whispered, awed by the sight.

His blue eyes ignited with a twinkling light. "Robert. My name is Robert."

"Robert, I guess I should introduce myself. My name is—"

"Anne," he chimed in merrily.

"How did you know?" Then she realized that Mrs. Jensen must have at least mentioned her name, too. Her neighbor had obviously failed in her job as Cupid's promotions director. When she'd invited Anne to meet her son's friend, she should have said, "Oh, by the way, he's the most gorgeous man you've ever met in your life."

"I saw the unicorn pendant hanging from your neck, Lady Anne. I'd recognize your father's emblem anywhere. But I wasn't expecting you so soon. Your herald sent word that you'd postponed your journey due to inclement weather. You shouldn't have risked the dangers of traveling alone."

Herald? *Lady* Anne? What was he talking about?

Anne pinched the bridge of her nose. "Robert, when you were driving up the road, did you see a cat? I heard a bell and thought it was from my cat's collar." She cocked her head and heard the noise again. Only this time there were several bells ringing in the distance. Were they church bells? The sound triggered a wave of vertigo. She really had taken quite a spill.

"Oh, my, I'm not feeling well." She swept a shaky hand over her tousled hair and decided to beat a hasty retreat to her home. But only after she'd thoroughly grilled this stranger. "Robert, when you were driving up the road, did you see a black cat? My cat is lost."

"Driving?"

"In your car. That was your car that hit me, wasn't it?" She glanced around but couldn't see much of anything in the pelting snow.

"My cart is over there, if that is what you mean."

His cart? Fighting a feeling that something was very wrong, she accepted his helping hand and stood, then dusted clumps of wet snow from the back of her cape. She allowed Robert to guide her with a hand on her elbow. She didn't want to slip and fall again. After walking a dozen yards, she finally understood what he'd meant, and she stopped dead in her tracks.

"What is this?"

"My cart. Please climb in. I'll follow behind on my palfrey. Have you no handmaidens? Well, no matter. We must move quickly before the storm grows worse. Besides, I don't want to linger out in the open without any men-at-arms. The forest nearby is rife with thieves."

Robert's words were a jumbled blur. Anne couldn't fathom their meaning. She was still staring dumbly at the cart. It was so odd. It didn't look anything like the trailers local farmers used. There were two bays whickering impatiently in front of the cart. Inside there were two benches on either side of the open-air vehicle. A young man with shoulder-length hair like Robert's held the reins on a bench up front. He wore a brown tunic type of outfit and dull-colored hose. Then Anne realized she'd seen a cart like this before. In a book on medieval transportation.

Confusion turned to relief. "Well, that explains it. Mrs. Jensen said you liked history. Are you a member of the Society for Creative Anachronism?"

"I am a member of the Order of the Garter," he said proudly. "But I have not heard of this Society of which you speak."

Anne's gaze found his horse, or palfrey, as he had called it. She blinked in astonishment. The animal was wearing a trapper, just like the ones she'd read about when researching her postcards. A bright red cape covered the horse from flanks to haunches. The trapper was adorned with an ornate crest—the same one that Robert wore on his chest.

"Well, then you must be from the Medieval Fair."

Robert's ruddy face cracked with a grin, revealing an exquisite pair of matching dimples. "The fair? Nay, my lady, the fair won't take place for another six months. And then only if the king grants us a license."

"*The king?*" Anne took a step backward. There was something about the way he had said it, with a faint tone of concern, as if the fair truly might not come to pass. He wasn't joking. She could see he was dead serious. This was not a man who would jest or bandy lies about. Anne's head began to spin. She felt suddenly as if she were on a roller coaster ride, and after a steep, clackity climb to the top, was now plunging at high speed to the ground. She couldn't seem to get her bearings.

"I want to go home. I want to crawl in bed until my headache goes away. I'm sorry, Robert. I must see if my cat is waiting for me. Mrs. Jensen's house is that way, a block down the road. Tell her I'll be over soon. I must go home."

Anne turned and hurried back across the road. She flung herself through a deep snow bank and across her yard until she nearly stumbled over a campfire. She came to a skittering stop and inhaled a whiff of wood smoke as it snaked skyward. Above the fire three sticks had been fashioned into a triangle from which hung a wrought-iron pot filled with bubbling stew.

"What the—?"

"E'en, now, yer ladyship." A woman in a tattered beige gown stepped out of a daub and wattle hut and drew up to the fire. She nodded respectfully to Anne, squatted down, and started to stir the meaty-smelling brew. "Can ye spare alms for a poor woman, yer ladyship?"

Anne stared into her weary, dirt-smudged face. The woman's hair hung to her shoulders in greasy strands. Anne began to shiver, violently. "Who are you? Where have you come from? Robert! Robert!" Was he responsible for this, too?

The dull-eyed woman glanced over her shoulder to the hut behind her. A grubby little boy poked his head out from behind the thatched door. "This is me home," the woman said. "We've paid our taxes to 'is lordship. We've a right to be 'ere."

Anne focused on the child. His cheeks were gaunt, his face nearly black with dirt, except for his lips, which shimmered with a tinge of blue.

"You're cold," Anne said. "Poor child."

She untied her cape and drew it off her shoulders. Heedless of the falling snow, she went to the boy, coaxed him out of the hut only long enough to drape her cloak over his shoulders.

"Here. Take it. Now go inside and warm yourself."

Robert came up behind her and placed his hands on her shoulders, gently pulling her away.

"That's enough, Lady Anne. You needn't give away your only protection from the cold. I will send my almoner to look after this family."

He smiled kindly at the peasant woman. "Do not worry, Mary Goodfellow. Her ladyship took a nasty spill on the way to Wittingham Castle. Now, come along, Anne."

There was no mistaking his patronizing tone. Anne turned on him, anger sparking from her green eyes. "Do you think I'm crazy? Is that it? Well, I'm not, I can assure you. I've never seen a child like this—this cold and hungry—near my home. I've never seen a child like this anywhere. I want answers, Robert. What is the date?"

"Why, 'tis the eve of our Savior's birth. Tonight we will light the Yule log."

"Yes, I know it is Christmas Eve." She pressed the tips of her fingers to her aching temples. "I mean, what is the year? What year is this?"

"Thirteen hundred and seventy-five. At least 'twas the last time I checked a calendar," he added with a wry smile.

"Thirteen-seventy-five!?" Anne screwed her eyes into a desperate and silent plea for the truth. "Robert, are you sure?"

But he had spoken truly. There was no mirth in his relentless gaze. Though she was reluctant to admit it, his answer was the only one that made sense. Somehow, some way, she had been catapulted back in time *600 years!*

"Well," she continued, licking her chafed lips, "all right. Fine. Okay. I can deal with this. I don't understand it, but I can surely accept it. I think. For now, anyway." She began to pace, her toes quickly growing numb in her slippers. "Now that I know the year, I suppose you should tell me where we are." She looked around the little peasant village she had stumbled on.

"Yorkshire."

"England?"

"Of course."

She turned her incredulous gaze back to Robert. "And who do you think I am?" She was prepared for any answer this time, no matter how astounding. "You knew my name. Have we met before?"

"Nay, Lady Anne. We have not met. But I was expecting you, though not until after this storm passed."

"So who am I, Duke Robert of Wittingham?"

His eyes twinkled again. "I am not a duke. I am an earl. Lord Robert will do. And you are Lady Anne Wharton. The woman I am to marry."

"I see," Anne replied calmly. Then her knees began to buckle. Her head seemed to weigh a million pounds, and she realized she was about to faint.

"Come hither, lady," he murmured, then scooped her into his arms. When she laid her head on his broad chest, she looked up into his eyes. They glowed with worry and the warmth of a fire.

"I want to go home, Robert."

"You *are* home," he murmured.

Chapter Three

The next morning, Lord Robert stomped his way toward Lady Anne's guest chamber. Torches lining the cold stone corridors fluttered in his wake. Servants in muted grays and browns scattered before their lord, who was dressed in a brilliant burgundy doublet. He knew that they knew he was in one of his notorious black moods.

How could the rumors about Lady Anne have been so wrong? Robert wondered, opening and closing his hands into fists. He had been taken aback completely by her pleasant demeanor, and he didn't like surprises. The Lady Anne he had found on the roadside was a beauty, and sweet in nature. Not plain and sour of disposition as he had been warned she would be.

Last month Robert had agreed to marry Anne, sight unseen, after his castellan and good friend, Sir Roger Downey, had been killed in battle. As earl, Robert had concluded then that enough blood had been shed in the border war being fought with his neighbor, Lord Geoffrey. Robert had accurately concluded that if he agreed to marry Lord Goeffrey's daughter, Lady Anne, the border confrontations would end immediately. And marrying a shrew seemed a small price to pay for peace after twenty years of discord.

But now he had discovered that the greatest prize in this match was the lady herself. Gods, he was a lucky man. So why wasn't he elated? Something about the whole matter didn't make sense. He hoped presently to find out exactly what was afoul.

When Robert finally arrived at Lady Anne's guest chamber, he raised a broad fist to knock on her door. But his hand halted in midair when he heard a high-pitched scream.

"Get your hands off of me!"

It was Lady Anne's voice. Robert's blood ran cold. He lifted the latch and kicked open the door.

"What goes here?" he shouted, bolting into the flickering shadows that danced in the chamber's firelight.

He found the barber-surgeon leaning over the lady's bed. Anne, lying prone, was staring in wide-eyed horror at the slithering leech poised in the graybeard's hand. Looking up at Robert with a start, the old man nearly dropped the leech, and Anne gasped in even greater horror.

Robert halted in place, confounded by the scene. "What is it, Lady Anne? What is the matter?" He'd thought she was being raped. No danger of that from old Barber Farley.

"He . . . he wants to put that disgusting thing on my arm!"

"I am just trying to bleed her, my lord. Her humor is exceptionally sanguinary. A good bloodletting will cure her confusion, methinks."

"Over my dead body!" Anne piped in with a shaky voice, her Irish temper thoroughly inflamed. "Get that gross thing away from me, or I'll scream again. Robert, *please* help me."

She turned to him with such a tortured look that his heart flip-flopped in his chest. Gods, she was beautiful! He'd noticed her lustrous green eyes in the snowstorm, and her pert little nose, which had been as red as a holly berry in the cold. Now he glimpsed her other lovely features at length—her long, reddish-gold hair that gleamed in the firelight, and wondrously high cheekbones that hinted of nobility and strength, and her rosebud lips, through which flowed the oddest words. *Gross.* He would have to travel more often to places where such words were used. Obviously he was too isolated on his Yorkshire estate.

But there was more that drew him to Lady Anne. Something he couldn't quite identify. A vulnerability that he knew he would do anything to protect—conquer castles, battle dragons, or fight to the death. And so when she said, "Please, my lord," once again with a quavering little voice, he leapt forward and pulled the barber-surgeon's hand away.

"Put your leeches aside, sir. The lady does not wish to be bled now."

"Or ever," Anne added.

"But, my lord, she needs to regain her strength."

"Then losing blood is the last thing I should be doing!"

At this absurd statement, Robert turned to Anne, his arms akimbo. "My dearest lady, Barber Farley is right. A good bleeding would do you wonders. But if you are disinclined, so be it. I will not allow it." He turned to the befuddled old man and added quietly, "She's just bumped her head. I'm sure she'll survive. Leave us now."

"Very good, my lord. If you think 'tis best." The barber-surgeon sniffed and pursed his lips, dropping the fat leech into a jar. "Good day."

Robert watched the door close behind him, then turned back to his betrothed. He studied Anne intently, aware that a strong current of energy flowed between them, like a moonbeam so thick he could cut it with a misericorde. The awareness warmed his belly, and more southern regions of his anatomy. He wanted to scoop her into his arms and hold her. She was that lovely, that open, so unlike all the other ladies he had ever met.

"There is something different about you, Lady Anne. I can't quite fathom what, but there is something very odd."

Beneath his intense gaze, her cheeks turned a lovely shade of pink. The pastel color was perfectly offset by the white, delicately embroidered gown he had provided for her.

Aware that his gaze was taking on a proprietary air, Anne self-consciously pulled her sheet nearly to her chin.

"How am I odd, Lord Robert?"

"I do not mean in any insulting way, Lady Anne. Your peculiarities are most refreshing. But before I elaborate, I should ask you—is my presence here disturbing you?"

Anne relaxed her arms and frowned up at him. "What do you mean?"

"Do you think me improper for being here alone with you?"

"Good Heavens, no!"

"See, that's what I mean. Most ladies would at least pretend they were offended by my presence in their bed chamber."

Oh, dear, Anne thought, *I'm already sticking out like a sore thumb.*

"Well, I don't exactly welcome you, my lord. Not in any sense that's improper," she improvised, trying to muster a prudish arch to her brow, "but it is your castle, after all. I am a stranger here and you are my only friend. And I am exceedingly curious about you. I'd like you to stay and talk to me."

"Good! There is much we have to discuss." Without preamble, he circled the bed and sank down on her left side.

His nearness was like a blast of wind; one that left her shivering and invigorated. The shadow from his towering figure was a balm on her forehead made from an ancient, long-forgotten recipe: three parts masculinity, one part sensuality. Perhaps she had died and gone to Heaven. If so, she was glad of it. She had never felt so alive.

She shut her eyes and ordered her swooning head to snap out of it. But her eyes peeped open again, unable to resist the dashingly handsome man at her side. His shoulder-length hair was windblown and free. He peered fearlessly at her over rugged cheekbones. Even his arms were tantalizing—they were corded with muscles and brushed with fine tawny down.

"Wh-what is it, my lord? What do you want to talk about?"

"We are to be married in twelve days, my lady. Don't you think we should get to know each other?"

Her nod was all the invitation he needed. Robert spoke rapidly, but with great passion, about his childhood and his hopes for the future. Anne learned that he came from a wealthy and powerful family in England. As the first son, he had inherited all three of his father's castles. But he had lost valuable land to Lady Anne's father when Robert's own brother, Godrick, had betrayed him. Recounting this, Robert's handsome, dimpled cheeks hardened with rage. Anne nearly shivered at his cold glare.

"That is the one thing I cannot tolerate, Anne. Deceit. Whatever you do to me, ill or otherwise, over the course of our marriage, you must never lie to me. Do you understand?"

He swung his head around until his visage loomed in her line of vision. Decades of betrayal, anger, and heartbreak carved deep slashes beneath his high cheekbones. "Do you understand?"

Anne swallowed thickly and nodded, then tilted her head speculatively. How in blazes would she survive the coming days pretending to be someone else without violating his rule against deceit? It was impossible. But what would she tell him? That she had traveled through time? That explanation would land her in the stocks and very likely on a stake with a nice big bonfire sizzling at her feet. He would either think she was mad and lock her in a tower somewhere, or conclude she was a witch.

Still, she did not want to hurt him as his brother had.

"Lord Robert, I . . . I am not the person you think I am."

His angry eyes met hers, then softened with resignation. "I was afraid of that. I thought you too good to be true. Did my brother send you? Did Godrick ask you to spy upon me?"

"No!" Anne nearly shouted, sitting upright. "I am not sent by your traitorous brother, or any other enemy. I would never intentionally betray you or harm you. I don't know how I got here."

Anne reached out and wrapped a hand over Robert's. She didn't care whether he thought the gesture too forward or improper. There was something about this man that made her drop her guard completely. It was as if she'd known him for years. Or perhaps it was that they were made for each other. He squeezed her hand and she felt a surge of excitement darting up her arm, infecting her heart with an incredible feeling of love.

Love? Yes, love. She realized in this strange warped place where time meant nothing, one could fall in love in no time at all.

"If you are not the person I think you are, then who are you?" he pressed. He leaned forward, peering more closely into her eyes, as if burrowing for the truth.

Anne relished the closeness. She inhaled his musky, male scent as his sweet breath fanned her cheeks. A coil of desire tickled up her neck. And she realized she didn't want to say anything that would ruin what they might have together. Even if that was only one night in each other's arms. Even if this was only a crazy dream.

"My name is Anne," she hedged. That was the truth. "I do not want to deceive you, Robert. I did not lie when I said my name was Anne."

"And you are a lady, are you not?"

"Well, I am not a peasant, if that is what you mean," she answered, at least partially truthful. How strange it must be to live in a society in which being a lady meant belonging to an exclusive social and economic class.

"That makes you Lady Anne, does it not?"

She looked into his stunning blue eyes, well past the provocative flecks of gold, deep into his soul. He did not want to know the truth any more than she did. He was looking for love as much as she, this man who had so willingly agreed to a political match with a woman he had never even met.

"Robert," she whispered, her eyes scouring his beautiful features, "does my name really matter?"

He slid forward and scooped her into his arms. "Not now," came his husky reply. His throat bobbed as he tried to swallow overwhelming desire and failed. "Not with you."

He pulled her gently against the mass of muscles rippling over his warrior's chest. His strong arms enclosed her like a cocoon. Then his mouth was upon hers, hard and insistent, stealing her breath away. She groaned. His lips were firm and kneading. His tongue dipped between her lips. A soft, wet touch. Anne gasped again. And then he pulled back.

"You set me on fire," he murmured.

He smiled a lazy half-smile, and glimpsing his easy confidence, she realized she would do anything this man asked. She trusted him completely. This was the man she had wished for all her life. This was a man who would fight for his lady's honor.

"I'd better go before I truly lose control."

"If you must," Anne whispered on a sweet sigh.

"I must help my steward find an appropriate Yule Log in my forest. There will be time later to sort out all the details of your arrival and our marriage-to-be. But first I want you to recover fully from your fall. I will see you anon in the Great Hall."

"Yes. Anon," she replied, and watched him depart with a mixture of utter contentment and vague uneasiness. He still thought she was Lady Anne Wharton. So be it. She would play the part if that's what it took to be near the man with whom she had so quickly fallen in love. She only prayed he would understand when he learned the truth.

Chapter Four

"Oh, you look lovely, my lady." The petite handmaiden designated to serve Anne clapped her small hands together and beamed at her new mistress with approval. "You'll take Lord Robert's breath away, I avow."

Anne smiled at the young woman and flushed with unexpected pride. She felt like a queen in her ornate gown. Yet somehow she was more comfortable than she had ever been in blue jeans and Reeboks. *Perhaps I was born in the wrong century,* she mused.

Trying to keep a level head and some remnant of her 20th-century skepticism, she frowned into the looking glass proffered by the handmaiden. "Don't you think the pearl fillet is putting it on a little thick?" Anne said.

"Putting it on a little what, my lady?"

Anne looked up at the befuddled handmaiden and saw a look that was becoming all too familiar. Several times since she'd arrived at the magnificent Wittingham Castle, people had stared at Anne as if they knew something wasn't quite right. Usually the looks followed conversations. While she somehow had managed to leave her American accent in the 20th century, she hadn't yet learned to stifle slang phrases. She would have to be more careful.

"What I mean, Rose, is that I think the headband, I mean the fillet, is a little too ornate."

"Oh no, my lady, 'tis perfect. See how it illuminates your lovely cheeks?"

"Maybe you're right," Anne said, pleased at her reflection. The pearl fillet sat on top of her reddish-blond hair like a tiara, holding her hair away from her face. The length of her wavy locks flowed down her back, as was acceptable for maidens, Rose informed her, but not for wives. And naturally Rose assumed her mistress was chaste.

The rest of Anne's outfit was equally elegant. She wore a high-necked kirtle made of deep blue velvet with tapered sleeves that hugged her narrow wrists. Over the tight-fitting kirtle she wore a flowing floor-length gown called a cote-hardie. The material was a stunning rose brocade high-lighted with silver thread. Her kirtle's high neckline and elegant sleeves peeked out from beneath that floral mass. Anne was sure she had never been so regal or beautiful in her life. And she wanted to be beautiful. For Robert. Never before had a man inspired that desire in her, not to mention other desires more carnal in nature.

What had come over her? She had enjoyed making love with David, but she'd never thought about him in that way outside of their bedroom. In the short time she'd known Robert, she could think of little else.

"I'm afraid I shall be late if we don't hurry along."

"Never you fear, my lady. Lord Robert has not yet re-turned with the Yule Log. And you're a special guest everyone will be happy to wait for." She gave Anne an im-petuous hug, then blushed. "We had heard such awful things about you, Lady Anne. I . . . I hope you will forgive my telling you so. Everyone is delighted to learn you are kind and friendly."

"Thank you, Rose." Anne accepted the compliment with a warm smile, then frowned at its implications. If the real Lady Anne were really a shrew, then they didn't have much in common. "Rose, did you by any chance hear anything else about Lady Anne? I mean about me, that is. For exam-ple, have there been any rumors linking . . . me . . . with an-other love interest?"

Did she have any lovers? Anne wanted to ask, but didn't dare.

"Nay, my lady. Everyone had heard you were such a shrew that no one would have you, no matter how enticing your marriage portion." The handmaiden's hands flew to her gaping mouth. "Oh, dear, I do run on. Forgive me, my lady, but the rumors were so clearly wrong."

"Do not worry, Rose, you do not offend me." Anne patted the girl's shoulder distractedly.

Her thoughts turned to Robert. If his fiancée were so undesirable, he would expect her to be a virgin. To continue masquerading as Lady Anne, she would have to make sure he didn't seduce her into his bed and learn the truth. And she would have to resist the urge to do likewise. Such a pity. Robert was the first man she'd felt she could truly love. Eventually she would have to find a way to be truthful if they were to have a real relationship. *If* she were going to be around that long.

This wasn't a dream, she had concluded. It felt all too real, especially the painful pinprick Rose had accidentally given her when fixing her hair. But how had she traveled through time? And when would she return to the future? *If* she returned to the future. That prospect saddened her. In many ways she didn't want to go back. But there were still so many unanswered questions. Too many to contemplate when she was about to join a party.

"Lead the way, Rose. I am ready."

Anne followed her handmaiden from the guest chamber through a maze of arched corridors. The stone walls exuded cold. The only hint of warmth came from torches flickering from wall sconces. Anne realized how spoiled she had been by central heating. She also quickly discerned that her elaborate gown was not so much an indulgence as a necessity to keep warm.

Wittingham Castle consisted of a large rectangular keep, with the Great Hall in one end and the women's bower and men's sleeping quarters on the other end. In between, there was a kitchen, a chapel, the lord's solar, the garrison, the brewery, and a dungeon. Servants scurried everywhere, eyes bright with Christmas cheer.

"Lord Robert and his knights will drag in the Yule Log any moment, my lady. We will wait for them in the Great

Hall," Rose said. She leaned into the heavy wooden arched doors to the hall until they swung open.

Anne stepped inside and exhaled in wonder. If there had been any doubt that this was Christmastime, the doubt was vanquished by the magnificent scene laid out before her widened eyes.

The entire hall was awash in pleasant smoke from a giant fireplace set in the far wall. Pine and sprigs of dried lilac burned in the blazing flames, exuding a sweet scent. That pleasant odor was nearly overwhelmed by the aroma of freshly baked sweet breads and hot spiced ale nearly overflowing from the wassail bowl.

The hall was jammed with merry revelers. They wore fantastic medieval costumes with ornate glittering masks. Although, Anne reminded herself, these were not costumes, but clothing. No doubt their finest. The very outfits Anne had read about when researching her postcards.

Many of the men wore silk and velvet houppelandes, some with hems trailing to the floor. The women wore flowing gowns similar to Anne's. Those who did not wear elaborate masks wore fillets with crimped veils or squarish headdresses known as chaplets, some with wimples swathed around their chins. Anne clearly had not overdressed, as she had feared.

"You must be Lady Anne," a feminine voice rose above the genial cacophony.

Anne turned to find a jolly-looking woman who filled her green satin gown to overflowing. The hair peeking from beneath her boxed hat was salt and pepper. She struck Anne as the sort who would know everything about the castle and discreetly share the best gossip.

"You may call me Gertrude," she warmly introduced herself. "I am the steward's wife, and I have acted as chatelaine for a good ten years, waiting patiently until Lord Robert did his duty and brought home a wife to run his castle. Come, let me introduce you while we wait for Robert and my husband. I trust they didn't stop in a tavern for a tankard of ale on their way back from the forest!"

Without waiting for acquiescence, Gertrude scooped her arm around Anne's waist and dragged her good-naturedly around the hall, giving her a proper introduction. Ann was relieved that Gertrude apparently saw nothing odd in either her behavior or her demeanor. In the presence of the steward's wife it was easy to pretend that she really did fit in and someday would truly be the lady of the castle.

When they had come full circle around the hall, they paused before the wassail bowl. There a page served them cups filled with spiced ale and an apple slice. Anne drank readily. It warmed her belly and relaxed her nerves. She wanted to feel at home. This was so much better than spending another Christmas alone. But where was Robert?

"He and my husband probably started their journey to the forest with a tour of the border. That will be a safe enough task now that Lord Robert has signed a truce with your father."

"Border?"

"Aye, Lady Anne, the border separating Robert's lands from your father's. Without your marriage, there would be no peace between your families. And with the money stolen from his coffers by his nasty brother Godrick, Robert likely could not afford to defend himself properly from any more assaults from your father."

Anne paled in the golden light of the hall. "My father and Robert at war? So, what would happen to Robert if he didn't marry Wharton's daughter?"

"I daresay your father might win the next battle and claim Robert's land for his own. Lord Robert might even fight to the death. He is that way, you know. Very chivalrous and noble."

Anne licked her lips, which had suddenly gone dry. *If he doesn't marry the real Lady Anne, he could lose his earldom, and perhaps even his life,* she thought, newly distressed. *I must tell him who I am. We cannot marry. He must marry Wharton's daughter. Even if she is a shrew.*

Three loud knocks vibrated against the hall's outer doors. Gertrude spun around, gleaming at Anne with a broad smile. "They're here! Lord Robert and my Kevin."

A sense of foreboding flooded Anne. Struggling against an impulse to flee, she pinched the bridge of her nose. "I must leave. I shouldn't be here." She turned to go, her full gown twirling around her legs with a rustle, but Gertrude grabbed her wrist.

"This is no time to be shy, my lady. The merrymaking is about to begin."

The doors flew open and amidst a swirl of snow entered Robert and his steward, Sir Kevin, strutting as they showed off the log they had just chopped down.

Robert was gaily, almost absurdly dressed. The toes of his shoes were coiled with bells attached at the tips. His red and green hose would have been comical if they weren't encasing such fine, muscular legs. He dashed off his cape, revealing a lush velvet doublet, which stopped at the top of his thighs. But what struck Anne the most was his hat. A *chapeau extraordinaire*. It was an odd creation that looked almost like a turban, or an oversized bird's nest. The cap was made of vines entwined with bright silks and boughs of holly dotted with red berries. Robert looked like a cross between a court jester and an ancient druid. He looked like the man she had painted in her postcard!

But Anne couldn't seem to focus on anything but his blue, blue eyes. They immediately trained on her. Her cheeks heated beneath his intense gaze, and all her worried thoughts of Wharton's daughter vanished.

"I am the Lord of Misrule!" Robert shouted with glee. His baritone voice echoed off the wooden beams holding up the ceiling. "In truth, I had hired a whimsical fellow from Horner's Green to play the part and oversee the festivities over the next fortnight. But the snowstorm precluded his arrival. Therefore, I am filling his shoes."

Robert thrust out one foot and tapped his heel on the rushes. The bell attached to his shoe jingled and the crowd broke into applause.

"Let the festivities begin!" Robert shouted.

The Christmas revelers cheered. Robert bowed before the freshly chopped log, as did Sir Kevin.

"But before we light the Yule Log," Robert added solemnly, holding up a finger for emphasis. "There is one introduction I must make."

Anne's heart began to pump madly beneath her gown as Robert strode toward her. She swooned to see the most dazzling and charming light she'd ever seen in anyone's eyes—two blue orbs twinkling at her and no one else. His lips were curled into a tantalizing smile, engaging his dimples full force. Anne's knees nearly crumbled at the pure charm wrought by this smile. His shoulder-length hair, dangling below his absurd hat, glistened with melted snowflakes. She wanted to run her hands through those long locks and inhale the leathery scent of him. Resist this man? It might well be impossible.

"Lady Anne," he murmured, and plucked her delicate artist's hands from the folds of her gown. "I would have thought it impossible, but you are even lovelier than before."

He pressed his lips to the knuckles of one of her hands. Her arm tingled, and she eagerly pictured him pressing those lips to hers.

"My lord, you are too kind," she said, her voice husky with desire.

"Lords and ladies, may I introduce to you Lady Anne Wharton, my betrothed. She will do us the honor of lighting the Yule Log this year."

Applause swelled again. Anne looked around at the smiling faces, so vibrant and alive. And it finally struck her. Not only was Robert the man she had painted in her postcard, she had used this setting as well. She had created this warm and cozy celebration. Or recreated it. Was this an elaborate fantasy of her own design? She wondered until Robert boldly kissed her on the mouth in a way no fantasy man could.

"I'm sorry," he murmured against her lips. "I know I am too bold, but I have been longing to do that ever since I left you this morning."

She gripped his wrought-iron arms for support. "I am not embarrassed, my lord. Believe me."

"Good. Very good." He gave her a saucy half-smile and turned to the crowd. "I am the Lord of Misrule! I can kiss maidens and pinch other men's wives and no one can stop me!"

"Hold now! Just try it!" several men shouted back, huge smiles betraying their threats.

Robert waved them off. He had no need of any other woman now that he had met the extraordinary Lady Anne. He instructed several pages to drag the enormous log to the fireplace. Half a dozen women swept forward and, laughing, decorated the ash tree trunk with colorful ribbons and sprigs of holly. The pages then threw the log onto the roaring fire while the revelers cheered. The steward handed Anne a burning faggot.

" 'Tis from last year's Yule fire," Robert explained. "Place the burning faggot onto the new Yule Log."

With his hand gently supporting hers, Anne did as she was instructed, touching the burning remains of last year's Yule Log to this year's, which hadn't yet ignited. When a ribbon caught fire, the crowd broke into renewed applause.

"Let the dancing begin! The Lord of Misrule commands that everyone dance!"

Three troubadours struck up a merry tune. Their nimble fingers danced over lute strings and flicked over drum skins. In mere seconds, it seemed, the hall had turned into a sea of skipping and twirling dancers.

Anne watched in wonder, laughing at the exhilarating merriment. She had never been to a party where people laughed and danced with such abandon. Somehow they seemed to know something that modern-day people didn't; they possessed an intensity she had never witnessed before.

Perhaps they celebrated because they knew each day was precious. While some lives in medieval times were long, many would be cut short by disease or mishap, particularly among the poor. Anne noted that members of the lower classes seemed to be having the most fun of all tonight.

Anne was pleased to see the miller, dressed in his simple brown tunic, slapping his knee to the beat of the music; and the scullions, who rested from their kitchen work, wiping goose fat from their hands and giggling madly as they took turns dancing around the great hall. All were welcome here on Christmas Eve.

But Anne wasn't naive. During the rest of the year, she was sure, the differences between rich and poor were rigidly kept, and she wondered: could she live in a world where people were not equal under the law? Could she live in a world where women had few rights, save for those granted them by a benevolent husband?

"You are not having fun?" Robert gently queried.

She looked up, startled by his sudden presence, and found him gazing down at her with concern.

"Do not worry, my Lord of Misrule, at your command I have had the time of my life. But my feet are hurting, and so I decided to rest a spell."

She had taken a seat on a bench in an arched recess, watching the festivities unfold before her marveling eyes. A torch fluttered overhead. Robert sat next to her and scooped her hand in his. She felt the gesture tingle all the way down to her tippy toes.

"Well, I hope you recover swiftly," he commented dryly. "I have special celebrations planned for every one of the Twelve Days of Christmas. Right up until Twelfth Night, when we will be married. I will send word to Cornwall to see if your family can still arrive in time for the nuptials. I understand your relatives are spending the holidays on the

coast. I still can't believe your father let you travel alone!
I'll send my herald to him on the morrow."

"No! I mean . . . let me contact my father."

"Very well. My herald will be at your service. But you
must send him quickly. It may already be too late. And I
don't want to delay the ceremony. It wouldn't do to give
your father a chance to change his mind."

Anne nodded, overcome with a flood of guilt. Robert had
to know the truth. He could not marry her. It would ruin his
plans for peace. He had to marry the real Lady Anne. But
what would she tell him when he asked her how she had
gotten here? If he even allowed her to explain.

During a lull in the music, Anne heard the distant chim-
ing of bells. It seemed that church bells rang out virtually
twenty-four hours a day. And suddenly, thinking of Niner's
bell, a stunning realization broke through the morass of
confusion.

"My lord, do the bells ring every hour every day year
round?"

"Nay, my lady, they ring every hour only during Christmas, between December 24th and January 6th. Otherwise
they ring only during the eight canonical hours of the day.
At Vespers, Sext, Matins, and so on. And of course on holy
days. But do you not know this yourself? Are there no
churches in your village or in your father's bailey?"

"I should know it, but I don't," she said frankly, biting
her lower lip as she calculated all the possibilities. "So the
bells ring continuously only during the Twelve Days of
Christmas. I was afraid of that."

It was the sound of bells that had lured her out of her
house, that had launched this whole bizarre journey through
time. Anne realized now that it was very likely the sound of
bells that was keeping her here.

"Robert, I took a course in religion once—"

"A course?" he said, frowning.

"I studied," she clarified for him. "I learned about other

religions. In some eastern religions, I am told, gurus teach their disciples that the soul travels on a current of sound."

"You speak of the infidels?"

"I suppose so. I think that's why in some religions people chant instead of pray. They're trying to tune into their soul, like a transmitter homing in on a frequency."

She caught his suspicious glance and squeezed his hand. "I'm sorry, I'm sure I must sound mad to you. How can I explain it? It would be as if, let's say in Westminster Cathedral, the choir members were so finely tuned to one another, their harmonies so precise, that they somehow reached through to Heaven simply on the pureness of their voices. I think that is what may have happened to me. I heard the bells, and they transported me somewhere I had never been before."

He stroked her cheek with the back of one hand. She saw the pity in his eyes.

"I'm not mad, Robert. I promise you."

"I didn't say you were, beautiful lady."

"You didn't have to. I could see it in your eyes. I know I may sound like a crazy prophet, but I promise to make sense soon. We will talk further about a great many things. But for now, I just want to enjoy your presence. I've never met a man like you before."

"And I have never, ever met a woman like you."

"Let me just ask you one last crazy question: precisely when will the bells stop ringing?"

"Precisely at midnight on Twelfth Night. Then life returns to normal."

"Normal," Anne whispered. Normal would put her back in the 20th century, alone in her isolated home. The thought left her with a hollow feeling in the pit of her stomach. "Robert, what about—"

"You said one last question, and I mean to hold you to it."

He leaned over and kissed her temple. Shivers of pleasure emanated across her face. His lips burned a pleasurable imprint on her skin. It felt so right that she nearly cried.

He withdrew and frowned at her quizzically.

"Is there something wrong?" she whispered, fearful he was regretting his affectionate gesture. She wanted him to want her as much as she craved him.

"Nay, nothing is wrong. But I have the uncanny feeling we've met before." He rose, reluctantly, she could tell, for he took his time releasing her hand. "My duties as Lord of Misrule are calling me. 'Tis time for me to start a game of Hot Cockles. But before I go, there is something, believe it or nay, that you *didn't* ask that I think you should know.

"Though I agreed to marry for political purposes, I have longed for a wife to love. That is why, at the ancient age of thirty, I am still a bachelor. I do believe I've been waiting all this time for you."

Anne tried and failed to swallow the enormous lump of emotion that had suddenly congealed in her throat. *I know I've been waiting for you,* she silently replied.

Chapter Five

The next morning, which was Christmas day, Anne attended the small private chapel in Robert's castle. She had always attended Mass on Christmas morning, and doing so now made her feel at home. But she was startled to realize that she would also be expected to go to Mass every day of the year. She'd had no idea of the great role religion played in medieval times.

It felt good to pray, to sort out her chaotic feelings. She had never been happier than she had been during the last twenty-four hours. But of course, happiness aside, this was all madness. She knew it all too well. How could she have traveled back through time? And why did she feel more at home here than she'd ever felt in Wisconsin?

"No disrespect meant, Heavenly Father, but what is going on?" she muttered to God as she knelt in the pew. "How did I get here? Why? Does this have something to do with Mother's death? With Annabelle? With Niner?"

Somehow the three had to be connected. But how?

Listening to the priest chanting in Latin, Anne thought of her grandmother. When Anne was a little girl, Grandma Ruth used to take her to Mass in downtown Milwaukee, where the Latin mumbo jumbo swelled to awesome decibels in the great cathedral.

"Grandma," she prayed now. "Are you up there in Heaven? Can you figure any of this out?"

Grandma had died when she was in her seventies. And about a month before she passed away, she would sit in her room and talk to people who had been dead for years. She apparently saw them as if they were still alive, sitting on her bed, holding conversations. Anne was convinced that those loved ones had in fact returned on some unseen level to escort Grandma to the other side, through the tunnel of light, or whatever it was that happened when you died.

Thinking of death, Anne recalled her mother with a twinge of longing. Before her mom had died last year, she had confessed to Anne that she had prayed to Grandma Ruth to help Anne find a husband. Lord, it sounded so corny. And Anne was a little embarrassed to think that others apparently thought she was so desperate to catch a man that she actually needed divine intervention.

Well, if Grandma Ruth was really looking down from Heaven, she'd be happy to know that Anne had finally found Mr. Right. But in the year 1375?

A spark of insight flashed behind her closed eyelids and she blinked them open, taking in the brilliant blues and reds of the stained glass window over the altar.

She had longed for a man who wasn't afraid to fight for her. "But I didn't mean it like this, Lord. I don't have to have a knight in shining armor battling it out on a battlefield. I was speaking figuratively."

Anne sighed with frustration. In a hushed moment, she thought of Niner. He had started this all. Was he somehow in cahoots with Mom and Annabelle? Were they all conniving to get her married off? Was Anne *that* desperate? Was love that important?

Yes, a voice answered deep inside her. *There is nothing more important than love.*

Anne blinked up at Robert. He was praying fervently. For what? Love? A conquest in battle? She wanted to know, she realized. She wanted to know *everything* about this strong, handsome, gentle man. Everything.

He looked down at her, blinking beneath his jutting brow, his blue eyes flashing like patches of sky. A flame burned deep in them, flaring to life in the darkness of the church, and Anne sensed with a shiver that soon she would know everything about him down to his skivvies. Or braies. Or whatever you called medieval underwear.

* * *

On the day after Christmas, Robert showed Anne every nook and cranny of the castle. She was amazed by its complexity. A castle was a miniature world. A complex maze of stone living quarters called a keep. That rectangular and jutting structure was surrounded by a wall demarcating the inner bailey. A wider circular stone wall made the so-called curtain surrounding the outer bailey.

The inner bailey contained the Lord's herb garden and a few fruit trees. There was a small area where Robert could practice hand-to-hand combat when he chose. In the outer bailey, there were stables containing fine stallions whickering in the frigid air, blowing clouds of steam from their nostrils. The farrier worked in the barn, hammering horse shoes. The miller came and went as he pleased, unless the porter drew up the drawbridge for safety purposes. There was never-ending activity. The almoner was especially busy, tossing leaves of bread to the lepers and poor people who begged for Christmas alms beyond the drawbridge.

Anne's heart wrenched to see the beggars, crippled and toothless. Till now, she had missed little of her old life. But there was so much that modern medicine could do for these people. If she remained in the past, she would spend the rest of her days regretting the help that she knew was available, but did not know enough to produce for these unfortunates. She had no idea how to grow mold cultures, for example, for penicillin.

"What is it, my lady?" Robert said softly.

She had been standing alone on the wall-walk atop the forty-foot-high stone curtain, gazing out at the setting sun while Robert conferred with his sentries. He had returned without a noise, and his voice startled her.

She caught her breath and pivoted, then caught her breath again when she saw the blazing red rays of the dying sun painted across his utterly masculine features.

"I was just thinking about . . . the world where I came from."

He brushed aside a tendril of hair that had fallen down

her cheek, escaping from her fillet. "I suppose it was another world. Though your father's estate borders mine, you
spent most of your youth in Cornwall, which is leagues
from here. Too far. I wish we'd met before now. How
many years more might we have had together?"

His voice was an intimate rasp. The sound drew her
focus to his lips, full and inviting. "I wish I'd met you before as well, Robert. In another time. Another place."

"Why?" he whispered, cupping her cheek with a hand.
"You sound sad saying that. What do you mean another
time?"

What should she tell him? He deserved to know the
truth. But would he believe her?

"Robert, I won't be here forever, you know."

"No one will be, sweet lady. Life is far too short."

"No, I mean . . . Oh, Robert, if I told you, you wouldn't
understand."

"Try me."

She frowned at him. "No, you tell me. Why did you
agree to this marriage with your bride sight unseen? What
if I had turned out to be the shrew everyone said I was?"

It was getting easier, pretending to be Wharton's daughter.

He shrugged. "A political match is to be expected, Anne.
Your father offered your hand as a way to end a hundred
years of enmity between our families and twenty years of
bloodshed. When my brother stole half the gold in my coffers, I realized I could not afford to defend my land forever.
It was time for peace."

"So, without marriage to Wharton's daughter, you might
well be defeated by Wharton in the coming days. You
could lose your castle."

He nodded, frowning. "Not until spring, anyway. No one
fights in the dead of winter." He turned away and leaned on
the waist high parapet, and stared at the red sun, which
seemed to be burning a hole in the horizon. "Avoiding war

was certainly my reason for agreeing to the marriage. But it is not the reason I will go through with it."

"I can't marry you, Robert." They were the saddest words she had ever uttered. She would have died for a man like Robert in her real life. No question. She would have snatched him up in a minute. But to claim him now, here, would mean his destruction. Wharton would realize Robert had insulted him by marrying someone other than his daughter, and the border skirmishes would resume with even greater force.

"For your own good, I cannot marry you."

"What are you saying?" He clutched her arms and tugged her closer. His sweet breath warmed her pinkened cheeks. "You do not expect me to let you go now, do you?"

"I am not the woman you think I am."

"So you say. But I still do not know what you mean. Anne, make sense, dear lady, or I shall go mad. You see, I have fallen in love with you."

He whispered on in a desperate rush, "Can a man love a woman so soon? With one look? With one glance in her wise and sweet eyes? So it has happened to me. I will fight for you to the death. I swear it. I would slay dragons, fight an army single-handedly. Just let me prove it."

His lips found hers and he kissed her with even greater intensity than before, for they knew each other better now. They had talked about their hopes and dreams until the wee hours last night: both wanted children—he ten, she two. Both loved to play chess and take baths—he said he indulged in a tub full of hot water once a week and nearly fell over when she confessed she sometimes bathed twice a day. Both loved literature—he had read Chaucer, and she had tried to quote passages from Shakespeare and Frost and Byron, as best as she could remember them. Her words had brought tears to his eyes, and he said he had never heard such beauty. They had held hands, sweetly, so much understanding pouring through their tingling fingers. And so, when he kissed her now, it was almost chaste. It was not lust that bound their hungry mouths together. It was the desire to consume each other, to erase all barriers, to join minds and souls on every level.

"I am in love with you," she muttered on a rushed gasp for air when the kiss ended. "I love you, Robert. I want to be with you forever."

The words hung between them, potent and profound. Her admission would be great under any circumstances, but all the more so in this time warp.

Realizing the commitment she had just made, if only internally, she threw herself into his powerful arms and laid her head against the falcon emblem adorning his coat of arms.

"Then so you shall be with me forever," he whispered ardently. "It is as simple as that. We will be married. You will be mine forever."

No, it will not be that simple, she thought. But she didn't want to dampen his joy by telling him so.

That night she lay in her canopy bed, listening to the last exhale of the dying fire. Her mind was filled with images of the merry mummers who had entertained them that evening. The Lord of Misrule had introduced the masked players after the meal, and the cozy evening was spent watching the dancers act out the birth of the Christ child. In their colorful silk costumes, the mummers played the parts of the Three Wise Men, Mary, and Joseph.

Anne had sat by Robert in a high-backed chair on the dais, enthralled, nibbling sugar sculptures and sipping sops and wine. It was so much fun, she hadn't wanted the night to end. And she had been reluctant to bid Robert goodnight. Would she still be here on the morrow? She supposed she would be, as long as the bells kept ringing. But she hated to spend any time away from him, even during a night's sleep, for she didn't know how long she would be here. Just like people in medieval times. Was that why she had been so happy since being transported back in time? Because she finally knew just how precious each day could be?

She blinked in the darkness of her chamber, staring at the canopy overhead, which was swathed with curtains. She heard the chains and pulleys of the drawbridge as it creaked shut for the night. She couldn't help wondering what was happening in Wisconsin. Was Mrs. Jensen wondering what had happened to her? Sadly, Mrs. Jensen was the only one who would even know she was gone. Her best friend from school would have called on Christmas Day and gotten no answer, but she wouldn't have worried that much. The guy Anne worked for at the greeting card company in Milwaukee was supposed to call between Christmas and New Year's Day to update his order. And that was it! The modern world would not fall apart because Anne Clancy had disappeared. There would be no serious blip in history. The nagging question in her mind was how would history be affected in the year thirteen hundred and seventy-five if she stayed?

Chapter Six

Chaste kisses turned to something far more primal on the fourth day of Christmas. The day of the boar hunt.

Anne joined Gertrude and the other ladies of the castle in a round, white tent trimmed with gold borders that was pitched at the edge of the forest bordering Wittingham Castle. Inside the tent, minstrels sang Christmas carols while outside Lord Robert and his knights prepared their horses and bows for the hunt.

"My lord, you will be careful?" Anne queried, appearing at his side amidst the mingling crowd. Hounds yipped and pranced around their feet in the dampened leaf-laden snow.

Robert looked up as he tugged on a stirrup and, seeing her, his eyes brightened. "Ah, Lady Anne!" With one free hand he lifted her gloved fingers to his lips. "There is no need to worry, dearest."

A servant handed both of them cups of hot mulled wine. Anne savored the warmth of the cup that penetrated her cheverel-leather gloves.

"But I *do* worry, Robert."

"Dear Lady, have you not heard? The Lord of Misrule is immortal. I will live forever." He winked at her, giving her a sexy half smile.

"Yes, I suppose you're right," Anne replied, smiling in kind. He had lived long enough to meet her. A mere 600 years!

She watched him load an arrow onto his powerful bow and mount up. His steed bore a flowing trapper adorned with his falcon emblem. Robert wore a shirt of mail and a blue cloak, but his head was bare, his long locks flowing and wild in the whipping wind. He was utterly dashing, Anne concluded, gazing up at him with unabashed adoration.

"To the hunt!" he shouted when the others were gathering their reins and hitching their spurred boots into their stirrups. "The one who pierces the boar's heart shall dance with Lady Anne tonight."

A chorus of masculine voices rose in a cheer, startling a flock of moorfowl that fluttered skyward from a nearby heath. Anne blushed and shot Robert a mocking "You'll pay for this later" look. As the men began to trot off, Robert leaned over his horse's withers and whispered for her ears alone: "Fear not, I will be the only one to dance with you tonight. I'm the best hunter by a furlong."

She grinned at his cocky boast, but had no doubt he spoke the truth.

"Be careful," she said again, more to herself than him, as a dozen horsed men galloped into the forest.

He did not hear her, but he looked back over his shoulder before disappearing into the haven of barren trees, just to make sure she cared enough to watch him ride out of sight, and she did not disappoint him.

The women went about their business, but returned an hour later when a breathless page announced that a boar had been killed. Anne was the first to return to the tent. As the others gathered, she hugged herself beneath her hooded woolen cloak, straining to see a glimpse of Robert through the stark beige treeline. For some reason, she had an ominous feeling about the hunt. Her stomach had been a jumbled skein of nerves ever since Robert had left.

Moments later, however, he reappeared, jubilant, holding one end of the spear on which the enormous boar had been impaled. Robert's steward, Sir Kevin, held the other end.

"My gentle ladies, we bring you the Christmas boar!" Robert shouted breathlessly.

The women broke into applause as the men filtered into the clearing. Their faces were ruddy and sweaty from a hard ride. Several began to sing when the minstrels broke into another joyful carol.

Robert handed over the wild pig to his squire and, dismounting, he came straight to Anne's side.

His hair was tousled and sweaty. His face was bright with joy and victory. But the sleeve of his doublet was torn. Anne's stomach, already queasy, did a somersault.

"You were hurt!"

"A mere scratch." He touched the torn material and glanced down at the drying blood. He shrugged and grabbed her hand. "Come, we will walk back to the castle through the woods. 'Tis too beautiful of a morning to rush back."

They walked a spell in companionable silence, their feet crunching in the snow that had fallen the day Anne had arrived. Birds flitted from branch to branch, chirping, looking for dried red berries.

At length, Robert cleared his throat and said, "I cannot lie to you, Anne. While my wound was a mere scratch, I came very close to being gored by the boar."

His voice was even and strong. He tightened his hand around hers. "I would have died had Kevin not come to my aid. And what astonished me the most is that I had only one regret when I thought my life might soon be over—that I would not spend a lifetime with you. As 'tis, I regret that we did not meet sooner. I am thirty years old and you are . . ."

"Twenty-seven."

Robert frowned. "That's odd. Your father said you were—"

"I am twenty-seven," she gently interrupted without explaining the reason for any discrepancy. "I suppose that makes me an old maid by your standards. But if it's childbearing you're concerned about, believe me, it's not too late."

He stopped and tucked a warm hand into the folds of her hood and stroked her temple. "You would be a treasure at any age. Not only will you bring peace to the borders, you bring me love."

Her heart hitched at this sweet proclamation. She would bring him love. That much was true. But peace?

"Robert, I am not the woman you think I am."

"I don't want to hear it, Anne. Truly."

He studied her with great sobriety. Then, when he was assured she would not spoil the moment with logic and ugly realities, he kissed her. His hot probing lips provided a delightful contrast to her cold skin. She did not even pretend to resist. She breathed in her new world—a burning campfire; his clean, cold skin; his sweet, warm breath. And when his tongue flickered between her lips, she opened them, welcoming him. He pulled her closer to the long, hard length of his well-muscled body. She coiled her arms around his broad shoulders and kissed him with an abandon that could signal only one thing—desire.

He ended the kiss and hugged her sweetly, then whispered in her ear. "Will you come to my chamber?"

She nodded. "Yes, Robert. I thought you would never ask."

Yes, even though he would learn she was not a virgin. Would he throw her out of the castle? Would he consider that reason to end the bargain with Wharton? Anne didn't care. She wanted to make love to this extraordinary man. In eight days the bells would be silenced, and she would be transported back to Wisconsin. Until then, she would love Robert as much as possible.

They walked the remainder of their journey in silent anticipation. When they returned to Wittingham Castle, Robert dismissed the pages waiting to help him change clothes after the hunt. Instead, Anne helped him strip his outfit.

Her hand shook when she lifted his heavy wool cloak from his broad shoulders. She laid it gently on a chair by the crackling fire. When her back was turned to him, she squeezed her eyes shut, remembering the last time she had been intimate with a man. With David. Her husband. She realized now that she and David had never truly been married in spirit. They were merely kids playacting their brief roles as man and wife. Anne also realized that if she and Robert were torn apart by some quirk of time or fate, they would be married forever, even without the blessing of a priest. Their souls had been waiting an eternity for this joining. She only hoped they could be together long enough to join their lives together permanently in holy matrimony.

Sighing with deep contentment, relaxing muscles that had been tight for years, Anne turned with an easy smile.

"What is it?" he whispered. He had pulled off his doublet and started to loosen the leather ties on the V neck of his shirt.

"I was just mentally putting the past in order so I can better enjoy the present." She pushed his large hands aside and deftly loosened his collar.

"What past is that, my love?"

"My past, which is your future, Robert." She clasped both his hands, tilting her head coyly to better view him in the golden firelight.

"Another riddle," he said. "I don't know what that means, Anne. All I know is that I love you. I fell in love with you the moment I saw you lying in the snow, your reddish-blond hair tousled against the white."

She had already loosened her hair from its fillet and veil, and he took advantage of her dishabille. He ran his fingers through her loose locks, skimming her scalp, and she shivered with pleasure.

"And when I first kissed you," he continued sensuously, "I wanted not only to swoop you in my arms and make love to you. I wanted to hold you and never let you go. There is music in my head when I look into your eyes. Music I cannot describe."

"A symphony," she offered, feeling as if an Alleluia chorus were exploding within.

"Again, I don't know what you mean. What is this word—symphony? You say things that make no sense. But what you don't say, what I see in your eyes, makes sense to me as no woman ever has. I need you, Anne. I will never let you go. You are mine. And mine alone."

He swooped down for one of his unique and overpowering kisses. When his hungry lips consumed hers, it was as if his entire being existed simply to kiss her. All sounds faded—the distant cry of the night sentry, the cooing of birds from the dovecote, laughter from the Great Hall, the giggle of servants scurrying down the corridor.

Anne parted her lips when he deepened the kiss and melted against his powerful form. Her hands slipped under his billowy shirt and skimmed up the leather-tight skin covering the ridges of his ribs, and then over the twisted skein of bulging muscles along his spine. When her mind cleared itself of the exquisite pleasure wrought by these sensations, logic reared and panicked her.

They were about to make love. He would know she wasn't a virgin. Doubtless he expected his bride to be chaste. When he discovered she wasn't, reality would have to be faced. The ugly reality that threatened to tear her away from this dreamland.

"Oh," Anne gasped when one of his hands encompassed a breast. Her nipples hardened beneath her low-cut velvet kirtle. She ran her hands over his high cheeks, feeling the faint stubble of a beard. She inhaled his musky scent, and inwardly threw all caution to the wind. She wanted him. Now. Logic be damned.

"Make love to me, Robert."

He looked at her, blue eyes smoldering with gray smoke, and nodded. In lusty and frantic desperation, they fell on the big canopy bed, disrobing as they went, tugging at each other's garments. When Anne's gown was crumbled around her waist, Robert fell into the soft cushions of her breasts, inhaling her womanly scent. His hot mouth found a cold, hard nipple, and suckled ardently.

Anne shivered and gasped and writhed as a searing fire burned between her thighs, unlike anything she had experienced before. "Robert," she mumbled incoherently. "Oh, Robert."

His torso was bare; his skin slick and hot on hers. He moved his mouth from her breasts to her lips again, his tongue plunging into her moist depths. And all the while he continued to disrobe them, first pulling her gown over her hips, them fumbling with his hose and braies, ripping the cloth from his loins. When he fell atop her again, there was no mistaking the large and stiff testimony to his all-consuming desire. It pressed against her thighs, which all too willingly spread before it.

"With this act, I thee wed, in my heart and in my soul," he whispered, his eyes hard and sincere, his mouth parted in panting need.

"I thee wed as well, my love," she whispered on half a breath.

He slid into her then, easily. He groaned in hot delight, and then stilled. He raised himself on his elbows and his demanding eyes found hers.

He knew. He knew he wasn't the first. She did not deny it. She stared back with all the honesty she possessed. She could not pretend to be ashamed that she had slept with a man before. She was too much the modern woman. Besides, with Robert it felt like the first time. Only better. She was who she was. Would a 14th-century man understand that?

Presently, the issue was moot, for raging desire once again took control. The faintly pained look that had flashed over his tanned face melted with a quiver of hungry need. He started to move inside of her, a slippery and urgent rhythm. Before she knew it, Anne rose to a fervent peak, the kind that held her in limbo for what seemed an eternity. And then she collapsed beneath him. Robert, panting and sweating, fell atop her moments later.

They were spent. His skin had melted into hers, it seemed. The pleasure and satisfaction were greater than she had even dreamed possible. They were one. Of one mind, one body. Together. Forever?

"You are not a virgin," he whispered into the pillow.

His voice was neutral, betraying no anger or hurt. But surely those emotions were eating him up.

"No, Robert, I am not a virgin."

"Who was the man who came before me?"

He rolled over and they stared into each other's eyes, their heads resting on the pillow.

"His name was David."

"Are you bearing his child?"

"No!"

He nodded, his face shuddering with relief. "My brother, Godrick, was once betrothed to a woman who came to him with child. He cast her off, and her father then beat her to death."

"Good lord!"

"I am glad you are not with child."

"Robert, my darling Robert, the circumstances of my previous . . . encounter . . . are hard to explain. But I want you to understand. And please, *please* listen before you reject what I say."

He nodded, and she began.

"I was born in Wisconsin, in the United States of America, in the 20th century. That's 600 years in the future."

He blinked, as if trying to focus on the unbelievable, but he did not interrupt her, and she continued.

"I was an only child, raised by my mother. In modern times, that is possible. Men and women have equal rights. Frequently they both work outside the home. There are no castles, by the way. And you can literally fly from one city to another."

She talked for more than an hour, explaining to Robert the impossible. He listened with rapt attention to everything, particularly when she discussed her brief marriage to David.

"The Church allowed you to end this union?" Robert asked incredulously. Jealousy strained his voice.

"The Church does not control society in my time. A divorce is easy to get. Almost too easy," she added on a melancholy note.

"Your husband willingly let you go?" Robert persisted.

"He did not want me anymore." The pain was still there. She heard the sadness in her whispered answer. But the hurt vanished when he leaned forward and kissed her fervently.

"I will never let you go, Anne. Never. Do you understand?"

Tears burned at the corners of her eyes and trickled down her temples to the hair splayed about the pillow. She nodded and laughed softly through her tears. "Yes, I do know. That is why I agreed to marry you. That's the only reason I am willing to give up the only world I have ever known. I sensed your commitment. And that is more important to me than anything."

She continued the story of her life, ending with the car accident, which was the last thing she remembered.

"But how?" Robert finally disengaged from their loose embrace. He sat at the edge of the bed, wiped a hand over his perspiring forehead, and then rested his forearms on his muscular legs. "How did you travel back in time?"

Anne sighed in relief. "So you believe me."

He shot her a steady look. "Of course. I would believe anything you say. Besides, there was something different about you from the start. I didn't want to acknowledge it. I wanted to believe that Lady Anne Wharton was beautiful and kind and not the shrew everyone had warned she would be. So I ignored all the incongruities."

"Lady Anne!" she groaned, covering her face with her hands. "Don't remind me of Wharton's daughter. She will arrive at Wittingham Castle as soon as the snow melts, Robert. You know she will. Then everyone will know I am not the person they thought I was. I could be burned as a witch!"

"I don't care what the others think," he said without hesitation. "You will be my wife."

"No, I won't." She sat up, a bit peaked by his dictatorial manner. "I don't care if you are the lord of the castle. You can't make me marry you. We still haven't exchanged our vows before a priest. I will always love you in my heart. In my heart of hearts, you will always be my husband, my true love. But if I interfere with history by legally marrying you, who knows what disaster may befall you. You were meant to marry Wharton's daughter."

He rose and began to pace. "You cannot say that with certainty. Who knows God's plan? Only Him. Or do you presume to His seat just because you have seen miracles of which I couldn't have dreamed."

Anne's cheeks flamed with color. "Please, Robert, don't act like the overbearing Lord of the Castle. I'm trying to do what is best for you. If you do not marry Wharton's daughter, the border skirmishes will continue and you may die on the battlefield. In my time, men commonly live to be seventy or eighty, and you are only thirty."

"That is a ripe age, Anne."

"No, Robert, you are young. Too young to die. Oh, I know people in medieval times live fast and hard. I've read all about it. In the early 1400s your country will win one of the most famous battles in all of history, the battle of Agincourt in France, led by Henry V, one of the greatest English monarchs of all time. He died at the age of thirty-five. I want you to live far longer than that, Robert. It is possible even in this day and age."

Robert paused, his anger replaced by intense curiosity. "Henry V. The son of whom?"

"Henry IV, the Usurper. He usurped the throne from King Richard, who was the son of— Oh, for Heaven's sake! What does it matter? I shouldn't even be telling you this. It will alter the way you act. And that will alter history."

She jumped up and started fumbling for her clothes, but he grabbed her bare arms and pulled her close.

"You will be my wife. I don't care about Wharton. I will fight him and I will win. It was foolish of me to think marrying a shrew would be a tolerable exchange for peace. I will fight for you, Anne, because I will be your husband. All I ask," he said, then choked on the next words. Blinking rapidly, he continued in a whisper. "All I ask is that you stay here. With me. In your past history. Promise me you will."

When she did not answer, he shook her. "Promise me!"

Tears flooded her eyes. "I can't. Not even if I wanted to."

Chapter Seven

"Wherefore not?" he had asked, and asked again each day for the next sennight, as he would call the week that followed. And always her answer seemed constrained and lifeless. Unlike the blossoming of their love.

Each night, before they retired to his chamber to make sweet love, Robert gave her a gift. Not six maids a-milking and seven lords a-leaping. His presents were much more thoughtful and beautiful. On the second day of Christmas her true love gave to her an ornate ivory comb to run through her long locks. On the third day, she received a small vial of exotic perfume from Persia. On the fourth day, her eyes feasted on a gift of brightly-colored ribbons. Day five: he surprised her with a finely-bred horse. On the sixth day of Christmas a more modest gift—a box of figs. The seventh day, which was New Year's Eve, she delighted in a stunningly ornate gown, the edges of which were bordered with pearls and gold stitching. And on the eighth day, after they had joined a wassailing procession through the local town, she received a glittering amethyst ring, which made her cry. The spigot opened when Robert said it represented the wedding ring he would slip on her finger on the Twelfth Day.

And through all the days and nights she spent with Robert—making love, learning how to run the castle, befriending his friends, learning to live with a cold privy and baths only once a week, if that much—through it all she came to one startling conclusion: she did not want to go back to her home in Wisconsin. She belonged here. No one would miss her. Oh, a few college friends, certainly, and Mrs. Jensen would worry about what had happened to her, but what other commitments did she have? Here she was needed. Robert needed her. And perhaps others. Perhaps she knew enough about sanitation to help save lives in a way that wouldn't interfere too much with the grand design.

Even if she could do nothing to stop the ravages of disease, she was willing to live a shorter life if it were a life filled to overflowing with joy and love. With love, each day was in itself an eternity. Time, after all, was an illusion. She thought of how long the days had seemed when she was a child, before she knew what time meant. Each day seemed to last a year. And summer vacations lasted an eternity. Only when she had gained the perspective that comes from age did it seem like she never had enough time in a day to accomplish all that she wanted. Only then did it seem that the years flew by with little fanfare. So it had to be possible to make time stand still. Anything was possible with love.

"I will not let you go," Robert said once again after giving her the ring.

She sighed and strolled to the embrasure in his solar, looking out at the dusky winter scene. Another bitter snowstorm was in progress, pelting the castle with two feet of endless white.

She shivered and turned to him with a love-torn expression. "Robert, I would give anything to stay with you here. But as I've said over and over, I did nothing to send myself back in time. I have no control over whether I will return to the future."

"Very well," Robert said with resignation, "let's go over this one more time. What proof do you have that you will return to your other life?"

"I don't have proof of anything. But it simply seems logical. All right, let's retrace the steps." She began to pace over the pleasantly-scented rushes on the floor while Robert sat on the hearth before the blazing fire. "I heard the bell from the cat's collar. I rushed into the street and was hit by what I thought was a car. It turns out that I was struck by one of the horses carrying your supply cart. When

I came to, I heard bells again. That sound somehow connected our worlds. Unfortunately, the bells, by your account, will stop ringing on midnight of Twelfth Night
because that is the end of the holiday season. If the bells
brought me here, then it logically follows that I will disappear when they grow silent."

"Then I will never let them stop ringing," Robert
growled with frustration. "I will pay someone to ring the
bells all year."

Anne considered this, then shook her head. "No, it's not
that simple. It can't be. There's something else in the odd
chain of events. Niner ran away the day Annabelle died,
which was the same day to the year that my mother died."

"Perhaps that is only coincidence," he offered.

"Perhaps. But I suspect Mom and Annabelle are in cahoots with Niner. Mom wanted me to be happily married."

"Then she doesn't want you to return to the future."

"Maybe. But there is another factor to consider. I had
done a lot of research on the medieval time period for my
Christmas postcards. To tell you the truth, I was obsessed
with the Middle Ages. When I painted the Lord of Misrule,
I drew my ideal man. I fell in love with the character who
looks just like . . ."

She stopped pacing and stared at his handsome, bold fea-
tures in the flickering firelight. "He looked just like you.
Does that mean you are a figment of my imagination?
Maybe this *is* a dream after all."

"I am real, Anne. If you are transported back to the future, which I hope you will not be, read your history books.
You will know I existed."

She began to pace, gnawing at her lower lip. "I know
you're real, Robert. I'm just considering all the possibilities. And when I do, I keep coming back to the bells.
There's something significant about that."

He stood and met her in the middle of the room. His towering figure loomed lovingly over her petite form. He

tucked a finger under her chin and forced her to look directly into his startlingly blue eyes.

"Your cat's bells and your mother may have contributed to this miraculous mystery. But I think you'd be wise to focus on your contribution."

"My contribution?"

"Your study of history. By your own admission, you were obsessed with this time period. Then be obsessed with me. Love me wholly, without condition, without fear or reservation. Keep your eye on love, and I believe you will never leave my side. If you love me completely, then not even death will part us."

Anne's heart swooned with love. "You are such a wise man, Robert. I do believe I am the luckiest woman in the world in *any* century."

He kissed her then, sweetly, infinitely. The kiss was a breath of pure meadow air, redolent with the scent of flowers; a cleansing rain storm; a deep, healing slumber. When it ended, Anne hugged him, until a nagging thought loomed in her head.

"We are forgetting the other problem," she said gloomily. "Lady Anne Wharton will be arriving any moment. On my way to your chamber, I heard the servants scurrying about in a rush of whispers. They said the sentries had sighted Wharton's traveling party on the south road. If she arrives tonight, I will not sleep with you. It would not be proper."

"I told you. I will not marry her."

"Then you will be challenged in battle by her father. I don't want you to die, Robert!"

"Anne, I—" His response was cut short by a rapid knock on the arched wooden door. "Enter!"

"My lord, Wharton's herald has arrived," said Robert's ruddy steward. He stepped aside, making way for a trim man who bore a blue cloak glistening with melting snowflakes. His coat of arms, peaking through the slit in the cape, was adorned with a unicorn. Anne clutched the unicorn pendant hanging from her neck, and her heart began to thump madly. She was here! The real Lady Anne had finally arrived.

"My lord," the herald said, bowing deeply. "I come with grim news. I was traveling with your betrothed, Lady Anne Wharton, along with her entourage. She had delayed her journey because of the first snowstorm. But we set out two days ago, when we were unexpectedly waylaid by a second storm. Sadly, my lord, Lady Anne and her handmaiden got separated in the blizzard. We . . . we found them both this morning at the edge of Cotter's Forest . . . dead, my lord."

"*Dead?*" Robert repeated.

"Aye, my lord, she had gotten lost in the forest and then plunged onto the road. But the snow was so thick, she did not see an oncoming cart and was trampled and left in its wake."

"She was struck by a cart?" Robert exchanged a potent glance with Anne. Could it be? Lady Anne struck the same way as his Anne? One Anne had survived, the other had perished.

"We've returned her body to her father's castle, but I came to inform you that . . . that there would be no wedding."

Robert pondered this incredible turn of events, rubbing a hand over his faint stubble of a beard. "Lord, may God send her soul quickly to Heaven. Please give Wharton my condolences. His only daughter . . . dead!"

"My lord bade me inform you, that the peace accord will still exist. He says he has no heart for any more death. He bids you peace."

Robert shot a glance at Anne, who, frowning, was still trying to sort out the impact of this tragedy.

"Thank him for me. Tell him the priest in town will say a year of masses in his daughter's honor. Meanwhile, tell no one else of this tragic news. I will inform everyone here at Wittingham Castle myself."

"Very good, Lord Robert. I leave you with thanks on my

lord's behalf," the herald said. He bowed again, then departed in the company of the steward.

When the door shut behind them, Robert rushed to Anne. He gripped her forearms and she gripped his in return, a flood of excitement rushing back and forth between them.

As he struggled to find the right words, her frowning visage blossomed into a glorious smile of joy. "Oh, Robert!"

"I hope God will forgive me," he managed to say at last, "I am sorry for her death. I truly am. But now there is nothing to stand between us, Anne. Nothing."

"Oh Robert, I would never have endangered your life. But now you are free."

She flung her perfect, strong, feminine body into his arms, and he thought his heart would burst with love for her.

"We will be married on Twelfth Night. I will tell the others after our wedding that you are not Wharton's daughter. I will need some time to explain your sudden appearance. If I am not careful, someone might accuse you of witchcraft, and then *your* life will be the one endangered."

There was only one thing that still threatened to keep them apart. One major, seemingly insurmountable obstacle—time itself. He had lectured Anne on love and faith. But deep inside, he still feared she would be ripped from his arms four days from now. He could not let that happen. He had to take matters into his own hands.

"Set up the chess board, my love. I would play a game with you tonight before we sleep. But first there is something I must do."

"What?" she inquired, a touch of concern wrinkling her smooth brow. "What is it?"

He shook his head. "I will tell you four days from now." He added grimly, "If you are still here."

Chapter Eight

On the morning of the Twelfth Day of Christmas, Anne stirred, but did not open her eyes immediately. It was a game she liked to play. She would listen, knowing that sounds in the morning were easier to hear because there were fewer distractions, like airplanes flying overhead, or noisy cars. She would listen and savor whatever dream she'd had. And her ruminations would turn to daydreams about the future.

This morning, however, instead of cars and planes, she heard sounds that she was just beginning to recognize. There was the clanking of the chains and pulleys when the porter ordered the drawbridge lowered, followed by a monstrous groan when the wooden bridge sank the last few inches and thudded into place. There was the giggle of children gathered to see a puppet show in the inner bailey, and the whirring of doves in the dovecote. And, of course, she heard bells. The sounds were precious to her, because she always heard them when she was lying in Robert's arms after a night of lovemaking.

And in the moment before her eyes fluttered open to begin the day, very likely her last day at Wittingham Castle, Anne knew beyond doubt that she wanted to stay here forever. This was her home. The only place she had truly felt complete. Robert had said she could stay if she meditated on their love.

"I believe in our love," she whispered. "I believe in our love." Then she smiled, thinking that perhaps she should click her heels together three times like Dorothy in the Wizard of Oz.

But what would she do here if she were able to stay? Of course she would love Robert. She would bear his children and raise them. She would act as chatelaine and see that the castle was properly cared for. Who knows, perhaps she would even defend his castle in his absence, as she had read some noblewomen did in wartime. But would that be enough to fulfill her? Fulfillment was probably something 14th-century women were too busy to think about.

If there were anything that she would miss about her old life other than central heating, it would be her artwork. But there was nothing to keep her from drawing and painting here. In fact, maybe there would be a way to record history through her art and preserve it for the future. Her postcards had been inspired by ancient art.

Putting her daydreaming aside, she blinked open her eyes, only to find Robert leaning on one of the posts at the end of their bed, staring at her with a loving look, a half-smile dimpling one cheek.

"You're ravishing when you sleep. Did you know that?"

"How long have you been standing there?"

"Not long enough."

She flushed with pleasure. "You've been up awhile?"

"Long enough to fetch you a modest wedding gift."

"Another gift?"

"Tonight we will be married, remember? 'Twill be Twelfth Night."

"How could I forget?"

"I thought I would mention it in case you planned to leave as abruptly as you arrived."

"I won't leave willingly."

He frowned at the unspoken reminder of the heartbreak that might well be awaiting them.

"Would you like to see your presents?"

"Yes." She sat up eagerly, feeling like a child at Christmas, and not at all the grown woman she was.

Robert reached down to the floor at the end of the bed and pulled up a big basket filled with velvet. He plucked out a small object—a broach—and handed it to her, sitting by her side.

"Oh, Robert, it's beautiful." She gazed at an intricately-cast silver pin inset with glittering jewels. She'd never seen anything so elegant outside of a museum. It was heavy in her hand, solid, like their love. "Thank you, my darling husband-to-be."

"I also mustered these for you." He pulled from the basket several rolled sheaves of parchment, a quill pen, and an ink pot. "You said you are an artist. I want you to draw. I will buy you some paint from the merchants who come to the fair this summer. I would like to see the world through your eyes."

A rush of emotion flooded her and she blinked back tears. She leaned over and hugged him tightly. "Oh, Robert, I love you so much. I did not know I was capable of such love. I only wish I had a gift for you," Anne said, withdrawing from his embrace.

"Oh, I'm not finished yet. There is yet another gift in my basket." He carefully parted the material and pointed inside. "See for yourself."

Anne leaned forward and then gasped with joy. "A kitten! Oh, it's adorable."

She reached in and scooped up a sleeping black furball. It was purring like a little engine. Stirred by the warmth of her hands, the kitten opened its big green eyes and yawned.

"I love cats, Robert. Especially black cats. It reminds me of . . ." Niner. She couldn't quite say it. She still got choked up whenever she thought of him. What ever had happened to her old friend? Did he ever return to her house?

"I had a cat that looked just like this," she said, swallowing a bittersweet lump of emotion that lodged in her throat.

"I know. You spoke of him the first day I met you. That's why I'm giving you another. I don't want you to miss anything about your old life."

"Ironically, my cat is the only living creature I'll truly miss. Sad to say, Robert, I didn't live a very exciting life until I met you."

"Well, the excitement is just beginning."

She smiled contentedly in the silence that followed. Bells

rang softly in the distance. It struck her suddenly that if she vanished tonight at midnight, he would have no keepsake to remind him of her. And she wished doubly that she had a wedding gift for him. But what did she have to give?

Suddenly, it struck her.

"Robert, are you free for a moment? I mean, do you have any pressing business as the lord of the castle, or even as the Lord of Misrule?"

"Nay, my lady, I am at your command."

"I want you to sit still for about a half hour. I'm going to draw a portrait of you in pen and ink. That will be my wedding gift to you."

She ordered him to pose in the sunlight that was beaming in a warm rectangle through the embrasure. The light infused his blue eyes with sparkling beauty and cast deep shadows below his rugged cheekbones. Of course, she could not translate the color with black ink, but she could render the shadows and light which dramatically exposed his strength and handsome features.

Inspired by her subject, she worked quickly, filled with joy to be drawing again. Less than half an hour later, she was done.

"Come see your wedding gift," she said, propping the picture on the table at which she had been working. She moved away and wiped her ink-stained fingers on a handkerchief. She looked around the room, giving her eyes a break from the minute lines she had drawn. She always liked to look away from her artwork for a few moments so she could view the finished project with fresh eyes.

" 'Tis a marvel," he said, and she could hear the glowing approval in his voice. "You have great skill."

"I'm glad you like it." She came to his side and tucked her arm through his. She focused on the portrait and then gasped.

"What is it? What is wrong?" he said.

"I've seen this drawing before."

"How can that be? Where?"

She racked her brain, and then it came to her. "In a history book. The one I used to research my postcards. I used this picture to inspire my rendering of the Lord of Misrule. The artist was anonymous. Oh my God, I can't believe this! Robert, I'm getting goose bumps. I drew this picture and it survived through 600 years of history as the work of an anonymous artist!"

Anne was thrilled to realize that at least one of her drawings had survived the test of time. But would there be others? Or was this portrait of a medieval figure the only one she would draw before being hurtled back through time?

Chapter Nine

The bride wore Christmas green.

Anne was surprised when her handmaiden procured the ornate gown, for she didn't know that medieval brides rarely wore white. The rich velvet fabric was lush and much more interesting than anything she had seen modern brides wear.

She met Robert just before dusk at the steps of the castle chapel with a dozen ladies-in-waiting trailing behind her. They were all dressed in their finest, for not only would there be a solemn marriage, but a wild and merry Twelfth Night celebration following the ceremony.

Anne held up the heavy folds of her gown and ascended the cold marble steps. Robert was waiting for her in a brilliant gold houppelande that hung to the top of his short boots. With a high black collar and a dashing hat, he looked positively resplendent.

Prodded by the priest, they said their vows at the church door. It seemed to Anne a peculiar custom, but she learned that it dated back many years to a time when the Roman Catholic Church was trying to establish its authority over marriages. If couples said their vows outside the church where everyone could see them, there would be no doubt that the union had been sanctified by a priest.

Afterward, they entered the church, and the priest celebrated Mass. Through it all, Anne was in a daze.

I'm married, she thought. *I'm married to the most extraordinary man I have ever met. And I have chosen to live with him in the year 1375. If I am lucky enough to stay here, I will never see my old home again. And I don't even care.*

But every moment of wonder and joy was accompanied by a moment of gripping fear. In approximately six hours, the Christmas bells would fall silent. Would she still be here?

She couldn't bear to think otherwise. And so when Robert kissed her to seal their marriage vows, she clung to him fervently, all the hopes and dreams of a lifetime pouring through her lips in a silent and desperate proclamation of her love.

After the wedding Mass, everyone went to the Great Hall for the Twelfth Night celebration. There was a giant wreath made of holly hanging over the fireplace. A table off to one side displayed ornate sugar sculptures depicting a nativity scene. Three minstrels sang Christmas carols and a jester played a lute, accompanying a dancing bear. Quickly, the mood of the crowd soared to a fevered pitch of joy.

Robert pushed his way through the throng to Anne, who was accepting congratulations from Lady Gertrude and Sir Kevin. During a lull in their conversation, Robert grabbed Anne by the wrist and pulled her, laughing, to the dais.

He still wore his gold wedding garb. But he had donned his garish Lord of Misrule chaplet, which, Anne concluded, looked not so much like a bird's nest, but like a cross between a hat and a wreath.

"Gentle lords and ladies, I welcome you to Twelfth Night here at Wittingham Castle," Robert pronounced, his commanding voice stilling the crowd. "In a moment we will play Hot Cockles. And we will have the most spectacular mummery you've ever witnessed. But first I must introduce you to my wife, Lady Anne, the Countess of Wittingham."

"Hear, hear!" several men shouted gaily and banged their tankards on the wooden tables. The others applauded enthusiastically.

"Once in a lifetime, nay, once in an eternity, a man finds a woman who is perfect in every way. Some say love is an indulgence. My father would have said that. But if we listen to the troubadours, we know that there is an ideal by which we all can live. The ideal of love, devotion, honor, and chivalry."

A shiver niggled up Anne's spine. She turned her gaze from his astonishingly handsome and poignant profile to the still burgundy surface of the wine in her goblet. She couldn't bear to look at him for too long. He was too precious to her. Here was a man who shared her ideal of true love. How very lucky she was.

"Sometimes two souls have been seeking each other for so long and hard that time itself becomes irrelevant," Robert continued, with a message that only Anne could truly appreciate. "When you are in love, a moment lasts an eternity. Six hundred years can fly by in the blink of an eye."

He looked down at Anne, beaming at her.

"I drink heartily tonight in honor of this marriage because I am the most fortunate man who ever lived."

The crowd broke into a cheer and Robert kissed her again, to the delight of everyone.

And so it went. Every moment was a joyous celebration. Robert and Anne danced until they nearly collapsed. They played wild games, and Robert even danced with the bear, which made Anne double over with laughter. But when ten o'clock drew near, the newlyweds made their way back to Robert's solar, and their fervent joy faded, replaced by melancholy and exquisite intimacy.

They made love as soon as the doors were closed. And then they made love again.

"I will love you forever," Robert whispered in her ear after they had collapsed in exhaustion. "If you leave, I will find you. Somehow. Some way."

"You must, Robert, you must come and find me," she whispered, clinging to him in her weariness.

After a few moments of stillness, listening to the crackling of the fire, Robert sat up in a rustle of sheets.

"Where are you going?" Anne inquired, groaning in complaint at the rush of cold air that hit her moist breasts.

"I am going to the chapel to ring the bells. I didn't have the heart to force the priest to do it on this bitter night."

"No, Robert." She sat up and tugged at his arm. "You cannot ring the bells forever."

"Why not?" he said defiantly, anger and fear breaking his voice. "I won't willingly let you go."

"You were right, Robert, when you said it is our love that matters most. The bells may have triggered my journey in time, but they are just an outward marker for something far more profound. If I am meant to be here, I will be here regardless of the bells. If love matters, then I will stay. We are not little gods who can manipulate history. And if we defy God's will, if we alter history as it is meant to be, we will pay the price. Now that I know I painted that portrait of you, I know that somehow I fit into your history, if even for only twelve days. Unfortunately, I didn't do enough research to know if I will be here longer. I don't know if I'll be able to paint more pictures of you. I pray to God it is so, but I won't defy God's will to do so. I don't care about the bells. I love you. Let that be enough."

His tanned, lean torso was taut with anger and the urge to defy the Creator. But she spoke wisely, and he knew it. Their love had to be enough. Slowly, his muscles melted and he crawled back into her arms. Tightly entwined, they gazed to the foot of the bed and beyond, where the fire glowed with hot, orange flames. Thus embraced, they waited for midnight. They merely waited.

About ten minutes before twelve, Anne heard a squeaky little mewing, and she remembered the kitten. She slipped out of bed, scooped him into her hands, and crawled back under the covers, taking care not to crush him. Together, silently, Robert and Anne petted the little creature. Anne thought of Niner. She had nurtured him as a kitten and through each of his eight close calls.

Eight times Niner had nearly been killed. Twice jumping from a tree, once nearly getting run over by a car, two times he'd been cornered and nearly eaten for dinner by Mrs.

Jensen's Doberman, once he'd licked some antifreeze and had had to be rushed to the animal hospital. She couldn't remember the other incidents, but she'd kept count. Eight brushes with death. Too bad he hadn't used up his ninth life. He'd had one left to spare.

"I could use nine lives," she whispered with a yawn.

"What?"

"If I had nine lives, I'd use one of them, no, strike that, I'd use all of them with you."

It was their last conversation. She had wanted to stay awake to hear the crier call out the stroke of midnight. But she grew groggier and groggier, and she couldn't manage to keep her eyes open. It was time to sleep. Time to trust in their love.

The last thing she remembered was looking into the kitten's green eyes. Then one of his eyes—only one—winked at her.

Finally, it all became clear.

Chapter Ten

Anne felt the first rays of dawn beaming down on her face, but she was so exhausted she couldn't manage to pry her eyes open. She knew this morning was important. She had been dying to find out what this dawn would hold. Was she still in Yorkshire? Or had she returned to Wisconsin?

All she had to do to find out was open her eyelids, but they felt like lead weights, and it was all she could do to keep from falling back asleep.

So she listened to the sounds as she always did when she had the leisure to loll around in bed. She heard a familiar crunch of gravel. Was it the sound of rubber car tires rolling over loose gravel? she wondered with dread.

Then she heard a Christmas carol. Had she left the Johnny Mathis CD on all night? she mused, fearing she was back in her old bed. She might have pressed the repeat button by accident.

And then she heard purring. *Niner!* Had he finally come home?

Excited by the prospect, her eyes flew open and she came face to face with—a kitten. The little black furball was fast asleep on her chest. It was the kitten Robert had given her. Then she saw movement from the corner of her eye and looked up.

"Robert! It's you!" She sprang up into a sitting position.

He wore a green velvet doublet and a broad, satisfied smile. "Aye, Lady Anne?"

"I'm still here in Yorkshire?"

"Aye, my darling."

"Then it really worked. Our love was strong enough to keep me here."

"Aye, my love."

"But I thought I heard the crunch of car tires on gravel."

" 'Twas just a cart filled with alms for the poor, trundling over the rocky road outside the castle."

"And I heard music. I thought it was my CD player."

"Just wandering minstrels, my love."

Overwhelmed with joy, she rose and quickly pulled on a robe to guard her body from the chill. Then she rushed into Robert's arms. He was warm and strong and smelled of wood smoke and fresh air.

"I'm still here," she murmured.

"Aye, my love. And I'll never let you go."

"Ahem! Forgive me for interrupting, my lord, but I think I finally have it figured out."

Anne and Robert turned to the door and found an old man with long gray hair and a beard. He was stooped over a cane carved with the head of Zeus. He clutched a large tome under one arm.

"I've been combing through the Emerald Tablet ever since your visit, Lord Robert. I think I finally know how to fulfill your request."

"Lady Anne," Robert said with a rumbling chuckle, "this is the castle alchemist, Brother Rupert. He was once a man of the cowl, but has spent the last five years studying the art of alchemy in my dungeon."

"Alchemy?"

"Aye, my lady," the old man offered, blinking his cloudy eyes and smiling with pride. " 'Tis my job to learn how to turn base metals into gold, to enrich my lord's coffers. The secrets are all here in the Emerald Tablet," he said, lifting the book for her viewing, "but I am afraid interpreting the alchemical secrets isn't as easy as it might seem. I haven't yet succeeded at my mission."

"Four days ago I called on Brother Rupert to see if there was a way he could help keep you here with me."

Anne smiled, now seeing amusement in their futile attempts to affect Fate. "I see."

"My job is to transmute metals, to turn silver into gold.

Lord Robert hoped I might be able to transmute time as well."

"And what did you discover, Brother Rupert?"

"Well, my lord, if I can find the eye of a newt and the toe of a frog, and then mix them with the urine of a mountain goat, I just might be able to do it."

"Just so it doesn't involve any leeches," Anne warned the old man.

At this stipulation, Robert burst out laughing. Anne joined in, leaving Brother Rupert very confused and a trifle insulted.

"Forgive us, good sir," Robert said when he'd regained his composure. "We will not need your services. Lady Anne is going nowhere. But I thank you for trying to help."

"Well, then, very good, Lord Robert. I will turn my attention back to gold."

He bowed and departed, leaving the lovers alone. They crawled back into bed and cuddled under the warm covers.

"So, love was the answer after all," Robert murmured, nestling her ear with hot lips.

"Yes, my darling husband. But in the end, I owe a big thanks to Niner. I've finally figured it out. Just before I fell asleep last night, this little furball here winked at me. He actually winked, just like Niner. You see, Robert, Niner gave me his ninth life so I could spend it with you. And this little guy," she said affectionately, scratching the kitten's ears, "this little guy is somehow holding Niner's spirit. Sort of a backwards reincarnation."

"I don't understand."

"Neither do I. But I'd recognize Niner's wink anywhere."

The kitten mewed from the end of the bed, seemingly in affirmation.

"I do not know or care how it happened, Anne. I'm just happy that I get to keep the love of my life."

He crawled on top of her, kissing her nape. It was obvious that they were going to make love again.

"Save some energy, Robert. I want you to pose for a long time this afternoon. I plan to draw a much more intricate portrait of you. I want to make sure future generations appreciate you as much as I do."

"Very good, my lady," Robert said, seeking her lips for another kiss, and soon they were making passionate love again.

The kitten settled down at the end of the bed, safe from the joyful thrashing of the lovers. Then he lowered one eyelid in a wink and began to purr contentedly.

A Gift of Light

Jo Beverley

A Gift of Light

"Sherry, do stop that noise!"

Kitty Mayhew was settled in her favorite wing chair, feet close to the fire, mending the tapestry work on one of her mother's chair-seats. The tiny stitches required all her concentration and she glanced up with a frown.

Her small, white cat ignored her, continuing to weave through the legs of a chair as if afflicted by fleas, yowling plaintively. There were no fleas—Kitty had checked her a dozen times in the past two days. She hadn't found any other problem, either. The cat clearly needed attention, however, so Kitty put her sewing aside and went to pick her up.

At her approach, Sherry crouched down, thrusting her rump at her, and making a peculiar growling kind of noise.

"Sherry!" When Kitty bent to pick her up, the cat leaped away and turned, almost as if about to scratch. What on earth . . . ?

Pol Cooper, her general maid, came in with the tea tray. A solid, round-cheeked young girl with bubbling, mousy hair, she was admirably even-tempered. "Is something the matter, miss?" she asked in her Kentish accent.

"I don't know." Sherry was now on the carpet in front of the fire, but instead of curling there contentedly as usual, she was writhing and making that strange sound that was more of a growl than a purr.

Pol cast a quizzical look at the cat, shook her head, and put down the tray. "Sit you down, Miss Kitty, and have a nice cup of tea."

"Perhaps Sherry's missing Mama," said Kitty, returning to her chair. "She was really her cat."

"It's been two months, miss, and she's only been like this for days."

"It takes time for these things to sink in." Smoothing her black mourning gown, Kitty knew she was really speaking of herself.

Pol poured the tea, adding milk and sugar to Kitty's taste, and bringing it to her. "I don't think cats are like that, miss."

"You're doubtlessly right. Do sit and have tea with me, Pol."

Pol obligingly poured herself a cup and sat in an upright chair. This had become a routine with them.

Kitty normally had three servants in her London house—Mr. and Mrs. Triscott, who served as cook-housekeeper and butler—and Pol, who was maid of all work. However, she had given the Triscotts permission to spend the Christmas season with their daughter, who'd married a well-to-do farmer down near Aylesbury. After all, so close to her mother's death, Kitty would be living quietly and Pol would be able to do all that was necessary.

Within days she'd decided it was silly to have Pol living alone in the servants' quarters and herself rattling lonely in the three-story house, so they'd begun this practice of sharing their tea and their simple meals. But, unspoken, certain rules had been decided upon—mainly by the maid.

Pol would prepare as if they were to drink and eat together, but she would not actually do so unless invited.

Pol would take tea with her employer, but she would not sit in an upholstered chair, which she considered the family chairs.

Pol would take dinner with Kitty, but she would still serve the food, acting as maid.

Also, Pol never initiated a topic of conversation.

"So," said Kitty, a little soothed by the tea, "what do you think is the matter with Sherry? Could she be sick?"

Sipping, Pol looked at Kitty over the rim of the cup. "Truth to tell, Miss Kitty, I think she's in heat."

"Too hot? But she likes to be by the fire."

"In *heat,* miss." Pol drank more tea, her brow slightly furrowed. "Wanting to have kittens, like."

"Wanting to . . ." Kitty stared at her cat, who for the moment was calm and relaxed. "But she's not the slightest bit bigger."

Pol sighed. "She's wanting to get in the family way, miss. She's wanting to meet a tomcat and let him have his wicked way with her. I'm not saying she wants *kittens* any more than most females want babies when they're wanting. But she's wanting."

Oh, of course. Kitty put down her cup, feeling foolish not to have thought of it herself. "I suppose cats come into season like other animals. Is that how they behave?"

"Reckon so, miss. There were any number of cats around the charity school."

"But she's so young! I had not expected . . . Surely that means she will go *out* of heat in due course."

"In due course, yes, miss."

"How long?"

Pol stood up and refilled both their cups. "I'm not rightly sure, miss. At the school, there were always toms about and it were sort of taken care of naturally, if you see what I mean. We always had lots of kittens around unless they drowned 'em."

Kitty took her refilled cup, her mouth slack with dismay. Not only was her pretty little cat behaving like the cheapest whore, but she could end up with kittens which would probably have to be drowned.

She remembered how entrancing Sherry had been as a tiny, large-eyed kitten. Could she bear to order such helpless creatures killed? She could never keep them all, however, and she knew how hard it was to find homes for them.

Kitty's mother had acquired Sherry from just such a clutch of unwanted kittens, driven by impulse in the period after the death of Kitty's father. The ball of white fur had been a comfort to them both, but Kitty didn't think she could depend on there being enough grieving families to provide homes for Sherry's offspring.

She sipped her tea. "At least there is no chance of kittens without a tom."

"Beggin' your pardon, miss, but haven't you heard the caterwaul the past few nights?"

"What caterwaul?"

"Well, I suppose you're at the front and I'm at the back. There's any number of toms hanging around arguing over her."

"Arguing . . . ! Now you mention it, I have heard something. I thought it was just some drunken revelers in a nearby street. Good heavens! How terrible. We must be very sure she doesn't get out."

Pol put down her cup, grinning. "She's going to like that just as much as any lovesick young lady would."

Kitty rolled her eyes, and Pol chuckled while gathering the cups. She then picked up the tray and returned below stairs.

Returning to her needlework, Kitty fretted over her poor cat. Sprawled in front of the sparking log fire, pure white and delicate, Sherry looked so young and innocent. The image of screeching males just waiting to get at her, fighting over the right to violate her even, was positively alarming. It was like something from the most barbaric periods of human history.

The house was secure, she assured herself, especially now that all the windows were closed for the winter. She would check before going to bed tonight, however, and make sure that no chink remained to allow rapacious tomcats to invade.

Then Sherry began to writhe again. A little while ago Kitty might have thought the cat was dreaming, or trying to scratch an itch. Now the movements could only be seen as voluptuous.

"Really, Sherry! Behave yourself."

How long would this go on? Perhaps there was a medicine for it, but Kitty wasn't sure she could bring herself to ask Dr. Whitworth about such a thing. She considered herself a well-educated woman, for both her parents had been scholars. She'd thought herself beyond being missish, but this situation was distinctly embarrassing.

As Sherry began to croon to herself, Kitty looked away, thankful that women were not plagued with such urges.

Then she remembered Pol's comment about lovesick young ladies. Of course the cat was not *love*sick. Kitty didn't really have a word for the state the cat was in. She did, however, have some friends who'd behaved in very silly ways when they thought themselves in love.

Not herself, of course. Life with her parents and their scholarly friends had avoided the peaks and valleys of romanticism.

She had encountered some supposed rakes, but they'd always seemed quite shallow, silly fellows, far too full of their own importance. Her friends had been inclined to sigh at the sight of a red coat, but military men had never turned her wits. Even the dashing Lord Byron, whom she'd met on a number of occasions, had not made her heart vary its normal, regular beat.

With his looks, that is. She had enjoyed his readings of his poetry.

She'd been comfortable with her phlegmatic attitude toward the opposite sex, but now it was a problem. Her situation was difficult, and the solution was doubtless to marry.

She had never expected to be left alone so soon. Her parents had not been old—they had died while only in their fifties. Both her parents had been only children, and so she had no close relatives at all.

Having lived here in Suffolk Street all her life, she was surrounded by friends. Friends, however, even old ones, are not quite the same as family, and she felt distressingly alone.

What was she to do?

She'd inherited all her parents' property, and now owned

the lease to this three-story terraced house. She could sell it for a substantial sum of money, but she had also inherited a comfortable income and had no need of more.

It was clearly ridiculous for a single lady to live here alone with four bedrooms, a handsome dining room, a spacious drawing room, and ample servants' quarters. On the other hand, what was the single lady to do? Was she supposed to move to a cottage out in the country where she knew no one?

What would she do there? Darn seat-covers?

Realizing that she'd not set a stitch for many minutes, Kitty restlessly put the needlework aside. She rose to pace the small room she had made her refuge when she found the drawing room to be just too big. This had been the family dining room—a small, easily-heated space with a round table that could include a couple of guests. She had brought in one comfortable chair and had it placed by the fireside, and was now perfectly suited.

This was all she needed, really—a bed chamber and a small room for sitting and dining.

Alone.

Was she to spend her life alone?

That was a miserable prospect. Yet the friends of her youth had already scattered, off to marriage or positions of some kind. And her parents' friends, kind though they were, could not be her true companions.

She was thinking of turning the house into sets of rooms which she could rent out to suitable ladies. That would use the space and perhaps provide a certain amount of companionship. It made sense, but Kitty was not ready to rip her lovely home apart.

Therefore, she was considering marriage. If she married a respectable professional man who didn't yet have a house of his own, she wouldn't have to leave here.

The trouble was, she had no idea how to go about acquiring such a husband.

Men certainly didn't cluster around her in a courting mood!

Happy in her life, and not of a romantic disposition, Kitty had rarely fretted about this. Now she stopped before the mirror to assess her attractions.

She was too pale, for a start. It wasn't a sign of ill-health, but had something to do with her dense skin not showing the blood. Her father had been much the same, but it hadn't appeared so strange on a man. Poets always seemed to be addressing blushing maidens, and Kitty never appeared to blush. The effect was even worse when she wore mourning.

The fact that her hair was straight and a pale ash blond didn't help, or that her brows and lashes were not much darker. When she was younger some friends had suggested cosmetics. She'd even tried, but perhaps there was an art to it, an art she didn't possess. She'd looked like a painted doll.

And she was too tall, and very slender. She'd often thought that if she could squash herself down about six inches, she'd be just right.

For years, she'd hoped that womanly curves would come in time. They hadn't. Her breasts were still small, her hips still narrow. Her mother had assured her that she had been just the same until giving birth. That was all very well, but Kitty was not going to have babies if she couldn't find a husband.

Everyone thought her frail. It was nonsense—she'd never had a day's serious illness. She could quite see, however, that a man would hesitate to think of marriage with a woman likely to be an invalid, or to die giving birth to their first child.

Among their friends, the fact that her mother had suffered a number of miscarriages and stillbirths after having Kitty had doubtless reinforced the idea. Doctor Whitworth had assured Kitty that build was not the cause, but a young lady could hardly go around sharing her doctor's assessment of her childbearing potential!

Though her father had been a scientist, her parents' circle included a number of poets, and poets seem to feel obliged to write odes to all the young ladies. Kitty had received her fair share, but they always seemed to include words like "pearly," "fragile," "delicate," and even "unearthly."

What man would want to marry an unearthly bride?

She turned away from the depressing mirror, trying to decide if she wanted to marry at all. Her parents had been very liberal, but as a wife, she would be subject to the authority of a husband. Then there was the fact that she would be obliged to be physically intimate whenever it pleased him.

Kitty was not naive or ignorant, for her parents had believed in full and frank discussion on all subjects. Her momentary confusion over Sherry's condition embarrassed her. She knew what the marriage bed involved, and had often looked at an eligible man trying to imagine being in bed with him, doing those things. It had never held the slightest appeal.

She had decided she was born to be a spinster and that it suited her. Now, however, the companionship, the belonging of marriage did have appeal. She was very lonely.

She shook herself and returned to her needlework. She was in an enviable position, after all. She was young—or youngish—healthy, with a comfortable income and her independence. From the situation of some of her friends, she knew she was very fortunate.

Her only problem lay in deciding what to do with all this good fortune. That shouldn't be too hard for an intelligent woman of sense and education.

That night, the tomcats woke her.

Pol's mention of it must have stuck in Kitty's mind, for she found herself unable to ignore the faint noise from the back of the house. Though she knew the male cats were competing among themselves, she began to hear their cater-

waul as voices, seductive male voices cajoling and be-
seeching the object of their desire to go out to them.

After a while, despite the chill of the house at night, she
leaped out of bed, dragged on her woolen robe, and went to
the back bedroom to peer out at the narrow garden.

The noise was much louder here, and she could hear
Sherry in the kitchen singing back. Doubtless, foolish female, she was telling the rascally toms that she'd be with
them in a moment if her human jailers would only let her
out.

Really! What would the neighbors think?

A half-moon glimmered on the frosted garden, showing
bushes, empty flower beds, and the two trees against the
back wall. At first, she couldn't see the offending toms at
all, but then she realized some frosty sparkles were the re-
flections in the cats' eyes. There must be a dozen or more!

Where did they all come from?

Then one shadow in the lawn resolved into a black cat
who appeared to be making the loudest noise. Another cat
crept out from the bushes. There was a brief, violent,
screeching battle, then the challenger retreated. The black
cat launched into an even more strident yowl—doubtless
one of triumph and warning to the rest.

Pol had been right. They were out there arguing over
Sherry, and the black tom seemed to have established su-
premacy.

Well, she thought, he could fight and screech all he
wanted, it would gain him nothing.

Now she thought of it, she knew the big tom. He'd been
around during the summer, stalking birds and generally behaving as if he owned the area. She rather thought he came
over from Wells Street.

Suffolk Street, where Kitty lived, was almost a border
between different parts of London. Her neighbors were all
members of the worthy professional class—doctors,
lawyers, and scholars.

Immediately beyond Kitty's back wall, however, the

Wells Street mews marked the beginning of fashionable London. The mews housed the horses and carriages of wealthy people, many of them titled. It offended her to think a rakish cat was invading from that world to attack a decent little kitty. Even if that kitty were behaving unwisely just at the moment.

The tomcat was doubtless a stable cat. In that case, people there should lock it up at night, and tomorrow she would make sure they did, wealth and title or not.

She returned to the warmth of her bed, glad of a plan of action. It took her hours to get back to sleep, however, for the lascivious chorus of the cats, once hardly noticed, was now like a screech right by her ear.

Ill-rested and disgruntled, the next morning Kitty prepared to beard Wells Street. Or at least, the Wells mews. Checking herself in the mirror, she decided that though black did not suit her, it gave her authority. Surely no one would refuse to help a poor, pale lady in deep mourning.

Slightly ashamed of using her mother's death in such a way, Kitty realized that she was nervous. Scared, even. She was not accustomed to leaving the house unescorted to approach strangers.

How strange. She'd never thought herself particularly protected. After all, she'd traveled widely with her parents as well as attended gatherings of many sorts all over London.

But she'd always been with her parents or with good friends.

She considered calling on someone to ask for their company, but then dismissed the idea. It was only two days to Christmas, and her closest friends were out of town. And anyway, if she needed an escort to talk to some servants about an unruly cat, how was she to manage her life?

Straightening her shoulders, she headed for the door.

"Oh, miss!" called Pol, dashing into the hall. "It's getting right overcast. Spitting even. Shouldn't you take an umbrella?"

Kitty opened the door and saw that the maid was right.

She reached for her umbrella in the stand by the door, only then realizing that it was pale cream with a lacy edge. It would look ridiculous with her black full-length spencer, gloves, and bonnet. Almost reluctantly, she picked out her father's substantial black one, tears stinging.

Two years ago they had been a contented family, then her father had taken that wasting disease. Within a year of his death, her mother had died of a seizure. Kitty couldn't help wondering if it had been from grief, for they had been a deeply devoted couple.

Out in the street, under the shield of the wide umbrella, Kitty fancied herself under the shield of her parents' wisdom and care. They would want her to handle this matter firmly and fairly, and so she would.

She walked briskly down Suffolk Street past a number of houses exactly like her own, exchanging greetings with two neighbors who were hurrying because of the spitting rain. At the corner, she turned right along Charles Street, and then right again onto Wells Street.

Wells Street was not on the way to anywhere Kitty normally went, and so she had rarely passed through it. Now, she assessed it nervously.

It was a little wider than Suffolk Street, both in the road and the pavements, which were edged with metal bollards to protect pedestrians from traffic. The houses, too, were larger, some even double-fronted. The metal railings around the steps down to the basement were often ornate, even gilded.

Nearly all the houses were closed for the Christmas season, however, the missing knockers indicating that their owners were away—doubtless at their country seats. The inhabitants of Wells Street were the kind of people who had two or even more homes.

Though her father had been a gentleman born—son of the younger son of a viscount—Kitty had not been raised to think rank of great importance. Now, however, the knowledge that the mews was for the care of the carriages and horses of the upper class just added to her weak uncertainty.

She squashed down nervousness and marched on.

Halfway along Wells Street, a lane passed between two houses, leading down to the mews. Kitty took it with firm steps. Small, plain houses lined this lane, and most of them seemed in normal use. Doubtless these inhabitants did not have country properties to remove to.

When Kitty walked into the open yard surrounded by the stables and carriage houses, she realized it was very quiet. Of course. With most of the wealthy families away, there'd be no need of their horses.

For a moment she thought she might be able to retreat with honor, but then she heard whistling from one of the buildings. With a sigh, she went to peer over the half-door. A middle-aged man was brushing a steaming horse.

Kitty was not much used to horses—they were just creatures who pulled coaches—but she knew this was a very fine beast. At least one of the grand and wealthy must be around.

"Excuse me," she said, and the whistling groom looked up, falling silent.

He touched his forelock. "Can I 'elp you, ma'am?"

Ma'am! How very old that sounded, to be sure.

"I am inquiring about a cat."

"A cat, ma'am? Don't reckon as we've had no kittens around 'ere recently." The horse nudged at him. "Beggin' your pardon, but I'd best keep rubbing 'im down." He returned to the long strokes and the horse seemed to soften with pleasure.

"I don't want to *acquire* a cat," Kitty said, fascinated by the sensuous rubbing and the animal's reaction. . . .

She pulled herself together and focused on the groom. "I want to know who owns the big, black tomcat who's been making a nuisance of himself the past few nights."

The man slid her a look. "Oh, that 'un. You'll have to go

to number fourteen about that, ma'am. If you can get 'em to drown the moggy, it'd be a blessing."

With a faint "Thank you" Kitty retreated back down the lane to Wells Street. She had no wish to sentence the poor animal to death. She just wanted it kept inside until Sherry had stopped attracting attention.

She realized that the light rain had stopped and put down her umbrella. There was even the chance of the sun breaking through the clouds. That was surely a good omen.

Chuckling at what her father would have said about such superstition, she retraced her steps, looking for number fourteen. Her mother might well have approved of her image, however. In her studies of customs and traditions, she'd often remarked on the symbolic importance of light.

Number fourteen turned out to be one of the larger houses, double-fronted, and with enough windows to cost its owner a handsome sum in window tax. The curtains were all drawn, however, and the gleaming door with a leaded fanlight lacked a knocker. At least she wasn't going to have to deal with a noble owner.

She went down the steps to the basement area.

The door here was plain, though in good repair, and a small window sat beside it. Kitty couldn't resist peeping through in an effort to discover what she must face.

She gasped.

It was some sort of servants' parlor, and before an extravagant fire sprawled that tom. It was not that which had caused her to gasp, however.

Two male servants lolled at the plain deal table in the middle of the room—a table scattered with cards and coins. A number of bottles stood there, too, along with two used wine glasses. Not only were the scoundrels drinking their master's wine and gambling, they were doing so when it was not yet noon!

Kitty reminded herself that it was no business of hers, but when she rapped on the door with the handle of her umbrella, it was in a particularly sharp and outraged manner.

She saw the two men look at each other—but without obvious alarm—then glance at the window. She refused to flinch. She looked back at them righteously. One—the slighter built—stood and came to open the door.

"Can I help you, ma'am?"

Ma'am again. It was beginning to irritate her. He spoke like an upper servant, however, and did not seem to be horribly foxed.

"Yes," she replied crisply. "I wish to speak to you about your cat."

He glanced back into the room, then said, "Yes, ma'am?"

"Invite the lady in, Ned," called the other man in a similar accent. "There's the devil of a draft and I'm still damp."

The man opened the door wider and stepped back.

Kitty hesitated. It seemed unwise to enter such a disorderly household, and yet it was true that the open door must be letting in a chilly blast. Telling herself that the groom in the mews must know where she was, she walked in a few steps so the man could close the door.

At least he was not large—only her own height. And though in shirtsleeves, he was not untidy. She guessed him to be a footman, or perhaps even a valet.

The other man, who showed no intention of rising, was more difficult to assess. Taller, she thought, and bigger-built, broad shoulders all too obvious under his loose-necked shirt. Then she realized the shirt clung to him slightly, and remembered him saying he was damp. A bathtub of dirty water sat close to the fire.

She was torn between approval of his cleanliness, and scandal at his lounging around in such disarray. After all, his shirt showed quite a bit of chest, and wasn't completely tucked in at the waist, and his damp, dark hair definitely needed combing.

His square chin and straight nose did give him a rakish kind of good looks, even in disorder.

But he knew it.

He was a rascally tomcat, and had doubtless been the ruin of many a poor maid.

Kitty turned from him to address the smaller man—Ned—whose very ordinary face and neat brown hair made him unalarming. "I have reason to believe that your cat has been making a nuisance of himself the past few nights." She emphasized the words by pointing at the somnolent cat with the umbrella.

"Oh. Ah. Quite likely, ma'am." A flicker of humor in Ned's eyes annoyed her.

"I must ask you to keep him in the house."

"Well, we'll try, ma'am. But he could break out of the Tower, that one."

Suddenly, the other man spoke. "How is it that you are sent tom-hunting, ma'am?"

Kitty turned to face him, glad for once of her dense skin which would conceal her fluster at his impudence. "I am not *sent*. The cat is spending its nights yowling beneath the windows of my house."

He smiled in a way that was not the slightest bit repentant or respectful. "Then you must have a tasty queen inside, ma'am."

"My name is Miss Mayhew," she snapped. "And I don't know what you mean."

Lazily, he poured more wine into his glass, and sipped from it, showing not a trace of shame. "A queen is a female cat, Miss Mayhew. I assume she is in heat. What's a poor male to do when a female is so needy?" He leaned down and scooped up the big black cat one-handed, cradling it in his arms. "Your gallantry is not appreciated, Rochester."

Rochester!

Kitty was again glad of her skin. The cat was named after the most notorious libertine of the Restoration period, and she could imagine who had named him that.

"The *gallantry*," she said frigidly, "is most certainly *not* appreciated."

"But look," said the wretch, turning the cat slightly to

show a mangled ear. "He's fought for his lady's honor. Doesn't that deserve some reward?"

If the cat had fought, it hadn't been for Sherry's *honor,* and the man knew it. But Kitty was not about to speak of that. "Kindly keep that cat indoors or I will resort to desperate measures."

She heard her own words with amazement, heard herself reinforce them by pounding the ferrule of the umbrella on the flagstone floor. She was sounding as if she'd try to kill the animal, whereas she was actually hard-pressed to swat a fly.

The man stroked his cat, watching her in disconcerting silence for a moment or two. Kitty could feel herself begin to sweat, for there was a distinctly dangerous glint in his eyes. Taking a firmer grip on the umbrella, she looked away from his face and found herself staring at one long finger smoothing the glossy, dark fur of the rascally cat.

Rascally cat.

Rascally owner.

"Very well."

Startled, she looked up to see a new expression on his face. It was almost serious, but not quite. Intent, perhaps?

"What did you say?"

"I said, very well, Miss Mayhew. We will do our best to keep Rochester indoors and your poor queen unpleasured."

Off-balance and hot with embarrassment, Kitty turned away from the wretched man and addressed the other. He, at least, had the grace to look ill-at-ease.

"Whose house is this? Who is your employer?"

"Er . . . this is the Earl of Felstowe's house, ma'am."

"Then if your cat bothers me again, the earl will hear from me!"

With that, Kitty escaped into the cool December air, which was welcome to her cheeks. They felt hot even though they would not be red. Marching back to her house, she silently berated the outrageous man. Impudent was too mild a word for him, and his employer should know how he behaved when the family was away.

By the time she turned onto Suffolk Street, however, she had cooled. It was not her business. She would not descend to tattletaling.

Unless, of course, that rakish tom returned to plague her.

The next night, Kitty was woken by the toms' chorus. Pulling on her long, white woolen robe, she went again to the back window. A glance out of the window showed that black tom caterwauling his mastery of the area, and his invitation to Sherry. Once again, Sherry was positively encouraging him.

Despite that, Kitty's anger aimed at the tom—the tom and his wretched, feckless owner.

It could not be so hard to keep one cat confined!

She knew that if the black cat disappeared, the others would stay, but they seemed much less aggressive and noisy. And anyway, she wanted to teach that servant a lesson.

With no precise idea of what she would do, Kitty returned to her room to pull on thick stockings and half boots. Her woolen robe would be adequate for a brief foray into the garden, for it was like a long, thick spencer. Since the night was frosty, she added her black leather gloves.

In the hall, she seized the umbrella, then headed down to the kitchen to find Sherry yowling and clawing at the door to get out.

"Oh, you disgraceful creature!" Kitty snapped. "Have some decorum."

In truth, though, she felt rather sorry for the cat. Needy, that man had said. Kitty couldn't imagine being in such a state of need, but she could imagine the desperation it might cause.

Sorry or not, she could not let Sherry dash out to become prey to all those males. Yet clearly, as soon as the door opened, she'd be gone.

Kitty crept up and seized the manic cat by the scruff of her neck. In typical cat fashion, Sherry went quiet, and Kitty dumped her in the corridor and slammed the door.

Immediately, the yowling and scratching started again.

Blowing out a breath, Kitty marched to the back door, swung it open, and stepped out. As she did so, however, the other door opened, and Pol said, "What's the matter, miss?"

"Shut it!" Kitty cried, but it was too late.

Before she herself could slam the back door, a streak of white shot past both of them and out into the dark of the garden.

Barely suppressing a scream, Kitty raced after. She rushed onto the lawn to see her wanton, intemperate cat writhing and crooning for the benefit of the toms circled around her.

Had she no sense?

"Sherry, for *shame*!" Kitty hissed, wanting to snatch her back to safety, but worried about the tomcats. Would they attack to keep their prisoner?

Then the black tom—Kitty could imagine him smirking—paced forward to claim his prize.

"You, you rogue. Don't you *dare*!"

She ran forward, sure she would be too late, but Sherry seemed to have second thoughts. She suddenly turned, and slashed out with her claws, spitting at him. He retreated, but seemed charmed rather than dismayed. Crouching, he wooed her with little chirping noises.

Kitty could almost hear sweet seductive words.

Sherry softened back into her seductive dance.

"No!" Kitty ran forward, swiping at Rochester with her umbrella.

The tom was snatched out of danger, just as Pol ran by and grabbed Sherry.

"Foiled again," said an amused voice. The Earl of Felstowe's impudent servant had his cat and was addressing him sympathetically. At least he was holding him firmly.

Neither cat was an easy prisoner, however, and Kitty noticed that her maid was only in her nightgown and a shawl. "Get back in the house, Pol. You'll catch your death."

"Here, Ned," said the cat's owner. "You'd best return Rochester to durance vile, too."

The smaller servant was there and took the cat. In moments Kitty was alone in a frosty garden with the man. Alone except for bushes full of frustrated tomcats. At least they'd broken their circle and gone quiet now that their ringleader was foiled.

"I warned you, sir!" she snapped. "I will not have my poor cat attacked like that."

"I think there's some question as to who attacked whom."

He was in a long dark coat of some kind and boots, but his shirt was still open-necked, maintaining his very rakish appearance.

"She attacked to defend herself!"

"Really? After displaying herself like a dancer in a brothel?"

"How dare you! I warn you, I intend to inform your master of everything. Not just the cat, but your making free with his wine stores, and lazing around all day gambling."

"I must congratulate you, Miss Mayhew."

"Congratulate? Why?" For some reason, Kitty felt she should retreat a few steps, but she would not allow such foolishness.

"For having the ear of God. I acknowledge no other master."

"Ah-ha!" she declared triumphantly. "I knew you had no right to be in that house."

"What greater right do you expect? I am the destined owner, the Earl of Felstowe's heir, Lord Chatterton, at your service." He gave her a brief, ironic bow.

Kitty should have scoffed, but she knew with frosty clarity that it was true. It explained his arrogance. And now that she thought about it, tonight he'd dropped the slightly servantish accent he'd assumed the other day.

Did he expect her to back down and grovel just because

he would one day be a belted earl? He'd soon discover his mistake.

"Then your behavior is a disgrace to your rank, my lord, and I'm sure your father would agree."

His lips twitched. "Do you intend to complain to him? I don't advise it. He too thinks only God has the right to dictate our conduct."

He moved closer and again Kitty resisted the urge to step back, though she was even less sure that that was wise.

She had met members of the nobility before. They did not awe her, but she knew he was probably speaking the truth. Many lords thought themselves above the law, and they were often correct. It was hard indeed to bring a court case against rank and privilege.

What could he do to her, though, here in her own garden?

She stiffened her spine and raised her chin. "Right is right, regardless of rank. If you didn't let your cat out deliberately, he escaped through your carelessness."

He didn't cower into repentance. "It was certainly tempting to let him out, understanding all too well his desperation, Miss Mayhew. A lovely queen so close is more than a male can be expected to resist. But I did not, and I will try to be a better jailer in the future. My word on it."

To her astonishment, he took her hand and brushed a kiss over the leather. She tried to tug free, but his hold was firm. "What a shame you are wearing black gloves."

"Wearing black gloves" was the common term for being in mourning, and she took it as such. "It is for my mother."

"My condolences, but I meant that they are the only dark thing about you, they and your trusty weapon. Otherwise, you are a perfect moon-maiden."

She pulled her hand sharply away, and did manage to free it. "Are you claiming I'm moon-mad?" She tugged her glove snugly back on her hand. "A lunatic?"

"Not at all. Just that you look as if you are made of moonbeams—moonbeams with frosty ornamentation. Quite delightful."

Kitty hissed in a breath. "If you tell me I am unearthly, my lord, I warn you, I am likely to correct the impression by hitting you over the head with this umbrella!"

He laughed, teeth white and healthy, eyes bright. "Oh, not unearthly at all." Then he knocked the umbrella out of her hand and seized her wrist.

Kitty swung at him, trying to hit or scratch, but he dodged and snared her in his arms.

She writhed, but he was much taller and stronger, and she was alarmingly helpless. She opened her mouth to scream, but then thought better of it. Did she really want her neighbors to discover her out in the garden in her night-wear, in the arms of a rakish lord!

"Please, my lord . . ." she whispered, hearing the tremor in her voice. She braced her hands against his chest and pushed.

To no effect.

"Please, what?" he whispered back, his features now in shadow. "I just want to show you that I don't think you un-earthly." He blew a tendril of hair off her face. "Or un-earthy, my moon-maiden."

Dear Lord, but her hair was in its nighttime plait and must be slipping loose, as it always did. Why this should seem the epitome of wantonness, she could not imagine.

"My lord . . ."

"Yes, my queen? My crystal moon-queen."

He was staring at her as if fascinated, but his use of the word "queen" had her struggling even more determinedly. "If you are even suggesting . . . !"

He controlled her without effort. "That you raced out here desperately seeking a randy tom? The thought never crossed my mind, Miss Mayhew." But he was laughing at her.

She kicked him, and made slight contact. He didn't relax his grip, but just trapped her head and kissed her.

Kitty had never been kissed before. She tried to squirm away, but he held her still and just rested his warm lips against hers. Breath playing against her mouth, he murmured, "Earth to earth, dear lady. Doesn't it feel pleasant to share earthy warmth?"

She was abruptly aware of the warmth of his body all along hers, of the warmth of his arms around her, and of the heat of his lips and his breath. Having no idea what to do or say, she stayed silent, trying to deal with the fact that she could be said to be enjoying this.

She was safe. She knew she was. He could not rape her here. He was behaving outrageously, but it was exciting to be a little outrageous for once in her life. A racy sizzle sparkled in her staid blood.

And he didn't think her unearthly. Nor had he addressed her as "ma'am" tonight.

He trailed his hot lips across her cheek to blow into her ear. She resisted the urge to squirm. One hand stroked her, stroked down her side from ribs to hip. The other played softly in the hair at the nape of her neck, and she remembered the way his finger had stroked the fur of his black cat. She rather thought the same finger was playing in her hair, in the same kind of movement.

She could, if she allowed it, turn soft like the cat, like the horse in the stables. . . .

"You have very dense skin," he said. "I noticed that. You don't easily show color. But everyone can be brought to the blush eventually. Are you blushing now? In moonlight, I would never know."

His lips returned to hers and kissed her again, hand firmly at the back of her neck, making it even harder not to slacken, not to let him hold her limp in his arms.

Perhaps she did.

One thumb rubbed up her jaw and his tongue tickled at her lips before he freed her mouth, still stroking.

"Shall I do more?" he murmured.

Kitty wrenched herself out of his arms, taking three steps back and fussing with her clothes. "Certainly not! You are a ruthless libertine, sir!"

But she knew he had let her go.

The moon picked out an expression of cynical humor. "Are you outraged? I do hope so. Now you know what to expect if you ever again try to harm my cat."

Kitty seized her umbrella, glad of the distance between them. That was all it had been—an assault designed to teach her a lesson? She could have wept, or scratched him, or belabored him with her weapon. She'd never been more embarrassed and outraged in her life.

"I would not normally even dream of attacking an innocent creature, my lord!"

"Oh, so he's innocent now, is he? Lucky fellow. I fear I am not so fortunate."

"You most certainly are not. You, my lord, are a wicked rake, and if you ever touch me again I will harm you in any way I can."

He grinned and gave her an elaborate bow. "I thank you for the warning, Miss Mayhew. I leave you now to comfort your poor, unpleasured queen."

Stunned by the feeling that he was referring to herself, Kitty watched him stroll off down the garden and nimbly climb the wall at the end. Then she fled back into the safety of her house.

Pol was there, holding Sherry so the cat couldn't try to escape again when the door was opened. "Are you all right, miss?"

Goodness knows what she looked like. "Yes, of course. I believe we will have to lock Sherry in one of the spare bedrooms at night."

"She'll likely shred it, miss."

"So be it." Kitty took possession of the "unpleasured queen" and carried her up to a spare bedroom, lecturing her all the way on the consequences of giving in to carnal urges.

The lecture, however, was to herself. Eventually, she settled into her still-warm bed knowing that she should have hated being captured and handled in such a way. In the beginning she had, or at least she'd been frightened. But she'd grown accustomed.

Rather quickly.

Yes, one could definitely become accustomed to being in a strong embrace.

With the right person, of course.

Which Lord Chatterton certainly was not, horrid man.

Resolutely, Kitty turned her mind to more general implications. Her adventure had made the option of marriage rather more attractive. She'd never quite thought of it, but the marriage act must involve more than just the insertion and planting of seed.

It must surely involve embracing, for example.

And kissing, she thought sleepily.

And perhaps even blowing in ears . . . ?

Kitty rose from her bed the next morning, disturbed and distressed by her own behavior—by her reactions, her thoughts, and her dreams.

It was all outrageous, and she would have no more of it. She repeated that sternly to Sherry when she let her out of the bedroom. Returning downstairs, however, Kitty paused by a window that looked out over the back garden, restlessly rubbing her arms and thinking of a dreamlike encounter.

The optimistic cats returned that night, and Kitty fancied she could pick out Rochester's dominant caterwaul. Of course, she should never have expected Lord Chatterton to pay any attention to her and actually control his cat.

Then the racket was cut short. Had one of the men taken action? She turned over in her bed and pulled the covers up over her ears, rejecting the temptation to go to a window to try to see which man it was.

It would be the servant, anyway.

In a very short while, the noise started up again, but different now, lacking the ringleader. It kept her awake and she lay there thinking—and it wasn't about the servant.

How strange that the heir to an earldom seemed to be lurking in his servants' quarters with the knocker off. It was especially strange so close to Christmas when most people were with family and friends. Perhaps he'd wasted his money on indulgence and gambling, and was now forced to hide from his creditors.

It was pretty reasonable, she told herself, to be curious about such a thing. It wasn't that she was particularly interested in the man himself.

She found a chance to find out a little more about Lord Chatterton and his family after church on Christmas Day. For once, Christmas was sunny and crisp, so despite the nip in the air, everyone was happy to linger for a while.

Dr. and Mrs. Whitworth, who lived three doors down from Kitty's house, paused to wish her a happy Christmas. They were a plump, solidly respectable couple who had spent evenings at her house in the past.

"I gather it was your mother's little white cat who attracted all that commotion, Miss Mayhew." The twinkle in the doctor's eye made Kitty feel quite hot.

"Yes, I'm afraid so."

"Poor little cat," said the doctor, still twinkling.

Perhaps, in private, she would ask him if there were something she could give Sherry to stop these fits. For now, she said, "The worst tom apparently belongs to the Earl of Felstowe's house on Wells Street."

"Indeed! Then you'll know where to complain if kittens arrive."

"There is no question of that, thank goodness." Kitty saw Mrs. Whitworth poke her elbow in her husband's ribs and give him a look.

The doctor cleared his throat. "Oh, aye. Well, the earl's not a bad sort, Miss Mayhew, though high in the instep. I've been called in to his servants now and then."

"I don't think he's in residence at the moment."

"No, likely not. He doesn't come to London often, as I understand it, but keeps the place in readiness. His heir uses it, mostly. Chatterton. He's turned up here in church, did you know? There he is. Over there, creating quite a flutter."

Kitty hardly heard the last words because she was staring

at Lord Chatterton. How had she missed him in church? Of course, he didn't have a pew here so must have sat toward the back.

He certainly couldn't be missed now, for he stood out in this plebeian crowd. It was partly height, though there were other tall men. It was largely presence. And, she realized, the fact that a number of people, including the vicar, were fawning all over him.

"Don't know that he's ever attended service at St. Caspian's before," said Mrs. Whitworth. "Or his father. Right and proper that he should, mind you, seeing as it's the parish church."

As if he felt eyes upon him, Lord Chatterton looked over. Then he smiled and bowed.

Kitty felt obliged to incline her head, though she'd dearly like to cut the man.

"Goodness, Miss Mayhew, do you know him?" asked Mrs. Whitworth.

Kitty forced a mild smile. "We spoke. About his cat, that is all. I fear he is arrogant."

"Such men generally are, my dear." With that and more good wishes, the couple moved on.

Kitty called Pol away from some friends and headed toward the lytchgate. She had to keep pausing to exchange greetings, but lingered as little as possible. With luck, people would think she was leaving quickly because the jollity of the season didn't mix well with her mourning. In fact, she wanted to escape before having to speak to a certain lord.

She felt that even thinking about him might summon him—like the devil, perhaps.

Therefore, she forced herself to think of other things. About the fact that she would miss St. Caspian's if she moved, for example. Most of these people had known her from birth. She certainly didn't imagine she would be happy away from here.

About dividing the house. It was doubtless the only practical solution. . . .

"Miss Mayhew."

She froze, then turned, wishing again that it were possible to cut him—to cut him like the reprobate he was.

"My lord?" She directed her eyes toward his right ear. He must have hurried to catch her. What would people think?

"How is your pretty little cat?"

"As before, my lord. We are keeping her closely confined."

"Poor little thing."

She glared at him, which meant she looked at him. Which was a mistake. Shaven, his dark hair neatly arranged, he was exceedingly handsome.

"Of course," he added with a teasing smile, "a tomcat is not dissuaded by an invisible queen, as you have seen. Despite our efforts, Rochester might bother you again. I can only promise to do my best to control him."

"Thank you, my lord." Kitty forced her eyes back into the safer position.

"You must feel free to call on me if there is any further *need*. At any time—day or night."

Need, indeed! Kitty wished she had her umbrella and the courage to bend it over his rascally head.

"I gather you worship here regularly," he said.

She glared directly at him. "Have you been asking people about me?"

"Just in general conversation. I have decided to get to know all my neighbors."

"I'm sure *they'll* be delighted."

His lips twitched. "Armed even without an umbrella," he murmured. "I gather you are well-known to all."

"I have attended this church since I was christened here, my lord. I have many friends." She gave it as a warning.

"How fortunate you are. I think I am converted to the notion of attending the local church, at least in the less fashionable times of year. Perhaps soon I, too, will have friends hereabouts."

Kitty couldn't imagine what he was up to, for the parishioners of St. Caspian's were hardly of his class. She only knew that she had to get away from him before doing something foolish.

She shot a final dart. "I'm sure most people here will be deeply gratified, my lord, at the honor of your attendance."

On the way home, Pol started a conversation for once. "That was the man who was out in the garden the other night, miss."

"Yes. He's the Earl of Felstowe's heir, Lord Chatterton."

"Lawks," said Pol, not obviously impressed. "You stayed out talking to him long enough."

"I was making my point about his cat."

"Oh." A few steps later, Pol said, "Beggin' your pardon, Miss Kitty, but you'd be best not to bandy words with the likes of him."

Kitty glanced at the maid. "Bandy words?"

"Like you were back there. Men take that as encouragement, they do."

Kitty was tempted to give the maid a sharp rebuke for impudence, but she feared she was right. "I hope never to even speak to him again."

"Oh," said Pol. Why did she sound disbelieving?

Because of her mother's death, Kitty passed Christmas Day just like any other. It depressed her, but more because it was final proof that her happy family life was over, than from missing company and special food. Next year, being out of mourning, she would doubtless celebrate Christmas in some way, but it would never be the same as it had been when her parents were alive.

Last year, only months after her father's death, Christmas had been quiet, too. She and her mother hadn't decorated the house or entertained at all. But the servants had deserved their Christmas dinner, and so they'd all enjoyed it. And in the evenings, Kitty and her mother had heard the servants singing traditional songs.

Christmas had been *there,* in the house.

And on Christmas Eve, her mother had lit a Yule candle.

Kitty's parents had started this tradition before she was born, a substitute for the Yule log which would never fit in their small hearth. They had a special mold, and made the candles themselves each year. Then, at midnight on Christmas Eve, they lit it in a special ceremony of light. They gave reverence to Christ, the light of the world, but also to more ancient gifts—those of sun and fire.

It was somewhat pagan, but Kitty's mother's special interest was ancient British traditions. She had felt that Yule—the celebration of light in the darkest time of year—was an important one to keep up.

The bit Kitty had always loved most was the extra prayer at the end, one of thanks for the warmth and brightness brought by family and friends. Last year, her mother had lit the candle, and they'd remembered Kitty's father. They'd cried, but it had been a healing moment. This year, however, being all alone, Kitty had lacked the heart to try to celebrate all on her own.

At the end of Christmas Day, she climbed into her bed, rather glad to have it over with. There were still the Twelve Days to get through, each with special memories, but surely the worst was over.

Then she found herself lying in the dark, waiting for the sound of Rochester serenading the object of his desire. The other cats were there, but not him. She went to the window and looked out. Sure enough, another cat was in the center of the lawn, a paler one.

For some reason, that seemed a depressing end to a dismal day.

Lord Chatterton had doubtless left town to spend Christmas with his family and had taken his cat with him. She should be glad. After all, she never wanted to speak to him again.

*   *   *

The very next day, however, Kitty found that she was going to have to speak to Lord Chatterton again. Just as she was getting into bed, a noise alerted her. Not cats, this time. An intruder!

Heart thumping, she crept downstairs, a poker in her hand.

In the kitchen, however, she found Pol taking off a shawl.

"Pol? Where on earth have you been?"

For once the girl looked flustered. "Out in the garden, miss."

"But it's ten o'clock!"

"It's a nice night, miss."

"It's *December*." Something about the girl made Kitty ask, "Have you been *meeting* someone?"

Pol's ready color flared and she studied her shoes. "Perhaps."

"Who?"

Pol looked up and bit her lip, but a smile fought to get out. "Ned. Ned Kingsman. His valet. Lord Chatterton's valet."

Kitty sat in a chair with a thump. "Pol! How could you be so wicked?"

" 'Tain't wicked, miss. We're courting." Pol's cheeks were red as rosy apples.

Suddenly Kitty felt as sorry for the maid as she had for her cat. "Oh, Pol. His intentions can't be honorable. He'll ruin you, that's all."

"I won't be ruined," Pol declared with some indignation. "And anyway, Ned's not like that."

"All men are like that," said Kitty, though she knew it was trite. "Off to bed with you, and we'll have no more of this."

But as she checked to see that the door was locked, Kitty knew she had no way to enforce her command. It was also clear that Pol was as incapable of being rational on this matter as Sherry had been.

The only thing to do was what they'd done with the cats—keep both would-be lovers closely confined until the madness passed.

That, however, would need the assistance of Ned's employer.

So the next morning, Kitty sent a neighbor's lad with a note requesting an appointment with Lord Chatterton at two in the afternoon. It seemed wise to insist on formality this time, but the prospect still made her shake with nervousness.

The boy returned with a terse acceptance on heavy, crested paper. That paper rather daunted Kitty, for it reminded her that he was, after all, far above her in social rank.

She could not fail Pol, however, so at a quarter to two, dressed in her usual black, Kitty left for her appointment. This time, she would definitely have preferred to take a companion as chaperone, but it was clearly impossible to take Pol. In fact, she hadn't told Pol where she was going.

After some thought, she had decided it would be embarrassing to have to discuss such matters in front of one of the neighbors. It shouldn't matter. This was not a social call, and surely even a rakish lord could not behave improperly at two in the afternoon.

When Kitty arrived at number fourteen Wells Street, she noted that some of the curtains were drawn back, and a polished brass knocker awaited her on the handsome door. With a steadying breath, Kitty applied it.

Almost immediately, Ned opened the door, neatly dressed in a valet's suit. "Good afternoon, Miss Mayhew."

Did he guess her errand? She supposed it was possible Pol had managed to sneak out and tell him she'd been caught. She studied the man and had to admit that he did not look like a wicked seducer of innocent maids. She'd been thinking much more of his master when she'd conjured up that image.

Like master like man, she reminded herself as he led her across a spacious hall and up wide, carpeted stairs.

But then, shouldn't it be like mistress like maid?

Lord Chatterton awaited her in the drawing room, a magnificent chamber with walls covered in Chinese silk, and windows draped with gold damask. The red, brown, and gold carpet was a work of art. Other works of art scattered the room. Could that really be a Caravaggio? And that sculpture. . . .

Kitty was tempted to gawk, and knew for sure that Lord Chatterton was not skulking from creditors. Even if he had outrun his funds, his family would rescue him. So why, she wondered again, had he been lurking in his own kitchen pretending to be out of town?

He certainly wasn't skulking now. As at church, he was dressed expensively in quiet elegance and looked in command of the world.

"Won't you be seated, Miss Mayhew."

Somewhat reluctantly, Kitty perched on a sofa, drawing off her gloves.

"Perhaps we can offer you tea."

Kitty almost refused, but then decided that tea seemed extremely safe. Surely nothing wicked could happen over tea. "Thank you."

Ned disappeared, and his master took a seat opposite her, crossing one pantalooned leg over the other. "How may I assist you, Miss Mayhew?"

His manner was exactly that of a noble lord giving a few moments to a lowly neighbor. It was as if he expected to be asked for a donation to the nearest orphanage.

Since Kitty took an interest in the local charity school that had produced Pol, she might as well ask for some money before leaving. If they were still on speaking terms, that was.

Annoyingly nervous, Kitty was shaping her words when he spoke again.

"If you have been pestered again by a caterwaul, Miss Mayhew, I assure you Rochester wasn't involved. We have him confined as if he were a traitor in the Tower."

Kitty met his eyes. "Then perhaps you should lock your man in there with him, my lord."

"Ned? You're suggesting that *Ned* is serenading your cat at night?"

He didn't believe that for a moment, she realized. She also saw, distractingly, that his eyes were a rich hazel, a color that was deceptively warm. A wicked rake should have cold eyes.

Keep your wits and your dignity, Kitty. "I am informing you, my lord, that your servant is trying to seduce my maid. Pol is a sweet, innocent girl raised in a charity school, and without protectors other than myself."

His brows rose. "You astonish me, Miss Mayhew."

But again, she decided, it was playacting. He was not at all surprised. Remembering him in disorder in his kitchen, she realized he was probably aiding and abetting his servant. Perhaps he intended to use poor Pol for his own low pleasures once she'd succumbed.

Rage might have tempted her to say things she shouldn't if Ned hadn't returned.

He carried a large silver tray holding not only a teapot and water jug, but a generous selection of cakes. He placed the tray on a side table and poured into pretty, gilt-edged cups. In moments, Kitty was being presented with her tea and the milk and sugar to add to it. Not long afterward, she was invited to select from among the cakes.

All this propriety gave her a chance to regain her composure. Her fancy was flying away with her. A nobleman— especially one like Lord Chatterton—would not sink so low as to ruin a kitchen maid.

Then she began to resent his silence. She was ill-at-ease and couldn't think of anything to say, but she was sure he was adept at small talk. The wretched man said nothing, however, so Kitty contemplated Ned again.

To all appearances he was an excellent servant. He moved about quietly and efficiently with none of the extremes— mincing or strutting—sometimes found. In looks he was tidy and unassuming, hardly well-armed for wicked seduction. Then she reminded herself that she'd first seen him lolling around over wine and cards at ten in the morning.

As soon as he left, Kitty fixed her host with a stern look, determined on a response to her demand.

He sipped his tea. "Where were we? Ah, yes. Ned as Casanova. Really, my dear Miss Mayhew, can you see it?"

"Since I have no idea what or who Casanova is, no."

"And everyone describes you as so well-educated!"

"Everyone . . . ? Have you been gossiping about me again, my lord?" Kitty was genuinely appalled. What would the world—her world—think if he'd been going around asking about her? She doubtless was as pale as usual, but her cheeks felt roasting hot.

"Gossip?" His regard was steady but with a glint in his eye. It must surely just be a reflection of the dancing flames of the fire. "Not at all. But on Christmas Day I found it possible to speak of you a little. Your father was a scholar, I believe, much interested in that mysterious force, electricity. Your mother assisted him in his work, but was also a scholar in her own right, with a great interest in ancient customs. They educated you at home, and widely, and you traveled with them wherever they went. You must miss them."

The last sentence broke through Kitty's bemusement like a blow. "My family is no concern of yours, my lord. I merely want your word that your servant will leave my maid alone."

"And I asked you if you saw him as Casanova. Clearly you do."

Kitty sighed theatrically. "I can only assume that Casanova is a character in a play, a rakish seducer. If so, then yes, I see your man in that mold. After all," she added, with a meaningful look at him, "not all rakes are as brash as toms about it."

He smiled. It almost turned into a grin. "Did I tell you, Miss Mayhew, that my name is Tom?"

Cheeks feeling as if they would blister from their own

inner heat, Kitty snapped, "How precognitive of your parents, my lord!"

He laughed, slumping back into his chair in a genuine abandonment of hilarity. He looked so wonderful in its glow that Kitty's cup and saucer tilted, splashing her skirt with the dregs.

She hastily put it on the small table by her hand and gave thanks to be wearing black. When she looked up again he had calmed, but the shimmer of laughter still lit him. "Casanova, my dear Miss Mayhew, was a real person, dead not twenty years ago. He loved women, and loved to persuade them into love with him, and wrote to tell about it. He claimed to make them all very, very happy."

Kitty gave thanks for an education that made her hard to shock. "Then I don't think your man is like him. He will make poor Pol very, very unhappy."

"Don't you think you should at least give him a chance?"

"Certainly not!"

"You don't seem to trust your maid very much."

Kitty resented that observation, though it was true. "She's young. Only eighteen. And an orphan. She's a very sensible girl, but I'm afraid that her head will be turned by your man's attentions. Any woman can be tempted by promises of love and tenderness, of a home and family. . . ."

She trailed off because of the way he was looking at her. Surely he didn't think those words applied to her!

He merely said, "Ned's intentions are honorable, Miss Mayhew. Apparently in the past week, while he has been acting as man-of-all-work to me, he has encountered your maid in the area—at the market, the butchers, and such. Out in the garden a few nights ago, he realized where she lived, and decided to pursue the acquaintance."

"Pursue!" pounced Kitty. "Exactly."

"With an eye to marriage, Miss Mayhew."

Kitty froze, staring at him. "You can't expect me to believe that."

"Of course I can."

He appeared serious. He must be a gifted actor.

"Firstly," she said, "personal servants rarely marry under the rank of butler and housekeeper. Secondly, upper servants—which your Ned clearly is—are as likely to marry a kitchen maid as . . ."

"As a lord is to marry the daughter of scholars?" he supplied helpfully.

"Certainly unlikely," she forced out, managing not to snarl. "But not of the depth of improbability of your Ned intending honorable matrimony with my Pol."

"But love can wipe away all social barriers, dear lady."

"Not in real life, *dear sir.*"

He considered her a moment. "Miss Mayhew, delightful as this verbal jousting is, let us be direct. Believe it or not, Edward Kingsman, my valet and occasional man-of-all-work—"

"Not to mention partner in all-night carousing," Kitty interrupted.

He sighed. "Are you holding that against him? My fault entirely, Miss Mayhew. I was restless and commanded his company. It is his job to do almost anything I command. What you saw, however, was the dregs of the night. I had been riding to clear my head, and had returned to bathe. I assure you that Ned disapproves of my occasional carouses as much as you would wish. May I continue?"

Daunted, Kitty nodded.

"Edward Kingsman believes himself in love with Polly Cooper, general maid at your house. Now, as you pointed out, she is really not worthy of this honor—"

Kitty opened her mouth to retort, then thought better of it.

"Or, at least," he amended with a smile, "could be said to be flattered by it. However, his regard is genuine. I gather that in the three years she has been in service at your house you have given her extra education and help. Apparently, she would be able to hold her own in a much higher level of the servants' world."

"Pol is the equal of anyone," Kitty said, though it sounded foolish to her own ears.

"In the eyes of God, I am sure you are right," he responded smoothly. "*I* am not sure this match is wise, though I would certainly be willing to arrange matters so that Ned could marry and stay in my service. *You* have doubts, too, as any sensible woman must. But it is hardly fair, Miss Mayhew, to forbid a match before we know if it is based on a genuine attraction."

Bludgeoned by reason, Kitty relented just a little. "So what do you suggest, my lord?"

"A courtship. I suggest we permit them to meet and learn about each other just as people of our own station would."

Such a marriage would be a wonderful thing for Pol, if it worked out. "I would like to believe that Mr. Kingsman's intentions are honorable, my lord, but I cannot put blind faith in that. What if we permit them to meet and . . . and he is less than honorable?"

"He gets her with child, you mean? I'd make him marry her, never fear."

"But would that be fair to her? Foolish though it is, a woman can be seduced without the man being an ideal husband. I would not want to see Pol trapped for life with an unpleasant and even resentful man because I allowed her too much freedom."

"I rather thought we'd outlawed slavery," he murmured.

"I beg your pardon?"

"If we can regulate the freedom of others, does not that make them slaves?"

"I would never have taken you for a radical freethinker, my lord!"

"You'd be astonished by the workings of my mind, my dear Miss Mayhew. Why not become acquainted with them as we allow our slaves to assess one another?"

"What?" Kitty was sweating, and the heat was stimulated by something in his eyes.

"I'm suggesting that we let Ned court Pol, and that we

act as chaperones. I'm sure it will be a tedious duty, but in the process we can each learn something of the other's mind."

"Chaperones," echoed Kitty. "But why two? One would suffice."

"Are you willing to entrust Pol to Ned with only me as guardian?"

Kitty most certainly was not. "Then perhaps I should be the chaperone."

"But can I abandon Ned to that arrangement?"

Kitty glared at him, but could see he meant to be difficult about it. And really, there was no reason to be nervous. She and Lord Chatterton would be chaperoned by Ned and Pol.

He smiled slightly, as if he could read her mind. "I am living here with just the one servant. It puzzles you, doesn't it? If you agree to my plan, I promise to explain it to you."

"I do not indulge in vulgar curiosity," Kitty lied. "But as you say, it is only fair to allow Pol and Ned to become acquainted. How is it to be arranged?"

"I suggest that each evening we four gather, alternating houses. We can talk, play cards, do whatever amuses us for a few hours. After some days of this, surely everyone will be clearer in their minds."

"Everyone?"

"Ned and Pol will know their minds, then. And we, Miss Mayhew, will know whether to approve or not."

Kitty was still unaccountably nervous. "I would think you would have other things to do with your evenings, my lord."

"Not just now, no. Well, Miss Mayhew?"

"How long is this to go on?"

"The servants here will begin to return on January sixth, the day after Twelfth Night."

"Mine will be back on the seventh."

"So, we have ten nights."

"It seems an imposition on you, my lord."

"No more of an imposition than it is for you, Miss Mayhew."

"But I live very quietly, especially now I am in mourning. You . . ."

"I?" Humor crinkled his eyes. "Perhaps I need a break from my life of endless dissipation. Have pity, Miss Mayhew. Ten days of healthy suppers with very little wine, and early bedtimes—I'll be fit as a fiddle by Twelfth Night."

He was fit as a fiddle now, no one could deny that. Kitty hadn't really thought of it, but he didn't look like a worn-out libertine.

That was irrelevant anyway. She must do what was best for Pol. She didn't think of her maid as a slave, but she did feel some responsibility. She could no more agree to her wandering about with a man unchaperoned than she could agree to such behavior for a young sister.

If she had a young sister, then chaperoned social activities would be exactly what was called for. She could see no reason to refuse the plan, though a part of her wanted to.

Very badly.

Another part of her, however, was suddenly looking forward to the next ten nights more than she could ever have imagined. "Very well, my lord. We will try it. But I reserve the right to put a stop to it if necessary."

"But of course. Perhaps after a few unclandestine meetings, both Ned and Pol will find the magic fading. Familiarity, after all, is said to breed contempt."

"And 'Sweets grown common lose their dear delight,' my lord? I think I understand your purpose now."

"And your Shakespeare caps my Aesop. You understand all too little, Miss Mayhew, despite your scholarly upbringing. So, tonight. Your house or mine?"

Kitty rose, pulling on her gloves to hide her fluster at the simple question. "Yours," she said, since she wasn't ready to have him invading her territory. "But what will people think to see me visiting your house every other night?"

"Not to mention my coming to yours. Perhaps," he said,

pulling the bell-rope, "through the garden and mews, like a hopeful tom? There's actually a gate, if you care to unlock it."

Kitty wished he would stop making these suggestive remarks. They didn't mean anything, but they unsettled her, and he knew it. She feared he not only intended this courtship to cool Ned and Pol's ardor, but to provide amusement for himself in teasing her.

Before she could put words to any of this, however, Ned was there, being informed of their plans. Kitty immediately felt ashamed of her earlier suspicions, for no one could doubt the shining delight that lit his face.

Just as Pol's face had glowed at merely speaking of him.

It was undoubtedly that plague called love.

So be it. As Kitty left the house, she decided to try to make this match work for Pol—regardless of Lord Chatterton's cynical intentions.

By way of exploration, Kitty returned the back way, finding that a narrow footpath from the mews led down the back of the gardens on Suffolk Street to Charles Street. It was clearly a well-used shortcut. As Lord Chatterton had said, there was a gate in her garden wall, but it was firmly locked and covered by ivy. She remembered it now from childhood explorations, but wondered if it could be opened after all these years.

She took the path down to Charles Street and returned home to explain the plan to Pol. Again, it was as if a candle lit behind the girl's eyes, they shone so. "Oh, Miss Kitty. Thank you! I know he's above me, but he's such a lovely man. . . ." Tears started. "Thank you. Thank you. . . ."

Kitty gathered the girl into a hug. "Don't make your eyes red, dear. And mark, this is just to let you become acquainted. You might find you don't like him so well, or he you."

Pol sniffed and blew her nose on a handkerchief, one of the ones Kitty had given her as a present. "I know that, miss. But at the moment, I just want to be able to spend time with him. I . . . I think of him all the time. I know it's daft, but I do. All the time."

Kitty laughed. "Sounds like love to me, Pol. It can fade, but why not enjoy it while you can?"

And that, she thought, was good advice for herself. She knew she was thinking of Lord Chatterton far too much, and was intrigued by his teasing ways. If she accepted that it was just in fun, she could enjoy it and give as good as she got.

Memories of that nighttime kiss flickered. She could bear a repeat of that, too. Perhaps while Ned and Pol were exploring their love, she could enjoy a safe little flirtation with a dashing nobleman. It was a chance not likely to come her way again.

And she could satisfy her curiosity, too. She did want to know why he was lurking almost alone in that magnificent house over Christmas.

"Very well," she said to Pol, "but if you want to go a-courting, we'd best find a way to open that gate. The gentlemen might be happy to climb the wall, but I most certainly am not."

It wasn't too hard. An old bunch of heavy keys provided one that turned the lock, though it took some squirts of oil to get it moving with ease. Kitty made short work of the ivy with a pair of garden shears, while Pol cut down two small bushes that had been planted where the path should be.

Kitty surveyed their work with satisfaction, but then laughed. "You know, we really should have made the men come over and do all this."

"Oh, no," said Pol. "I think we each have to take care of our own ground."

And that seemed very wise indeed.

That evening, Kitty decided that she hadn't been in such a fluster since her first dance as a girl of sixteen. And it wasn't even as if she had anything to be flustered about. Not only was she a mere chaperone tonight, but her wardrobe offered only four black dresses, all of virtually the same plain design. None of them was suited to an evening with a lord.

An evening with a lord.

She acknowledged that she wasn't merely a chaperone. Lord Chatterton seemed inclined to flirt with her, and she was determined to enjoy the experience.

She was still in mourning, however, so she squashed the temptation to add some jewelry, and arranged her hair in its normal smooth knot high on her head. Then she grimaced at her plain reflection.

He might have been inclined to flirt with her in the garden, when she was roughly dressed and her hair was flying loose. Now, however, she was Kitty Mayhew again, a woman men showed no amorous interest in at all.

How tempting to dress wildly and leave her hair flowing loose. She laughed at the absurd idea.

She did wish her hair would hold a curl, however. For fashion, she needed tight curls around her face, but she'd learned young that nothing would compel her hair to hold curls for an evening. She'd had nearly a decade to become used to that fact, so why did it torment her now?

And why, for heaven's sake, was she even thinking of digging out her mother's old curling iron?

Irritated by her own folly, she set her black straw bonnet firmly on top of her head and went to find Pol.

She had to admit to curiosity as to what her maid would wear to go courting. Over the years, Kitty had given her a number of gowns to alter and refurbish for herself. Pol was shorter, and so the gowns did fit with a little hemming.

Kitty was pleased to see that the girl had not given in to any extravagant impulses. She wore a cream muslin gown that Kitty remembered, but which was now pleasantly trimmed with embroidered red flowers around hem and neckline and on the inset panel at the front of the bodice. The low neck was filled with a soft, white chemisette. On her head she wore a red cloth toque that enclosed all her hair but a few curls at the front, and they were disguised by a pretty pleated frill.

It was just the sort of headdress a nimble-fingered lady could make for herself, and very fetching. Kitty couldn't help thinking that such a frill would soften her own looks without curls.

"Pol, you look delightful," she said honestly. "I think perhaps I should promote you to lady's maid."

Pol's color was already excited, and now it deepened. "I do like to make pretty clothes, miss. But . . ."

Kitty grinned. "But you're hoping not to be in my employ much longer. Very well. Let's go on our adventure."

Merely adding large warm shawls to their outfits, they slipped out the back door and crept across the dark garden. Kitty felt like a housebreaker, and the crunch of frosted grass beneath her half boots sounded like a fusillade of arms. She half-expected the neighbors to fling up their windows, crying, "What's amiss? Who goes there?"

When the gate hinges squealed, she cringed, caught between the urge to stand stock still hoping to be invisible, and to run through before they were caught. This whole area of London, however, remained undisturbed.

Still, as they stepped carefully down the narrow footpath, Kitty wondered if she was demented to have agreed to this plan. What would her parents have thought?

She was sure they would have supported Pol's chances of a good and loving marriage, but she doubted they'd have liked the means. Perhaps she should have insisted that all the wooing take place in her house. It was too late now, for they were into the Wells Street garden and approaching the kitchen door.

At the merest tap it flew open and Ned ushered them in, quickly taking their shawls. Nothing ardent was said or done, and yet something—something bright as the hearthfire on the copper pots—danced between the two blushing servants.

Kitty experienced a sudden, startling stab of emptiness. She had never felt anything like that. She had never—not even for a fleeting moment—been so important to a man.

"Where is Lord Chatterton?" she asked.

"In the drawing room, miss." Ned pulled an uneasy face. "I thought down here. He said up there."

Perhaps he'd felt the same qualms that Kitty did and wanted to keep things formal. "And why not?" she said with a smile.

As she followed Ned up plain servants' stairs, however, she suddenly worried that Lord Chatterton might have dressed for an evening entertainment. She would feel even more out of place.

He was, however, in day dress, and seemingly prepared to be the perfect host. Two sofas had been arranged on either side of the fire, and he smoothly arranged it so that Ned and Pol ended up on one, with he and Kitty on the other.

Soon after, the nervous valet went off to make tea. Pol made a move to help him but Lord Chatterton prevented it by engaging her in conversation. Kitty played her part, but she marveled at how easily he chatted to Pol, with whom he could have little in common.

Kitty was not of a tongue-tied nature, but she generally spent her time with friends, or with people gathered for a shared interest—political reform, perhaps, or gas lighting. Now she observed in action an expert at getting along with strangers.

Casually, lightly, he talked of a range of subjects that required only the occasional, "Yes, my lord," or "I don't think so, my lord," from the uncomfortable maid. As soon as he found one that sparked a touch of interest, however, he settled to develop it.

With surprised admiration, Kitty saw him draw Pol out to talk about the state of some nearby roads and the unreliability of the supply of fresh fish in the city. Soon the maid was easy enough to let loose a few pithy comments about some business in Parliament.

Kitty's parents had always encouraged their servants to read the newspapers and journals that came into the house, and Kitty had continued that tradition. She hadn't been aware, however, of how much use Pol was making of them.

By the time Ned came back—and he had clearly hurried—the object of his affections was leaning forward and giving his employer her firm opinions on the electoral system, and the exclusion of women from it.

"I agree," Lord Chatterton said, unruffled. "There does seem little logic in excluding women from the vote. However, it would not help you, Pol, for servants cannot vote. There is a property qualification."

"But if I were to become a property owner, I would have as much interest in good government as any similar man, my lord."

"Do you have ambitions to become a property owner?"

Pol leaned back slightly. "I have ambitions," she said. "What person does not?"

"Oh, many lack ambition. Perhaps most, if ambition includes the real intent to work toward a goal. But here is the tea."

Once they were settled to tea and cake, he managed the talk again, finding childhood accounts for everyone to share. After a while, whether by his management or natural forces, Ned and Pol were talking together, and he turned to Kitty.

"Would you care to take a stroll around the room, Miss Mayhew?"

In her own small house, the suggestion would be ridiculous, but this room was large enough to provide a circuit of sorts. His main purpose, clearly, was to give Ned and Pol more privacy while maintaining the chaperonage.

Kitty was thawing. Really, he was acting with wonderful kindness. She had clearly misjudged him, and she agreed willingly to his suggestion.

They rose and began to stroll down one side of the room. "You were raised entirely in London, Miss Mayhew?"

"Yes, my lord. We visited the sea every year, however."

"Brighton?"

"Good heavens, no! Far too racy. Eastbourne. It is still little more than a village, but very pretty. I suppose you grew up in the country."

"At Oakhurst, yes. Park, woods, lake, trout stream. I admit it was splendid."

As they turned to cross in front of the long windows, Kitty took a rash step. "Then why are you not there now?"

Distinctly, he cooled. "It's hardly fishing season."

"It is, however, season for gathering bay and holly, and hosting the tenants in Christmas festivities." It struck her for the first time that there was not a trace of Christmas decoration in this house.

There was none in hers, either, but that was because of mourning. Perhaps he was in mourning. Men often gave up outward signs quite quickly.

"My parents have such things in hand."

"Then should you not be there?" She immediately realized it was impertinent, and wished she could take the words back. "I mean, is it not a time to be with family, my lord?"

"Then why are you alone, Miss Mayhew?" It was clearly intended as a silencing attack.

Kitty almost smirked, but managed a soulful impression. "Alas, my lord, I have no family."

It struck home and he stopped to face her. They were now in the corner behind the courting couple, whose heads were close as they talked softly. "No family? That's impossible."

"I suppose it does depend how far out into the family tree one wants to cast, my lord. But I have no siblings, no aunts and uncles, no cousins, and no grandparents alive."

"Miss Mayhew, you'll have me in tears."

It was a joking comment, but she could see that he was genuinely moved by her situation. Perhaps this was more evidence of kindness. If he valued family, however, why was he here alone while his family celebrated at their country seat?

"Tell me about your family, then, my lord."

They continued their stroll. "I have two brothers and one

sister. Mary is married. Harold is in the army, Charles in the Church."

"Down at your home?"

"No," he said with a wry smile. "Charles has decided to take religion very seriously and has been living in a northern mill town. My parents are fit to tear their hair out over it."

"And your sister? Is she at your home with your parents?"

"She has her own home."

"So your parents will be alone for Christmas. How sad." She couldn't help a note of censure.

"Did I give you permission to poke into my family's affairs, Miss Mayhew?"

A distinct tremor of nervousness shot through Kitty, but she kept her chin up. "Do I need it? You did say you would tell me why you are here alone."

"Ah, so I did."

They were close to the door to an adjacent room, and he turned the knob, then gestured her through.

Kitty hesitated.

"We'll leave the door open," he said. "If either of our charges screams, we can rush back in. Don't you think, though, that they might be permitted to steal a kiss?"

Kitty knew nothing about this kind of chaperonage, but she supposed that as long as she and Lord Chatterton were in the same room, Ned and Pol wouldn't feel free to kiss. She went with him, therefore, into a simple anteroom that lacked any sense of being a true living space. It also lacked a fire, and was distinctly chilly.

"It hardly seems worth the time to find your shawl, does it?" The next thing she knew, she was in his arms.

"My lord!" But Kitty hissed it, not wanting to disturb the courting couple.

"I'm just blending our body heat, Miss Mayhew. Relax."

It was true that he was doing nothing other than holding her close, and that his warmth was welcome. Even so, the feel of his body against hers was . . . distracting.

"Perhaps it's time to go back," she whispered into his shoulder.

"Have pity. A good kiss takes time. But," he added, "perhaps you don't know that."

Kitty was not at all surprised when he shifted their bodies slightly and tilted her head toward his.

"No protests, Miss Mayhew?" He was intent again, a little amused, and devastatingly handsome.

Kitty's heart was thundering, but it pleased her to surprise him. "No. I, too, am chaperoned. If necessary, I will scream."

"But a kiss won't cause you to scream?" His lips were only inches from hers now and she could feel his breath.

"I don't think so. My experience of kissing is somewhat limited."

"Ah." She couldn't see his lips anymore, but his eyes smiled. "And being of a scholarly disposition, you would like to learn more."

"You have it exactly, my lord."

"In the interests of science, then. . . ."

The kiss in the garden, she realized, had not been a real kiss. It had been perhaps a challenge, a test, a tease, but not a kiss. This, she thought, was a real kiss.

Perhaps it was the way he held her: encompassing, but without any need to control or restrain.

Perhaps it was the way he sampled her, like a person stepping into the sea for the first time, exploring each sensation before going deeper.

Perhaps it was the way she responded, exploring gently in her turn, fascinated by the soft warmth of his lips, the hint of his teeth, the first touch of his tongue.

She knew she was relaxed against his arms, soothed and softened into a state ripe for further adventures. Improper adventures. She recognized, therefore, that it was time to end it.

Gently, for she was not offended, she straightened and moved back, taking a deep breath to steady herself. "I think, my lord, that if Ned and Pol are doing that, we should go and interrupt."

"How true." He looked gratifyingly unsteady himself as he led her back into the other room, saying, "Do you play cards, Miss Mayhew?"

He spoke rather loudly, and after a moment Kitty realized he was alerting the other couple. When they entered the warm drawing room, Ned and Pol were sitting side by side, hand in hand and rather flushed.

Kitty wondered if she were flushed, then realized her skin would hide it. "You're rather good at this," she murmured to the man by her side.

"At what, dear lady? Kissing, or playing gooseberry?" A teasing wink disarmed her outrage. "As for the matter, I have a sister, remember. I've seen it in operation. Had to play my part now and then."

Soon they were at a card table, enjoying a simple gambling game for outrageous stakes. Lord Chatterton cheated, and soon Pol learned from him, with both Ned and Kitty protesting at their tricks. Kitty laughed more than she had in a year, and enjoyed herself perhaps more than she could ever remember.

At one crystal moment, she realized that she could love to live like this. But this moment was a momentary sparkle, like the stars from fireworks, enduring only for a moment.

Soon Pol would be the maid again, and she the mistress. Lord Chatterton would have his servants back and live as a noble should. He would attend splendid balls, dine with important people, and if he played cards, it would be for more moderate stakes, but real ones.

Kitty would be alone again, perhaps without even Pol for company.

She shrugged off the touch of sadness. She had this moment, with perhaps more of them to come before Twelfth Night. She would enjoy them while she could.

At ten o'clock, as they prepared to return home, they found a sleek black tomcat waiting by the back door.

"Is your cat safe?" he asked Kitty as he arranged her shawl around her shoulders.

"I believe so."

"Then I'll let him out. He's not used to being confined at night."

"What if he sets up his serenade outside our house again?"

He smiled down at her. "Then you can imagine him my minstrel, sent to serenade you, my queen of the night."

Kitty sucked in an unsteady breath. "You are a wicked man, my lord."

"Aren't all toms?"

The two men escorted them back, the tomcat slipping ahead into Kitty's garden. His owner opened the gate and Kitty went through with him before realizing Ned and Pol had hesitated on the other side.

"Another kiss?" she asked in humorous comment.

"Why not?" he said with a smile.

Kitty didn't pretend to struggle as he cradled her head and kissed her warmly in a way that created an excellent illusion of tender care.

"Good night, dear lady," he murmured afterward. "I wish I could believe that you will dream of me."

She shivered slightly at his tone. "Will you dream of me?"

"Oh, undoubtedly." He kissed her hand, looking into her eyes. "Pale, slender, and bathed in starshine."

Kitty did step back at that, freeing herself and pulling her shawl close around her. He hadn't said "naked," but she'd heard it.

Perhaps she was playing a much more dangerous game than she'd thought.

If there was danger, it was elusive, for the courtship progressed as it had begun. While London celebrated the Twelve Days of Christmas, Kitty, Lord Chatterton, Ned, and Pol met each evening to talk and play games.

And to kiss.

Or at least, Lord Chatterton kissed Kitty. She could only assume that Ned was kissing Pol. It would be intrusive to ask.

Surely they must be kissing, for they showed no sign of tiring of each other. In fact, Pol began to act as if she'd given her wits into Ned's keeping, the way she wandered around during the day letting things burn and boil.

Kitty did feel a little absentminded herself now and then. She felt different, different all over. Sometimes she caught herself stroking her own body, imagining a man's arms around her. Thank heavens there was no one to see!

Perhaps the sanest creature in the house was Sherry, now restored to disinterest in the male of the species. This didn't prevent some of the toms from lurking and squabbling in the garden, but most of them had clearly left for more promising spots.

Rochester stayed around, however, occasionally cater-wauling his claim to his territory, sounding remarkably like a lover serenading beneath the window of his beloved.

One restless night, hearing the black cat yowling and seeing Sherry's disdain, Kitty made this a lesson for herself. If she ever felt tempted to croon at beguiling Lord Chatterton, she should remember that he was just suffering a temporary interest.

It would pass when his normal life resumed, and that would be tomorrow. She was sleepless tonight because tomorrow was Twelfth Night. The next day their servants would begin to return, and normal order would be restored. The adventure would be over.

She'd planned to enjoy it, and she had. She had not planned to fall in love with the man.

He was a wonderful companion, though, able to talk of almost anything, and able to listen just as well. He could occasionally show a biting wit, but he seemed kind and not the slightest bit haughty. And his kisses were a work of art.

The past few nights Kitty had found herself wishing he would do more. Thank heavens she was too shy to act on her impulses herself, or she'd be behaving as wantonly as

Sherry had in heat! She was not an animal, though, and could control herself. Since there was no question of marriage between them, she must not let him ruin her.

Let him.

With a sigh, she had to admit that Lord Chatterton had made no attempt to ruin her, which was part of her wicked dissatisfaction.

Was it possible to be just a little bit ruined?

Oh, you foolish woman.

Twelfth Night. Her saner part rejoiced that the Christmas season was almost over, and her madness with it.

This reminded her, however, that she still didn't know why an earl's heir was stuck in his house with no servants except for Ned. He'd promised to tell her, and he would.

Tonight.

That night, Kitty greeted Lord Chatterton and Ned, hoping her feelings did not show. She found that these days she couldn't help her excitement every time she saw him. She felt as if she must be quivering with it. In addition, tears threatened because this was the last of their magical evenings.

On top of that was a kind of relief that the madness and temptation would soon be over and she could be cool and calm again.

As usual, they sat in her drawing room, chatting. Then Lord Chatterton said, "You have a piano. Do you play?"

"Yes." Kitty hadn't suggested it because Pol didn't know how, and she didn't want to make a distinction between them.

"Would you not play a piece or two for us?"

Asked directly, Kitty could not refuse, and went to the instrument. He followed, and raised the lid for her. She realized then that it was another clever way to give Ned and Pol some privacy, and smiled as she took her seat.

She played a number of pieces from memory, enjoying herself. In fact, she lost herself in the music so that she was surprised, looking up, to see him leaning on the piano, watching her.

The look in his eyes could turn her foolish—if she were a foolish woman.

"Do you sing?" he asked softly.

"Not well, I'm afraid."

"I do. Could you accompany me?"

"To what? I don't have music for many songs."

"Let's see."

She rose and he flipped through the music in the bench. "Ah. This one?"

He'd pulled out Tom Moore's "Believe Me, If All Those Endearing Young Charms." She was certainly familiar with it, for her father had loved to sing it, generally with his eyes on her mother. For a moment she could not bear the thought of hearing it again, but then, like a healing salve, she decided she would let it bring back sweet memories.

She ran through the melody once, reminding her fingers, and then he joined her.

> "Believe me, if all those endearing young charms
> Which I gaze on so fondly today,
> Were to change by tomorrow and fleet in my arms,
> Like fairy gifts fading away,
> Thou would'st still be adored as this moment thou art,
> Let thy loveliness fade as it will,
> And around the dear ruin, each wish of my heart
> Would entwine itself verdantly still."

He had a beautiful baritone voice and he acted well, too, singing to her as if he meant the words. Embarrassed, Kitty looked away for a moment and saw Ned gazing into Pol's shining eyes, honestly feeling the words.

Oh, love, how sweet it could be.

As her beloved sang on, she let her eyes lock with his, creating an impossible fairy moment to treasure all her days.

As soon as the song ended, however, she leaped up, closed the instrument, and moved away from it.

"We've made a Twelfth Night cake, so you must eat

some of it and make a wish." Impulsively, she added, "We really should have punch with it, too."

"I'll make some," said Pol, jumping up.

"I'll help," said Ned. "No woman knows how to make punch right."

"Do you say so!"

"I do indeed."

They disappeared, squabbling as lovers do, leaving Kitty alone with Lord Chatterton.

She shared a smile with him over their charges, but then looked away. She really didn't know how to behave with him these days, or how to react to anything.

He went to put another log on the fire, then stayed there. He often did that these days, she realized, left her side when they were alone.

Did he think she'd leap on him?

Were her feelings obvious?

In defense, she headed toward the question he'd once promised to answer. "So, my lord. At your family's country seat—at Oakhurst—are they celebrating Twelfth Night with punch and cake, and with shots fired around the apple trees?"

He stood, brushing his hands together. "The tenants doubtless are." His tone was cool.

"But not your family?"

"My parents do not approve of pagan rites."

"And you?" she asked, rather shocked.

"I find nothing of worth in such things. In fact," he added, almost with bravado, "I detest Christmas."

"Detest . . ."

"Why gape? I took you for a sensible woman. Christmas is merely a plague that comes back every year. If it escapes false sentimentality, it is only to plunge into crude bawdiness."

"It's a celebration of the birth of Christ!"

His lips twisted into an unpleasant smile. "With punch, cake, and shots fired around trees? Not to mention Yule logs, holly, and mistletoe. It's pagan, Miss Mayhew, and might be slightly more bearable if everyone acknowledged that."

"It is a blend of many things, my lord, all of them good."

His brows rose. "What possible good is there in the Lord of Misrule?"

Kitty had never been in a household that followed the tradition of appointing someone to rule throughout Christmas, forcing others to entertain, or to suffer fanciful punishments. "It is just a game, which surely brings family and friends together in laughter. That is suitable for Christmas."

"Laughter? Only at other people's embarrassment. If it brings people together, it is in enjoying the humiliation of those they dislike, despise, or envy."

Kitty looked up at him in dismay, fighting tears.

"I never took you for a sentimental fool," he said harshly. "I suppose you like this new fashion for creches, too. Simpering plaster madonnas praying over babies that never cry or spit."

Kitty was too dismayed to tell him that she did like them, very much indeed. It was as if a stranger stood before her.

She sought refuge in her original question. "But this doesn't explain why you are skulking all alone in your basement, my lord."

"Does it not? My dear Miss Mayhew, have you ever tried to escape Christmas? The servants insist on it. Street vendors wish you a merry Christmas—expecting a penny for it, of course. Even my most irreligious friends end up singing sentimental hymns over a wassail bowl."

Hurt was rapidly turning to anger. "No doubt I have offended you by ordering punch!"

"I'll endure it as long as you forgo the hymns. At least you seem sane in most respects. You have no silly trappings here."

"In fact, I enjoy Christmas, my lord, and I think it cruel of you to deprive poor Ned of it just to suit your whim."

His jaw tightened. "I pay him to endure my cruelties. And my damnable interference. Which reminds me that I had better go and interrupt whatever is keeping them."

He stalked out, and Kitty stared at the closed door,

shocked and saddened. She had been deceived, for she couldn't really like anyone who detested Christmas. She certainly couldn't *love* such a person.

She sat staring into the fire, feeling as if she'd suffered another death. Slowly, however, her hurt and anger changed into pity. How horrible not to see the blessings of the season.

Her memories were full of wonderful Christmases in this house. Of greenery and kissing boughs; plum pudding and mince pies; carols and stories; and chestnuts roasting in the grate.

Of laughter and song.

Song. *Believe me . . .*

She wiped away a tear. No matter what little problems had fretted her family, at Christmas they'd always found joy. Each year her family and friends had renewed their warm feelings, like new logs placed on a spiritual fire.

Had he never felt that?

Did he really reject Yule as entirely pagan?

When he returned with the servants and the punch, he said, rather stiffly, "I'm sorry. I've upset you. I thought you of a similar mind."

"Well, I'm not. It's just that I'm in mourning."

"So normally you would be romping to the end of twelve days of mayhem?"

That didn't quite describe her family's practices, but she said, "Yes."

"Then I am disappointed in you, Miss Mayhew."

It didn't seem charitable to snap that she was even more disappointed in him, and Kitty could see concern written on the faces of Pol and Ned. So she put it aside, accepting a glass of punch and a piece of cake. As she ate, she made the traditional wish, and her wish was for him, that he could somehow one day find the light and blessings of Christmas.

Superficially everything eased, and they sat to play hazard for millions of guineas. Since Kitty didn't actually like the dice game, she felt pleasantly virtuous. Unhappiness simmered in her, however, so when Lord Chatterton and Ned rose to leave, she stayed them.

"It *is* Twelfth Night," she said with a challenging look at him. "Why not stay to see the end of Christmas?"

"If only I could," he muttered.

But Ned—perhaps obliviously, or perhaps rebelliously—said, "Aye, why not?"

"Oh, and we've some chestnuts," added Pol, bright-eyed. "We could roast some and sing some songs."

When the two of them disappeared in search of chestnuts, Lord Chatterton snapped, "I could throttle you."

"For making you endure some roasted chestnuts and an hour more of my company?"

"For spoiling everything with Christmas." She was pulled to her feet.

"What—!"

And kissed.

It was short, rough, and rather unpleasant. When it stopped, she said, "Why?"

"I might as well have some benefit—kissing beneath the mistletoe for example."

"But we have none."

"I, at least, have an imagination. Try to guess what I'm imagining now."

He kissed her again, just as roughly, but something in the way he held her to him, pressed her to him, shaped her to him, left her shaken rather than annoyed. She could guess what he was imagining, and it stirred visions in her own mind.

Visions of entwined naked bodies from Renaissance masters and Grecian urns.

Voices made them break apart to stare dazedly at each other, wicked notions still dancing between their minds. Kitty's heart was galloping high in her chest and she felt she could hardly breathe. Or that at least her breath should be visible as a wavering, broken line of light between his lips and hers.

Ned and Pol came in, chattering, carrying a big bowl of chestnuts and a cellar of salt.

Kitty caught a mischievous, assessing look from both servants, followed with a shared smile of knowing amusement. Just who was chaperoning whom?

But chaperoning would imply courtship.

She glanced at Lord Chatterton. He, however, had turned away to study a landscape on the wall, as if attempting to reject the company.

No, no courtship. What a foolish thought. He'd kissed her that way as an attack, as he had done that first time in the garden. Perhaps he'd hoped to be thrown out so he could retreat with honor.

So, she'd make him endure it.

Kitty joined Ned and Pol on the floor in front of the fire and placed a chestnut in the embers. Rebelliously, she began one of her favorite seasonal hymns.

"The race that long in darkness pined
    Have seen a glorious light . . ."

Pol joined in, for the whole household had sung this at some point during the Christmas season. She saw Ned glance at his employer, but then he began to sing, too, in quite a pleasant voice.

Kitty refused to look at the man who detested Christmas.

If he wanted to sulk, let him.

He didn't sing, but suddenly he sat beside her, close beside, so his legs brushed hers and his body was *there* all along her. He even leaned past her, pressing against her, to place a chestnut on the edge of the fire. "I will think of a suitable revenge," he murmured into her ear.

"For what sin now?"

"Carol singing."

She turned and met his eyes. "If you're so set on revenge, my lord, I shall have to do something to *really* deserve it."

She stood and went off to find her Yule candle.

She had made one this year, continuing the family tradition even though she hadn't intended to use it. Traditions were hard to break, and all her life she'd helped her mother make the special candle, which was eighteen inches high and as thick as her arm.

She took it off a shelf in the pantry, missing her mother so dreadfully that she thought she'd just collapse into tears. She fought it, though, knowing Mama would want her to light the candle in celebration of the joy and optimism of the season, not with the sadness of loss. She placed it securely in its silver holder and returned to the drawing room.

She confessed to herself that she was a little nervous. In talk of Christmas, Lord Chatterton had seemed almost violent. What would he do about this?

She paused just inside the door to study him.

He was lounging on the carpet, picking morsels of roasted chestnut out of the skin, his long, strong body edged by the light from the fire. Perhaps because he was so close to the fire, he'd taken off his jacket and cravat, so he resembled the rakish man she'd first encountered.

Or perhaps it was just another cut of his revenge. He must know his attractions and how to use them.

He looked up at her, and his expression reminded her of their first meeting, too, while something in his lazy, sprawled elegance reminded her of his rakish cat.

"A candle, Miss Mayhew?" he drawled. "And such a big one. Are we to sink even lower?"

"A Yule candle," she said defiantly, and continued into the room—only to halt when she saw Pol. The maid was actually in Ned's lap, laughing and letting him feed her with bits of chestnut. At Kitty's stare Pol bit her lip and straightened, but not much.

"I think we have light enough," Lord Chatterton said, dragging her attention back to him.

"Not for long." Kitty decided she really couldn't lecture

Pol just at this moment, and set about extinguishing the candles.

She slid a wary glance at the man who didn't like Christmas, half-expecting him to stop her by force. He just continued to pick apart chestnuts and chew on the meat while watching her in a way that made her feel . . .

. . . feel undressed, she realized!

So, *that* was his true revenge.

How extraordinary that he could do it.

And he was even managing to look undressed himself, look naked. She could imagine his body beneath the clothes, as if he were a statue from ancient Rome.

Forcing her eyes away, she put out the last candle so that only the firelight broke the darkness. The clock sounded the quarter to midnight. Christmas was almost over.

She headed for the mantelpiece, intending to place the candle there as usual. She, her parents, and any guests, had always stood around in front of the fire to watch the candle be lit. That was the way it should be done, the respectable way. But she looked at Pol and Ned, so cozy together, and at Lord Chatterton lounging in arrogant ease, and wasn't sure she could get them up and neatly arranged in time.

With an apologetic prayer to her mother, she surrendered to a new way and settled back down onto the carpet.

But everything else would be done properly, she resolved, even if she was twelve days late. Traditions were the glue that bound both family and society, or so her mother had claimed.

She placed the candle on the carpet. "Gather round."

Ned and Pol slid over quickly enough, though almost as if stuck together. *He* was slower, but shifted slightly so as to form part of the circle. His resistance lay beside her like a deep shadow, and she felt almost guilty at forcing this on him.

She looked at the candle, but spoke for him, longing to convert him. "It has always been a tradition in our house to light a Yule candle. To celebrate both the birth of our Savior and the blessedness of light."

"I hesitate to object," he said, still eating, "but shouldn't Yule be celebrated on the shortest day of the year? You're rather late, Miss Mayhew."

"Since ancient times, my lord," Kitty said tightly, "Yule has been combined with Christmas, as is fitting. After all, Christ is a light to the world."

"Even so, Miss Mayhew, you are rather late."

"I know it. The candle should be lit on Christmas Eve, but this year I didn't . . . I am in mourning. But I now see I was wrong not to follow tradition. Tradition, even pagan tradition, is very important."

He said nothing more, but she began to tremble. She knew now that he would not welcome this at all. He wouldn't be moved and change his mind about Christmas. He would just see this as pagan, unseemly, or even *sentimental*.

She'd thought to convert him, but now she feared that he might change her, might ruin this for her.

She thrust that out of her mind and summoned the words her mother had always said. Immediately, she was back in this moment last year, remembering how they had dedicated this tradition to the memory of her father. . . .

Tears threatened, but she fought them. She would do this for both her parents, and tomorrow she would begin to make something good, something bright, of her life.

"The world fell into darkness," she said, unable to clear her throat enough to avoid huskiness. "Then God sent His son to be a light—light to show the spiritual way, but also to bring warmth and brightness to our hearts. This recalls a more ancient gift, a gift dating back to creation, when God gave His world the sun, and then fire. Fire—the means to make light even in the longest, darkest times of winter, just as Christ's love will bring grace into even the most joyless, sinful soul. Let us celebrate, therefore, the gift of light."

She handed Pol the spill. "The youngest should light the candle."

As Pol turned to the fire, Kitty continued, her voice clearer now. "But there are other gifts for which we give thanks as the candle glows—the daily gifts of love and joy, the treasures of our family and friends."

Features serious, Pol put the splint to the wick. It caught, and in moments the flame spread up in its perfect mellow shape, weaving slightly with the movement of the air, touching each face with warmth.

"Let us give thanks to God, therefore, for sending His son to be our light, but also for the heavenly sun, for fire, for love, and for joy in our family and friends."

She sat staring into the gentle flame, thinking of her mother speaking the words last year, of the tears that had run down her mother's cheeks. . . .

She wasn't aware of her own tears until he brushed them away.

She started, turning to him, braced for something hurtful. His expression was sober, though, as he kissed her lips, gently, comfortingly, there on the carpet in front of the servants.

She should have objected, but surrendered to tenderness.

"You really feel that, don't you?" he said at last.

"The kiss?"

"The light."

She turned to look at the candle, still within his arms. "Oh, yes."

She thought he wouldn't say anything else, and hoped in a way that he wouldn't.

"It's not that I don't love my family," he said, as gruffly as she had spoken. "It's just that Christmas . . ."

"But why? Why Christmas?" She looked back at him, needing to know.

He studied her, this alien male who'd brought her down to her drawing room carpet. "Come sit in my lap and I'll tell you."

Kitty stiffened and glanced at the servants.

They'd gone!

"We should—"

"No, we shouldn't. Their attachment is genuine and they'll be married soon enough. What are you frightened of?"

"You."

He cocked his head. "Why? I promise not to force you to anything."

"You make me feel . . ." She bit back the words and muttered, "You might not have to use force."

He smiled and some of the blessed light was in it. "Then I promise not to let you ruin yourself with me, Miss Mayhew, no matter how *heated* you become." He held out a hand. "Come."

She shouldn't. She knew she shouldn't. But she put her hand in his and allowed him to draw her into his lap. "Kitty," she said. "My name is Kitty."

He laughed. "How very appropriate. I will use it only if you call me Tom." He settled her there, back against him, facing the fire, warm all around. His arms encircled her, hands resting over hers, and one thumb rubbed against her skin.

"Tom," she said shyly, but loving this moment. It seemed as blessed as fire on the coldest winter's night. "Now, tell me why you hate Christmas."

He spoke softly, right against her ear. "Christmas," he said. "I don't know where it all went wrong. Perhaps in childhood. We were taught many things by excellent tutors, but not about Christmas. Christmas isn't celebrated at Oakhurst."

She shifted slightly so she could see him. "You did *nothing* to mark the season?"

"We went to Christmas Day service in the chapel, of course. We were certainly taught the religious significance of the day. But my parents don't approve of the more pagan aspects of the season. They are completely appalled by kissing boughs."

"My parents weren't comfortable with them, either. If it hadn't been for my mother's belief in the importance of customs, we wouldn't have had one. As it was, no one was allowed to do more than kiss on the cheek."

He kissed her lightly on the cheek. "Compromise. Very wise."

"My parents *were* wise. They were wonderful." She stopped there, for she wanted to learn more about him and why he disliked Christmas. "I can see that you didn't grow up with much feeling for Christmas—"

"Ah, but there you are wrong," he interrupted. "My parents couldn't ban festivities from the neighborhood, and children are curious creatures. Each of us had a governess or tutor, and a personal servant. Then there were the maids and footmen who cared for our rooms, not to mention the grooms who taught us to ride, groundsmen who took us fishing, and the people who talked to us when we went down to the village. The result was, of course, that in the weeks before Christmas we were surrounded by excited talk of the celebrations. It became the paradise we were barred from."

Kitty was dazed by this glimpse into a noble household, and saddened by the gulf it illuminated between them. But she pursued her inquiry. "You must have reached an age to choose for yourself."

"I tried at sixteen. I sneaked down to the village to watch the Christmas Eve mummers. They were too frightened of my parents' disapproval, however, and took me straight home. I received a blistering lecture and strict confinement to my room on lean rations for the Twelve Days."

Kitty couldn't think of anything to say.

"You mustn't think badly of my parents," he said. "We received excellent care and education, and all other normal fun was permitted—games, sports, fishing, riding. They just have strong feelings about pagan ceremonies. They'd love to ban well-blessing, and All Hallows' bonfires, and especially the maypole, with its quite risqué connotations."

Kitty chuckled, for her mother had discussed the symbolism of the maypole dance. "Your parents and my mother would certainly have had brisk arguments."

"Indeed." He smiled. "I would have loved to have seen it. But nothing would change their minds, I'm sure. And I can see their point. Most of those pagan traditions have quite improper aspects."

"Fertility rites," Kitty agreed. "Like rice and flowers at weddings." But she realized they were in danger of drifting away from him and Christmas. "So, did you never try traditional Christmas to see if you liked it?"

"Oh, yes. Once I came of age, I threw off the shackles. I spent Christmas with a school friend who'd always made me envious with his stories of romping jollity."

She could see it hadn't been pleasant. "What happened?"

"Romping jollity." He grimaced slightly. "I discovered I am my parents' son. I couldn't blend the crudeness of it with the holiness of the season. It was more than that, though. It was the hypocrisy."

"Hypocrisy? They weren't really enjoying themselves?"

"Oh, I'm sure they were. But everything they were doing . . . They kissed under the mistletoe—and on the lips, of course. But mostly there was no affection in it. Often it was used to tease and torment those who didn't want to be kissed at all. The Lord of Misrule used his power to embarrass. When the wassailers came, the gentry made fun of them as yokels. Despite the Yule log in the grate, there was no light in it. No light at all."

Kitty placed her hand over his. "I think you are a good man, my lord."

"Tom."

"Tom," she said with a smile.

"Good in places," he admitted, but grinned. "Just don't forget the bad spots, Kitty."

She didn't. She was shiveringly aware of them all the time. "But that was when you were twenty-one. Have you hidden from Christmas ever since? How old are you?"

She immediately felt she shouldn't have asked, but he answered. "Twenty-seven. And you?"

She'd thought him a little older, perhaps because of his sophistication. "Twenty-five."

"Well matched for friendship, then."

That warmed her, even though she was aware of a foolish part that wanted more.

"So," she asked. "What have you done with Christmas for the past six years?"

He shifted back a little so he could lean against the sofa, drawing her closer against him. She hadn't been aware until then how tense he had been. "Let me see. Year two I returned, chastened, home. However, I still couldn't feel that that was all Christmas had to offer. Year three I spent with my newly-married sister. She had thrown herself into romping Christmas with enthusiasm, and there was some spontaneity and joy in it. Unfortunately, she'd invited some of her best friends along."

"Why was that a problem?"

"Because I was clearly the main offering at the Christmas feast."

"What?"

He touched her nose with his finger. "My dear Kitty, I've been a juicy quarry for the Marriage Chase all my adult life, and Christmas is prime hunting season. All that family feeling, not to mention all those kissing boughs, and the things an obliging Lord of Misrule can make people do."

"How horrible for you."

"It's not comfortable, no. Where was I? Year four I spent in Melton at an orgy. That seemed safe enough, and it was. But I found I missed the real parts of Christmas. On the other hand, when the drink-soaked, debauched company slid into singing Christmas hymns, I was offended."

"An orgy," echoed Kitty, trying not to show that she was shocked. He'd calmly laid before her the grandeur of a noble household, but this unbalanced her even more.

An orgy!

She swallowed. "I've . . . er . . . never known anyone who admitted to being at an . . . an . . ."

"Orgy." His eyes twinkled with laughter at her embarrassment. "I don't suppose you have. They have their moments, but are not really all they're cracked up to be. Where was I?"

Shamefully, she would have liked to know more, but she said, "Year five, I believe."

"Year five I found quite a good solution. I spent it in Scotland, where they make far less of Christmas Day, then left for England on New Year's Eve—their Hogmanay. But it all felt wrong. So, the last two years, I've hidden away."

Kitty took his hand firmly in hers. "You haven't been trying to hide from Christmas, you know. You've been searching for it."

He stared at her for a moment. "Perhaps I have at that. But I fear it isn't there for the finding."

"Perhaps it cannot be *found*. Perhaps," she added, as much for herself as for him, "part of growing up is that we have to make our own traditions, including Christmas."

"At my parents' house?"

"No, at your *own*. Do you not have a home?"

He looked rather startled by the idea. "No. I use my father's houses. I suppose I could have a set of rooms. . . ."

"No. You need a home." She turned between his legs to face him. "It could be many years before you become earl. Are you to be a waif all that time, living in your father's houses and hiding in the basement every Christmas?"

He touched her cheek, an almost dazed look in his eyes. "How wise you are. But I'm not sure I know how to make a home, never mind Christmas." He brushed her lower lip softly with his thumb and frowned thoughtfully. "Could you help me, Kitty? Help me make a home, a real home. Teach me how to celebrate a real Christmas there, a Christmas full of light."

It touched her to smiling, but a somewhat sad smile. It would be bittersweet to work with him on these things, for one day it would be done and they'd part.

"You don't seem pleased," he said, almost hesitantly. "You have doubts about me?"

She puzzled over it a moment. "Oh, about your behavior? No, of course not. I'm sure you won't go beyond what is proper."

"I don't suppose I will." Then suddenly he laughed. "Kitty, you goose. Don't you realize I just asked you to marry me?"

"What?" She knelt up straight. "You did not!"

"I . . ." He sucked in a breath and cradled her head between his hands. "Pay attention, Miss Mayhew. I have fallen in love with you. No, not fallen—slid slowly, gently, wonderfully into love with you. I want to spend the rest of my life with you as my wife. But I am being very practical, too. I am trying to claim the one person who can help me create what I most want—a loving home, and endless joy-filled, light-filled Christmases. Say yes."

It was a command, so Kitty said, "Yes." Then, "No! I mean, I don't know. My lord—Tom—you've drunk too much punch. I'm no wife for a nobleman."

"I'll teach you anything you need to know, while you teach me all the things I need to know. My father's a healthy man. We should have decades to live quite simply. I like this house, for example."

"You want to live *here*?"

"It's a home already. Warmth has soaked into the bricks and wood, into the very air here." He winked at her. "I'm marrying you for your house, Miss Mayhew."

Kitty stared at him breathless, beginning, tentatively, to believe.

"But in return," he said—and a touch of anxiety in his eyes could make her weep—"I can offer you a country estate. I own a pleasant property near Uckfield, with a neat house just big enough for a reasonable family. I'm sure we could create an excellent Christmas there. Yule logs, and mistletoe—but just with kissing on the cheek, of course. Except for us, when the children aren't watching."

"Children . . . ?"

"Children would be inevitable, I think, after all that kissing. Delightfully inevitable. Add in some mince pies, plum pudding and wassailers—whom we will enjoy, of course. We'll have holly, ivy, bay, and rosemary all over the place, and a Lord of Misrule who doesn't abuse his powers. On Christmas Eve we'll light a Yule candle, and the children will stand around, eyes shining, and sing in praise of the light . . . say yes."

"Yes," said Kitty, dazzled by the sweetest vision of her life. "Yes, please. If you're sure you're not affected by the punch."

"I'm affected by the light," he said, smiling as brightly as if lit from within. He brushed his lips softly against hers. "I am entranced by my moonlight queen, my candlelight angel, my firelight wanton. . . ."

"Wanton?" Kitty gasped.

"Wanton," he said, rolling her to the floor beneath him and kissing her with fiery heat.

There was something about being kissed in the horizontal, thought Kitty, about a man's weight over her. Something wonderful.

Something perhaps not even wicked since he wanted to marry her.

He wanted to *marry* her!

Like kindling to fire, she kissed him back, igniting a flame that swelled. . . .

Until someone cleared his throat.

Ned and Pol were there, looking embarrassed but resolute.

"Tom," she said, since he seemed too interested in her breasts to notice. "Tom!"

He stopped, looked at her, and grimaced ruefully. "I suppose our chaperones have returned."

"*Our* chaperones?"

Laughing, he leaped to his feet and helped her up, straightening her dress. "Of course. Did you ever imagine that Ned and Pol would do anything even slightly improper? Or that they weren't made for each other? These past ten days have been for us, my love. I've been courting you." He kissed her with aching tenderness, then turned to the servants. "It's all right. We're to be married."

"So I should hope, my lord," said Ned rather primly. "Pol and I, of course, also intend to wed. And to *wait* till we're wed."

Kitty tightened her lips on a smile. "So do we, I'm sure. And I think I'm going to need a lady's maid. Could I interest you in the position, Pol?"

Pol's smile could light the dim room. "Oh, miss! Thank you, miss!"

"And we're all going to divide our time between here and a lovely house near Uckfield, where we'll create the most wonderful Christmases imaginable."

Tom tucked a tendril of her hair behind her ear, causing a frisson to pass through her. "With a journey or two, I think. France, Holland, Italy. The morning light on the Grand Canal in Venice is not to be missed. Perhaps that should be our wedding journey. . . ."

"It sounds wonderful." Kitty wanted to ask how *soon* it could be.

At that moment, Sherry slipped in to step neatly between legs and candle. With a rather disdainful look at the humans, she curled up before the leaping fire. It was hard to imagine her wanton behavior of weeks before. In fact, thought Kitty, suppressing a giggle, they could almost be said to have changed places!

"I really think," she said, "that amid all this contentment, we should let Rochester and Sherry free to enjoy each other."

"He'll have to wait until she's in the mood, or be ripped to shreds." Tom nuzzled close to Kitty's ear. "Isn't it nice, my moonlight queen, that we poor human toms don't have so few shining moments. . . ."

Home for the Holidays

Barbara Bretton

Prologue

As a rule, Sebastian endured Christmas with the good grace for which the best cats were known. He never indulged in merrymaking. His self-defined role as elder statesman precluded such a loss of dignity. Instead he held himself aloof and watched with great indulgence as his humans did the strangest things.

Once a year, around the first snowstorm, they opened the front doors wide and dragged in a big pine tree from outside. The same people who scolded him when he came in with muddy paws ignored bugs and dirt and sap and set the tree right smack in the middle of the living room carpet. They hung round, shiny objects from the branches and strung twinkling lights from top to bottom. Then, when that was all done, they placed boxes underneath the lowest branches. Everyone who came to visit gathered around the tree to sing songs and drink something called eggnog and give each other presents that weren't half as much fun as catnip or a ball of yarn. All things considered, it was a most puzzling time of the year.

At Christmastime a cat had to learn how to cope, or he'd find himself with a Santa Claus hat on his head and a ribbon around his neck, posing for some stupid Christmas card picture that would embarrass him for the rest of his days.

The dog and the parrot were perfectly happy to make fools of themselves and wear all manner of ridiculous outfits to make the humans laugh, but not Sebastian. The first person who tried to make him wear snow boots or a bow in his fur would find himself picking kitty litter out of his teeth for a year.

Sebastian did not suffer fools gladly. Christmas was not his favorite time of year. He preferred Thanksgiving, thank you very much, with that big juicy dead bird on the table and lots of leftovers. When Christmas got too loud and confusing, he retreated to his hiding place in the Girl's room where a cat in his golden years could sleep in peace and quiet until things got back to normal again.

This year, however, something was wrong. There was no tree, no sparkly packages, no friends and relatives gathered around singing songs to torment the ears of innocent cats. The Boy and Girl moped around in their rooms, and not even talk of Santa Claus could make them smile.

And their parents weren't smiling either. When the changes all began, the man slept downstairs on the sofa while she had the big bed all to herself. Sebastian, with the sensibilities of a diplomat, had tried to divide his attentions between the two of them, but his twelve-year-old legs weren't what they used to be. The stairs took their toll on his rickety knees and made him wheeze like a bulldog, so most of the time he slept on the landing in order to be near them both.

Finally a time came when he didn't have to do that any longer, because the man packed his bags and moved to something called a hotel. The family dog refused to believe anything was wrong. The parrot thought Sebastian was making a mountain out of a molehill, but Sebastian knew in his ancient bones that change was in the wind. He had been around since the beginning and he knew how it used to be when they were happy. There had been so much laughter in the little cottage that he couldn't hear himself purr. Now he couldn't remember the last time he'd even seen them smile.

He found himself dreaming about the little cottage where he'd first lived with them and how happy they'd been. It was as if the cottage itself were somehow calling him back home. The woman used to sing while she cooked dinner, and sometimes the man came into the kitchen and drew her into his arms and they danced around the floor. Sebastian would even get into the act. He'd wind his way between their ankles until, laughing, they would bend down and stroke his fur just the way he liked it. Ah, those were the days. . . .

He'd been young then, and fast. A better mouser never lived than Sebastian in his prime. He'd bring his treasures home proudly and place them on the front porch, but she never seemed to appreciate them the way Sebastian thought she should.

Sebastian didn't do much mousing anymore, and his birding days were a thing of the past. He hadn't gone exploring in longer than he could remember, content instead to stay close to home in case he was needed. Sometimes he thought he caught the mourning doves laughing at him as he lay on the back steps and sunned himself. He pretended he didn't notice them waddling by, but he did. It was a sad day when a proud cat like Sebastian couldn't catch a mourning dove, but time marched on, and, like it or not, there wasn't anything he could do about it.

Not long ago a sign appeared in the front yard, and every day strange people marched through the house. Sebastian refused to acknowledge their presence as they peeked in closets and peered under the beds. He didn't know exactly what was going on, but he knew enough to know it meant that life was about to change.

He hadn't seen his people together in a long time. The man hadn't been around much since the sign appeared. The other day Sebastian had heard his voice through the answering machine, and he'd winced as the dog danced about with delight. Poor Charlie just didn't understand the difference between a machine and the real thing. For a minute Sebastian had wished he didn't either. He wanted to believe that his people would be together again, and things would be the way they used to be, but he was starting to suspect it never would.

When the big long truck pulled into the driveway that morning, Sebastian knew it was all over. He sat in the foyer and watched with growing dismay as the televisions vanished into the truck, along with the piano and dishes and even the paintings on the walls.

A snowy boot nudged his flank. "Move, fatso."

Sebastian aimed a malevolent look in the man's direction, but he didn't budge an inch. It was his house. Let old Snow Boots move.

"Hey, tubs." The brown boot nudged a little harder. "I got a twelve-foot couch to move. Get your furry ass out of my way."

Sebastian considered turning the man's pants into confetti but thought better of it. Instead, he leaped onto the sofa with a surprising display of agility and curled up in the corner as if he hadn't a care in the world. He was having trouble catching his breath, but he refused to let on.

"Hey, lady!" the man bellowed. "Do something about this cat, will you?"

"Sebastian!" She appeared in the doorway. "Scat! Stay out of the moving man's way."

Sebastian arched his back and hissed. Scat? Since when did she tell him to scat? She'd never embarrassed him in front of strangers before, and he didn't like it one bit.

"Bad cat!" Her voice shook as if she'd been crying. "Don't you ever do anything right?"

Her words cut him to the quick. He jumped down from the sofa, landing hard on his paws. Pain shot up his legs and along his back. He was getting too old for gymnastics. He waited for her to come see if he'd hurt himself, but she turned away as if she'd forgotten he was even there. That hurt most of all.

"You gonna stand there all day, fatso?" the moving man asked, aiming that boot in Sebastian's direction one more time. "You heard what the lady said. Now scat!"

Sebastian couldn't help himself. There was only so much a cat could take before he defended his honor. With one graceful swing of his paw, he turned the moron's right pants leg into a windsock and then he marched out the front door, tail held high. Maybe next time the man would think twice before insulting an innocent feline who was just minding his own business.

He strutted out onto the porch and surveyed his domain. Snow. Everywhere he looked . . . on the porch, the driveway, the yard. Sebastian's whiskers quivered with distaste. He hated snow. It was cold and wet and reminded him of baths and other indignities. Maybe if he looked pathetic enough she would come out and rescue him. An apology would be nice, but he wouldn't insist.

He waited patiently, watching as tables and chairs and beds and tables disappeared into the big truck parked in the driveway. It seemed a very strange thing to do, and he was pondering the mystery when he suddenly remembered the last time something just like this had happened to him.

The Boy and Girl had been babies then, too little to do anything but sleep and eat and cry. Sebastian would have suggested they leave the babies behind, but his people had a strange fondness for the little roundheads, a fondness Sebastian learned to share only after they were out of diapers. In his opinion, litterboxes made a great deal more sense.

He remembered that summer as if it were yesterday. All of their furniture had disappeared into a truck that time, too, only back then there hadn't been quite as much of it—and most of what they had boasted claw marks.

"Don't look so sad, Sebastian," she had said, chucking him under the chin. "You'll love the new house!"

"Wait until you see the backyard, old boy," the man had said with a laugh. "Slower birds and plumper mice and lots of shady places to take a nap."

Was that the last time they'd all been happy? he wondered now. The man worked harder than ever and was home less and less. She worked harder, too, sitting alone at the computer late at night while the Boy and Girl slept. Sebastian never saw them curled up side by side on the sofa or dancing in the kitchen or heard them laughing together in their room late at night.

The moving men bellowed something behind him. Sebastian scampered down the icy stairs and darted under the porch, just in time to avoid being flattened by work boots and the big couch from the den. Snow brushed against his belly and made him shiver. He hated the cold almost as much as he hated the 3-cans-for-a-dollar cat food his people sometimes foisted on him. At his age he should be curled up in front of a roaring fire with a platter of sliced veal and gravy, claiming his rightful place in the family.

Wasn't it bad enough that the man didn't live with them any more or that she sometimes cried herself to sleep when she thought no one could hear her? Now they wouldn't even have a home, and everyone knew you couldn't be a family if you didn't have a place where you could be together.

The cottage on Burnt Sugar Hill.

For days Sebastian had felt the pull of the old place. It had grown stronger with time until it was almost irresistible. And now he finally thought he knew why: the secret to being a family was in its four walls, and somehow Sebastian had to lead his people back home before it was too late.

Chapter One

Jill Whittaker crouched down and fastened the top snap on her daughter's bright red down jacket. "There," she said, sitting back on her heels and smiling. "Now you look perfect."

Six-year-old Tori beamed at her mother. "I know."

Jill laughed and turned to Tori's twin brother Michael. She tugged at the Christmas green scarf around his neck. "And I suppose you look perfect, too?"

Michael's dark brows knit together over the bridge of his straight nose, and for a moment Jill thought her heart would break. He was a miniature version of his father, with the same blue eyes and serious nature.

"Boys don't look perfect," Michael said, casting a curious glance toward his sister. "Only babies do that."

Tori punched him in the arm. He grabbed for her knit cap. Tori was about to retaliate with a swift kick learned at karate class, but Jill intervened.

"It's Christmas Eve," she said in her most sternly maternal tone of voice. "If you don't behave, Santa might think twice about coming to visit."

The twins were instantly chastened. Jill breathed a sigh of relief, but that relief was short-lived.

"Santa can't visit if we don't live here anymore," Tori pointed out.

Michael nodded vigorously. "We'll be at Aunt Patsy's."

"What if Santa can't find us?" Tori went on, her small face pinched with worry. "What if he doesn't know we're moving and he looks for us here and can't find us?"

"Santa knows everything," Michael said. His eyes met Jill's. "Doesn't he, Mommy?"

"I sent Santa a change-of-address form," Jill said, congratulating herself on a quick save. "He knows we'll be at Aunt Patsy's tonight."

The children watched her face carefully, searching for the slightest indication that she'd spun her story from whole cloth. They were at the age where they desperately wanted to believe in Santa Claus and the Easter Bunny and the Tooth Fairy, but were getting old enough to suspect something wasn't quite right.

"What about Daddy?" Michael asked, looking more like David than ever. "How will Santa find him?"

She swallowed hard against a terrible wave of sadness. "You know how Daddy leaves messages on the answering machine when we're out?" They nodded. "Well, Daddy left Santa a message and told him he was going to San Francisco."

Tori's lower lip began to tremble. "I don't want Daddy to go to San 'Risco."

"Call Daddy," Michael ordered Jill. "Tell him Santa said he shouldn't go."

And you thought labor was going to be the tough part. "Sometimes mommies and daddies have to live someplace else in order to do their jobs," she said carefully, wondering how much of the explanation was actually getting through. The only thing Tori and Michael knew was that their daddy was going away. To them, that was all that was important. "Isn't that what Daddy told you yesterday when you spent the day with him?"

"Daddy said we can come to San 'Risco and see a gold bridge," Michael said.

"Bridges aren't gold," Tori said, shaking her head. "You're dumb."

"Am not!"

"Yes, you are."

Michael pulled at Tori's scarf, and the little girl let out a shriek that could wake the dead, while Jill wondered why nobody ever told you the truth about parenthood. Oh, they shared all the details about pregnancy and childbirth. And you could find a million books about colic and teething and the terrible twos. But nobody ever mentioned moments like this when only a white lie—or a ticket to Tahiti—would do.

Her neighbor Phyllis tapped on the open front door. "Quakerbridge Mall taxi, at your service."

"Hi, Phyl." Jill stood up and tugged at the hem of her sweatshirt. "Great timing," she said, sotto voce. "We were heading into dangerous territory."

Phyllis winked at Jill, then turned to the kids. "Get your mittens, kittens, and let's hit the road. Santa's elves have two candy canes with your names on them waiting for you."

The twins scampered off toward the kitchen.

"Keep the door closed," Jill called out. "Don't let Sebastian or Charlie get loose." With the movers traipsing in and out all morning, she'd had to keep a sharp eye on their menagerie.

"So how are you doing, girl?" Phyllis asked, her gray eyes warm with concern.

"I just dodged another one of those tricky Santa Claus questions. If I make it through this Christmas, I'll kiss Rudolph right on his bright red nose."

"You'll make it," Phyllis said, "but I wish you'd change your mind about moving."

"I have to move, Phyl." She drew in a steadying breath. "I can't stay here now."

"The old neighborhood just won't be the same without you. Believe me, if there was something we could do to convince you to stay here, we—" Phyllis shook her head and pulled a crumpled tissue from her coat pocket.

"Don't you dare!" Jill wagged a finger at her friend and neighbor. "If you cry, I'll cry, too." The kids had already seen enough tears to last them a lifetime. She wouldn't do that to them, not on Christmas Eve.

Phyllis crossed her heart, but her eyes still glittered with tears. "By the way, what was Sebastian doing out by the Zimmerman house?"

"Sebastian?" Jill frowned. "He's in the kitchen with Charlie and Juanita."

"It sure looked just like him," Phyllis said. "A big fluffy cat with mutton-chop jowls."

Jill shook her head. "It couldn't possibly be Sebastian. He's been inside all day."

Phyllis looked dubious. "I'm telling you, honey, if it wasn't Sebastian, it was his long-lost twin brother."

"Maine coon cats aren't *that* unusual," Jill said. "Besides, Sebastian hasn't wandered off in at least a year." David said it was because Sebastian was getting older, but Jill liked to believe it was only because he'd grown lazy.

The kids bounded back into the room, and minutes later Phyllis and her tribe disappeared down the snowy street.

The movers finished loading the furniture from the second-story bedrooms and began to dismantle the family room. She leaned against the wall in the foyer and watched as they pulled pictures from the wall, unfastened curtains, and carried the artifacts of a family to the moving van parked in the driveway.

It shouldn't be this easy to end a marriage, she thought. The whole enterprise had been so without ceremony, just a series of solitary meetings in a lawyer's office that culminated in a frenzy of signatures on documents. There she was, about to say goodbye to the only man she'd ever loved, and she hadn't even seen him in weeks. *My choice,* she thought. *My regrets.*

"Ma'am, we need you to sign this." The job-site supervisor appeared at her elbow.

"I'm sorry," she said, blinking in surprise. "What was that?"

He pushed a clipboard toward her. "You have to okay the lunch break. We thought we'd push through until we finish, then grab something after. The snow's supposed to really kick in this afternoon, and with it being Christmas Eve and all—"

"Sure." She scribbled her name on the appropriate line. "You should all be home where you belong."

He countersigned the paper, then gave her the yellow copy. "Hell of a day to move."

"Yeah," she said softly. "It is at that."

Christmas Eve had always been their day, hers and

David's. They'd met and fallen in love on Christmas Eve thirteen years ago, and it seemed as if most of the milestones of their life together had happened on December 24th. Sebastian had come to live with them on Christmas Eve. And it was Christmas Eve when they had discovered that Jill was expecting the twins, after being told she would never get pregnant.

So it seemed strangely fitting that Christmas Eve was the day their marriage ended.

It's not too late, that persistent voice inside her heart reminded her. *The divorce isn't final until the stroke of midnight.* There was still time for one last miracle.

This whole thing had gathered speed over the past few months like a runaway train. She hadn't meant to ask David for a divorce. The words had leaped from her mouth, almost of their own volition, and once they were out she couldn't find a way to pull them back. She had been trying to shock him into admitting they had a problem, that somehow they had grown apart and the day would come when it would be too late to bridge the divide.

She should have known that you didn't back a proud man like her husband into an emotional corner that way. He'd come to tell her about his new assignment in San Francisco, and she'd turned it into a "the job or me" confrontation. Money didn't have the same resonance with her as it did with David. She had grown up rich, the only child of a broken marriage where money was substituted for love every chance her parents got. David had grown up without love or money, a foster kid lost in the system until he was too old to be of value to anyone but himself. Everything he'd accomplished—from graduating Princeton to gaining a top position with a leading architectural firm—had been accomplished by virtue of brains and backbreaking work.

No man loved his family more than David did, but no matter how hard Jill tried, she couldn't make him see that he was more important to them than the hefty salary he commanded. Whether or not he realized it, David hadn't been happy for a very long time. He was a gifted architect who was being wasted at his firm. It was probably naive of her to believe that there was a spiritual aspect to architecture, but once, a long time ago, he had believed that, too. David wasn't meant to be designing malls for greedy San Francisco investors; he was meant to be creating beautiful environments that enriched the spirit.

When he came home and told her they'd be leaving for a two-year assignment in San Francisco, something inside Jill had snapped. If he'd seemed happy about the project, she might not have reacted that way, but he'd talked only about the raise in salary that came with the job. She remembered the fire in his eyes when he began work on a design he loved, the joy he brought to the drafting table, the sense of fulfillment that permeated the entire house.

And she missed it . . . almost as much as she missed him.

She knew she could pick up the phone and call David, tell him she'd been wrong, that she'd follow him anywhere, even to San Francisco if that was what he wanted. She could tell him that she liked seeing him put in eighty-hour weeks at the office, that it didn't bother her to see him poring over his architectural drawings until three or four in the morning. She could even tell him that she didn't mind sleeping alone.

She could tell him all of that and more, but she would be lying. She missed him desperately. She missed *them*, the way they used to be when they were happy. Couple by couple, she'd watched their friends divorce, but she'd never in a million years thought it would happen to them. They were special. Everyone had said so. They were the couple everyone turned to for advice, the couple everyone thought would be together for the long haul.

"I might as well book the restaurant now for your Golden Anniversary party," her sister Patsy had said years ago. "I've never seen two people more right for each other."

Or more wrong.

"Coming through!" Two movers, carting the dining room breakfront, filled the doorway.

"Sorry." She fled for the kitchen. She wasn't usually so

docile, but suddenly the house felt as if it belonged more to the movers than to her. A big pine tree should be standing in front of the family room window, its branches decorated with the wooden ornaments the twins had made last summer. White lights should be twinkling among the ornaments and draped across the mantel. There should be brightly wrapped packages beneath the tree and stockings hung by the fireplace.

But most of all, there should be love.

Charlie, the huge floppy-eared mutt they'd found at a shelter, threw himself at Jill the moment she swung open the kitchen door. "I'm glad to see you, too," she said, giving the dog a big hug. He looked longingly toward the door that separated him from all the action in the other rooms. "You're better off in here, Charlie," she said, giving him a biscuit from her pocket. "They might pack you up with the china and carry you away."

Juanita, a dainty green conure, let out a wolf whistle followed by a raucous laugh. "Me, too," she said, bobbing her sleek head. "Me, too."

Jill tossed her a dog biscuit that she caught neatly in her beak. "You didn't think I'd forget about you, did you?" Juanita didn't answer. She was too busy enjoying her treat.

"I know what you're thinking, Sebastian." Jill reached into her other pocket for the cat's favorite snack. "Stop sulking, and we'll call a truce." She knew she'd been sharp-tempered with him earlier, and Sebastian tended to hold a grudge. "Come on, sweetie. You know I didn't mean to hurt your feelings."

A tingle of apprehension moved across her shoulders. No matter how annoyed he was, Sebastian would never turn up his nose at food. She quickly surveyed the kitchen, opening the cabinets and peering into the pantry. No sign of him. Okay, it was nothing to worry about. He was probably hiding in the laundry room or in one of the bathrooms. No sign of him there either. The tingle of apprehension escalated sharply.

"Stay calm," she told herself as Charlie and Juanita

watched her with curiosity. The house was almost empty. How difficult could it be to find a twenty-pound Maine coon cat in an empty house?

She searched from top to bottom, but there was no sign of Sebastian. How could she have been so careless? When she'd chastised him earlier for getting underfoot, she should have hustled him back into the kitchen where he belonged. But she'd been distracted and weepy, and now Sebastian was missing because of it.

The mover's rep found her standing on the back porch without a coat, looking for paw prints in the snow.

"We're all done," he said. "I need you to sign one more form, then we're out of here."

She scribbled her name again and handed back the clipboard. "Did you see my cat anywhere?"

"Your cat?" He frowned. "Do you mean that big guy who was getting underfoot?"

"Yes. Have you seen him?"

"Not since you told him to get lost."

Her heart sank. "You're sure you haven't seen him anywhere?"

"Not me," he said. "Let me ask some of the crew."

Jill followed him around the side of the house to where the movers were tying down the last few pieces of furniture.

"Hey, guys, her cat's missing. Anybody see him?"

They all shrugged except one.

"The son of a gun got me good," he said, extending his left leg. "Shredded my pants with those claws of his."

Jill groaned. Definitely Sebastian's handiwork. "I'm so sorry. Please add that to my bill."

"Darn right," the mover said. "You better put that thing on a leash."

"I will if I can find him." *When I find him,* she corrected herself. Sebastian had been with them forever. David had found him in the pet shop one Christmas Eve and brought him home in the beat-up leather backpack he'd used as a book bag. She loved all of the pets who'd made their home with them, but Sebastian was her special favorite. He had been with her from the beginning and—

She forced the thought from her mind. She refused to even contemplate it.

The movers climbed into the truck, and moments later, the truck rumbled down the street. The next time she saw her furniture would be at her town house the day after Christmas. She wished she could muster up some enthusiasm for the prospect. It was a perfectly lovely town house with a sunny kitchen and three bedrooms, but it wasn't home, and she knew it never would be.

She searched the front yard for paw prints in the snow or some indication—anything!—that Sebastian had been there, but she found nothing.

Wrapping her arms around her chest, she hurried back into the house. "Okay," she said out loud, "don't get crazy. He used to do this all the time. It's no big deal." So why did she have the feeling that there was something different this time, almost as if Sebastian had no intention of ever coming back?

There was only one other person on the face of the earth who felt about Sebastian the way she did. Taking a deep breath, she dialed David's office.

"Denise, this is Jill. Is David there?" She cradled the receiver against her shoulder. "I didn't realize he was flying to San Francisco tonight . . . yes, it's important . . . please tell him I called." She hung up, feeling as if she'd run face first into a brick wall. He was leaving tonight? She hadn't realized he was in such a hurry to get to his new assignment.

She paced the kitchen, then reached for the phone again and dialed the hotel where David had been staying for the last three months.

"Mr. Whittaker checked out this morning," the operator said. "Have a nice day."

"Damn!" she whispered, hanging up the phone. Why did everything have to be so complicated? It hadn't always been this hard. . . .

THEN

"I can do this," Jill told herself as she dropped a dime into the pay phone at Palmer Square. The world was changing, even if her parents refused to believe it. Girls called guys all the time these days. It wasn't as if she were asking for a date. All she needed was a ride to New York City.

"Hello?" The male voice was slightly husky and very appealing.

"David Whittaker, please."

"You've got him."

She clutched the phone to her ear. "Uh, hi. My name is Jill Aylesworth. I—um, Sandi Vitelli gave me your number. She said you were driving up to New York tomorrow morning and—"

"You need a ride?"

"I do," she said, trying to sound as though she did this sort of thing every day of the week. "I'd be happy to pay for gas and any—"

"Ten bucks."

"Oh. Well, of course. Gas money plus ten dollars. That sounds fair." A rumbly chuckle, not at all unpleasant, tickled her ear. "Did I say something funny?"

"You agreed to the first price I mentioned."

"It was a good price."

"It was a lousy price. You could've had the ride for gas money."

"You should have told me that."

"Then I'd miss out on the ten bucks and I have a feeling I need it a hell of a lot more than you do."

"How would you know whether or not I need the ten dollars?" she countered, temper rising. "You don't know anything about me."

"If you needed it, you would have bargained with me."

"Maybe I'm just a nice person."

"If you are, it's because you can afford it."

"This has been a lovely conversation, but I've had quite enough. Good—"

"Hey, don't get upset."

"Don't get upset?" She stared at the phone as if it had sprouted horns and a tail. "You've made a fistful of insulting assumptions about me and you tell me not to get upset? If you're one of those working-class types who think rich people are the enemy, then—"

"I'm sorry."

Her temper deflated like a popped balloon. "You are?"

"Yes," he said. "I have a weird sense of humor. It's an acquired taste."

She found herself grinning at the phone. "I've been told I have no sense of humor."

"Sounds like we're made for each other. We could elope tomorrow instead of driving up to New York."

"Sounds great," she said, feeling suddenly lighthearted. "I'll pay for the gas, and you can pay for the marriage license."

She'd never bantered that way before. Usually the witty response occurred to her the day after she needed it. It felt good to make a guy laugh, even if she'd probably never see him again after they reached New York City tomorrow afternoon.

"Full circle," she said as the memory shimmered, then faded away. They fell in love on Christmas Eve and now, on Christmas Eve thirteen years later, they would finally say good-bye.

Chapter Two

How the hell was it possible to sweat when it was twenty degrees outside and snowing?

David Whittaker wasn't a scientist, but it seemed to him that he was doing something pretty damn extraordinary. The heater was turned off. He'd cracked the window a good two inches. He had the feeling that nothing short of a new ice age could stop the twin beads of sweat from trickling down his temples.

His assistant's message had been short and sweet. *Jill called. She said it was important. Call her back.* Ten words, nine of them words of one syllable. You'd think it would take more than that to screw up your body's thermostat. *How did she sound, Denise? Happy? Sad? Do you think there's a chance?*

He told himself it was no big deal, that she was probably calling about the house or the car or some document that needed his signature. She'd avoided him at every turn during the last two months. The kids relayed his messages, her attorney answered his questions—her voice on the answering machine was as close as he got to making contact.

And now this. Out of nowhere she'd called him. His imagination was running riot. *Come back home, David . . . I love you, David . . . we can't get along without you, David. . . .* There were at least a dozen variations on that same theme, and not one of them stood a chance in hell of coming true.

He turned off the main road and negotiated the hill that led to Eagle Ridge Drive. The snow was coming down hard and fast, and he wished he was driving the Jeep.

The driveway curved gently off Eagle Ridge, and he eased into the turn. He always stopped at the same spot, just far enough back that he could get a good look at the house.

He used to tell himself he was checking for gutter problems or trouble with the siding, but the truth was he just wanted to sit there and revel in the fact that the house and the gutters and the siding were his. His house. His home. The one place on earth where he would always belong.

When he was a little boy, he'd dreamed about the house he would own when he grew up. He spent hours lying on whatever bed his current foster family had provided, imagining the house from the basement up. He knew every detail of the foundation, every bend and twist of pipe. He knew what kind of insulation the walls would have, the kind of wiring he'd run. It would be two stories high with wide windows and a front porch where kids could while away a summer afternoon. It would be the kind of house those same kids came back to after they were grown, a welcoming house that greeted you with open arms and pulled you inside.

One day he'd meet a girl, and his heart would burst open like a piñata, spilling gold coins and diamonds at her feet. He would sweep her up into his arms and carry her away to the house of his dreams, where they would have six children and live happily ever after.

That's exactly how he'd felt when he'd met Jill Aylesworth thirteen years ago today. He glanced at his watch. Almost to the hour. The irony of the situation wasn't lost on him.

"It's now or never," he told himself as he shut off the ignition. Sitting out there staring at the house wasn't going to change things. She either wanted to get back with him or she didn't, and the only way to find out was to get his sorry butt out of that car and knock on the front door.

He tried to ignore the big yellow FOR SALE sign stuck in the snowy front yard, but it wasn't easy. The house he'd dreamed about wasn't for sale.

"David! Oh, thank God, you're here!" As always, the sight of her stole his breath away. Her coppery hair was pinned atop her head in a tumble of curls, and she wore jeans and a sweatshirt. No makeup. A smudge of dirt on her cheek. She was still the most beautiful woman he'd ever known.

His spirits soared, but he couldn't let her see that. "Denise gave me your message," he said. He paused a second, waiting for her to throw herself into his arms. "Are the kids okay?"

"They're fine." She seemed distracted.

"Where are they?"

"Phyllis took them to Quakerbridge to see Santa so I could deal with the movers."

She was staring over his shoulder, practically looking right through him. That didn't bode well for a Hollywood-style reconciliation.

"Uh, Jill, it's snowing out here. Mind if I come in?" *It's Christmas Eve, Jilly. Don't you remember what that used to mean to us?*

Her cheeks reddened, and she motioned him into the foyer. "Sorry," she said.

"So what's wrong?" he asked as he shook snow from his hair. "Did I forget to sign something?"

"It's Sebastian," she said, her chin trembling. "He's gone."

"Gone?" He glanced toward the living room, expecting to see Sebastian sprawled on the rug in front of the fireplace. There was no rug and no Sebastian. "Are you sure?"

"He weighs twenty-two pounds," she said, her tears shifting quickly to anger. Every now and then he was reminded that she wasn't a redhead for nothing. "He's pretty hard to miss."

"You know how he likes to hide in Tori's room. Maybe—"

She shook her head.

"What about the basement? That place under the stairs where we used to keep the Christmas decorations."

"Sebastian's gone, David, and if we don't find him before the kids get back, they'll—" She turned her head, and he saw her do something to her eyes with a tissue.

In the old days he would have pulled her into his arms and kissed away her tears. He hated standing there, helpless to comfort her, but he no longer had the right. She'd made that perfectly clear when she'd filed for divorce.

"This isn't the first time he's taken off like this," he pointed out after her tears subsided. "In the old days, he was gone more than he was here. You know he always comes back home." *Home.*

"I know," she managed, "but the kids and I are spending tonight at my sister Patsy's house in Philadelphia. Unless Sebastian knows about Amtrak, he'll never find us."

"Damn it," he said, dragging a hand through his snow-damp hair. "The timing stinks. I'm flying out to San Francisco tonight."

"Denise told me." She paused for a moment. "What's the rush?"

"The Japanese consortium is holding an open house tomorrow afternoon at the building site."

"You sure wouldn't want to miss a big event like that."

"There's nothing holding me here." *Is there, Jilly?*

"No," she said lightly, "nothing at all."

He tried to put a positive spin on her words but failed miserably. *You're a jerk, Whittaker. It's over. You'd better get used to it.*

"About Sebastian," he said. "Where have you looked for him?"

"My car is being serviced," she said, "so I couldn't get very far. I checked the yards and the woods behind the house."

He checked his watch.

"I know you're a busy man," she said, her words clipped. "I wouldn't have bothered you if I'd realized you were leaving tonight."

"I have a few hours," he said. "We'll see what we can do."

"I'll get my coat."

He stood awkwardly in the foyer, feeling like a stranger in his own house. The walls were stripped bare. The furniture was gone. All that was left were a few cardboard boxes and a bright red suitcase he remembered from years ago. He sniffed the air. The house didn't even smell right anymore. Jill used to keep a pot of spices simmering on the back of the stove at Christmastime, a blend of pine and cinnamon and apple that smelled like home and love. Now all he could smell was sadness.

He turned and went outside to wait by the car.

How could you spend over one-third of your life with a man and feel as if you'd never really known him at all?

David hadn't so much as blinked a blue eye when she'd told him that Sebastian was gone. Sebastian had been with them since their first married Christmas. He'd appointed himself the twins' official guardian angel the first moment he'd laid eyes on them. First words, first steps, first communions—Sebastian had been there for all of them.

Okay, so maybe this wasn't the first time Sebastian had wandered off, but even David had to admit that the cat had stuck close to home the last year or two. David had acted as though Sebastian had wandered down the hall to take a nap.

What happened to us? she wondered as she slipped into her coat. How had they ended up one of those miserable marital statistics you heard about on TV talk shows? Once upon a time David had been her knight in shining armor, ready to slay dragons and lay them at her feet. He was everything she'd wanted in a man: strong and idealistic and passionate about life. Passionate about her. Had there really been a time when they couldn't get enough of each other, when they couldn't be apart for more than an hour without hungering for the other's touch? The thought was so alien that it seemed more like someone else's memory than her own.

He was outside, brushing snow off the windshield of his Porsche. She could almost see the waves of impatience rolling up the driveway toward her. He hated to be kept waiting for anything. It was as if he'd been born with a stopwatch in his hand and he'd been hurrying to catch up ever since, as if he were perennially five minutes behind the pack. She'd often wondered if it had to do with the fact that he'd grown up without a family of his own. She couldn't imagine how he had felt, growing up in foster home after foster home. Her own life had been shamefully blessed in comparison.

"I'll always take care of you," he'd said when they had gotten married.

"We'll take care of each other," she'd started to reply, but the serious look in his eyes had stilled her words. He needed to take care of her, she'd realized, more than she needed to be taken care of.

THEN

"You look fine, Davey," Jill said as she smoothed the shoulders of his sport coat. "Nobody's going to know you got the jacket at the consignment shop."

"Your father will know," he said, glaring at his reflection in the bedroom mirror. "The second I walk into the restaurant, he'll know this is a thrift shop special."

"So what if he does?" she said. "We're students. Nobody expects students to be rich."

"You're rich," he said with a shake of his head. "At least you were until you married me."

"Ancient history," she said lightly. "I knew my trust fund would be canceled if I got married and I'd do the same thing all over again."

He searched her face for reassurance. "I never wanted your money," he said, "but—"

"You're not going to start that nonsense again, are you?" She couldn't keep the exasperation from her voice. "I know you didn't marry me for my money. You married me for my cooking." Her lack of culinary expertise had made for interesting dining during the last six months.

His serious expression didn't brighten one iota. "Look at how we're living, Jill." His gesture took in the entire four-room cottage. "You had more space in the dorm, for crying out loud."

"Maybe I did," she said, twining her arms around his neck, "but you're much more fun than my last roommate."

"I'll make it up to you someday, Jilly, I swear to you. You'll never regret marrying me."

"I wish you wouldn't talk like that. You're the most wonderful person I've ever known. You're decent and kind and smart and ambitious"—she grinned up at him—"and you love me more than anyone has ever loved me in my entire life."

His kiss was long and slow and intoxicating. She rose up slightly on her toes and pressed her body close to his.

"Let's skip dinner," she said, tracing his beautiful mouth with the tip of her index finger. She laughed at the horrified expression on his face. "I'm only kidding, David."

"Your old man hates me enough as it is. If we blew off the dinner invitation, I'd be on the FBI's Most Wanted list."

"I don't care what he thinks," Jill said, feeling her jaw set into a stubborn—and very familiar—line. "The only reason I said yes to this dinner was because you said we had to accept it."

"He's your family. I'm not going to cut you off from your own parents."

"My father hasn't been a real part of my life since I was five years old, when he walked out on my mother." He'd gone on to raise two more families and whether he ever gave more than a passing thought to the little girl he'd left behind, Jill couldn't fathom a guess. And, to her delight, she found that it no longer hurt. Her parents had done the best they could with the emotional tools they had to work with. No amount of wishing could change the past, but now that she loved David she knew the future would be as golden as the simple ring that circled the third finger on her left hand.

So they would see her father tonight, and he would do

what he always did. He would tell charming stories and make everyone laugh, and before he paid the tab, half the restaurant would be in love with him. He would never ask David about his studies or try to find out why she'd fallen in love with the serious young man with the vivid blue eyes, and even if Jill told him, her father would never understand.

David had been as good as his word. Discipline and determination moved him steadily up the ranks at Bailey, Haverford, and Macmillan, and now he was being rewarded with a plum two-year assignment in San Francisco, designing a soulless metro complex for a Japanese consortium.

Reward. There was a funny word for you. Whatever happened to Christmas bonuses and a corner office? You didn't reward a man by uprooting his family from their home and shipping them to the other side of the country like lawn furniture.

Not that it mattered anymore. They could be sending him to Saturn for all the difference it made. Tomorrow she wouldn't be part of his family. She'd be part of his past.

David motioned for her to hurry as she stepped out the front door. She ignored him, taking great pains to make certain the door was locked and the welcome mat was properly straightened. He waved again, more impatiently than before. She muttered something rude under her breath.

"I thought you said you checked the backyard."

Her hackles rose a little higher. "I did check the backyard."

"So what's that by the swing set?"

"Snow."

"Look again."

"I see lots of snow and a blot of brown near the—" She stopped. "Oh, God! Do you think—?"

He didn't answer, but the set of his jaw confirmed her worst suspicions as they started across the yard.

"You look," she said, stopping a few feet away "I'm too scared."

Their eyes met, and he nodded. *You're scared too,* she thought, and for a moment her heart went out to him. It wasn't often these days when they found themselves in sync. She remembered how it used to be when they thought and acted like one person instead of two very separate individuals. But that was a very long time ago.

David bent down and reached under the snow while Jill squeezed her eyes shut.

"I thought you said it was missing."

"Sebastian isn't an 'it.'"

"I'm talking about my backpack."

"For the last time, David, I don't know where—" She opened her eyes. "You found your backpack!"

He shook snow off the old leather bag. "Not funny, Jill."

"You don't think I—"

The look on his face spoke volumes.

"David!" Her voice bristled with outrage. "Believe it or not, I buried my last backpack some time around puberty."

He was inspecting the wet leather. "What the hell? There are tooth marks on this thing!"

"Don't even think it," she warned. "You're on thin ice as it is."

He pushed the backpack toward her. "What do you call those scratches?"

"I call them tooth marks." She pushed the bag back toward David. "How could you not have tooth marks on it? Don't you remember? Sebastian came home in that bag." Her tone softened despite herself as more memories pushed into her heart. "The twins spent a lot of time in there, too, come to think of it." She could still see their tiny faces peeking out from the backpack as their daddy proudly walked down Main Street with his kids. She'd been so happy, so filled with joy in those days that she'd wanted to reach out and stop time. She should have. She should have found a way to hold those perfect days close because they were gone and they would never come again.

Chapter Three

"The thing to do is blitz the neighborhood," David said as Jill fastened her seat belt. "Let people know Sebastian's out there."

"I called everyone," she said. "No one has seen him today."

"You got hold of everyone?" He tried not to sound skeptical.

"All but the Reillys. They're spending the holidays in Aspen."

"Their store is doing that well?" He remembered when Mitch and Katie had taken a second mortgage on their home to help finance their kitchenware shop at the mall. He'd never known a couple better suited to carving their own path in business. Or in life, for that matter. In some ways they reminded him of himself and Jill before they had drifted apart.

"The Reillys are a great team," Jill said as he backed the Porsche down the driveway. "They set a goal and they achieved it."

"Most new ventures fail," he pointed out. "They're not out of the woods yet."

She looked at him, an odd expression on her face. "Kind of like marriage, wouldn't you say?"

"That isn't what I meant."

"Are you sure?"

"No," he said after a moment. "I'm not." He'd found himself speaking in metaphors a lot lately, as if he needed words to cushion him from harsh reality.

He hadn't needed anything to cushion him from reality in the old days. Reality had suited him down to the ground. . . .

THEN

The store clerk looked at David and let out a loud, exasperated sigh. "I can set my clock by you college boys. Come eight o'clock on Christmas Eve you're banging on my door, looking to buy anything that isn't nailed down." He shook his head sadly. "Where's your brain, boy? It's not like Christmas snuck up on you."

David knew what the guy was thinking, that he was some thoughtless yuppie type, racing in for a last-minute present for a girl he barely knew.

"Listen," he said, leaning across the counter, "Christmas didn't sneak up on me, it steamrollered over me. I'm in school six hours a day, I study for another six, and pull an eight-hour shift driving a hack, and that doesn't count eating, sleeping, and wishing I wasn't too tired to make love to my wife. If you want to lump me in with all the rest of the SOBs, then go ahead. I don't care. But I *do* care about making sure my wife isn't disappointed tomorrow morning."

The guy blinked and backed up a step. "Hey, sorry if I misread you, kid." He squinted in David's direction. "Aren't you a little young to be married?"

"You want to see my driver's license?"

"No reason to be insulted. Just asking a question."

What David wanted to do was pop the guy one and walk out the door, but that wasn't going to take care of the problem. Jilly deserved something wonderful. "I'm looking for Chanel No. 5."

"Don't have any."

"Shalimar?" He could almost see the sneer on her father's face.

"All out."

"How about Charlie?"

"That was the first to go."

The guy didn't have gloves, scarves, flowers, or slippers either. "We still have can openers and pressure cookers."

David shook his head. "Forget it." He stuffed his money

into his backpack and slung the leather bag over his shoulder. "I'll take my business someplace else."

"Good luck," the clerk said. "The pet shop's the only other place open, and they're down to their last iguana."

David refused to be discouraged. Something happened to people when they got older. He didn't know if it was disappointment or jealousy or just bone-deep nastiness, but newlyweds seemed to bring out the worst in some people.

We'll never be like that, he thought as he trudged down the street in the blinding snow. He and Jill were special . . . together they were downright magical. Ten years from now they would be exactly the same as they were today, except even more in love.

Jill had said they shouldn't exchange gifts. "The rent is due in a week, and I don't want to let the Zimmermans down. They've been so kind to us."

And she was right. Their landlords Claire and Eddie Zimmerman treated them like the children they'd never had. They'd remembered Jill's and David's birthdays, invited them over for Thanksgiving dinner, and provided shoulders to lean on. David would never do anything to disappoint them. He'd saved the twenty dollars by skipping lunches and two haircuts, because putting a smile on Jill's face was worth a couple of hunger pangs any day. After all she'd given up for him, it was the least he could do.

He walked the length of Main Street, first one side and then the other. Even the all-night drugstore was shut tight as a drum. The lights in the pet shop were still on, but somehow he didn't think Jill would welcome an iguana into the family with open arms.

One day, when they had a house of their own, the big house of his dreams, they'd go to a shelter and take in as many dogs and cats and parakeets as the place had, but that day was still a long way off.

A brisk wind was blowing the snow straight into his eyes. It was the kind of wind that whistled up your sleeves and down the collar of your jacket and made it feel twice as cold as it really was. Some day they'd have two cars, both of them brand spanking new with heaters that could keep you warm in the coldest weather, and stereo speakers and a tape deck and—

"Yowch!" His feet slid out from under him, and he sailed up into the air and landed butt first on the pavement. His backpack skidded to a stop a few feet away. He scrambled to his feet and brushed the snow off his pants, wishing he'd worn snowshoes instead of Reeboks. He bent down to retrieve his backpack when he made the mistake of glancing at the pet shop window.

One lone kitten slept peacefully on a bed of shredded newspaper. He curled up into a little ball of fluff with his head resting on a knot of Christmas red yarn. Talk about tugging on the old consumer heartstrings, David thought. One adorable kitten asleep in the window was all you needed to lure customers in by the carload.

But why would they need to lure customers in at nine o'clock on Christmas Eve when anyone with a brain was home decorating the tree?

The kitten opened one sleepy eye and looked straight at David.

Oh, no, you don't, he thought. *You've got the wrong guy. We can't afford to keep you in kibble.*

The kitten yawned, then washed a tiny paw with its little pink tongue.

What do you do, practice those moves in the mirror? David didn't even like cats, but he was smiling ear to ear as he watched the fluffy creature toddle over to get a sip of water from the dish in the corner.

He supposed it wouldn't hurt to go in and take a closer look. He knew all about these bait and switch techniques. Consumer affairs reporters gave it a lot of play during the holidays. He'd express an interest in the kitten on display, and they'd tell him the kitten in question had just been sold to John Doe, but wouldn't David love to see the purebred

Himalayan with the special $1,000 price tag? At least he'd know the little guy had a home.

"We're closing in five minutes," a cheery female voice greeted him. "If you think you know what you want—"

"That kitten in the window," he said as a round-faced little woman popped out of the back room. "I suppose he's spoken for."

Her smile broadened. "Sebastian?" she said. "You like our sweet boy?"

"He's pretty cute," David acknowledged. "I imagine he's going to make some little kid's Christmas." *Okay, lady. Now tell me about the Himalayan with my name on it. . . .*

"How I wish that were true," the woman said with a sigh. "All of his littermates sold, but Sebastian hasn't had much luck."

"You're kidding." She was shooting his theories all to hell.

"You see," she lowered her voice, "Sebastian has a bit of a personality problem."

"A kitten with a personality problem?"

She nodded. "Sebastian hates people. It's his only flaw."

"How old is he?"

"Nine weeks today."

"Nine weeks old, and he's already decided the whole human race isn't fit to use his litter box?"

"I'm afraid that's the size of it. I'm the only one he'll allow to handle him, and then only after he lodges a loud and angry protest."

He glanced from the woman to the kitten and back again. "Let me see him, please."

She reached into the window for Sebastian then yelped and jumped back. "You little—"

She caught herself and flashed a sunny smile in David's direction. "That dickens has one heck of a temper." She grabbed the cat, then thrust him, squawking and scratching, toward David.

She hates the poor guy, David thought as he took the kitten from her. *No wonder he's unhappy.* "Hey, boy." He scratched the kitten behind the right ear and was rewarded with a cross between a growl and a purr.

"I don't believe it," the woman said. "He likes you." She crooked a finger toward the kitten. "Sweet Sebastian—"

Sebastian's hiss was loud enough to peel paint.

"It's pretty clear he doesn't like *you*," David said as the kitten nudged his finger for another scratch.

She looked at her watch. "It's nine o'clock," she said. "If there's nothing I can do for you, you can put Sebastian back so I can close up."

"You're going to leave him in the window?"

She nodded.

"But you're closed tomorrow."

"He has food and water."

"It's *Christmas*."

"Sebastian doesn't know that."

"But you do."

She fixed him with an icy stare. "If you're so concerned with his welfare, why don't you buy him? God knows, nobody else is likely to."

Five minutes later, he was the proud owner of a nine-week-old Maine coon cat with an attitude. That grinch of a saleswoman refused to lend him a blanket to keep the kitten warm, so David yanked off his scarf and lined his backpack with it, then settled Sebastian down for the cold walk home. No hissing. No scratching. No fuss. The kitten nestled in as if he belonged there.

"You picked one hell of a time to develop a personality," David said as he cradled the bundle close to his chest and started walking home. He'd slip the backpack on just before he reached the apartment. "If you'd played your cards right, you could've been a doctor's cat."

Sebastian yawned and closed his eyes. David could almost swear he saw the kitten smile.

                    *   *   *

Jill threw herself into his arms the moment he came through the front door.

"I was so worried about you!" She peppered his face with kisses. "It's almost ten o'clock! Where have you *been*?"

He grabbed her hands and kissed them. "Vanilla?" he asked, laughing.

"The last batch of Christmas cookies is in the oven. We may be poor, but our gifts are the best in town."

He nuzzled against the side of her neck. "So are you."

She sighed and leaned into him, all warmth and softness.

"I'm full of snow," he said. "I'm melting all over you."

"I don't care." Her blue eyes twinkled with mischief. "I—" She tilted her head to the left. "What was that?"

He had the feeling his own eyes were twinkling with mischief, too. "What was what?"

"That noise." She frowned. "Listen . . . it sounds like a tiny outboard motor."

"I don't hear anything," he said, although the sound was getting louder by the second.

"David, it sounds like it's coming from you."

"I'm battery-operated," he said, unable to hold back his grin. "Did I forget to tell you that?"

"I'm serious." She grabbed for the zipper of his parka. "What are you hiding?"

"Nothing," he said, all wide-eyed innocence. "Why do you think I'm hiding something?"

She wouldn't be deterred. She tugged at his jacket, and finally he had to come clean.

"Close your eyes," he said. "I have a surprise."

Her face was aglow. "I love surprises."

"You may not love this one."

"You know I love everything you do."

"You may change your mind after tonight." Just because Sebastian seemed to think he was palatable, it didn't mean Jill would pass muster.

"You're making me crazy! What is it?"

"Close your eyes," he said again, "and you'll find out."

He watched as she squeezed her eyes shut, then slid off the backpack. "You can open your eyes now."

She did. "Where is it?"

He handed her the backpack.

"David!" She sounded disappointed. "I don't want your backpack."

"Open it up."

Her brows slid together, and he knew her temper was beginning to boil. Leave it to Sebastian to save the day. He picked that moment to wake up and poke his head out to see what was going on.

Jill let out a shriek of pure delight. "Oh, David!" She scooped up Sebastian and cradled him against her chest. "A kitten!"

"You're kidding," David said, afraid to check out the condition of the backpack *post* Sebastian. "Where did he come from?"

"He's beautiful," she crooned, kissing the top of the kitten's head. "Look at those mutton chops and that fluffy striped tail! Does he have a name?"

"Sebastian."

"Sebastian?" She grinned. "I think it suits him."

Sebastian did, too. He meowed once, loudly, then started to purr again, a loud and happy hum of pure pleasure.

"So you like him?"

"I *love* him," she said. "But I thought you said we shouldn't get a pet until we're settled in a house."

He told her about the pet shop and about Sebastian's "problem."

"That's so cruel!" Her eyes glittered with angry tears. "How could she even think about leaving a sweet little kitten alone in the store on Christmas?"

It occurred to him suddenly that the little lady in the pet shop might have scammed him royally, but Sebastian looked up at him, and damned if it didn't seem as if he winked.

"It's official," Jill said, hugging them both. "Now we're really a family."

"David." Jill's voice, sharp with curiosity, brought him back to the present. "What's the matter with you? Jake Malloy is waving us over."

"I saw him," David said, lying through his teeth. "I was about to pull into his driveway when you said that."

She shot him a look but said nothing. The marriage might be over, but she was still a wife.

Jake was standing near the mailbox. He was one of the neighborhood's nosier residents, the kind of guy who would poke around in your garbage, given half a chance. David whirred down the driver's side window.

"So what's up?" he asked.

"I hear you're looking for Samson," Jake said.

"Sebastian," David corrected him.

"The fat cat, right?"

"That's the one. You seen him?"

Jake nodded, eyeing Jill with open curiosity. David could see the wheels of gossip turning.

"By the Zimmermans' house," Jake said, still eyeing Jill. "He was standing in the foot of the driveway, eating something."

"Sounds like Sebastian to me. Thanks for letting us know."

Jake poked his head into the car. "I thought that was you, Jill."

She peered around David and smiled. "Good to see you, Jake. Merry Christmas."

"Yeah, Merry Christmas," said Jake in his usual gracious manner. "So what's the story?"

Jill's smile flickered. "Excuse me?"

"The story," Jake repeated, eyeing David in the same curious way. "Looks to me like the divorce is off."

"Can we get going?" David asked. "If we're going to nab Sebastian, we'd better move before he takes off again."

Jake looked from Jill to David. "Been a long time since I saw the two of you together."

David couldn't bite back his anger. "Take a good look, Malloy, because it's going to be your last."

He gunned the engine and pulled out of the driveway.

"That was a rotten thing to say, David." Jill shot him a withering glance.

"He had it coming."

"He made an observation."

"A *stupid* observation."

"You didn't have to bite his head off."

"He's lucky I didn't push him into a snowbank."

"What *is* your problem?" she demanded. "The man was only trying to help us find Sebastian . . . assuming you even give a damn."

He started to tell her that he had been thinking about Sebastian, about the little kitten with the big attitude who'd helped them take their first step toward being a family, but then he thought better of it. Why bother? After tomorrow they wouldn't be a family anymore.

Chapter Four

Claire Zimmerman peered at Jill and David through her storm door for a moment, then a huge smile spread across her face. "This is the best Christmas present I could possibly have!" The elderly woman flung open the door and motioned them inside. "When did it happen? I want all the details, every single one of them."

Jill exchanged glances with David. "Claire," she said carefully, steeping into the warm foyer, "I think you're jumping to conclusions."

Claire's round face didn't lose a glimmer of happiness. "Of course I jumped to conclusions—and what better conclusion could I possibly jump to when the two of you show up on my doorstep on Christmas Eve?"

Oh, Lord, thought Jill, wishing the floor would open up and swallow her whole. Claire Zimmerman was the last person she wanted to disappoint.

"Claire, please—"

"Eddie!" Claire called up the stairs. "Come down here this instant! I have a wonderful surprise for you."

"*Say* something," Jill hissed to David. He gave her the deer-in-the-headlights stare she'd first seen when he coached her in the delivery room.

Eddie lumbered down the stairs, all two hundred and fifty pounds of him poured into a Santa Claus suit complete with fluffy white beard. "Ho ho ho!" he bellowed, patting his unpadded belly with gusto. "Best Santa Claus in town six years running."

Jill couldn't help smiling. "Looks like you'll make it seven, Eddie."

"Eddie," said Claire in her most wifely tone of voice, "don't you notice something special?"

Eddie's eyes widened. "Well, saints alive! If the two

lovebirds aren't back together again, and just in time for Christmas."

"It's a miracle, that's what it is," said Claire, dabbing her eyes with the edge of her apron. "We've been praying for it since you told us you were getting a divorce. I just knew God was listening and wouldn't let us down. . . ."

THEN

The cottage was set back from the road. It was a small doll-like house, with dark green shutters and window boxes and rosebushes planted everywhere. The rosebushes were snow-covered now, but Jill could imagine how beautiful they would look come spring.

"It's wonderful," Jill whispered.

"We can't afford it," David said. "C'mon, Jilly. We'd better go."

"No!" She tugged at his hand. "The Zimmermans are expecting us. We told them we'd be here at two o'clock. The least we can do is keep our promise."

"I don't like that look in your eyes," David said, his blue eyes serious. "Look at this place, Jilly. Do you really think we can swing something like this?"

"I don't know, but it doesn't cost anything to look."

"You've got your hopes up—I don't want you to be disappointed."

"I'm a big girl, David. I can take a little disappointment. Let's meet the Zimmermans and see what they have to say."

Everything about the cottage enchanted Jill: the rosebushes, the sunny kitchen, the Zimmermans themselves. Eddie and Claire were a well-to-do childless couple in their late sixties. The cottage was the first house they'd ever owned and, hopelessly romantic, they'd held onto it through the years for sentimental reasons.

"Laurel and Vincent moved away six weeks ago," Claire said as they sipped hot cocoa in the kitchen.

"Why did they move?" David asked in the edgy tone of

voice he used when he was worried about money. He shot Jill a look. *They probably couldn't afford the place.*

Jill shot him a look of her own. *Just be quiet and listen.*

Claire, oblivious to the nonverbal byplay, gave them both a beatific smile. "Laurel gave birth to a beautiful baby girl on Easter Sunday. Their new house has a wonderful nursery for little Elizabeth."

"A baby!" Jill sighed with delight. "How wonderful."

"Oh, it was, it was," Claire assured her. "This cottage is a very lucky place for babies." Her faded blue eyes grew misty, and she patted her husband's hand.

Jill's heart ached for them. How awful it must be to want a baby and never be blessed with one.

David stood up. "Listen, we're probably wasting your time. We don't have a lot of money, Mr. Zimmerman. It's a good bet we can't afford this place."

"David!" Jill's cheeks reddened with embarrassment.

Mr. Zimmerman wasn't the slightest bit perturbed. "No, no, Mrs. Whittaker. I admire a man who puts his cards on the table that way." He stood up and faced David. "One hundred dollars a month. You do the yard work in the summer, snow removal in the winter."

"You're kidding," David said. "Aren't you?"

"Do I look like I'm kidding?" Mr. Zimmerman said, smiling.

Jill's heart was pounding so hard she thought she'd faint. "One hundred dollars?" she asked, her voice nothing more than a squeak.

"If that's too much, we'll lower it to seventy-five," Mrs. Zimmerman said. "Life has been very kind to us. If we can help a young couple get started, that's enough for us."

Jill turned to David. "We'll never find a more perfect place."

David nodded, and she threw her arms around him. "What about Sebastian?"

She swallowed. "I—um, I hope this isn't a problem, but

we have a cat . . . a kitten, really. His name is Sebastian, and—"

"The more the merrier," Claire said. "We have quite a menagerie ourselves."

Mr. Zimmerman extended his hand to David. "Then it's a deal?"

David shook the older man's hand. "It's a deal."

And with those words, Jill and David were welcomed into the Zimmermans' cottage . . . and into their hearts.

"Oh, Claire . . ." Jill's voice broke, and she cursed her emotions for betraying her. She hated disappointing Claire this way. "There hasn't been a miracle. Sebastian is missing. We were hoping he might have come here."

Poor Claire. Her big smile faltered then faded entirely. Every line and wrinkle on her eighty-year-old face fell into sharp relief. Eddie patted her on the shoulder and whispered something only his wife could hear. It was such a natural gesture, so much a part of their sixty years together, that it came close to breaking Jill's heart.

That's all I ever wanted, she thought, feeling older than Claire, older than the world. *Just to know I could grow old with him.*

"Sebastian," Eddie prompted, meeting Jill's eyes. "Has the old boy run off again?"

Jill nodded. She didn't dare look at Claire, because if she did, she knew she'd start crying. "The movers were here this morning, and he got underfoot. I scolded him and I guess he decided to teach me a lesson."

"He's a sly one, Sebastian is." Eddie chuckled. "Though I can't much imagine him traipsing through the snow. Seems to me he's more the warm fire and cozy blanket type nowadays."

"Did you look under the porch?" Claire asked, her voice warm with concern. "I'll bet you he's hiding under there, waiting for all the commotion to die down."

"I'm sure we looked under the porch." She turned to David. "Didn't we?"

"I think so," he said. He didn't sound any more sure than she felt.

"I thought he might come here," Jill offered. "He's known you since he was a kitten. You two have been so kind to him when we've gone away on vacation." The Zimmermans had opened up their beautiful home to Sebastian and the rest of the menagerie and given them the run of the place. Jill shuddered just thinking about Sebastian grooming himself on one of their Aubusson carpets, but neither Claire nor Eddie worried a whit.

"We love having him stay with us," Claire said, patting her on the arm. "Maine coon cats don't take well to being cooped up in a kennel. Besides, what's this big old house for if we can't fill it with the people and things we love?"

"Apparently Maine coon cats don't take too well to moving, either," Jill said. "We have to find him before the kids come home from the mall. They've been through so much. If Sebastian—" She refused to finish the sentence, but everyone knew how it would have ended.

"Let me make us all some hot chocolate," Claire said. "We'll come up with a plan."

"That's so kind of you," Jill said, "but we can't stay. We have to keep looking. The kids will be home at five, and Sebastian—"

"We understand," said Eddie. "We'll spread the word through the neighborhood. If everyone pitches in, the old boy will be home before you know it."

Impulsively, Jill hugged Claire, then Eddie, while tears streamed down her cheeks. She hadn't cried this much in years. "I'm going to miss you so much," she said. "You two are family."

"You're not moving that far away," Claire said, her own eyes wet with tears. "We'll still see each other."

"You can't get rid of us that easily," Eddie said. "Flemington is a hop, skip, and a jump from here."

Jill nodded, but she knew that by tomorrow everything would be different.

David stepped forward and extended his hand. "I guess this is good-bye, then," he said.

"Safe trip to San Francisco," Eddie said, shaking David's hand briefly. "I hope you find what you're looking for."

Claire said nothing at all, just dabbed at her eyes with the hem of her apron.

"What did he mean, he hopes I find what I'm looking for?" David asked as they made their way down the driveway to the car.

"I think he meant exactly what he said." She pulled her collar up around her neck and burrowed deep.

They reached the car. He opened the passenger door for her, then walked around to the driver's side.

"So I'm the bad guy in this," he said a few moments later as they swung around the Zimmermans' circular driveway and headed back toward the main road.

"I didn't hear anyone say that."

"Come on, Jill. You saw what happened back there. They couldn't wait to see me leave."

"They were disappointed. They thought we'd reconciled. You can't blame them for being upset."

"So why take it out on me? Last I heard, it takes two to reconcile."

She drew in a deep breath. "You're the one who's moving across the country."

"You and the kids could have moved with me."

"Sure," she said, her hackles rising in anger. "Uproot them from school, take them away from their friends, leave our families behind. Sounds like a great idea to me."

"They're only six years old, Jill. They'd make friends wherever they lived."

"My home is here." *Our home, you fool, if you'd just open your eyes.*

"So why are you selling the house?"

"Because—" She stopped short. *Because I don't want to*

live there without you. "Forget it," she said finally. "We agreed to sell the house and split the profits, and that's what I'm doing."

He grew noticeably tightjawed. "You're making a mistake."

She arched a brow. "I could say the same thing to you."

Seeing Eddie and Claire had stirred up memories of their first years together. She had loved David so deeply, so freely, without boundaries or reservation. And he had loved her the same in return. So where on earth had it all gone wrong?

She supposed it hardly mattered. Their house was up for sale. Their divorce would be final at midnight. And Sebastian, who had been there from the very beginning, was gone. *A clean sweep,* she thought. Too bad it wasn't what she wanted.

They rode in silence for a few hundred yards, then David slammed on the brakes at the intersection of the main road and the Zimmermans' street. The Porsche went into a gentle skid. Jill's arm reached out automatically to protect him. His arm reached out at the same time to protect her.

Jill cleared her throat. "You stopped for a reason?"

"I'll let you know." He swung open the door and climbed out. She watched as he walked around to the front of the car, then bent down to retrieve something in the intersection.

"Since when do you have the instincts of a bloodhound?" she said when he slid behind the wheel again. "You're the man who can't find his car keys when they're in the ignition."

He held out his hand. "Sebastian's collar."

Her heart lurched as she grabbed for the object. No doubt about it. Sebastian's identification was clearly marked inside. "It's in perfect shape," she said. "Someone must have unhooked it for him."

"I saw paw prints," David said. "Heading toward town."

"Like little snowshoes?" Sebastian's paws were made for traveling snowy paths.

"Exactly like snowshoes," David said. "It's got to be Sebastian."

He turned the car in the direction of town.

"You know what they're going to think, don't you?"

He glanced at her, puzzled. "That we're looking for Sebastian."

She shook her head. "That we're back together again. Just like Jake Malloy thought."

Some of the stiffness eased from his jaw. "That shouldn't be a problem," he said. "We'll tell them that nothing has changed. We're together because we're trying to find Sebastian."

"You make it sound simple."

"It *is* simple, Jill."

"That's what's wrong with men," she said, more amused than annoyed. "You're oblivious to nuance."

"What's that supposed to mean?"

She started to laugh despite herself. "If you have to ask—"

"That's what's wrong with women," he said. She wasn't sure where he fell on the amusement/annoyance scale. "You waste too much time worrying about things like nuance. Sometimes you have to act first and analyze later. Remember the day Sebastian terrorized the butcher shop and they called the police? We didn't waste too much time analyzing why he dragged all the filet mignons out of the front case and into the street."

"I'd forgotten all about that."

David's grin was rueful. "I haven't. It cost $372 that we didn't have."

Another rush of memories came back to her. "You did Frank's yard work that whole summer."

"And you wrote all of his advertising copy."

"'Succulent leg of lamb—on sale Wednesday only.'" She rolled her eyes. "I was a veritable wordsmith."

"You haven't done too badly for yourself, Jill."

His statement caught her off guard. He rarely mentioned her writing. He'd thrown a party for her when she'd sold her first book, but there'd been a haunted look in his eyes that she'd never forgotten. He said that her money was her money, and he continued to support the family on his earnings alone. Their accountant knew a hundred percent more about her income than did her husband.

David saw the surprise on Jill's face, and he regretted saying anything at all. He was proud as hell of all she'd accomplished. He knew how hard it was to get a book published. Competition was fierce, and it took guts as well as talent to succeed. Every time he tried to tell her how much he admired her achievements, the words caught in his throat, and he was tumbled back to those early days when they were poor and struggling. She'd given up so much when she married him: money and social standing and whatever tenuous connection she'd had with her family.

THEN

Eight months to the day after David began working at the biggest architectural firm in the state, he made dinner reservations for two at the Peacock Inn.

"Have you lost your mind?" Jill asked, clearly shocked, when he called to tell her what he'd done. "We can't afford the Peacock Inn. We don't even *know* anyone who can afford the Peacock Inn."

"Trust me," he said, pride almost bursting through his chest. "I'll pick you up at the office at six."

He pulled up in front of the rambling colonial building that housed Baxter Publishing, the small textbook firm where Jill had worked since their marriage. He was three minutes early. He knew she would be three minutes late. Their marriage had been a series of compromises, some easy and some not so, and he couldn't imagine it any other way.

She trusted him with her life. He trusted her with his heart. She lifted him up when his optimism flagged. He held her close when the world was too much with them. People said that marriage made romance disappear, that the grind of everyday life extinguished the spark of passion, but they were wrong. Marriage had taken two lonely people and turned them into one entity, a team in heart and spirit. A team that only death could part.

"Champagne?" Jill said as the waiter brought the chilled bottle for his inspection. "Our anniversary isn't until September."

"You need an occasion to drink champagne?"

"On our budget, we need an occasion to drink beer."

He smiled but said nothing. Good news deserved to be savored. He motioned the waiter to leave the champagne and, with great ceremony, David popped the cork himself, then filled the crystal flutes with the golden liquid.

"To the future," he said.

They touched glasses.

"To the future," Jill echoed. Then, "You're making me a nervous wreck, David. The Peacock Inn. Taittinger's. You must have robbed a bank to pay for this."

He leaned forward. Her hair shimmered in the candlelight, glowing like burnished copper. There was no sight on earth that could compare to his wife's face. He was consumed with love for her, for everything she was, and for all he knew, she would be, too, now that he could finally give her the chance.

"How much do you like your job, Jilly?"

Her brows drew together. "It's okay. Ed Cavanagh is easy to work for. The editors are pleasant enough. *Why* are you asking me this, David?"

"Because I think you should quit."

He'd never seen a jaw sag open before, but damned if Jill's jaw didn't do exactly that.

"I must be hallucinating," she said, staring at him. *"Quit?"*

"Quit."

"How much champagne have you had tonight?"

He lifted his glass. "It's still almost full."

"Then you must have lost your mind."

"I haven't lost my mind. In fact, I've never felt more sane in my life."

"I'm glad one of us can say that, because I feel like I'm trapped in the Twilight Zone and Rod Serling is about to serve our salads."

He reached for her hand. "I'm doing the O'Neal house."

"Oh, David . . ." Her beautiful face came to life, as if all the candle power in the room were centered in her eyes. "You worked so hard for this. I'm so happy!"

"*We* worked hard," he corrected her. "We did it as a team. I wouldn't have made it through without you, Jilly, and that's the God's truth."

"You're not going to toss me aside and run off with an assistant?" Her words were soft and teasing. "I hear that's what all you successful architects do."

"Not this one." He raised her hand to his lips. "I have everything I want right here."

He told her about the corner studio and the expense account, and then he told her the best part of all.

"It means a lot more money," he said, "enough for you to quit work. You can start working on that novel you've always wanted to write."

She didn't believe him at first. Hell, he could hardly believe it himself.

"I wish—" She stopped.

"What do you wish, Jilly?" He'd give her the moon and stars if he could. "Tell me."

"A baby," she whispered.

His smile faded. "A baby?"

"I know a baby's a huge expense, but don't you see, Davey, it's time. We've been married almost three years. You have a wonderful job. We're young and healthy and—"

She stopped midsentence and watched him as he reached into his pocket and withdrew a small brown paper bag.

"What's that?" she asked as he pushed it across the table.

"Open it and see."

She reached inside and pulled out a paperback book named *Five Thousand Names For Your New Baby*. She stared at it for a few seconds, then leaped from her chair and threw her arms around him. "Oh, David!" She pressed kisses all over his face. "We're going to make a baby!"

That night David had believed heaven was within his reach. Making love to Jill had always been incredible, but that night it became a sacrament. She'd slept in his arms afterward, a gentle smile on her face, and he'd found himself glancing more than once at her flat belly and imagining how beautiful she would be when she was great with child.

He wondered how they would have felt if they'd known how painful and heartbreaking the road to conception would be. They'd been so young and filled with hope, so damn unprepared for failure. These days miracles came with a healthy price tag, and he'd worked long hours to make sure that that was one burden Jill didn't have to shoulder.

Who would've figured the good times would be what finally did them in?

David found a parking spot near the post office. He angled the Porsche in on the first try. "The snow's piled up against the curb," he said. "You'd better slide out on my side."

He reached for her hand as she swung her legs from the car.

"Thank you," she said in a very formal voice, "but I can manage on my own."

"There's ice," he said. "I don't want you to slip."

"Thank you again," she said, even more formally, "but I'm quite sure-footed."

"The hell you are."

"What's that supposed to mean?"

"The Marinos' Christmas party, 1992."

Her face flamed. "High heels and black ice don't mix. It could happen to anybody."

"There was no ice, Jill."

"*Black* ice," she repeated. "The kind you can't see."

"That was the Christmas it rained."

"I really hate it when you're right," she muttered, but she took his hand anyway.

Neither one was wearing gloves, and the initial shock of skin against skin stole her breath away. How could she have forgotten? David didn't have artist's hands. He had big workman's hands, broad-palmed and callused from sports and yard work. She'd fallen in love with those hands the day she'd met him, imagining how it would feel to have him touch her . . . to hold her close.

Once upon a time she'd believed his hands held magic in their grasp, but now she knew better. Not even those hands had been able to keep their family from breaking apart, and that was the only magic she cared about.

Chapter Five

The car barreled down on Sebastian from nowhere. He heard the squeal of brakes, and he leaped up onto a snowdrift along the shoulder just seconds ahead of the tires.

"You trying to get killed?" the driver yelled through his open window. "Stupid cat."

Stupid cat? Sebastian glared at the driver from his perch atop the snowdrift. He wasn't the one who had trouble staying in his lane. He could drive better than that human, and he didn't even have opposable thumbs.

Maybe he would lie there for a few minutes and survey his surroundings. It wasn't that he needed to catch his breath, mind you. He simply wanted to admire the view from up there. Sebastian's chest swelled with pride. That was the kind of leap a young cat could make without thinking twice, but at Sebastian's age it was cause for celebration.

A blue jay darted overhead, swooping down low enough so Sebastian could make out the markings on his throat and belly. He considered taking a halfhearted swipe at him with a paw, but then thought better of it. It was Christmas Eve, after all, and contrary to public opinion, cats had a kind and loving nature, even when it came to birds.

His humans were about to make the biggest mistake people could make, and it seemed to Sebastian that he was the only one who knew it. He'd been there for them when they thought they'd never have babies. Many a tear had fallen onto his thick fur, but he had kept their sorrows to himself. And later, when the babies finally came and with them turmoil and change, his people remembered the nights Sebastian had kept their secrets and loved him all the more for that. They were a family, after all, the whole lot of them: humans and cat, dog and bird.

Sebastian didn't much like getting older, but knowing the family would be together after he was gone made him feel better about the whole thing.

Now he didn't even have that to hold onto anymore.

A lesser cat, one of those sniveling Siamese or overbred Abyssinians, might throw in the towel, but not Sebastian. No Maine coon cat worth his salt would give up without a fight. He was descended from fine stock, from the great cats Deuteronomy and Checquers, strong and sturdy cats with broad backs meant to carry burdens.

But what good was fighting if you didn't choose your battle well?

The cottage was still calling to him, so loud he could barely hear himself think. He had to get there . . . had to bring his people home if they were to have a chance at a happy ending.

Family was worth fighting for. People didn't think cats understood that, but they were wrong. As far as Sebastian could see, it was the humans who needed to be reminded.

And what better place to be reminded than the cottage on Burnt Sugar Hill where it all began?

Christmas Eve cheer had hit Main Street full force. Lights twinkled everywhere. Holly and poinsettia festooned store windows. Carolers from the high school were gathered in the town square by the gazebo, and the merry sounds of "Jingle Bells" and "Rudolph, the Red-Nosed Reindeer" filled the air.

"New outfits," David commented as they waved to Mrs. Palumbo, the chorus leader. "Looks like the fund-raiser was a success."

"I'm glad they picked the red jackets," Jill said. "The green was too dreary." Both she and David had donated their time and money to the cause.

"Hi, Jill. Hi, David." Carol Bonnier from Greg's Grocery waved to them from across the street. "Merry Christmas!"

"Merry Christmas," Jill called out, and David echoed the sentiment.

"Glad to see you two together!"

Jill had never realized that the woman had the lungs of a prize-winning hog caller. She cringed as passers-by took notice of the conversation.

"I knew that divorce nonsense wouldn't last," Carol bellowed. "You two are made for each other."

Jill and David exchanged glances.

"I gave Sebastian some chicken when he popped by the market," she continued at full bellow. "Hope you don't mind."

They were across the street in a flash.

"You saw Sebastian?" Jill demanded of the bewildered woman. "Where? When?"

"At the market. Maybe an hour ago." Carol thought for a moment. "It must have been around lunchtime. I brought some leftover chicken with me, and all of a sudden there Sebastian was, begging."

"Where did he go after he left the market?" David asked.

"He ate the chicken, then turned around and waltzed back out the door the same way he came in. Marge at the hardware store mentioned seeing him, too, but—wait, you two! I want to hear about the reconciliation!"

They tore down the street and burst into Foster Hardware.

"I don't believe my eyes!" Marge, the owner, let out a whoop of delight. "You're back together again."

"Sebastian," Jill said, her cheeks flaming. "Have you seen him?"

"Oh, sure I have, honey. He shared my tuna sandwich with me."

"When?" David asked. They were beginning to sound like the cops on "Dragnet."

"About an hour ago," Marge said. "I was thrilled to see my old friend. He doesn't make many trips into town these days."

"He shouldn't have made this one," Jill said. "We can't find him, Marge, and we're frantic."

"Well, I wish I'd paid more attention when he left, but Mr. Jensen came in looking for a crescent wrench, and you know how talkative he is."

"No apologies necessary, Marge." Jill was so disappointed she could cry.

"Wait a minute!" Marge's face lit up again. "I'm sure I saw him headed toward Frank's Meat Mart."

"Oh, no," Jill murmured. "That's all we need."

"Frank's a dear," Marge said, patting Jill's hand. "He forgave Sebastian for that mishap with the filet mignons ages ago."

David started inching toward the door. "Thanks for the help, Marge."

"Now, just you wait a minute!" Marge barred their exit with her ample body. "You can't leave here without telling me all the wonderful details." She winked broadly. "So . . . ?"

Jill nudged David. In the best tradition of husbands everywhere, he didn't say a word.

"Well, Marge," Jill began, "I'm afraid there really isn't much to tell you."

Marge winked again. "Nothing you can tell me in mixed company!" Her laugh was downright bawdy. "It does my heart good to see you two together again. We've all been talking these last few months, trying to figure out what it would take to get you two to see the light—looks like you managed just fine on your own."

Jill took a deep breath and plunged in. "Marge, this isn't what you think."

"Oh, honey"—a third wink in case they'd missed the previous two—"of course it is. A fool could see how happy you are."

"Marge, I think you've had a bit too much eggnog. David and I aren't getting back together again. We're just trying to find Sebastian before the kids get home from the mall."

Marge's jolly face sagged like a fallen soufflé. She sighed deeply. "Guess I'm one of a dying breed," she said, looking from Jill to David. "My hubby calls me an incurable romantic." Another sigh. "All I want is for everyone to be as happy as Archie and I are."

"Archie is a lucky man," David said with a perfectly straight face.

Jill suppressed a snort of laughter. Archie was Marge's fifth husband. The other four had headed for the hills before the first anniversary.

"Well, Merry Christmas anyway," Marge said, "although I must say you've put quite a damper on my holiday mood."

"She certainly told us off," Jill said as they escaped the hardware store. "You'd think we were divorcing just to spite her."

"Maybe she wanted us to ask for tips on how to have a happy marriage," David said. "You've got to admit she's had enough experience."

"She means well."

"She's a loud-mouthed snoop who spends half her life spreading gossip and the other half creating it."

"I never knew you spent so much time analyzing Marge Foster."

"Marge is easy to figure out," he said. "It's the rest of your sex that has me stumped."

Jill stopped in her tracks. "Uh-oh. Frank's standing in the doorway of the butcher shop, and he doesn't look happy to see us."

Frank was obviously fuming mad. For a second Jill thought she saw steam swirling over his head. No doubt about it: Sebastian had paid him a visit.

"Merry Christmas, Mr. DeMarco," Jill said pleasantly.

"Merry Christmas, my butt." Frank aimed a glare at both of them. "That damn cat of yours wished me a merry

Christmas, and now I'm out two crown roasts and a tender-loin. Don't you people feed that animal?"

"Name your price, Frank." David pulled his wallet out. "Just tell us where Sebastian went from here."

Frank treated them to a five-minute tirade against poor Sebastian before he accepted a one-hundred-dollar bill and their apologies. What he didn't do was tell them where Sebastian was headed when he had departed.

"Good for Sebastian," Jill said as the butcher door slammed shut. "I'm only sorry he didn't grab the turkeys, too."

They started walking again, and Jill shivered. "It's getting worse out," she said, looking up at the heavy, cream-colored sky. The wind had picked up considerably, and the temperature was dropping fast. She met David's eyes. "He'll never make it through the night. Not in this weather."

David took her hand. She felt the same bone-deep shock of recognition as she had before, and she didn't pull away.

"Cats have nine lives, remember? He hasn't used up more than four or five."

She laughed despite her fear. "Four or five, huh? I would've figured a solid seven."

"Five, max. Our Sebastian was born under a lucky star."

"Twelve years ago tonight," she whispered. "I'll never forget when he popped out of the backpack . . . I fell in love right on the spot."

"Remember how his nose got out of joint when the kids were born? He disappeared for three days after I started carrying the twins around in his backpack."

"Sebastian got over it," she said, smiling at the memories. "He loves the kids now. He's been sleeping on the foot of Tori's bed since—"

Since you left. She didn't say the words aloud but then she didn't have to. They hung in the air between them just the same.

They asked about Sebastian at the barber shop, the hair

salon, the deli, the video store, and the dry cleaners. The same thing happened every time. The second their old friends and neighbors saw Jill and David together they made the inevitable leap in logic, only to have their hopes dashed.

Jill's nerves were shot. In less than a half hour, she and David had fueled more gossip than "Entertainment Tonight" and *The National Enquirer* combined.

"If one more person tells me how thrilled they are to see us together, I'll scream."

"They're looking for a happy ending, Jilly. You can't blame them for that."

"It doesn't bother you?" she demanded as they stopped in front of the bank.

"This is a small town. It comes with the territory."

Jill made a face. "So says the man who's leaving for San Francisco."

He checked his watch. "What time is Phyllis bringing the kids back?"

"Around five," Jill said. He was probably counting the minutes until he left for the airport.

"It's getting late."

Tears burned against her lids. "You're right," she said, pushing her hair off her face with an impatient gesture. "I should get home."

"If I wasn't expected at the open house tomorrow, I'd change my plane reservations."

"I'm sure you would."

"What the hell is that supposed to mean?"

"Exactly what I said."

"Damn it, Jill, Sebastian is every bit as important to me as he is to you."

"I know that."

"You're doing it again."

"Doing what?"

"That." He glowered at her. "Saying the right thing in the wrong tone of voice."

"Sorry if I've offended you."

"If you've got something to say, say it. You never used to be shy."

"I want to go home," she said, tears threatening. "Maybe Sebastian is there."

"We haven't checked with Don at the pharmacy."

"I'm not going in there."

"Since when?"

"I said no and I meant it."

He looked at her for a long time, then turned and walked away.

"David!" she called. "Where are you going?"

He didn't answer. He didn't stop. He headed straight for the pharmacy.

A wave of anger swept over her. If he didn't remember, she wasn't about to remind him.

THEN

"You buy it," Jill said to David as they loitered in Aisle 3 of Tudor Pharmacy, pretending they were choosing Christmas cards.

"You're embarrassed?" He sounded amused, faintly surprised.

"Of course I'm not embarrassed." She hesitated, feeling almost afraid to say the words, in case she woke up the gods of bad karma. "I'm superstitious."

"What?" Grinning, he leaned closer. "You're mumbling, Jill. You never mumble."

She gave him a gentle elbow in the ribs. "I'm superstitious," she repeated. "Okay? I'm not proud of it, but there you are." All week long she'd knocked on wood, tossed salt over her shoulder, and turned her back on black cats. She knew she was wishing for the impossible, but who said miracles didn't happen? Somehow she knew this time it would all be different.

He pretended to study the array of home pregnancy tests on the shelf. "Which one has the magic?" She heard the fear and pride and longing in his voice and knew a fierce moment of love so deep and strong it almost frightened her.

She pointed toward a blue box and followed him to the cashier.

The next morning they waited together for the results.

"Five minutes takes a hell of a long time," David said, staring at the special receptacle that came with the test.

She squeezed his hand. "I have a feeling," she whispered. "A good feeling."

He looked at her, his expression both curious and hopeful. "So do I," he said.

They woke up before dawn the next morning.

"Merry Christmas Eve," he said, kissing her gently.

"Merry Christmas Eve," she said, then disappeared into the bathroom with the package.

"We're going to be lucky this time, Jilly," he said as they waited. "Christmas Eve is our day."

"I know," she whispered. They'd met on Christmas Eve. Sebastian came into their lives on Christmas Eve. Maybe God would bless them with a miracle on Christmas Eve.

The clock ticked. Their hearts thundered. Then the moment came.

"I can't look," she said, burying her face against his shoulder. Finally, after all these years, a doctor had offered them a chance at heaven. Things were different for them now. David was earning a good salary, and they had plowed most of it into exploring every medical avenue available that might lead them closer to a healthy, happy baby. They'd weathered disappointment after disappointment by holding tight to each other and to their dream of parenthood, but the experience had taken its toll.

She loved him so much, and he deserved the family he yearned for. The family he'd never had as a child. If her body failed her this time, she didn't know if she would be able to bear it.

The timer dinged.

"Oh, David, would you—?"

He nodded, then stood up and walked into the bathroom. She closed her eyes against the shattering of a dream. *Please, God,* she prayed. *Please, please . . .* She heard her husband draw in a deep breath and then she heard nothing. An anguished moan escaped her lips, but then she looked up to see the most beautiful sight on earth. David knelt in front of her, tears streaming down his lean cheeks as he held out the plastic vial. A black ring shimmered at the bottom . . . a beautiful, glorious black ring!

They laughed and cried and held each other close that morning, whispering words of love and joy that seemed to shimmer in the air around them. She felt drunk with ecstasy, as if some rare and wondrous nectar of the gods bubbled through her veins, making her one with the universe and everyone in it.

He placed a gentle hand against her belly, and she laughed and covered his hand with hers. She had loved him as long as she could remember. From the first moment, she'd known that this was the man she would grow old with, the man in whose arms she wanted to die.

The man who would be the father of her child.

No wonder Jill didn't want to go into the pharmacy, David thought. There were ghosts in there. And not just any ghosts. He wouldn't have minded Mrs. Adelson, who had lived up the hill, or Old Man Martinson, who had died three years ago. Seeing them again would have been okay. The ghosts he'd seen in the pharmacy were of a different kind, and they were a hell of a lot more dangerous.

He saw himself in that old drugstore and he saw Jill. He saw them as they'd been back at the beginning, young and poor and happy. He saw them picking up the Sunday paper and choosing anniversary cards. He saw them buying home pregnancy tests the way other people bought lottery tickets, praying the day would come when they finally hit the jackpot.

"Surprised to see you," Don the pharmacist said from behind the counter. "Thought you were on your way to the city by the Bay."

"Tonight," he said.

"Sorry to hear you're still going. I feel like I watched you and Jill grow up. Never thought it would come to this."

"Neither did I," David said.

"You got yourself another woman?"

He shook his head. "Jill's a tough act to follow."

"So what's the problem? You love her. She loves you. Why the divorce?"

"She loves me?" David asked. "What makes you think she still loves me?"

Don tossed him a sprig of mistletoe. "Ask her."

"Ask her," David said, clutching the mistletoe. "I'm going to ask her."

He bolted for the door.

"Hey!" the pharmacist called out. "Didn't you want something?"

"My wife," he said. He wanted her love, her friendship, her company. He was going to take her in his arms and ask her if she loved him and if he didn't like her answer first time around, he was going to kiss her soundly and ask her again.

The whole town couldn't be wrong. He and Jill belonged together. They had belonged together since their first phone conversation, their first car ride, their first kiss. And he wasn't going to just ask her about love, he was going to tell her how he felt, tell her all the things he hadn't told her for too damn long—that he loved her and needed her and that there had to be some way to put it all back together again.

She wasn't in front of the store where he'd left her.

He looked up one side of the street then down the other.

She wasn't anywhere.

"Damn it, Jill!" He dragged a hand through his hair. "Where are you?"

First his cat, and now his wife. He was beginning to see a pattern emerging. He still had the car keys, so she couldn't have gone far. Maybe she'd spotted Sebastian and had gone off in pursuit. He noticed Ted Weinstein watching him from the bakery window and he darted into the shop.

"Have you seen Jill?"

"Son of a gun," said Ted, grabbing his hand and shaking it. "It's true. You two are back together."

"Not yet," David said, "but we will be if I can find out where she went."

"That way," Ted said, pointing north. "Toward Burnt Sugar Hill."

Burnt Sugar Hill. It made sense. There was a shortcut that would take her back to their house. David planted a kiss on the baker's weathered cheek. "I owe you, Ted. Big time."

Ted made a face and wiped off the kiss with the back of his hand. "Send a greeting card. This kissing stuff is too continental for me."

David ran through the snowy streets. He didn't feel the cold. He didn't slip on the ice. He ran faster than he'd ever run before, as if somebody had attached jet skis to the bottoms of his shoes. Somebody was watching over him, the goddess of stupid husbands who'd almost let the best woman on earth walk away without a fight.

So what if she got mad or slapped his face or said she never wanted to speak to him again. She'd already said she wanted a divorce. There was nothing else she could do that would hurt him more than that.

"Jilly!" She was halfway to Burnt Sugar Hill. "Wait up!"

If anything, she walked faster. Her head was ducked low against the wind and snow. Her hands were plunged deep into her pockets.

"Jilly!" His strides ate up the distance. "Stop!"

She broke into a run. What the hell was going on? He pulled up even with her.

"We've got to talk." He sounded winded but sincere.

She darted off the road and started up the hill. "Go to hell," she said.

Was that some kind of secret code for "I love you"?

His foot caught on an exposed tree trunk, and he stumbled.

"Serves you right," she called over her shoulder. "You rat."

"This isn't funny, Jill." He grabbed her forearm. "I love—"

Chapter Six

Jill hadn't meant to flip David over her shoulder, but she'd been named Karate Mom of the Week and she couldn't pass up a golden opportunity like that. He had her so angry, she could probably break boards with her pinky.

"You threw me like a Frisbee," he said as he lay on his back in a snowdrift, gasping for air. "Where did you learn to do that?"

"Mommy & Me karate classes. Want to see what I can do with my feet?"

"Thanks, but I've had enough bodily injury for one day." He held out his hand. "Help me up, will you?"

She shook her head and took a step back. "I wasn't born yesterday."

His blue eyes were wide and innocent. "I'm not exactly in an offensive position, Jill."

She hesitated. She'd never caused anyone bodily harm before.

"You're the one who flipped me." He really did look helpless, lying there like a macho snow angel. "My butt's getting numb."

"I suppose I owe you that much." She reached for his hand, and a second later found herself lying next to him in the snowdrift. "You rat! You tricked me."

"Stubborn redhead."

Her fingers curled around some snow. "What was that?"

"You heard me."

"I'm hoping I heard wrong."

He met her fierce look with one of his own. "I called you a stubborn redhead."

"Take it back."

"The hell I will. You're the most stubborn woman I've ever known."

"You pigheaded lout. How dare you call me stubborn!"

"You were born stubborn and you'll die stubborn."

Furious, she scrambled to her knees. "I said take it back."

"Make me."

"You asked for it, Whittaker!" She reared back and aimed her snowball right between his eyes.

She wanted to pelt him with snowballs until he couldn't see straight. She wanted to bury him in snow up to his nostrils until he realized what a stupid fool he'd been. She wanted him to throw himself at her feet and beg her forgiveness. And then she would withhold it until he really began to squirm.

He lobbed a few snowballs in her direction.

"That's pathetic," she taunted, gaining confidence by the second. "Is that the best you can do?"

She landed another missile right between his eyes.

Splat!

Splat!

He was starting to look like a polar bear. "Jilly—"

"Don't call me that! You lost the right to call me that."

"I don't want a divorce."

"Well, that's too damn bad," she said, trying to ignore the foolish explosion of hope inside her heart. "You should have thought about that before you accepted that project in San Francisco."

"I had to make the decision on the spot. I thought you liked San Francisco."

"Everyone likes San Francisco." She let out a shriek of frustration. "Don't you get it, you fool? This isn't about San Francisco, David, this is about *you*."

"About me?" David forgot about the snowballs. Of all the things he'd expected her to say, that was at the bottom of the list.

"You don't want that job in San Francisco any more than I want you to take it."

"How do you figure that?"

"Oh, David—" She tossed another snowball in his direction, but it lacked conviction. He told himself that that was a good sign. "If you're going to leave us for some stupid job, at least leave us for a job that's worthy of you."

"You don't know what you're talking about."

"I know all I need to know. I know you haven't been happy for a long time. I know it's all wrong for you to put your heart and soul into some design-by-committee project. I know you're a brilliant, passionate architect and you're being wasted—"

"Damn it, Jill, don't you get it? It was go to San Francisco or leave the firm."

"You should have turned and walked out the door the minute they gave you that ultimatum."

Deadbeats did things like that. Sons-of-bitches who walked out on their families and let their son bounce from foster home to foster home. The way his father had done to him. "You and the kids are my responsibility."

"Why don't you let me be your partner rather than just your responsibility?"

"You've always been my partner," he said as the truth of her words pounded inside his brain. "You gave up a lot for me, Jilly—I owe you."

"You owe me." Her voice was soft, ineffably sad. He wondered if it was finally too late. "If that's what you think our marriage was about, then there really isn't any hope for us."

She turned and started to walk away, and he knew that if he let her go, nothing else that happened in his life would matter a damn.

"Jilly."

She hesitated.

"You could have had an easier life with someone else."

"Maybe," she admitted, "but I couldn't have had a happier one."

He reached for her hand. She entwined her fingers with his. There was still a chance . . . there had to be.

"Tell me you want to go to San Francisco," she whispered. "Tell me that I'm wrong, that this project is important to you. Tell me that this job in San Francisco will make you happy, and I'll get the kids and follow you."

The truth was staring him in the face, and he couldn't avoid it any longer. "You're right about the job," he said. "It's a lousy project, and I'd be a pawn of the Japanese consortium, but if I want to stay on with the company, this is part of the deal."

"And you call *me* stubborn." The faintest beginnings of a smile flickered at the corners of her mouth. "We're supposed to be a team, you fool. We were a team when you got that first big promotion. We were a team when I quit my job to write my book. We were a team all those years when it seemed like we'd never have a baby. Why should this be any different?"

"You went through hell to have the twins," he said, remembering. "The doctors, the surgeries—"

"And you worked around the clock to make it possible. We did it together, the same way we can do this. The same way we can do anything we put our minds and hearts to."

He doesn't hear you, Jill. He doesn't understand. Her heart sank. David was looking right through her as if she weren't even there. She pulled her hand away. "David," she snapped, "the least you can do is pay attention." This was their future she was talking about. Their children's future.

"Sebastian," he said, pointing. "Look!"

"Oh, my God!" A fluffy cat with huge muttonchops and a bushy striped tail stood on the top of the hill, looking down on them.

Sebastian didn't so much as blink as they slowly made their way up the snowy hill to where he stood. When they were within ten feet of him, he turned and bolted, running faster than he'd run in years, straight through the open front door of the cottage.

It looked exactly the same as always. Same shutters, same window boxes, same aura of love and magic.

David and Jill exchanged glances.

"There are a lot of memories in that cottage," she said.

"I know," he said, reaching for her hand. "But I can take it if you can."

They crossed the threshold, and the years seemed to fall away.

"I can almost see us," Jill whispered, "the way we used to be."

David nodded. "By the window, where we used to watch the sunrise."

"Oh, Davey," she said. "We look so young."

"We look so happy."

"We *were* happy."

"We didn't have a pot to pee in."

"We had everything we needed." She drew in a deep breath. "We had each other."

"You deserved more," he said, his voice breaking. "You deserved all the things you left behind when you married me."

"I left loneliness behind," she said.

"You left a way of life I couldn't provide for you."

"I didn't want that way of life. I wanted love . . . I wanted you."

"I love you, Jilly." He gently drew her into his arms. "Everything I've ever done in life, I've done for you. When you asked for the divorce, I thought—"

"Shh." She raised up on tiptoe and placed her index finger against his lips. "I never really wanted a divorce." She told him how much she'd missed him, how much she hated the way they'd drifted apart. "All I wanted to do was make you open your eyes and realize we need you more than we need your paycheck." She hadn't expected the avalanche of emotions her words would set into motion.

"Took me long enough, didn't it?" He shook his head. "When I think how close I came to losing you and the kids—"

"You couldn't lose us," she said. "We're your family."

Her heart beat painfully, wondrously, inside her chest as she saw the smile light up her husband's beloved face.

"You're my life," he said, and in those simple words, she heard their future. "Everything I was or am or will ever be—it's all for you, Jilly. All because of you."

He lowered his head and kissed her with all the passion and pain a heart could bear. They had come so close to losing everything that mattered, everything that was real and true and lasting.

"We might be in for some more tough times," he said, stroking her hair back from her face.

"Maybe not that tough," she said, her eyes twinkling. "I'm a lot more successful than you realize." She quoted him a figure. She saw the look of fear flicker behind his eyes. "I'm with you because I want to be, Davey. Not because I have to be."

"Give me a year," he said, his voice husky with emotion, "and I'll give you some competition."

"Give me your heart," she whispered, "and I'll give you my life."

Sebastian meowed from atop a kitchen chair.

"You big, wonderful cat!" Jill forced him to endure a hug.

David scratched Sebastian behind the ear. "We owe you, fella. There'll be a Christmas catnip bonus in your stocking tonight."

"Oh, my God!" Jill cried. "It's almost five o'clock . . . it's Christmas Eve . . . the kids . . . we've got to get home!"

She reached down to scoop up Sebastian, but he leaped from her arms and darted toward the living room.

"What's his problem?" David asked as Jill hurried after the cat. "We're taking him home to a warm house and a full dinner bowl. You'd think he had something better to do."

Jill's laugh floated toward him as he reached her side. "He does have something better to do, Davey—look!"

"You old son of a gun," he said, shaking his head. "Who would have guessed you had it in you?"

Sebastian stood guard while a beautiful tortoiseshell cat nursed a quartet of kittens, one of whom bore a strong resemblance to a certain Maine coon cat.

Jill looked at David. David looked at Sebastian. Sebastian's chest seemed to swell with pride.

"If I didn't know better," Jill said to Sebastian, "I'd think you planned this whole thing to bring us back together." She met David's eyes. "That's impossible, right?"

He hesitated. "If you'd asked me that this morning, I would have laughed."

"David—"

"Look at the evidence, Jilly. We're here in the cottage with Sebastian and his offspring. Pretty incredible, if you ask me."

"And we're together," she said, as a sense of wonder built inside her heart. "You wouldn't think a cat could—"

David looked at the little kitten who was Sebastian's mirror image. "I'm starting to think anything's possible on Christmas Eve." He drew her into his arms. "We found each other on Christmas Eve, didn't we?"

"Twice," she said, as her heart soared. "And this time I'm not letting go."

Epilogue

Outside the snow fell steadily, brushing against the window like angel wings. There was music in the air and more than a touch of magic. It was Christmas Eve, and Sebastian's family was home where they belonged.

The Boy and Girl were settled upstairs in sleeping bags. His people had told them that Santa Claus had come early and had brought them a wonderful surprise. Who could resist kittens? Even Sebastian had a soft spot for the little balls of fluff. And Princess wasn't bad, herself. He was only a cat, after all. He couldn't help being partial to a pair of big eyes and a silky coat.

Ah, but that one kitten—he was really something special. Sebastian knew it wasn't simply his pride speaking or his vanity. That little Maine coon cat was the one he'd been waiting for. The kitten was strong and curious and brave. Sebastian could teach him things, important things, like how sometimes a cat had to do the impossible to keep his family together. It was an important lesson, and he would see to it that the little one learned it well.

"We're going outside for a minute," the man said to him. "You take care of things for us, you old devil."

The woman kissed the top of Sebastian's head, then followed the man out the door. Sebastian leaped onto the windowsill and watched as they made their way through the deep snow to the wooden sign that had been in the front yard for months now. She pulled it out of the ground and handed it to the man, who broke it over his knee and threw the pieces as far away as he could. Then, to Sebastian's delight, they wrapped their arms around each other, and he knew that they would be out there a long time.

His son meowed. Sebastian leaped down from the windowsill and pressed his nose against a tiny ear. One day you'll love them as much as I do, he thought. When I'm gone, you'll be here to take care of them and keep them safe from harm.

Sebastian yawned. He wasn't at all tired, but maybe a short nap wasn't such a bad idea. Tomorrow was Christmas, and he knew how his humans were about Christmas. He'd be lucky if he managed to get any rest at all. Funny how Christmas had managed to come, even though there was no tree or twinkling lights or presents stacked up higher than a cat could jump.

Maybe Christmas was more than presents and laughter. Maybe it had something to do with the feeling inside his heart that seemed to grow stronger each year that he spent with his people. His family.

Sebastian yawned again and decided it would feel nice to lie next to the fire and dream. He settled his ancient bones near the fireplace and was about to doze off when his son curled up next to him, his sturdy little body pressed close to Sebastian's side.

The front door squeaked open then shut, and he heard the sounds of whispers and laughter from his people. He had waited a long time to hear the house echo again with those sounds, and he congratulated himself on a job well done. There would be a lot of happy Christmases spent in this house, and he intended to be around a long time to enjoy them.

Life was good, Sebastian thought, as he fell asleep next to his son. Very good indeed.

The Gift of Christmas Past

Lynn Kurland

Prologue

"Dames," Bruno said, with a regretful shake of his head. "Whatcha gonna do wit 'em?"

Sir Maximillian Sweetums swished his tail twice, settled himself more comfortably on his cloud, and admitted to himself that he quite had to agree with his companion—as indelicately put as the sentiment had been.

"Ah, dear Bruno," Sir Sweetums said, "there's the rub. Women don't like to be 'done with.' Especially The Abigail. A most forthright and independent spirit, she is."

"It ain't like you ain't tried, Boss," Bruno offered. "Before you, uh, I mean while you was still, uh—"

Sir Sweetums held up his well-manicured white paw to spare the blushing bulldog further embarrassment.

"Yes, I understand." It was very impolite to mention to a feline that his nine lives were up, but Sir Sweetums overlooked the faux pas. After all, he'd lived his turns to the fullest, using his considerable wits and wiles to their best advantage.

He'd had a different charge during each of his nine lives, and he'd seen eight of those mortal charges successfully settled. It was Number Nine who had, and continued, to elude his superior matchmaking skills. The Abigail. He'd tried, oh, how he'd tried.

He'd made an unmentionable deposit into the toolbox of a less-than-desirable handyman The Abigail had taken a fancy to. He'd leaped off the back of the couch over an insufferable attorney, snatching the man's hairpiece and wresting it to the ground. Snags in gabardine trousers, bloodcurdling yowls, sneak attacks from the bushes—they had served only to keep the undesirables from The Abigail. But a suitor to suit? Sir Sweetums wrinkled his aristocratic nose disdainfully. Nary a one, dear reader, nary a one!

That was before. Two years into his post-ninth life and subsequent Guardian Feline Association membership, Sir Sweetums had found the Right One for The Abigail.

Now it was just a question of bringing them together.

"Hey, Boss, uh, is you ready to go yet?"

Sir Sweetums tucked a bit of stray fur behind his left ear. "Yes, my friend, I believe the time has come. You saw to the details?"

"Yeah, Boss. Dat movie's on right now. Only how come dey don't have no parts for no Guardian Animals in dat one?"

"Perhaps The Capra was allergic."

A thoughtful expression descended onto the bulldog's pudgy face. "Yeah," he said, nodding slowly. "Maybe dat's it." He looked up at Sir Sweetums and snapped to attention when he saw the feline was poised to jump. "Anyting' else, Boss, befores you go? Some Tenda Viddles? A sawsah of haf n' haf?"

Sir Sweetums was already leaping down athletically from the cloud. "No time, dear Bruno," he called back. "We mustn't keep Fate waiting any longer!"

"Good luck, Boss! You's gonna need it," Bruno added, in an undertone. "Dames," he said, with a slow shake of his head. "Whatcha gonna do wit 'em?"

Chapter One

It *wasn't* a wonderful life.

Abigail Moira Garrett stood on the bridge and stared down into the murky waters below her. She couldn't even find a decently rushing river to throw herself into. The best she could do was Murphy's Pond and the little one-lane bridge that arched over the narrow end of it. Instead of meeting her end in a torrent of water, she'd probably do no better than strangle herself in the marshy weeds below. It was indicative of how her life had been going lately.

It had all started last Monday. Her power had gone off during the night, causing her to sleep until ten A.M. The phone call from her boss had been what had woken her. He'd told her not to bother coming in. Ever.

If only it had stopped there. But it hadn't. And why? Because she'd uttered the words, "It can't get any worse than this." Those were magical words, guaranteed to prove the utterer wrong, words that drew every contrary force in the universe to zero in on the speaker with single-minded intensity.

Tuesday she'd been informed that because of a glitch in the system, it would take several weeks to collect unemployment.

Wednesday she'd been informed that she wouldn't be getting any unemployment because her Social Security number didn't exist. If she wanted to take it up with the Social Security office, their number was . . .

Thursday, her landlord had told her he wanted her out. Being between jobs, she had now become a freeloader and he wasn't taking any chances on her. Chest pains had begun that night.

On Friday her fiancé, whom she had always considered boyishly charming, boyishly mannered, and boyishly handsome, had left her a note telling her that since she no longer had a job and wouldn't be able to support him in the style to which he wanted to become accustomed after they married, he was moving on to greener pastures. To the woman in the apartment next door, to be exact.

And now, on top of everything else, Christmas was three days away. Christmas was meant to be spent with family, basking in the glow of friendship, food, and hearthfire. All she had to bask in was the odor of sweat socks that permeated her apartment, despite her attempts to dispel it. She had no family, no hopes for posterity anytime soon and, most especially, no cat.

She dragged her sleeve across her eyes. This was her second catless Christmas. She should have been used to it by now, but she wasn't. Just how was one to make the acquaintance of Sir Maximillian Sweetums, live with him for ten years, then be expected to live without him? One day he'd been there and the next, *poof,* he'd been gone. She'd cried for days, looked for weeks, hoped for months. But no Sir Sweetums.

And now that darned movie had just made matters worse. She had watched George Bailey lose it all, then regain it in the most Christmassy, heartfelt of ways. It certainly had been a wonderful life for him. All watching it had done for her was make her realize just exactly what she didn't have. Good grief, she didn't even have a Social Security number anymore!

She stepped up on the first rung of the railing and stared down into the placid waters. All right, now was the time to get ahold of herself and make a few decisions. She had no intentions of jumping—not that she would have done herself much harm anyway. Well, short of getting strangled in Mr. Murphy's weeds, that is. No, she had come to face death and figure out just what it was she had to live for.

She threw out her hands as a gust of wind unbalanced her. Okay, so maybe this was a little drastic, but she was a Garrett and Garretts never did things by halves. That's what her father had always told her and she had taken it to heart.

Her dad ought to have known. He'd fallen off Mt. Everest at age seventy.

She stared out over the placid pond and contemplated her situation. So, she'd lost her job. She didn't like typing for a living and she hated fetching her boss coffee. She would find something else. And her apartment was hazardous to her sense of smell. She could do better.

Her fiancé Brett could be replaced as well. What did she need with a perpetual Peter Pan who had three times as many clothes as she did, wore gallons of cologne and deep down in his boyish heart of hearts was certain she should be supporting him while he found himself? Maybe she'd look for a different kind of guy this time, one who didn't mind working and wouldn't hog all her closet space. She crossed her heart as she made her vow. *No one who dresses better, smells nicer, or works less than I do.*

So maybe her life was in the toilet. At least she was still in the bowl, not flushed out on her way to the sewer. She could go on for another few days.

Oh, but Sir Sweetums. Abby swayed on the railing, shivering. He was irreplaceable. Even after two years, she still felt his loss. Who was she supposed to talk to now while she gardened in that little plot downstairs? Who would greet her at the end of each day with a meow that said, "and just where have you been, Miss? I positively demand your attention!" Who would wake her up in the morning with dignified pats on her cheek with his soft paw?

Meow!

Abby gasped as she saw something take a swan dive into the pond. She climbed up to the top of the railing for a better look. That had to have been a cat. It had definitely meowed and those headlights had most certainly highlighted a tail.

Headlights? A very large truck traveling at an unsafe speed rumbled over the one-lane bridge, leaving behind a hefty gust of wind. Abby made windmill-like motions with her arms as she fought to keep herself balanced on that skinny railing.

"Hey, I wasn't through sorting out my life!" she exclaimed, fighting the air.

It was no use.

Darkness engulfed her. She didn't see the pond coming, but she certainly felt it. Her breath departed with a rush as she plunged down into the water. She sank like a rock. Her chest burned with the effort of holding what little breath she still possessed.

Time stopped and she lost all sense of direction. It occurred to her, fleetingly, that Murphy's Pond wasn't that deep. Maybe she had bonked her head on a stiff bit of pond scum and was now hallucinating. Or worse.

An eternity later, her feet touched solid, though squishy, ground. With strength born of pure panic, she pushed off from the gooey pond bottom and clawed her way to the surface. She started to lose consciousness and she fought it with all her strength. No halves for this Garrett.

She burst through the surface and gulped in great lungfuls of air. She flailed about in the water to keep afloat, grateful she was breathing air and not water. Finally, she managed to stop coughing long enough to catch her breath.

And then she wished she hadn't.

The smell was blinding. Her teeth started to chatter. Maybe she had died and been sent straight along to hell. Was this what hell smelled like?

Well, at least there was dry land in sight. It was possible she had just drifted to a different part of Mr. Murphy's pond. Things floated by her, but she didn't stick around to investigate. Pond scum was better left unexamined at close range. She swam to the bank and heaved herself out of the water. She rolled over onto her back and closed her eyes, content to be on terra firma, still breathing, still conscious.

She had to get hold of herself. Life just wasn't that bad. Lots of people had it worse. *She* could have had it worse. She could have married Brett and watched her closet space dwindle to nothing. She could have been fetching Mr. Schlessinger coffee until she was as personable as the cactus plants he kept on his windowsill. Life had given her the chance to start over. It would be very un-Garrett-like not to take the do-over and run like hell with it.

She took a last deep breath. She needed to get up, find her car and go home. Maybe she'd stop at the Mini Mart and get a small snack. Something chocolate. Something very bad for her. Yes, that was the ticket. She sat up, pushed her hair out of her eyes and looked back over the pond, wondering just where she'd wound up.

She froze.

Then her jaw went slack.

It seemed that the moon had come out. How nice. It illuminated the countryside quite well. She blinked. Then she rubbed her eyes.

She wasn't sitting on the bank of Murphy's Pond. She was sitting on the bank of a moat.

She looked to her left. What should have been the bridge over the narrow end of the pond, wasn't. It looked like a drawbridge. She followed it across the water, then looked up. She blinked some more, but it didn't help.

All right, so maybe she *had* died and gone to hell. But she'd always assumed hell was very warm, what with all that fire and brimstone dotting the landscape. She definitely wasn't warm and she definitely wasn't looking at brimstone. She was looking at a castle.

She groaned and flopped back onto the grass. *Faint, damn it!* she commanded herself.

Shoot. It was that blasted Garrett constitution coming to the fore. Garretts never fainted. But did they lose their minds? Abby turned that thought over in her head for a few minutes. She didn't know of anyone in the family having lost it. Lots of deaths of Garretts of grandparent vintage driving at unsafe speeds, skiing down unsafe hills, climbing up things better admired from a distance. But no incontinence, incapacity, or insanity.

Meow.

Abby sat up so fast, she saw stars. She put her hand to her head. Once the world had settled back down to normal rotation, she looked around frantically.

"Sir Sweetums?" Abby called.

Meow, came the answer, to her left.

Abby looked, then did a double take. "Sir Sweetums!" She jumped to her feet. "It's you!"

There, not twenty feet from her, sat her beloved Sir Maximillian Sweetums, staring at her with what could only be described as his dignified kitty look. He flicked his ears at her.

Abby took a step forward, then froze. What did this mean? Surely Sir Sweetums hadn't been packed off to hell. But she had the feeling he just couldn't be alive. Did that mean she was dead, too?

Without further ado, she pulled back and slapped herself smartly across the face.

"Yeouch!" she exclaimed, rubbing her cheek. Well, that answered a few questions. Though Sir Sweetums might have left his corporeal self behind, she certainly hadn't.

But, whatever his status, His Maximillianness was obviously in a hurry to be off somewhere. He gave her another meow, then hopped up on all fours, did a graceful leap to change his direction, and headed toward the drawbridge.

"Hey," Abby said, "wait!"

And Sir Sweetums, being himself, ignored her. That was the thing about cats; they had minds of their own.

"Sir Sweetums, wait!"

The blasted cat was now on the drawbridge and heading straight for the castle.

The castle?

"I'll deal with that later," Abby promised herself.

Later—when she figured out why the moonlight was shining down on walls topped with towers and those little slits that looked just about big enough for a man to squeeze through and either shoot something at you, or fling boiling oil at you. Later—when she'd decided just what she was: dead or alive, in heaven or hell. Later—when she'd had a bath to remove the lovely fragrance of *eau de sewer* from her hair and clothes.

"Hey, stop!" Abby exclaimed, thumping across the drawbridge. She pulled up short at the sight of the gate. It looked suspiciously like something she'd seen in a documentary on medieval castles. Abby took a deep breath and added that little detail to her list of things to worry about later. Now she had to catch her fleeing feline before he slipped through the gate grates.

She made a diving leap for Sir Sweetums' tail. She wound up flat on her face in a puddle of mud, clutching a fistful of what should have been cat hair.

She jumped to her feet and took hold of the gate, peering through the grates. They were about ten inches square—big enough for her to see through, but definitely not big enough to squeeze through.

"Sir Sweetums," she crooned, in her best come-here-I-have-some-half-and-half-in-your-favorite-china-bowl voice.

Nothing. Drat.

"Come on, Max," she tried, in her best aw-shucks-cut-me-some-slack voice.

Not even a swish of a tail to let her know she'd been heard.

"Get back over here, you stupid cat!" she hollered.

That wasn't working either. No cat. No castle owners either. Well, maybe they were asleep.

She thought about waiting for morning to call for help but all it took was one good whiff of herself to decide that *that* wasn't an option. Maybe that was all part of hell, too. Phantom cats, sewer-like stench clinging to one's clothes, delusional surroundings.

She rubbed her muddy cheek thoughtfully. It was still sore. She felt far too corporeal for the afterlife. Nope, she wasn't dead. Totally in control of her faculties was debatable, but she'd give that more thought later.

What she wanted now was a hot bath and a mug of Swiss Miss with mini marshmallows. She was a damsel in definite distress. Maybe there was a handsome knight inside ready to rescue her from her less than best-dressed self.

She started to yell.

Chapter Two

Miles shifted in his chair, shoved his feet closer to the fire blazing in the middle of the great hall, and tried to fall asleep. He had a bed, but he'd shunned it in favor of the hard chair. He likely could have contented himself with merely choking on the abundance of smoke in his hall, but somehow this dual torture had suited him. Of course had he remained at his sire's keep, he could have been sitting in a more comfortable chair, enjoying the festivities of the season in a smokeless hall. Artanc was a thoroughly modern place, with hearths set into the walls and flues to carry the smoke outside.

But Miles had sought discomfort and Speningethorpe certainly provided him with that. It was, politely, a bloody sty. Miles knew he was fortunate to have arrived and found the place possessing a roof. But he'd wanted it. He'd all but demanded it. He'd wanted a place of refuge. What with the pair of years he'd just survived, peace and quiet was what he'd needed, no matter the condition of the surroundings.

He never should have made the journey to the Holy Land. Aye, that was the start to all his troubles. Now, staring back on the ruins of his life, he wondered why his reasons had seemed so compelling at the time. It wasn't as if he'd had to prove himself to his sire, or to the rest of the countryside, for that matter. He vaguely remembered a desire to see what his father and brothers had seen on their travels.

Perhaps the tale would have finished peaceably if he'd been able to keep his bloody mouth shut on his way home. Soured and disillusioned after returning from Jerusalem, he'd let his tongue run free at the expense of a former French Crusader. If he'd but known whom he'd been insulting!

He shook aside his thoughts. It did no good to dwell on the past. He'd escaped France with his flesh unscorched and he had his grandfather to thank for that. He'd been home for four months already; it was past time he sent word and thanked the man for the timely rescue. He would, just as soon as he'd brooded enough to suit himself. That time surely wouldn't come before the celebrations were over. Had he ever possessed any desire to celebrate the birth of the Lord, he had it no longer. He'd seen too many atrocities committed for the sake of preserving holy relics. Nay, what he wanted was silence, far away from his family, far away from their joy and laughter. He had no heart for such things.

His father hadn't argued with him. But then, Rhys of Artane had had his own taste of war and such, and he understood. He'd asked no questions, simply given into Miles's demand for the desolate bit of soil without comment. His only action had been to see stores sent along after the fact by a generously-manned garrison. Miles had kept the foodstuffs, but sent the men back. He would hear about that soon enough. He smiled grimly. His father would be provoked mightily by the act. Hopefully his mother had the furnishings secured well.

The wood popped, startling him. He shifted in his chair, then paused. Was that a voice?

Surely his father wouldn't have ridden from Artane so soon. Miles frowned. He would have to investigate, obviously. He pushed himself to his feet, feeling far older than his score and four years. The saints pity him if he ever reached his sire's age. He was exhausted already by living.

He walked to the hall door, then unbolted it by heaving a wooden beam from its iron brackets. He set the beam aside and pulled the heavy door back.

There was most definitely someone at the gates. Miles sighed heavily and returned to his chair for his sword. It would have been wise to don at least a mail shirt, but he had no squire to aid him, nor any energy to arm himself by himself. A sword and a frown would have to suffice. He snatched a torch from a sconce on the wall and left the great hall. Perhaps he'd been too hasty in his decision to leave the servants behind. It was much easier to ask who was at the gates than to discover the truth of the matter for oneself.

Miles walked toward the lone gatehouse in the bailey wall. There were times he wondered why anyone had bothered with even the one wall surrounding the keep. Speningethorpe was very assailable, a fact he didn't think on overmuch. Who would want the place?

"Open up, damn it!"

Miles stopped in the gatehouse tunnel, too surprised to do anything else but stare. There was some sort of creature pounding on his portcullis, babbling things in a rapid, obviously irritated manner.

The creature stopped its tirade and then hopped up and down.

"Oh, someone's home! Great. Can you open this gate? I lost my cat inside. At least I think it's my cat. He looks like Sir Sweetums, but I don't know how that can be." The being stopped speaking suddenly and looked at him.

Miles looked back. He took another step closer, holding out the torch.

"Am I in hell?" the creature asked, uncertainly.

Miles almost smiled. "Near to it, certainly."

"Really?" This was said with a gasp.

Miles took another step forward. The being before him was covered with muck. He frowned. Perhaps it was a demon come to torment him. The saints knew he deserved it. He'd committed enough sins in his youth to warrant a legion of demons haunting him for the rest of his days.

But did demons smell so foul? That was a point he wasn't sure on. He considered it as he gave the mud-covered harpy before him another look. It had to be a harpy. He'd heard of such creatures roaming about in Greece. They were part woman, part bird. This being certainly chirped like the latter. She spoke the peasant's tongue, poorly, and her accent was passing strange. Miles frowned. Had she truly come from Greece? Then how had she come to be standing outside his gates?

"Look, can't you at least open up? I'm freezing and I stink."

Miles considered. "Indeed, there is a most foul odor that attends you."

"I went for a swim in your moat."

"Ah," he said. "That explains much."

The harpy frowned at him. Miles took a step closer to her. She was a very plump harpy, indeed. Her arms were excessively puffy, as was her middle. She had scrawny legs, though. No doubt in keeping with her bird-like half. He stared at her legs thoughtfully. She wore very strange hose. Even stranger shoes. He leaned closer. Her foot coverings might have been white at one time. It was hard to tell their present color by torchlight, but he had little trouble identifying the stench.

"Hey," the being chirped at him, "would you just let me in?"

He hesitated. "Are you truly a harpy?"

The creature scowled at him. "Of course not. Who are you? The gatekeeper of hell?"

Miles laughed, in spite of himself. "You insult both me and my fine hall, and now I am to let you inside?"

The woman, who claimed not to be a harpy, looked at him with a frown. "Hall?"

"Speningethorpe," he clarified.

"And just where is that?" she demanded.

He shrugged. "It depends on the year, and who is king. 'Tis near Hadrian's wall. Some years it finds itself in England, some years in Scotland. A lovely place, really, if you've no use for creature comforts."

The woman swayed. "England? Scotland?"

"Aye," Miles said.

The woman sat down with a thump. "I'm dreaming."

Miles wrinkled his nose. "Nay, I think you aren't. I know I'm not."

The woman looked up at him. He thought she might be on the verge of tears. It was hard to tell with all that mud on her face.

"I'm having a very bad day," she whispered.

"Demoiselle, your wits are most definitely addled. 'Tis no longer daytime. 'Tis well past midnight."

She nodded numbly. "You're right."

Miles looked down at her and, despite his better judgment, felt a small stirring of pity. She was shivering. What she truly was, he couldn't tell, but she had come banging on his gates in the middle of the night seeking refuge. How could he refuse her?

He jammed the torch into a wall sconce, then turned back and looked at her.

"Are you alone?"

She nodded again, silently.

"No retainers lie in wait, ready to storm my keep and take it by force after I let you in?"

She looked up at him and blinked. "Retainers?"

"Men-at-arms."

"No. Just me and my stinky self."

Miles almost smiled. "Very well, then. The both of you may come in. I'll raise the gate just far enough for you to wriggle under, agreed?"

"Whatever you say."

Miles propped his sword up against the wall and trudged up the steps to the upper floor of the gatehouse. For all he knew, the woman could be lying. She could very possibly be a decoy some Lowland laird had sent to prepare the way for an assault.

He found himself cranking up the portcullis just the same.

"Are you inside?" he called down.

He heard a faint answer in the affirmative. He released the crank and the portcullis slammed home. Miles thumped down the circular steps. He realized as he retrieved his sword and the torch that he was relieved to find both still in their place. The years had taken their toll, he thought with a regretful sigh.

Well, at least the woman was still alone and not accompanied by two score of armed men. That wouldn't have done much for his mood. His guest was standing just inside the gate. She smiled at him, seemingly a little self-conscious.

"I'm sorry to barge in on you like this. I need a bath and then I'd like to look for my cat."

"Cat?" His nose began to twitch at the very thought of such a beast. He rubbed the possibly offended appendage almost without thought. "Cat, did you say?"

"You're allergic?" she asked.

"Allergic?"

She looked at him closely. "You know, you sneeze when you smell one?"

"Aye, that I do, demoiselle. If your beastie has wandered into my keep, I daresay we'll have no trouble locating him."

She laughed. Miles found himself smiling in response. Saints above, he was going daft. He'd just let a stranger inside his gates without demanding to know aught of her business save that she was seeking a missing feline. Her person did nothing to recommend her—especially since it was all he could do to breathe the same air she occupied. But her laugh was enchanting.

Without warning, Miles felt a surge of good humor well up in him. 'Twas true he could have remained at Artane and joined in the festivities eventually, but if he had, he wouldn't be standing at his gates with this woman. Beyond reason, he couldn't help but think he'd made the right choice.

He made her a small bow. "Miles of Artane, lately of Speningethorpe, your servant." He straightened and gave her his best lordly look. She didn't respond. He cleared his throat. Perhaps she merely needed something else to be impressed by. No sense in not making use of his connections. "My sire is Rhys de Piaget," he said. "Lord of Artane."

She looked at him blankly.

"You know him not?" Miles asked, surprised. His father's reputation stretched from Hadrian's wall to the Holy Land. And what reputation Rhys hadn't managed to spread, Miles' older brothers Robin and Nicholas had seen to. Surely this woman knew something of his family.

Her mouth worked, but nothing came out.

"Saints, lady, even the lairds in the Lowlands know of my sire."

She swallowed. "I think I'm really losing it here."

Miles frowned. "What have you lost?"

"My mind." She shook her head, as if that would somehow solve the problem. It must not have helped, because she gathered herself together and gave the whole of her a good, hard shake.

Miles hastily backed up to avoid wearing what she'd shaken off.

"Look," she said with a frown, "I'm confused. Now, am I in hell, or not? Telling me the truth is the least you can do."

"Nay, lady, you are not in hell," he said. "As I said before, you are at Speningethorpe. 'Tis in the north of England, on the Scottish border."

"And you're Miles of Ar-something, lately of this other Spending place, right?"

Close enough. "Aye."

She shook her head. "Impossible. I can't be in England. I was in Freezing Bluff, Michigan, half an hour ago. I fell into a pond." She was starting to wheeze. "I couldn't have resurfaced in England. Things like this just don't happen!" Her voice was growing increasingly frantic.

"Perhaps the chill has bewildered you," he offered.

"I'm not bewildered! I smell too bad to be bewildered!"

He had to agree, but he refrained from saying so.

"England! Geez! And backwoods England at that!"

"Backwoods?" he echoed.

"Backwoods," she repeated. She looked at him accusingly. "I bet you don't have running water, do you?"

Miles gestured apologetically toward the moat. "I fear the water runs nowhere. Hence the less than pleasing smell—"

"Or a phone?"

"Phone?" he echoed.

"Oh, great!" she exclaimed. "This is just *great!* No phone, no running water. I bet I'll have to haul my own water for a bath too, right?"

"Nay, lady. I will see to that for you." Let her think he was being polite. In reality, he didn't want her moving overmuch inside. She was sopping wet and he didn't want moat water being dripped all over his hall, sty that it was. Having the cesspit emptied into the moat had seemed a fine deterrent to attackers at the time, but he wondered about the wisdom of it now.

"Look," she said, planting her hands on her fluffy waist, "I appreciate the hospitality, such as it is, but what I really need from you is a bath, some hot chocolate and a bed, pretty much in that order. Sir Sweetums will have to wait until tomorrow. Things will look brighter in the morning."

She said the last as if she dared him to disagree with her.

So he nodded, as if he did agree with her.

"And then I'll figure out where the hell I am."

He nodded again. Whatever else she planned, she certainly needed a bath. Perhaps her wits would return with a bit of cleanliness.

"Garretts never have hysterics," she said sternly, wagging her finger at him.

"Ah," he said, wisely. "Good to know." The saints only knew what hysterics were, but he had the feeling he should be relieved the woman before him never had them.

"You are a Garrett?" he surmised.

"Abigail Moira Garrett."

"Abigail," he repeated.

"Right. But don't call me that. Only my grandmother called me that, and only when I was doing something I shouldn't have been. Call me Abby."

"I like Abigail better," he stated.

She gave him a dark look. "Well, we'll work on that later. Now, let's go get that bath, shall we?"

Miles watched her march off toward the stables. He smiled in spite of himself. The saints only knew from whence this creature had sprung, but that didn't trouble him. He'd seen many strange things in his travels. He liked her spirit. She made him smile with her bluster and babble.

"Miles?"

"Aye, Abigail?"

"I can't see where I'm going," she said, sounding as if that were entirely his doing.

"That shouldn't matter, as the direction you've chosen is the wrong one. The great hall is this way."

She appeared within the circle of his torchlight again. "Great hall? What's so great about it? Do you have central heat? What, no phone but a great furnace?"

Miles didn't even attempt to understand her. He inclined his head to his right. "This way, my lady. I'll see to a bath for you."

He led her to the hall, ushered her inside and rehung the torch. He set the bar back across the door. That was when he heard her begin to wheeze again.

"Garretts do not faint. Garretts do not faint."

"I'll be back for you when the tub is filled," he said, giving her his most reassuring smile. "Things will look better after a bath."

She nodded. "Garretts do not faint," she answered.

Miles laughed to himself as he crossed the hall to the entrance to the kitchens. If she continued to tell herself that, she just might believe it.

Chapter Three

Abby sat in a crude wooden washtub and contemplated life and its mysteries. It gave her a headache, but she contemplated just the same. Garretts didn't shy away from the difficult.

No phone, no electricity, and no Mini Mart down the street. Things were looking grim. She looked around her and the grimness increased. Had she stumbled upon a pocket of backwoodsiness so undiscovered that it resembled something from the Middle Ages? The fire in the hearth gave enough light to illuminate a kitchen containing stone floors, rough-hewn tables and crude black kettles. Not exactly *Better Homes and Gardens* worthy.

Abby stood up and rinsed off with water of questionable cleanliness. She wasn't sure she felt much better. Even the soap Miles had given her was gross. She decided right then that she was a low fat person, especially when it came to soap. At least she thought she'd just washed with a glob of animal fat. She filed that away with half a dozen other things she would digest later. On the brighter side, though, at least she didn't smell so much like a sewer anymore. She'd splurge on a fancy bar of soap when she got home.

She dried off with a completely inadequate piece of cloth, then looked at what Miles had given her to wear: coarse homespun tights and a coarse linen tunic. Not exactly off-the-rack garments, but they would do. She put the clothes on, *sans* her dripping wet underthings, and found, not surprisingly, that Miles' hand-me-downs were much too large. They might have fit if she'd kept her oversized down coat on under them, but there was no wearing that at present. She kept the tights hitched up with one hand while she dumped her clothes and coat into the washtub with the other. She'd let them soak for a while. She didn't want to wash her leather Keds, but she had no choice. She dunked them in the tub a few times with everything else.

"Hachoo!"

The sneeze echoed in the great hall. Abby dropped her shoes in the tub and ran for the doorway. She slipped and skidded her way out into the large gathering hall. Miles was standing by the wood piled high in the middle of the room, sneezing for all he was worth. He looked at her and scowled.

"Dab cat," he said, dragging his sleeve across his furiously tearing eyes.

"Where?" Abby said, looking around frantically. "Sir Sweetums! Here, kitty, kitty."

She saw a flash of something head toward the back of the hall.

"Damn cat," she exclaimed, taking a firm grip on her borrowed clothes and giving chase. "Come back here!"

"Abigail, wait!"

Oh, like Miles would be any help in catching the spirited feline. Abby scrambled up the tight, circular stairs, almost losing her balance and the bottom half of her clothes.

"Here, kitty, kitty—whoa!"

She would have fallen face first into nothingness if it hadn't been for that arm suddenly around her waist, pulling her back from the gaping hole that was the top of the stairs.

"We're missing some of the passageway and a good deal of roof," Miles said, panting. "By the saints, woman, you frightened me!"

His fingers investigated a bit more around her waist. Abby would have elbowed him, but her situation was too precarious.

"What happened to your middle?" he asked. "And your arms?" He frisked her expertly. "Saints, I thought you were excessively plump!"

"That was my down coat, you creep. Stop groping me!"

"Hrumph," he said. His fingers stilled, but he didn't

move. "Just what manner of woman are you, Abigail Garrett?"

"One on the verge of heart failure—if Garretts had heart failure, which we do not. Now, can we please go back downstairs? It's really drafty up here." She looked out into the shadows. "And I've lost Sir Sweetums again." She had the most ridiculous urge to sit down and cry. "Just when I thought I had him. But how can I have him? He's gone." An unbidden tear slipped down her cheek. "I'm losing it." She sighed heavily. "I'll be the first in my family to go that way, you know. Garretts never lose it. We die in flamboyant, reckless ways. We never go quietly. Except me. I'm such a familial failure."

"The only place you are going, Abigail, is to a chair before the fire. You'll catch the ague here in this night air."

"Don't call me Abigail."

He grunted. "Turn around and keep hold of my hand. These stairs are steep."

Abby followed him, because he had her hand in his and didn't seem to want to let go. She didn't want to go downstairs. She wanted to keep her eyes peeled for her cat, who should have been chasing butterflies in heaven. Instead, he was causing an allergic reaction to an inhabitant of hell.

"I'm tired," she said.

And with that, she pitched forward. She felt herself be caught and lifted.

"Saints, woman, but you are a mystery."

"I can't handle any more tonight," Abby whispered.

She felt herself lowered onto something relatively soft.

"Then take your rest, slight one. Things will look better in the morning."

Abby thought they just might, especially since the last thing she heard was a sneeze.

Abby woke, stretched, and shuddered. What a lousy night. And what an awful dream! Too many chocolate chips eaten straight from the bag. She'd have to coat them in cookie dough the next time around to diffuse the impact.

She rolled out of bed with her eyes closed, mentally halfway to the shower before her feet hit the floor.

"Oof!" the floor exclaimed.

Abby stumbled as the floor under her feet moved. She would have hit the ground if it hadn't been for those hands that came out of nowhere and caught her. How it happened she couldn't have said, but she soon found herself sprawled out over a long, impressively muscled form, staring down into dark eyes. She looked in them for several moments before she figured out their color. Gray. Dark gray. Like storm clouds.

So, it wasn't a dream. Miles of Spend-whatever held her up just far enough for her to get a good look at his face. She really felt as though she should be polite and get up, but she found she just couldn't.

The torchlight from last night just hadn't done justice to this guy. Maybe she'd been distracted at the time by the clamoring her sense of smell had set up. She must have smelled *very* badly. It was the only possible reason she could have done anything besides gape at the man she was currently using as a beanbag.

She propped her elbows up on his chest and took advantage of her vantage point. He was a stunner, even if he was a little bit on the unkempt side thanks to an abundance of shaggy dark hair and a stubble-covered chin. He was beautiful in a rough, mountain man kind of way. He probably lived off the land for months at a time. No fighting for mirror space with this guy, no sir. Abby felt her blood pressure increase at the thought. He probably limited his toilette to dragging his hands through his hair a few times each day and shaving when his face got too itchy. She had the feeling he didn't use hairspray or mousse—which meant her feet wouldn't stick to his bathroom floor. Oh, yes, this was her kind of man. Handsome *and* low-maintenance.

"Hmmm," she said.

"Hmmm," he replied.

He was giving her the same once-over. He reached up and fingered her hair. It was unruly hair, she knew, and she opened her mouth to make an excuse for the riot of auburn curls, when he met her gaze and smiled.

"You have beautiful hair, Abigail."

Okay, if he wanted to like it, he was welcome to.

"Indeed, you clean up very passably."

"What do you mean I clean up just passably?" she demanded. "I was giving you much higher marks than that."

He grinned. "Indeed."

Abby tried to hold onto her annoyance, but it didn't last long against the dimple that appeared in his cheek.

"Oh, you *are* cute," she said, feeling a little breathless.

"I take that to mean you find me tolerable to look at."

"Who, you? Of course not. I was just talking about your dimple. The rest of you isn't even passable."

He laughed. "Disrespectful wench. You've no idea who you're insulting."

"At least I gave you credit for one decent feature," she grumbled. She started to move off him, then got a good look at his floor. "Geez, Miles, what's the deal with your living room here? Are you planning on bringing barnyard animals inside anytime soon?"

He sighed. "I know the rushes need changing."

"Yeech," she said, climbing gingerly onto the bed. It was then she realized that she'd slept on a bed while he'd slept on a blanket on the floor. On the rotting hay, rather. She frowned at him. "Why didn't you just go sleep in another bed?"

"There is no other bed."

"Well," she said, slowly, "I appreciate the gallant gesture, but you wouldn't have had to make it if you didn't run such a lousy hotel. You know, inn," she clarified at his blank look.

He shook his head, with a small smile. "This is no inn, my lady."

"Spend-whatever. If that isn't a name for an inn, I don't know what is."

"Speningethorpe. 'Tis the name of my hall. I know 'tisn't much, but it gave me peace and quiet."

"Until last night."

He shrugged. "Perhaps too much peace and quiet isn't a good thing."

"All right," she said, crossing her legs underneath herself, "if you don't run an inn, what do you do? Is it just you here?" At that moment a surprisingly distressing thought occurred to her. "Are you married?" she demanded. She looked around. "Is there a wife hiding in here somewhere? This is all I need—"

A large hand came to rest over her mouth. Miles sat up, then took his hand away.

"Nay, no wife. Women do not like me."

"Really?" she asked, looking at him and finding that very hard to believe. "Good grief, is everyone blind here in backwoods England?" She clapped her own hand over her mouth when she realized what she'd said. "I meant—"

He was grinning. "I know what you meant, Abigail. And I thank you for the compliment. But even though I am a knight with land of my own, women don't care overmuch for my past accomplishments."

"And just what would those be?" Great. Out of all the places she could have resurfaced, she'd resurfaced in the moat of someone with questionable past accomplishments.

But at least he had accomplishments. And what was this business about being a knight? Maybe that was why he carried a sword. Abby looked at him thoughtfully. It couldn't hurt to reserve judgment until she found out more about him. She realized that she was already stacking him up against her Ideal Man list, but she could hardly help herself. After all, he had given her the only bed in his house. He was easily the most appealing man she had seen in years. He liked her hair. He had a great accent. He wasn't much of a housekeeper, but that could be fixed. The first thing to do was move the barn-like *accoutrements* outside—

"—burn me at the stake—"

"Huh?" she exclaimed, tuning back in. "Run that one by me again."

He looked at her with a frown. "Haven't you been listening?"

"No. I've been cataloging your good points. I don't think this is one of them."

He shook his head with a slow smile. "I was telling you that I'd just recently escaped being burned at the stake. For heresy."

"For *what?*"

"Heresy—which was a lie, of course. I had simply made the grave error of expressing my views on the Crusades," Miles said. "I was traveling through France this past fall, having just returned from the Holy Land, where I saw and heard tell of ruthless slaughter. To be sure, I could find nothing to recommend the whole Crusading affair. One night I sought shelter at an inn. I slipped well into my cups, but came back to myself a goodly while after I'd already disparaged my table companion, a man I soon learned was a former Crusader and a powerful French count."

"And what did he do to you? Threaten a lawsuit?" Trouble with the law, Abby noted. That could definitely be a mark in the negative column.

Miles smiled. "The law had nothing to do with it, my lady. He sent for his bishop, threw together an impromptu inquisition—of souls without any authority, I might add—and convicted me of both heresy and witchcraft."

"Witchcraft?" Abby eased herself back on the bed. There was no doubt about *that* being a red flag.

He snorted. "Aye, if you can stomach that. The count's witnesses—paid for handsomely, of course—claimed they had seen me conversing with my familiar."

"And that would be?"

"A fluffy black cat."

Abby laughed. "Oh, right. That would have been a pretty one-sided conversation, what with you sneezing your head off."

Miles smiled. "I laughed as well, at first. I sobered abruptly when I saw the wood piled high around the stake and one of the count's men standing there with a lit torch."

"Good grief," she said, "they really weren't going to do it, were they? What kind of backwater town were you in, anyway? Hadn't they ever heard of Amnesty International? Human rights activists would have been all over this."

"I daresay the count's men had heard of many things, yet they fully intended to do the man's bidding. They secured me to the post, but not without a goodly struggle on my part."

Abby was speechless. What was the world coming to? She made a mental note to avoid rural France as a travel destination.

"The count had taken the torch himself and was giving me a last fanatical spewing forth of religious prattle when a miracle occurred."

Abby found she was clutching the edge of the bed with both hands. "What?" she breathed. "A downpour?"

Miles laughed. " 'Twould have been fitting, to be sure. Nay, 'twas my grandsire, whom I had been traveling to meet. His men overcame the count's, he set me free and I fled like a kicked whelp, not even bothering to offer him a kiss of peace. Needless to say, my journeying in France was thereafter very short-lived."

"Did you tell the police about that guy? What a nutcase!"

"Police?" he echoed, stumbling over the word. "What is that?"

Abby frowned. "You know, the authorities."

"Ah," Miles said, nodding, "you mean Louis. Nay, I did not think it wise to chance a visit to court. My grandsire sent word a fortnight after I arrived home telling me that he'd seen the matter settled." Miles smiled pleasantly. "The crusty old goat has something of a reputation. I daresay he applied the sword liberally, as well as informing the king of what went on."

"Sword?" Well, Miles seemed to have one handy. Maybe his entire family had a thing about metal. "And what do you mean he informed the king?" she asked. "What king?"

"Louis. Louis IX, King of France."

"But France doesn't have a king," she pointed out.

"Aye, it does."

"No, it doesn't. It has a president."

"Nay, it has a king. Louis IX. A good king, as far as they go."

Abby scrambled to her feet, careful to keep them on blanket-covered floor. As an afterthought, she made a grab for her tights to keep them from falling to her knees.

"France does *not* have a king," she insisted.

Miles jumped to his feet just as quickly.

"How can you not know of King Louis?" he asked.

"What is he, some fringe guy trying to overthrow the government?"

"He's the bloody king of that whole realm!" Miles exclaimed. He looked at her as if she'd lost her mind. "Next you will tell me that you know nothing of Henry."

"Henry who?"

"Henry III, King of England!"

"No, no, no," she said, shaking her head. "Henry isn't king. There's little prince *Harry,* but he's just the spare heir. Elizabeth is queen. There's that whole Chuck and Di mess, but let's not even go into that."

"Elizabeth? Who is Elizabeth?"

He was starting to sound as exasperated as she felt.

"All right," she said, taking a deep breath. "Let's start from the beginning. And can we go sit by the fire? I'm cold."

"Gladly," Miles said. He shoved his feet into boots, then clomped over to the pile of logs in the middle of the room and built up the fire.

Abby tiptoed gingerly into the kitchen and put on her

Keds. They weren't as dry as they could have been, but it beat the heck out of wearing more of Miles' floor on the bottoms of her tights than she was already. She squished her way over to the fire to face her scowling host.

Miles folded his arms across his chest. "Let us see if we cannot untangle this snarl inside your head."

"My head?" she said. "I'm not the one who's confused."

"Aye, but you are!"

"I am not! France does *not* have a king, and neither does England. England has a queen and her name is Elizabeth!"

"It has a king and his name is *Henry!*"

Abby smirked. "I'd say let's turn on the TV and see what the local newscaster says, but I'll bet you don't have a TV either, do you?"

"Nay, I do not," he said, stiffly. "Nor would I have one."

"Ha," she said. "You don't even know what a TV is."

He scowled fiercely. "Aye, I do."

"Do not."

"How would you know what I do and do not know?"

"You don't have any electricity, bucko. It's a dead give-away."

He growled at her. "You are a most infuriating woman."

"Really?" she said, surprised. She smiled suddenly. "How nice. I've always wanted to be infuriating. It looks like the Garrett blood is really coming out. My grandmother would be so proud."

"I think I'd like to wring it all from you, for 'tis most—ha . . . ha . . . hachoo!"

Abby barely stepped aside in time to avoid the product of his violent sneeze. She grabbed his arm.

"Hush," she whispered, frantically. "Sir Sweetums has to be nearby."

Miles panted through his mouth. "Sir Sweetubs? What kind of a nabe is that for a bloody cat?"

"It's a term of endearment. Like this: sweetie pie, honey bunch, snookums." She tickled him under the chin for ef fect. "See?"

Miles scowled. "I see noth—ha . . . ha—"

Abby put her finger under his nose to plug it. "Don't even think about it, toots. We've got a kitty to find. Don't make any sudden moves."

She kept her finger under his nose as they turned slowly in a circle.

"See anything?" she whispered.

"Nay."

"Keep looking."

They turned another circle and Miles froze suddenly. "There," he said, softly.

Sir Sweetums was sitting next to the hall door.

"Perhaps he will cobe if you call to hib," Miles said, breathing through his mouth. He was obviously fighting his sneeze.

"Here, kitty, kitty," Abby said. She beckoned. "Come here, Sir Sweetums. Miles won't hurt you. He likes cats."

Miles muffled a sneeze in his sleeve.

"All right, his nose doesn't, but the rest of him does."

Abby took a step forward. Sir Sweetums got to his feet, gave her a meow she couldn't quite interpret, turned on his heel and, with his tail held high, walked through the door.

Through the closed door.

Miles staggered. He threw his arms around her and clutched her.

"Merciful St. Michael," he breathed. "I did not see what I just saw."

Abby would have felt the same way, but she had inside information. It was hard to swallow, but she had the feeling Sir Maximillian Sweetums was a ghost. She held onto her shaking host and wondered just how to break the news to him.

"Things of this nature do not happen," Miles said, his voice hushed. " 'Tis a modern age. I do not believe what I have just seen."

Abby looked up at him. "Honey, I think you're living in the past. Everyone else has indoor plumbing."

"How much more modern an age can it be?" he asked, returning her look, his eyes wide. "I don't care overmuch for his politics, but King Henry is a most forward-thinking monarch."

She rolled her eyes. "Oh, brother. Not that again."

"Aye, that again," he said, some of the color returning to his face. He released his deathgrip on her and stepped back a pace. "Saints, woman, where have you been?"

"Out to lunch," she returned, "obviously."

"Henry rules England," he insisted.

"No, he doesn't."

"By the very saints of heaven, you are a stubborn maid! Have you forgotten the bloody year? Who else would sit the throne in 1238?"

Abby blinked. "Huh?"

Miles clapped his free hand to his head. "That swim addled your wits, Abigail."

"What did you say before?" she managed. "What year?"

"1238. The Year of Our Lord 1238!"

Abby kept breathing. She knew that because she had to remind herself to do it. In, out, in, out. Twelve-thirty-*eight*, twelve-thirty-*eight*. She breathed in and out to that rhythm.

It couldn't be true. She looked around her at the stone room. There weren't any fireplaces; just Miles' bonfire in the middle of the room. No electricity, no central heat, no carpet. The walls were bare, leaving their stone selves fully open to perusal. No twentieth-century construction job there.

She looked down. There was stone beneath her feet, what she could feel of it beneath the layer of scum and hay. She looked around again. There were a pair of crude wooden tables near the walls, and chairs that looked rustically crafted. But that was the extent of the furniture. She took a deep breath. Well, the place certainly *smelled* like 1238.

She looked up at Miles. He stood in homespun clothing exactly like hers, wearing a very medieval frown. He didn't have the benefit of modern grooming aids, if his finger-combed hair and non-ironed tunic were any clue. He'd definitely been packing a sword the night before. He'd said he was a knight. Could that be true too?

Abby looked toward the door. Maybe if she stepped outside into the fresh air, she might have a different perspective on things.

She wanted to saunter across the great hall casually, but she had the feeling it had come out as more of a frantic get-me-the-hell-back-to-my-century kind of run.

She struggled with the heavy wooden beam that obviously served as a dead bolt in 1238. Heavy hands came to rest on her shoulders.

"Abigail—"

"Let me out!" she shrieked.

"Abigail—" he said, starting to sound a bit concerned.

Abby wasn't just a bit concerned. She was on the verge of having hysterics—and she was starting not to care just exactly what Garretts did and did not do.

"Please!" she begged.

Miles heaved the beam aside and opened the door, in spite of her attempts to help. She ran outside.

It was raining. She slogged straight into three inches of muck.

"Yuck!" she exclaimed.

She would have run anywhere just to be running, but she couldn't seem to get her feet unstuck from the goo.

"Abigail."

Before she could tell Miles just what had her so frantic, she found herself turned around bodily and gathered against a very firm, very warm body. Without giving his good or bad points any more thought, she threw her arms around him and clung.

"Oh, man," she said, feeling herself beginning to wheeze again. It was a nasty habit she'd gotten into lately. She was certain wheezing was something no respectable Garrett ever found herself doing. "Oh, man, oh, man," she wheezed again.

"By the saints, you're trembling," Miles said, sounding surprised. He stroked her back with his large hand. "There's nothing to fear, Abigail."

"It's 1238!" she exclaimed against his very rough, very un-department-store-like shirt.

"See?" Miles said, obviously trying to sound soothing. "You've remembered the year. 'Tis a most encouraging sign. I'm certain 'twas simply a bit of chill that seeped into your head and addled your wits for a time. Reason is most definitely returning to you."

Abby felt her tights beginning to slip and she made a grab for them before they migrated any further south. She tilted her head back and looked at Miles.

"It really is 1238, isn't it?" she whispered. "And you really are Miles of Spendingthorn—"

"Speningethorpe—"

"Whatever, and you really are a knight, aren't you?"

"For what it is worth, aye, I am."

Well, stranger things had happened. Like Sir Sweetums walking through a thick, wooden plank of a door.

Then there was her trip down into Murphy's Pond the night before to consider. That had taken an awfully long time, hadn't it?

But seven hundred years?

She rested her nose against Miles' chest and contemplated. Garretts didn't faint. Garretts didn't run away from difficulties. Garretts didn't lose their marbles.

Funny, she'd never heard anything about Garretts not time-traveling.

She looked up at Miles. "You don't believe in witches, do you?"

He smiled faintly. "Having come within scorching distance of a healthy bonfire myself, I would have to say nay, I do not believe in witches."

"Then I think you should sit down."

"Why?"

"Because you're going to fall down when I tell you what I have to tell you. It'll hurt less if you're closer to the ground."

Miles looked at her archly. "The de Piagets of Artane do not faint."

Abby reached up and patted him on his beautiful cheek. "There's a first time for everything, toots."

"Toots? Why do you persist in calling me that?"

Abby took his hand and pulled him back inside the hall. He'd just have to trust her on this one.

And she definitely hoped he'd meant what he'd said about the witch thing, or she was certain her revelations would land her in the fire.

Chapter Four

Miles frowned to himself as he allowed Abigail to pull him back inside his hall. Something had obviously troubled her deeply, if her frantic flight from his fire was any indication. But what? She had looked at him as if she were seeing a ghost.

He realized abruptly that he was allowing himself to be led and he dug in his heels. Abigail stopped and looked at him with that same, almost frantic look. Miles held his ground.

"Whatever you have to tell me, you may most certainly tell me while we are standing. Indeed, I insist upon it."

He looked down at her as he said it, and wondered if *she* shouldn't be the one sitting down. She was very pale. Saints, had she suffered some sort of injury that had damaged her mind so that she barely remembered the date?

He lifted his hands and cupped her face, rubbing his thumbs gently across her cheeks. Her skin was so soft and fair. Perhaps she was a nobleman's daughter who had become lost and wandered into his moat. Never mind how she was dressed. It was possible her sire employed seamstresses with very odd ideas on fashion. He should have questioned her sooner about her family, but he'd been too bemused by her actions the night before, then too unsettled by the appearance and disappearance of her cat today to think too deeply.

She caught his right hand and looked at it. "You have more calluses on this hand than the other."

"Of course," he said.

"Why?"

" 'Tis my swordarm, Abigail." He put his callused hand to her brow. She wasn't feverish. Indeed, she was chilled. "Perhaps we should repair to the fire," he said, pulling her

in that direction, "then you should tell me of yourself. Forgive me for not having asked sooner. Your sire will no
doubt be grieved over your loss. I will take you to him as
soon as may be—"

"Honey," she said, "I think you should sit."

"Why do you call me honey?" he asked, finding himself
being urged toward a chair. He sat to humor her.

"It's a term of endearment."

"Like Sir Sweetums?" he asked. "Saints, what a name!"

He would have expressed himself further on that, but
Abigail had pulled up a stool in front of him and sat. The
tunic he had given her to wear fell off one of her shoulders.
It was exceedingly distracting.

He looked at her face and instantly ceased to mark what
she said. He knew her lips were moving, but he couldn't
concentrate on her strangely-accented words. There were
surely a score of things that puzzled him about her, but he
couldn't seem to focus his thoughts on a bloody one of
them. All he could do was gaze at the woman before him
and marvel.

Saying she cleaned up passing well was an understate-
ment. Where she had come by that riotous mass of hair he
did not know, but it certainly suited her. He could almost
hear her saying it: "Garrett hair is never obedient." He
smiled at the thought. Indeed, Abigail's hair seemed to be a
reflection of the woman herself—beyond the bounds of reason or propriety.

And if her spirit hadn't intrigued him, her comeliness
certainly would have. He found himself entirely distracted
by thoughts of running hands and mouth over that bit of
shoulder she couldn't seem to keep covered up. He followed the curve of her shoulder out to her arm and down to
her hand. It was then he realized she was snapping her fingers at him.

"The lights are on but nobody's home," she was saying.

"Ah," he stalled, "I was thinking on your words."

She jerked up her tunic over her shoulder. *His* tunic—his

clothing that was covering her lithe body, much as he wanted to be doing. Miles was on the verge of allowing himself to be distracted by that thought when Abigail waved at him.

"Come on, Miles," she said, sounding exasperated. "Pay attention. I'm trying to tell you something very important."

He blinked at her. "Oh."

She sighed with exaggerated patience. "Are you with me now?"

"Indeed, we are sitting here together."

She dropped her face to her hands and laughed. Miles couldn't help himself. He reached out and ran his hand over her hair. It was pleasingly soft to the touch. It was not so dark as his, and with somewhat of a reddish tint to it. It was hair he wished he could sink his hands into as he sank another part of himself—

"Good grief!" Abigail exclaimed, jerking back upright. "Can't you just concentrate on what I'm saying for five minutes?"

"I'd rather concentrate on kissing you, if it's all the same to you," he offered.

"No," she said, firmly. "I'm serious about this."

And, suddenly, the truth struck him like a blow. He sat back and felt the blood leave his face. She was betrothed. How could he not have seen it before? Either that, or she was wed. She was no simpering maid who had to rely on her sire for every breath she took and every word to come out of her mouth. Abigail was far too sure of herself. She was likely of an age with his own score and four years, surely old enough to have been wed several years.

"Go ahead," he said, flatly. "Tell me of him."

"Who, Brett? How do you know about Brett?"

Damn. Knowing he had surmised correctly was no consolation.

"I assumed," he said curtly.

He should have stayed at Artane. What in hell's name had possessed him to come here? To hold Abigail Moira

Garrett in his arms and feel himself falling in love with her unruly hair and indomitable spirit? What had made him think she might even be free? What fool would let her go, once he had her?

And who had he been to think she might want him? Lord of his own hall though he might have been—but what a hall! The farmland surrounding his keep had lain fallow for years. The forests were likely thick with thieves. And it wasn't as if he could go to the continent to better his situation. There was most certainly no welcome for him in France, despite how generous Louis might be with his understanding. He had been accused of witchcraft. What would Abigail want with a husband of that ilk?

"—and when I lost my job, he broke up with me and took off. Next door, to be exact. To Bunny Ann Bartlett's apartment."

But, oh, to have had the chance to try to win her. He looked at her and, to his surprise, felt himself longing for the chance like he'd longed for nothing else in years, save his knight's spurs. To hear his name come from those lush lips with the same tones of love as she used when speaking of her husband—

"—a total putz. He kept bottles of hairspray and mousse at my apartment for emergency touch-ups. There were times I had to take a putty knife to the bathroom floor just to get the stuff up—"

To be the one she gazed at with longing, to be the one she welcomed to her bed each night—

"—of course, I think it's because I wouldn't sleep with him. Garretts don't do that until after marriage, you know. So, he left me. Bunny probably hit the sheets with him the minute he walked through her door."

Miles blinked. He realized he hadn't heard everything she'd said. And he'd understood even less.

"Bunny?" he asked.

"Brett's new girlfriend. They're getting married soon."

"Your husband is marrying someone else?"

Abigail looked at him as if he'd lost his mind. "Husband! Are you kidding? I never would have married that creep! I only got engaged to him because I was so miserable after Sir Sweetums met his unhappy kitty end. I knew Brett never really wanted to marry me. He was just using me for my ultra hold mousse."

Miles shook his head, feeling mightily confused. "Then you aren't wed?"

"Of course not!"

"Oh," he said.

Then he understood.

"Aaahh," he said, feeling himself start to smile. He couldn't help it. A feeling of relief started at his toes and worked its way upward until it settled on his mouth. "The saints be praised for that!"

Abigail leaned forward and felt his forehead. "You aren't feverish," she muttered.

"Indeed, I am most certainly not," he said, grasping her hand and hauling her onto his lap. He beamed at her. "And you are not wed."

"Boy, nothing gets by you, does it?"

He ignored her mocking tone in favor of contemplating his next action. "I believe I've heard enough," he announced. "I'm going to kiss you now."

She eluded his lips and managed to slip out of his arms and plant herself back on her stool. Miles frowned.

"Perhaps I was unclear—" he began, reaching for her again.

"Miles!"

"What?" he said, feeling his frown settle into a scowl.

"You can't kiss me. You haven't heard what I have to tell you."

"You aren't wed. What else could I possibly need to know?"

She clapped her hands on her knees, then rose with exaggerated care. "I am having a serious case of low blood sugar and you are *not* helping matters. I need something to eat. I don't suppose you have anything with chocolate in it, do you?"

"Chocolate?"

"Of course not," she groaned and walked off toward the kitchen. "It's too early in time for chocolate."

Miles followed after her grumbling self into his pitifully kept kitchen. He watched her rummage through the stores his father's men had unloaded onto one of the tables, and found himself wondering just what it was she had to tell him. Had she left her home without permission? There was her former fiancé to consider. The betrothal had been broken, obviously, but was that enough to have made her flee her home?

"Abigail," he said, "perhaps then you should tell me of your sire. I will no doubt need to get word to him that you are well." There, now he would have the entire tale.

She turned around with a loaf of bread in her hand. "You can't," she said, softly. "He's dead."

"Oh," Miles said, quietly. "Forgive me."

She smiled. "You couldn't have known."

Miles moved to stand next to her. He broke off a hunk of bread. "Did he die well?"

"He fell off the side of a mountain. My mother fell off trying to catch him."

"A glorious and astounding finish, as is right. I'm sorry, though, Abigail. You must miss them very much."

She shrugged and chewed slowly.

"No other family? Uncles? Aunts? Siblings?"

She swallowed and looked up at him. "They're a bit too far away to contact."

"Word can be sent."

She shook her head.

He frowned. "The world is not that large, Abigail, and I have seen a great deal of it. Now where is this place you come from—Frozen Muff?"

"Freezing Bluff. It's in Michigan."

That was surely no place he'd ever heard of, but he was loath to admit his ignorance.

"Scotland," he guessed.

"Not even close."

"Hmmm," he said, frowning. "Where exactly is Freezing Bluff, if not in the north?"

Abigail set her bread aside. She took Miles' bread away from him and put it on the table, too. Then she looked up at him slowly.

"*Where* isn't exactly the right question." She paused for a goodly while, then looked at him soberly. "*When* is, though."

He frowned. "What mean you by that?"

She clasped her hands behind her back. "I think you're right about Henry. He probably was king in 1238."

"I see you've finally come to your senses—what mean you was? He still *is.*"

"If you're living in 1238."

"Which I am." Saints, perhaps that swim *had* truly addled her wits.

"Which I wasn't—yesterday."

Miles shook his head. "I don't understand."

"Elizabeth is queen in my day."

"Your day?"

"1996."

"1996?" he whispered.

"The Year of Our Lord 1996," Abby said, slowly and distinctly. "Seven hundred years in the future."

Miles blinked. He looked at her head. No horns. He reached out and put his hands on her shoulders. She looked perfectly sane. She felt perfectly normal.

"1996," he repeated. The very numbers felt foreign on his tongue.

He looked at Abigail again. Was it possible? Could she have been living and breathing in another time one moment, then found herself alive in his time the next? Saints above, the thought left him with his head spinning.

Indeed, the entire room seemed to be spinning.

"Miles!"

He felt Abigail throw her arms around him. It didn't help. The stone of the kitchen floor came up to meet him. Abruptly.

"Oof," he managed, as Abigail landed on his stomach.

"I saved your head," she panted.

"My gratitude," Miles said, realizing that indeed her fingers were between his head and the unyielding floor. "Truly."

"I thought men from Artane didn't faint."

Miles could only manage a grunt. Words were beyond him. He was lying on his kitchen floor with a woman sprawled over him who supposedly lived in a time well past when the world should have ended. With great effort, he flopped his arms around her and held on. She felt like a true woman. She spoke a bit strangely, and used words he had to puzzle out, but now knowing her background, he could understand it. Background? Saints, her background was his foreground. Her past was his future. He groaned. He didn't spare much effort in doubting her. If he could believe he'd seen her cat walk *through* his hall door, he could believe this. But, by the saints, the very thought of it hurt his head.

And then the truth of the matter struck him with the force of a charging horse.

He couldn't keep her.

He groaned again, from deep within his soul. Merciful St. Christopher, he could not keep her! How could he, when she belonged in another time so completely foreign to his? She had a life there, a life that should be lived. How could he sentence her to a life at Speningethorpe? It wasn't even Artane, with its modern comforts, that he offered. His hall was no better than a stable. Surely she was used to luxuries he couldn't iamgine. How could he rob her of that?

He pushed her gently away and struggled to sit up.

"I'll find a way to send you back," he said, flatly. "Today."

"What?"

"Back home!" he snapped, looking at her with a glare. "I'll find a way to get you back to your home. Damnation, Abigail, I'll do it as soon as I've caught my breath."

"You'll send me back?" she asked.

Miles gritted his teeth. "Of course!" He lurched to his feet and grasped the table for support. "As bloody quick as I can!"

She was silent for several moments, long enough for him to catch his breath and regain his balance. His vision cleared just in time to see her expression of hurt change to one of anger. He hardly had time to unravel the mystery of that change when he was assaulted by a barrage of words.

"Oh, great!" she exclaimed, scrambling to her feet. "This is just great! You don't want me either!" She started to pace in front of him. "First it's my boss who gives me the old heave-ho, though I hated that job and his stupid cactus plants anyway. Then my landlord wants me out. Peter Pan takes a hike because I can't pay for his upkeep anymore. Hell's bells, not even the Social Security office wants anything to do with me! Just what's wrong with me, anyway?" She stopped, looked at him with another accusing glance, then poked him sharply in the chest. "You tell me that, Mr. I-just-barely-escaped-the-Inquisition knight from Spendingthorn."

"Speningethorpe."

"Whatever," she snarled.

"Ah . . . ," he began.

"Never mind," she said, her eyes blazing. "I don't want you either. Your house is a mess. You don't even have a job. I'm *not* going to work my fingers to the bone to feed and clothe another boyfriend. Forget it. I'm finding my cat," she said, sticking her nose up in the air, "and *going.*" She turned away from him smartly. "Sir Sweetums, get over here *right now!*"

Miles watched with open mouth as she stomped from his kitchen. And, much as he hated to admit it, he hadn't understood a thing she'd said. Except for the part about the Inquisition.

Oh, and that she thought he didn't want her.

Which had to mean, and he congratulated himself on the ability to deduce this, that she wanted *him*.

And while he was indulging in realizations, he realized that while she might have only come to want him recently, he'd wanted her from the moment he'd clapped eyes on her formerly fluffy self standing at his gates. Harpy or no, he had very much wanted to understand all there was to understand about Abigail Moira Garrett. He wanted it even more now. And if it meant keeping her in the glorious Year of Our Lord 1238, then so be it.

He stepped out into the great hall and watched as she hitched up her hose and stomped across the great hall, hollering for her bloody cat. What an enchanting woman. Hell, he didn't care if she was an enchant*ed* woman. He wanted her.

And Miles de Piaget always got what he wanted.

He would invite her to stay. Indeed, he would all but demand that she stay.

He strode forward. It took four long strides to catch up to her, another to position himself properly, and half another to sweep her squeaking self up into his arms. He looked down into her beautiful face and gave her his most lordly look. He knew it wasn't as convincing as his sire's, but since Abigail had nothing to compare it to, it would do.

"The future will just have to go on without you," he announced.

She blinked. "I beg your pardon."

"Petered pain is something you'll not have to bear again."

"Petered pain?"

"Aye," he said, firmly.

"Oh," she whispered. Then she smiled, a gentle smile. "You mean Peter Pan."

"Whatever," he said, with an imperious look. "And that so-shall sec . . . sec—"

"Social Security," she supplied.

"Aye, that. You'll have no need of it. Whatever it is," he added. "You will have me."

"I will?"

"Whether you like it or no."

"I see."

He grunted. "So you do."

He stalked back to the fire. Abigail's arms stole around his neck and it broke his heart. How could she think no one wanted her?

He set her down on her feet near the fire, put his hand under her chin, and lifted her face up.

"I assume this agrees with you," he stated.

She looked up at him solemnly. "I didn't think you were giving me any choice in the matter."

"I'm not. I intend to woo you fiercely. I am merely assuming the idea agrees with you."

A small smile touched her mouth. "I suppose the future isn't all it's cracked up to be."

"Especially when the glorious Year of Our Lord 1238 provides one with such exceeding luxuries," he said, indicating his pitiful hall with a grand sweep of his arm.

"Well . . . now that you mention it—"

He didn't wish to hear what she intended to mention, so, like the good soldier he was, he marched straight into the fray without hesitation. He lowered his head and covered her mouth with his.

She shivered.

And then she kissed him back.

Miles' senses reeled. He gathered Abigail close and wrapped his arms around her. He smiled to himself as he remembered his first sight of her and how plump a harpy she had seemed. She was definitely not fluffy now. He could work on that later. Visions of half a dozen little Abigail-like creatures scampering about his hall calling "here, kitty, kitty," sprang up in his mind. He lifted his head and blinked.

"Miles, I think—"

He captured her mouth again. Thinking was not something he wanted to do much more of for the moment. Later he would give thought to little dark-haired, gray-eyed waifs and their mother running roughshod over his hall and his heart. For now, he was far too lost in Abigail's arms.

Miles could hardly believe the events of the past several hours. He'd come to Speningethorpe a se'nnight before, determined to wither away to an intolerable, bitter old man. Without warning, Abigail had come splashing down into his moat and changed his life completely. Perhaps there was more to Sir Sweetums than met the eye.

Whatever the case, Miles knew he had made the right choice. Perhaps the sailing would be a bit rough at first, what with them both coming from different worlds. Already her cat had done damage to his nose. The saints only knew what wreckage Abigail would leave of his heart. But surely it would be worth the effort.

The smell of something burning finally caught his attention. And that warmth on his backside he had thought to be Abigail's hand had suddenly turned into something else entirely.

"Merde!" he shouted.

"Drop and roll!" Abigail said, shoving him. "Drop and roll, you idiot!"

He dropped and she rolled him. He soon found himself face down on the floor. There was a fine draft blowing over his backside.

"The fire got your tights too, I'm afraid," Abigail said. "What a shame. Your bum is looking kind of red—"

Miles whipped over so he was sitting, bare-arsed, on the floor. He felt furious color suffuse his cheeks. Abigail laughed.

"Oh, Miles," she said, shaking her head.

He grunted and scowled to save his pride. Abigail leaned forward and kissed him on the cheek.

"You're very cute."

Well, he knew that was a compliment. A pity he'd had to scorch his arse to wring one from her! To soothe his burned backside and assuage his bruised ego, he hauled her into his lap and looked at her purposefully.

"I will need to be appeased," he announced.

She put her arms around his neck. "And just how is that done in 1238?"

"I will show you."

"I had the feeling you would."

Miles kissed her. In time he forgot the pain of his toasted backside. He forgot that, by the saints, he was some seven hundred years older than the woman in his arms. He was almost distracted enough to bypass giving thought to what he would tell his father about her when he took her to Artane.

"Hey," Abigail said, looking at him with a frown, "keep your mind on the task at hand. Really, Miles. It can't be that taxing."

He threw back his head and laughed. Perhaps this was truly the gift he'd needed most for Christmas—a woman who had no reason to tread lightly near him. He looked at Abigail and smiled.

"My lady, you amaze me."

"Of course I do. What other twentieth-century girls have you met lately?"

He smiled and kissed her again. She was certainly the only one, the saints be praised. He doubted he would survive the wooing of another.

His nose began to twitch, but he stuck his finger under it and kept his mouth pressed tightly against Abigail's. With any luck that blasted cat would keep his distance until Abigail was properly wooed.

And if Miles ever caught up with Sir Sweetums, he would offer him a saucer of the finest cream in gratitude.

Chapter Five

Abby sat cross-legged on the table in the kitchen and watched Miles cut up vegetables for a stew.

"Do you know what you're doing?" she asked, doubtfully.

He looked up from under his eyebrows. "I cooked many a meal for myself in my travels. We will not starve."

"But how well will we eat?"

Miles very carefully set the knife down, crossed the two steps that separated her resting place from his working area of the table, and stopped in front of her.

"Oh, no you don't—"

She wasn't fast enough. She didn't even get a chance to give him her kissing-won't-solve-all-our-problems speech before a very warm, very firm mouth came down on hers. She shivered. It was a mouth minus its previous surrounding accompaniment of whiskers. Miles had shaved once he'd learned modern guys did it every day. Abby had vowed solemnly to herself not to overuse that keep-up-with-the-twentieth-century-Joneses strategy too often. But it was worth it for this. Kissing a bewhiskered Miles was great, but this was earth-shattering.

And he'd dispensed early on with that closed-mouthed kissing business. He was going straight for the jugular and didn't seem to care which way he got there, inside her mouth or out. Abby thought he might be wishing he could just crawl inside her and this was the best he could get for the moment. She hadn't given him her Garretts-don't-do-it-before-marriage speech, but they hadn't gotten that far yet. She sincerely hoped they got that far eventually.

Abby blinked when Miles lifted his head.

"Finished?" she croaked.

"Do you doubt my skill in the kitchens?"

She shook her head, wide-eyed.

He smiled in the most self-satisfied of ways and returned to his chopping. Abby rubbed her finger thoughtfully over her bottom lip. Maybe kissing *would* solve quite a few things.

Abby looked at Miles chopping diligently. Just how had she gotten so lucky? She had been rescued by a fantastic-looking man who got so distracted by kissing her that he set his own clothes on fire. He was stacking up oh-so-nicely against her Ideal Man list. It was almost enough to make her forget about going home.

Home. She turned the thought over in her mind. Modern conveniences waltzed before her mind's eye and she examined each in turn. Somehow they just didn't seem that appealing. Phones were noisy, fast food was unhealthy, and life in the corporate world spent basking under fluorescent lights gave her headaches. She'd always liked camping, which was a good thing, since Miles' castle was about on that same level of civilization.

And there probably wasn't any use in thinking about it. She had no guarantee that diving into Miles' moat would leave her resurfacing in Murphy's Pond.

On the other hand, what future did she have in the past? Miles certainly hadn't mentioned marriage. He was definitely shaping up to be someone she could share her life with, but was he free to choose his wife? Her knowledge of the marital practices of medieval nobility was scant, unfortunately. Even if he could choose, who was to say he'd want her?

"Where go you?"

Abby hadn't realized she had gotten off the table until Miles spoke.

"Just out," she said, moving toward the kitchen door. Maybe a little distance would soothe her smarting feelings. She was losing it. Why in the world did she think—

"You sound as if you need to be convinced to stay," he

stated, snagging her hand. "Come you back here, my lady, and let me see to it."

Abby let him pull her back, turn her around, and gather her into his arms.

"Abigail," he said softly, "what ails you?"

She put her arms around him and shook her head. "Nothing."

"Do you miss your home?"

"No."

He lifted her face up. Abby met his dark gray eyes and almost wanted to cry. Why be dumped here if she couldn't have him?

"Saints, but you Garretts are a stubborn lot," he said, smiling down at her. "You are resisting my wooing. You leave me with no choice but to pour more energies into it. Perhaps without the distractions of supper to prepare."

Well, wooing sounded good. Maybe it was best to just give things a few more days. After all, she might find out she really didn't like him very much.

He released her, dumped the rest of his vegetables into the pot, hung it over the fire, then turned back to her with a purposeful gleam in his eye.

"Is that all that needs to go in there?" she asked.

He shrugged and advanced.

"What if it tastes lousy?"

"You'll never notice."

"Why not?"

"Because you'll be too distracted by my surliness if you do not give me your complete attention."

"One of these days, Miles de Piaget, kissing me into submission isn't going to wor—"

But, oh, it was working at present. With her last coherent thought, Abby knew the day she decided she didn't like him would be the day they'd need snow tires in hell.

*   *   *

An hour later, Abby held up a dollar bill to the firelight. "This is George Washington. He was the first president of the United States."

"No king?"

"Nope. That's why we said 'no thank you' to England in the 1700s. We're all for life, liberty and the pursuit of happiness without a monarchy to tell us how to go about it."

Miles looked with interest at her wallet that sat between them on the blanket near the fire. Abby had appropriated his sleeping blanket as a carpet. The chair was too uncomfortable for sitting, and the floor too disgusting for intimate contact.

"What else have you in that small purse?" he asked.

"Not as many things as I would like," Abby said with a sigh.

She had her little wallet on a string, her gloves, and her keys. Her sunglasses had been stuffed inside her coat. The only other things she'd had in her pocket were a plastic bag of gourmet jelly beans and some soggy lint. But he'd been fascinated by it all. She'd been fairly certain he'd believed her when he'd hit the floor in the kitchen, but there was nothing like a bit of substantial evidence to slam the door on doubt.

He'd examined her jeans closely, seemingly very impressed by the pockets and copper rivets. Her down coat was still dripping wet, but she had the feeling they'd be fighting over that once it was dry. Her underwear and bra she'd finally had to rip out of his hands. It was then she'd given him her Garretts-don't-do-it-before-marriage speech. She'd expected protests. Instead, she'd gotten a puzzled look.

"Of course you don't," had been his only comment.

So, now they were sitting in front of his bonfire, examining the contents of her wallet and munching on Jelly Bellies.

"Aaack," Miles said, chewing gingerly. "What sort is this one?"

She leaned forward and smelled. "Buttered popcorn, I think."

"Nasty." He swallowed with a gulp. "Is there this chocolate you spoke of?" he asked, poking around in the bag hopefully.

"I wish," she said with feeling. She'd had one lemon jelly bean and given the rest to Miles. Unless sugar found itself mixed in with a generous amount of cocoa, she wasn't all that interested. Now, if it had been a bag of M&M's she'd been packing, Miles would have been limited to a small taste and lots of sniffs. "Chocolate doesn't even get to England until the seventeenth century. Trust me. *This* is history I know about."

"Where does it come from?"

"They grow it in Africa."

"Oh," he said, sounding almost as regretful as she felt. "A bit of a journey."

"You didn't see any on your travels?"

He shook his head. "Not that I remember."

Abby leaned back against the chair legs. "What made you decide to go to Jerusalem?"

"I wanted to see the places my father had been in his youth, I suppose. My father had gone on the Lionheart's crusade, first as page, then squire to a Norman lord. My brothers followed in his footsteps to the Holy Land, even though there was no glorious war for them to wage." He smiled faintly. "I think I simply had a young man's desire to see the world and discover its mysteries. Instead, I saw cities ravaged by war, women without husbands, children without fathers." He shrugged. "I don't think fighting over relics was the message the Christ left behind Him. Perhaps I found it even more ironic because I overlooked the city of Jerusalem on Christmas day."

"I take it that count you insulted didn't feel the same way about it?"

Miles smiled. "Indeed, he did not. And I am not shy

about expressing my opinions, whether I am in my cups or not."

"Was your grandfather upset with you?"

"Nay. You see, of all his grandsons, he says I remind him overmuch of himself." He smiled modestly, then continued. "My eldest brother, Robin, would rather grumble and curse under his breath. Nicholas is a peacemaker and rarely says aught to offend. My younger brothers are giddy maids, talking of nothing but whatever ladyloves they are currently wooing." He smiled again. "I, on the other hand, am surly and moody and generally make certain others know that."

"Oh, boy, surly *and* moody," she said, with delight. "And to think I could have landed in the moat of someone who was merely agreeable and deferring."

"And how dull you would have found him to be," he said with a grin. "My grandsire shares my temperament. I am his favorite, of course."

"Of course," she agreed, dryly. "You were just lucky he happened by when he did."

"It is perhaps more than luck. I learned later one of his servants had been passing by and heard me telling the count rather loudly that he was a mindless twit."

"Oh, Miles," she laughed. "You'd make a terrible diplomat."

"Aye," he agreed. " 'Tis fortunate I'll never pursue that calling."

"Then what is it you intend to pursue?" She knew it was a loaded question, but she couldn't stop herself from asking it.

His smile deepened. "I intend to pursue you, of course."

"Really?" she squeaked. She cleared her throat and tried again in a more dignified tone. "Really," she said, hoping it sounded casual.

He nodded. "Aye. But how is a twentieth-century girl wooed? Gifts?"

"Well, it is almost Christmas."

He frowned. "And you plan on making me participate in the festivities?"

"If I can do it, so can you." She had her own reasons for finding Christmas difficult, but she managed each year. Miles could, too. "We could spruce up the place a little."

"Aye," he agreed, sounding reluctant.

"Come on, grumpy. It'll be fun."

"Fun?" he echoed doubtfully.

"As in enjoyable, entertaining. We'll do some cleaning and sprucing and you'll feel much better about the season. Trust me. And while we're cleaning, I'll tell you the story of Ebeneezer Scrooge." She laughed. "Talk about the Ghost of Christmas Past! Boy, this puts a whole new spin on that one."

Miles only blinked at her.

"We may have to forgo the gifts," she continued. "I would have put those Jelly Bellies in your stocking, but you ate them all."

Miles burped discreetly. "And they were delicious. Is that how 'tis done in your day? Sprucing and giving?"

"Pretty much."

He reached over, put his hand behind her head and pulled her toward him. "You are the best gift I could have asked for," he murmured against her lips. "I need nothing else."

Abby closed her eyes as he kissed her. Was it possible to fall in love with someone so soon?

It was much later that she managed to catch her breath enough to ask if he thought the stew was finished.

"Do you care?" he asked, with a twinkle in his eye. "My appetite is running more toward more of your mouth. I can guarantee it is more tasty than what boils in yon pot."

"Who needs food?" Abby managed.

And that was the last thing she said for a very long time.

Chapter Six

Miles struggled to fashion the soft straw into a bow. "Will this do?" he asked, holding it up.

"Well, it isn't raffia, but we'll survive."

Miles handed her the bow, then leaned his elbows on the table and watched her rummaging through his stores for other appropriately Christmassy items, as she called them.

He'd slept poorly the night before. He'd been tempted to blame it on his stew. It had been, in a word, inedible. More than likely it had been sleeping so close to Abigail and not touching her. Garretts didn't do that sort of thing before marriage—not that he'd expected anything else. He wouldn't take her until he'd wed her. The thought of it sent a thrill of something through him; he wasn't sure if it was excitement or terror. He'd always known he would take a wife sooner or later. It had certainly suited his brothers well enough, though the wooing of their ladies had been tumultuous.

Miles stole a look at Abigail and wondered if the courting of her would take such a toll on him. He didn't think so. She looked fairly serene as she sifted through his things. Perhaps she would accept him well enough as time went on.

He watched her and couldn't help but smile. It seemed a better thing to do than shake his head, which was what he had been doing since she'd started telling him future things the eve before. Airplanes, cars, trains, microwaves; the list was endless. It would take him a lifetime to draw from her all the things she took for granted, things he hadn't even imagined, well-traveled though he might have been.

"Abigail, what sort of work did you do in your day?" he asked.

"I was a secretary for an insurance salesman," she said, frowning at a bow. She flashed him a brief smile. "People paid this man a certain amount of money each month just in case they died or their house went up in flames. If that happened, then he would replace the house or pay the family money to compensate for the deceased. I wrote out all his correspondence and things on a machine called a computer. And I watered his plants. I hated it."

"What would you rather have been doing?"

"Anything but that." She fingered a fig. "I always wanted to be a gardener. I love to watch things grow. A family would have been nice, too."

"I see," he said. No wonder she had found Brett so lacking. The man obviously didn't share her sentiments about marriage. But why was she so concerned with sprucing and giving? Was that all part of it?

"Why is this Christmassy fuss so important to you?" he asked.

He might not have noticed her hesitation if he hadn't been watching her so closely. But he noticed it, and he certainly noticed the false smile she put on for his benefit.

"'Tis the season, ho, ho, ho, and all that," she said, brightly.

"Hmmm," Miles said, thoughtfully. She was lying, obviously. He looked at her sad little pile of straw bows, then back up at her.

"How did you celebrate in your time?"

"Oh, there's a lot to it. You have to decorate the house with a tree and ornaments and greenery. All the family gets together and there's lots of food and laughter." She gave another piece of straw a hard yank. "It's the family togetherness thing."

Miles reached out and put his hand over hers. "Abigail, I want to know how *you* celebrated."

She looked away. "I went to my grandmother's. Until she and my granddad died."

"Then it must have been quite festive. Tell me of your siblings. What a clan you must have been with a houseful of Garretts."

"Oh, it was a houseful, all right," she said. "I don't have any brothers or sisters, but I have lots of cousins and aunts and uncles. They would all show up with gifts and things."

"And what of your parents?"

Abby shrugged. "They usually took me there and left me. They never stayed." She smiled at him briefly. "They always had other things to do."

Miles' chest tightened. He tried to pull her into his arms, but she wouldn't come.

"I was something of a surprise," she said, walking over to the kitchen hearth. "They had me after they'd been married almost twenty years. They had never wanted children and it was too inconvenient to fit me into their lifestyle, I guess."

"Oh, Abigail," Miles said softly.

"Don't," she said, holding up her hand. "I didn't tell you so you could feel sorry for me. I've had a great life. My grandparents were wonderful. I didn't need my mom and dad to make my life any better than it was."

He digested that for a few minutes. This obviously went deeper than that.

"So these Christmassy items remind you of your grandparents?"

She shrugged. "I suppose. Or maybe I just want what they had."

Miles understood. His father worshipped his mother and she him. They had their disagreements, surely, but there had never been a time that Miles had doubted their love for each other. Not that every household in England ran thusly. Most marriages were made to form alliances and were likely devoid of love. Miles knew his parents were something of an exception. Abigail obviously wanted such an exceptional marriage. Miles smiled to himself. And him right there to give it to her. Life was indeed miraculous.

"I want the whole enchilada," she was saying. "I want a husband who loves me. I want children. I want real Christmases with lights and a tree and my own family there around me. I want a fireplace."

Miles considered the last. 'Twas obvious improvements would have to be made to the hall.

"And while we're talking about marriage, let me be perfectly clear on this. I want a husband who will stick by me when things get rough, who won't bail at the first sign of trouble." She shot him a challenging look.

"Bail?"

"Leave. Run away."

"Ah, I see."

"So you do."

She had planted her hands on her waist again. Miles had the feeling she was gearing up for battle. He was beginning to suspect he might be the enemy.

"Then you don't want a man who would run off when things became difficult," he offered, wanting to make sure he understood.

"That's right, bucko."

"Anything else?"

She held up her hand and began using her fingers to tick off her items of importance.

"He can't dress better than I do, he can't smell better than I do, and he has to have a job."

"A job?"

"An occupation. He can't just sit around the house watching TV all day and expect me to pay all the bills."

Miles clasped his hands behind his back. "And?"

She was silent for a moment. "He has to love me," she said, quietly.

Well, that was done easily enough. Miles suspected he'd fallen in love with her the first time she'd begun to wheeze.

The occupation item was a problem. Miles leaned back against the worktable and stared thoughtfully at the ceiling. He could build Speningethorpe up and turn it into a profitable estate, but would that be enough for Abigail? 'Twas certain he would have to do something with his hands so as not to appear idle. Perhaps he would send for his hounds. He'd bred them in his youth, as he'd managed to keep himself home until he was almost two-and-ten. Aye, there was always a market for a finely-trained hound.

And if hounds weren't substantial enough, he would look to horses. His mother had a fine eye for horseflesh. When he took Abigail to Artane, he would seek his mother's opinion on the matter.

Miles considered Abigail's other items. It was certain he wasn't dressed better than she; he was wearing his oldest pair of hose. They were worn through at the knee, but better bare knees than a bare arse, to his mind. He was quite certain she smelled far better than he did. She certainly would once he took to cleaning out the kennels.

All in all, he thought he just might suit.

He flashed her a brief smile and started toward the great hall. There was no time like the present to see the future accounted for. It was just barely midday. If he rode hard, he could be to Seakirk Abbey and back by dawn. The abbot would likely be there for the Christmas celebrations. Miles had no qualms about using whatever tactics were necessary to see the man on a horse heading north with him. No doubt his own reputation as a convicted heretic would serve him. His elder brothers had already spread the tale from one end of the isle to the other, embellishing it with each retelling. Miles had been livid at first, especially since they had found it to be such a fine jest. Now, he thought the blot on his past just might serve him well.

"Where are you going?"

The desperate tone of Abigail's voice made him pause. He looked at her as he threw his cloak around his shoulders and pulled on his gloves.

"I've things to see to."

Her jaw went slack. "Just like that?"

"Abigail, I've a task to see to—"

"I bare my soul to you," she said, sounding irritated, "and all you can do is walk away?"

"Abigail—"

"Great!" she exclaimed. "This is just *great!*"

He paused and considered. If he told her what he was about, heaven only knew what she would say. She might say she thought he should take a swim in his moat. Worse yet, she might leave.

He couldn't bring himself to think about that. Only last night he had begun to realize just what he would be asking her to give up to remain with him.

He couldn't bear the thought of having her say him nay.

Aye, 'twas best he had the priest handy when he informed her of his intentions. Garretts never did things by halves, and neither did de Piagets.

"There's wood enough for the fire," he said, "so you shouldn't freeze—"

"It's about the sex thing, isn't it," she demanded.

"Well, aye," he said, with a nod, "that's part of it, surely." He certainly wouldn't take her 'til he'd wed her and the sooner he'd wed her, the happier he would be.

"Ooohh," she said, grinding her teeth. She picked up a piece of wood and heaved it at him. "You're such a jerk!"

Miles ducked, his eyes wide. "Abigail—"

"Go," she shouted, pointing to the door. "Just leave if you're going!"

Miles thought it best to do just that, while he was still in one piece. And when Abigail reached for another heavy stick of wood, he did the most sensible thing he could think of.

He bolted for the door.

He'd barely pulled the hall door to when he heard the thump of wood striking it on the other side. So he'd left his dignity behind. He would smile as he told his children how difficult it had been to woo their mother. It would make a fine tale.

He was halfway to the stables before he realized in how precarious a situation he was leaving his lady. He couldn't allow her to remain in a keep with an unbarred door and no men to protect her.

He turned back to the hall and pushed on the door. There was no budging it. Abigail had obviously made use of the crossbeam. Well, perhaps that would do. He would make as much haste as possible. The sooner he was home, priest in tow, the better he would like it.

Assuming, however, he didn't have to break down his own door to get to his bride.

He smiled as he strode to the stables. What a fine life it promised to be!

Chapter Seven

Abby threw another log onto the fire, then dragged her hand across her eyes.

"What a jerk," she said, with a snuffle against her sleeve. "He's no better than the rest of them."

She could hardly believe Miles had just walked out, leaving her behind to ponder the reasons for his hotfooted departure. Maybe her soul-baring had scared him. Abby scowled. Coward. And he'd flat-out admitted that part of it was the sex thing. And after how readily he'd accepted it before, as if he would have been surprised at anything else! She scowled again. For all she knew, he'd just been toying with her.

Abby moved closer to the fire, with a muttered curse. It had been a very bad day. After Miles had left around noon, she'd spent the afternoon pacing and raging. Then she'd cried. When she'd tired of that, she had retreated to Miles's chair. She'd been sitting there since dusk, cursing both his inadequate bonfire and the day she'd landed in his moat. After slandering his hall and his person to her satisfaction, she'd simply sat and pondered life and its mysteries, shaking her head. Her grandmother had always shaken her head a lot. Abby was beginning to understand why.

Miles' actions baffled her. She had been prepared for him to lose it when she'd told him where and when she'd come from. But when she had told him her tiny little dream of home and hearth to call her own, not only had he not given her dream the proper respect and attention it deserved, he'd walked out on her. And on Christmas Eve, of all times! Tonight was the night to have people around her who cared for her. All she had was an empty castle. She had no Christmas tree, no twinkling lights, and no presents.

Hell's bells, she didn't even have any fruitcake to worry about disposing of!

But that wasn't the worst of it. Much as she didn't want to admit it, what she didn't have was what she wanted the most.

Miles.

She'd always wondered if there were such a thing as meeting a person and knowing immediately he was the Right One. She'd never experienced it before. She was very familiar with attraction to the Wrong One. She would meet a man, think he was handsome, then ten minutes later start making excuses for his glaring flaws. But no amount of fiddling had ever turned any of those men into the Right One.

With Miles, it had been completely different. One minute she'd been chewing him out for not having indoor plumbing, the next she'd been comparing him to her Ideal Man requirements and finding nothing lacking. Until today. Running out on her was a big check mark on the Red Flag side of the list. If he didn't love her enough to stay, he just wouldn't do.

Besides, what did she want with primitive old medieval England anyway? No running water, no phone, and no History Channel on cable. Hell, she was *living* the History Channel.

She needed modern comforts. Hot showers. Soap that came pre-wrapped and contained moisturizers with long, scientific names. Craft stores, where she could buy makings for Christmas decorations. Good grief, even simple things like flipping a switch for lights, indoor plumbing, central heat . . . the Mini Mart!

Well, time was awastin'. She jumped to her feet purposefully and headed toward the door. She'd just go home. There wasn't anything there for her either, but at least she'd be miserable in comfort. It was definitely a step up from being miserable in a drafty old castle that was ratty even by medieval standards!

She put her shoulder under the crossbeam and gave it a

shove over to her left. It took several tries, but finally she managed to slide it far enough to one side that all it took was a good push upward to tip it out of the remaining bracket. She took hold of the iron door ring and started to pull.

"Meow."

Abby paused, then shook her head. "That's not going to work this time. I'm late for my date with the moat."

"I say, old girl, *meow!*"

Abby whirled around, fully expecting to see someone behind her.

She was alone.

This was way too spooky. She took a few hesitant steps out into the middle of the room, searching the shadows. Then she squeaked in surprise.

Sir Sweetums sat on the bottom step of Miles' circular stairway. He swished his tail impatiently, then turned and disappeared upward into the shadows.

"I'm going to regret this," Abby muttered under her breath.

She crossed the room, then climbed up the circular stairs. She waited until her eyes had adjusted fully. The moon was full, which helped. But one of these days Miles was really going to have to do something about a roof over this part of his castle—

"Really, my dear, you are the most stubborn of women."

Abby shrieked and jumped back. All she succeeded in doing was smacking herself smartly against the stone of the stairwell.

"Who's there?" she said, her voice warbling like a bird's.

" 'Tis I," a cultured voice said from the darkness. "Your beloved Sir Sweetums."

Against her better judgment, Abby strained to see into the shadowy hallway across from her. What she really needed to be doing was getting up and looking for a weapon, not peering into the shadows to catch a glimpse of a ghostly cat who seemed to be having delusions of conversation. Maybe that big cleaver in the kitchen would be protection enough.

And then, before she could gather her limbs together and move, Sir Sweetums himself appeared across the gaping hole that separated the stairwell from what should have been, and likely would be again, a hallway leading to bedrooms.

Abby sank down onto a step and gaped at him in amazement. "Sir Sweetums?" she managed.

"But of course," he said, giving his paw a delicate lick and skimming said paw alongside his nose. He finished with his ablutions and looked at her. "Who else?"

"Ooooh," Abby said, clutching the rock on either side of her. "I've really lost it this time. Garretts aren't supposed to hallucinate!"

"No hallucination, dearest Abigail," Sir Sweetums said, placidly. "Just me, come to bring you to your senses. I've been trying for years, since the moment you lost your wits over that pimply-faced chap named Mad Dog McGee when you were twelve."

Garretts never whimpered. Abby thought moaning might not be a blot against her, so she did it thoroughly.

"No vapors, I beg of you!" Sir Sweetums exclaimed, holding up his paw.

"You're talking," Abby said, hoarsely. She shook her head. "I'm talking to a cat. I can't believe this."

"We've talked before," Sir Sweetums pointed out. "I have many fond memories of conversing whilst I stalked the butterfly bush and you puttered amongst the hollyhocks—"

"That was different. You were using words like 'meow' and 'prrrr.' You weren't going on about me puttering amongst my hollyhocks." Abby glared at him. "This is unnatural!"

" 'Tis the season for giving, my dear, and this is the gift given to animals each year from midnight on the eve of the Christ Child's birth to sunrise the next morning."

"But you aren't alive," Abby whispered. "I know you aren't."

"Ah," Sir Sweetums agreed, with a nod, "there's the heart of it. I wished I could have come to you and told you, but once a feline enters the Guardian's association, he cannot go back. Unless he has further work to do." Sir Sweetums cocked his head to one side. "And to be sure, I had further work to do with you, my girl!"

Abby leaned back against the stone and shivered once. When it had passed, she took a deep breath and let it out again.

"All right," she said. "I can handle this." She laughed, in spite of herself. "I'm living in 1238. If I can believe that, I can believe I'm talking to you." She looked at her very beloved Sir Sweetums and felt her eyes begin to water. "I missed you so much."

Sir Sweetums coughed, a little uncomfortably it seemed to her. "Of course, my dear."

"Did you miss me?"

"Of course, my dear," he said, gently. "Out of the mortals I had charge of during my nine lives, you were my favorite. Didn't you know?"

Abby smiled through her tears. "No, I didn't know. But thanks for telling me."

Sir Sweetums smiled, as only a cat can smile. "My pleasure. Now, on to the reason I am here. You really must get hold of yourself in regards to The Miles. He is a perfectly acceptable human. Indeed, I would have to say he is the best of the matches you could have made."

"He's a total jerk," she grumbled.

"Strong-willed," Sir Sweetums countered. "Sure of himself and unafraid to speak his mind."

"He may speak, but he doesn't listen. I told him my most precious dream yesterday morning and he didn't even acknowledge it!"

"Maybe he was giving thought to your words."

"Hrumph," she said, unappeased. "If that's true, why did he leave?"

"When he returns, you'll ask."

"I'm not going to be here when he gets back."

"Tsk, tsk," Sir Sweetums said. "My dearest Abigail, you don't think I brought you all the way here just to have you leave, do you?"

"You?" she screeched. *"You're* the one responsible for this?"

"Who else?" he said, with a modest little smile.

"Why?" she exclaimed. "Why in the world did you drag me all the way here?"

"Because this is where you need to be," he said, simply.

"Right. Without chocolate, my superfirm mattress, and running water. Thanks a lot."

Sir Sweetums shook his head patiently. "Really, my dear. Those are things you can live without."

"No, I can't. I'm going home."

"Conveniences there may be in the future, dear girl, but who awaits there to share those conveniences with you?"

Well, he had a point there. Abby scowled and remained silent. She was not going to let a cat, no matter how much she loved him, talk her into remaining in miserable old medieval England.

"Abigail," Sir Sweetums said gently, "Miles is a dashedly fine chap."

"He's a convicted heretic!"

"Abigail," Sir Sweetums chided, "you know the truth of that."

"Well, then . . . he's always trying to kiss me into submission," she finished, triumphantly. "It's barbaric."

"Consider his upbringing, my dear! The man is a knight. He is used to taking what he wants, when he wants it."

"And what if I don't want to be taken?" she said, feeling peevish. Peevish was good. It beat the heck out of feeling hurt.

"Then tell him so. But I rather suspect you would find you like it."

"I'm surrounded by chauvinists," she muttered—peevishly.

Sir Sweetums looked unruffled. "Think on the alternatives you've had in the past, my dear. What of Brett? Would he have fought for you? Exerted himself to do anything but help you spend your funds and deplete your pantry?"

"No," she admitted reluctantly.

"And what of those other insufferable fops you managed to find yourself keeping company with? Anyone there who had the spine to care for you?"

"Lord over me, you mean."

Sir Sweetums conceded the point with a graceful nod. "As The Miles does. Perfectly acceptable behavior for a medieval knight. A most modern medieval knight, if I were to venture an opinion. He's quite liberal-minded in his thinking, my dear. I've no doubt that you two will see eye to eye in the end."

"He has a big check mark in the Red Flag column," she insisted. "Running out is the kiss of death with me."

"Perhaps he had affairs to see to."

"It would have been nice to have been told, you know. How are we supposed to work things out, not that I'm sure I want to, when he isn't even around?"

"You've waited all this time for him, my dear. What are a few more hours in the grander scheme of things?"

Abby looked at her most beloved of cats and, in spite of herself, found she had to agree with him. Maybe Miles had left for a reason. A good reason.

"It'd better be a *damn* good reason," she muttered. "And he'd better come rolling back in here before long, or I'll give my second thoughts a second thought!"

A throat cleared itself from immediately behind her. "Actually, my lady, there was very little rolling involved. I walked in quite well on my own two feet."

Abby whipped around to look at Miles, who was standing at the crook of the stairs. He climbed up another step or two. He smiled at her, then his gaze drifted across the gap to Sir Sweetums.

Miles sneezed.

"Likewise, I'm sure," Sir Sweetums said, with a swish of his tail.

Abby couldn't decide who to watch. Miles looked like he was going to faint again—she knew that look. She put out her hand to steady him.

"That's Sir Sweetums," she supplied.

"So I gathered."

"He's talking. But only until sunrise."

"How positively lovely," Miles managed.

Sir Sweetums grimaced. "Ye gads, boy, get on with this, won't you? 'Tis almost dawn. I'd like to see The Abigail comfortably settled before the night is out."

"Maybe I don't want to be comfortably settled," Abby interjected.

"Sir Miles?" Sir Sweetums prompted.

Miles came up another step and knelt. Abby stiffened her spine and reminded herself of all the reasons she had to be angry with him.

"Abby?" he said, quietly.

Oh, great. *Now* he decided to call her Abby. She scowled at him.

"This isn't going to work."

He looked at her solemnly. "Just what about me doesn't suit? My visage? 'Tis too ugly to be gazed at for the rest of your life?" He flexed an arm for her benefit. "Too scrawny? Too frail? Here, come sniff me."

She leaned close, then wrinkled her nose. "All right, so you don't smell too great. What have you been doing?"

"I've been riding hard since midday yesterday. Now, in what other thing do I fail?"

"You dress better than I do. A very important issue with me."

Miles plunked a small, jangly bag in her lap. "Hire a seamstress. Anything else?"

Abby fingered the money in the bag. She looked at Sir Sweetums, who was watching her silently. Then she looked up at the stars; she couldn't look at Miles.

"I want it all," she said, quietly. "Kids, a garden, Christmas." She cleared her throat. "And a husband who loves me."

"And I would not?" he asked.

She looked at him. "You left. What am I supposed to understand from that? I tell you what is most important to me, you ignore me, and then you leave."

"I went to fetch a priest."

She frowned at him. "Why? So you could have me exorcised?"

Miles smiled. "Nay, Abby, so he could see us properly wed."

She blinked.

"Wed?" she asked.

"Aye."

"I—"

He took her hand in both of his. "I want you, Abby, in my life and in my bed. I vow always to smell more poorly than you. I give you my solemn word that you will always have the majority of garments in our trunk." He lifted his hand and touched her cheek. "I want to give you what you want, Abby. I want to give you a home and a family."

She looked at him. It was hard, but she made herself look at him and ask about what meant the most to her.

"And what about love? Between us?"

He smiled, and the tenderness of it went straight to her heart. "I think I began to fall in love with you from the moment I first clapped eyes on you standing at my gates. Every breath I've taken since then has just convinced me that life with you is infinitely more joyful than life without you." He raised her hand to his lips. "My sweet Abby, how can you think I would offer you any less?"

"Oh, Miles," she said. It was all she'd ever wanted to hear. She threw her arms around his neck, closed her eyes and let her tears slip down her cheeks. "Oh, Miles."

"I want you to stay," he whispered, putting his arms around her and hugging her. "I'm half-afraid to ask you to give up the future for me." He pulled back and looked at her. "Will you? I haven't much to offer you, yet."

She looped her arms around his neck and smiled at him, feeling joy well up in her heart. "All I really want," she said, blinking back the tears that stung her eyes, "is you."

"You won't miss chocolate?"

"I hear making love is a good substitute."

Miles laughed. "Perhaps in our travels someday we'll learn the truth of it. Until then, can you make do?"

"Yes."

"And you'll wed me?"

"Yes."

"Finally," Sir Sweetums exclaimed, triumphantly. "Well done, Miles, old boy! Finally, someone to take care of my beloved Abigail!"

"I don't need to be taken care of—"

Miles kissed her.

"See?" Abby mumbled. She made a concentrated effort to pull away so she could point out that such barbaric practices were most definitely not in the agreement, but somehow she found herself mesmerized by the feeling of his mouth on hers.

All right. If he wanted to kiss her into submission, she'd let him. Now and then.

"Perhaps, Sir Sweetums," Miles said, when he let her up for air, "Abby might be more amenable to the idea of keeping me in line, rather than the opposite."

Sir Sweetums considered. "Well, Garretts *do* do that sort of thing."

Miles' eyes began to water. "The first thing she might do is remove me from your presence, my good cat. No offense, of course."

Sir Sweetums drew back at Miles' hearty sneeze. "Well, yes, perhaps that would be wise. I'll be on my way now."

"Oh," Abby said, holding out her hand, "don't go."

"But I must, my dear. You are safely settled. My task is finished."

"But," Abby said, "don't you want to see how our lives turn out? What if we have rotten kids?"

Sir Sweetums smiled again, a cheshire cat smile. "I'm a permanent member of the Guardian Feline Association, my dear. We're always about, lending a paw when needed. Now that you're here, I daresay I'll be popping into medieval England more regularly."

"Always on Christmas Eve," Miles said with another sneeze. "I doubt anything else during the year will give me quite the same start as watching you speak."

Sir Sweetums lifted a paw in farewell. "Until next year, then. God be with you, my dears!"

Sir Sweetums vanished. Abby looked at Miles with a watery smile.

"Hell of a cat, huh?"

Miles laughed. "Indeed, my love, he certainly is. Now, I believe you and I have some unfinished business below with a priest."

She followed him down the tight staircase to find the priest standing near Miles' inadequate bonfire, shivering. Abby took one last look around the hall and shook her head. The place was a dump. It made her apartment look like a four-star hotel suite.

Then Miles stopped, looked down at her, and smiled. He held out his hand for her.

Abby put her hand in his. The floor squished under her Keds as she let Miles lead her to the priest. Maybe she would ask for a shovel for Christmas next year. Why hadn't she thought to stuff a can of disinfectant in her jacket before she'd left the twentieth century?

Abby came to from her contemplation of Miles' floor to find the priest looking at her, waiting for her to give some sort of answer in the affirmative to the question of whether or not she wanted Miles and medieval England for the rest of her life.

She looked up at Miles. "Shouldn't your parents be here?"

Miles shrugged. "They'll learn of it soon enough."

Abby looked at the abbot, who seemed to be warning her with his eyes alone that she was sentencing herself to a life with a condemned heretic and shouldn't she really give it a few more minutes' thought?

"I'll take him," she blurted out.

Miles hustled the priest out the door before anyone had a chance to say anything else. Abby squished her way closer to the bonfire. She'd just gotten herself married to a man some seven hundred years older than she. Talk about a May-December romance! She shivered. Hopefully his family was as open-minded as he seemed to be. She heard Miles stomping his feet outside the front door and she took a deep breath. He didn't seem to be worried about what his parents would say. They would just have to cross that bridge when they came to it.

Abby rolled her eyes. Hadn't a bridge been what had started her entire adventure?

The front door opened and Abby gave up worrying about Miles' parents. She was married now and Garretts did do it after they were married. Frequently. With enthusiasm. Her grandmother had been very clear on that.

Abby stood up straight and planted her hands on her waist. No time like the present to get down to business.

And what wonderful business it promised to be.

Chapter Eight

Miles saw the abbot comfortably ensconced in the gate-house, then returned to the hall. He stood at the threshold and looked back over his bailey. Already, his mind was overflowing with ideas for improvement. He couldn't subject Abigail to life in these conditions. He would make Speningethorpe as modern as he could, for Abigail's sake.

He stomped his muddy boots to clean them, entered his hall, and closed the door behind him. Abigail was standing next to the fire, hands on her waist. Ah, so she was prepared to do battle again. Miles leaned back against the wood and smiled. Saints, what a woman he was blessed with. His life with her would be one joy after another.

After they survived the next few hours, that is. Miles folded his arms across his chest and contemplated his next action. They were wed legally enough. To be sure, he wanted to bed her, but was it too soon?

"Hey," she said, frowning. "Why are you over there?"

"I'm watching you," he replied, with a smile.

"I'm cuter up close."

Miles laughed as he crossed the floor. "You're fetching from any distance, my lady." He pulled her into his arms and held her close. "God bless that bloody Sir Sweetums for bringing you to me."

"I couldn't agree more."

Miles held her for several minutes in silence. After a time, he began to feel quite warm. He jerked away from Abigail and gave himself the once-over to make sure none of him was on fire. Abigail was looking at him as if he'd lost his wits.

"I was growing warm," he offered.

Her eyes twinkled merrily. "Nothing seems to be smol-dering, Miles."

He looked at her, feeling exceedingly uncomfortable. What was he to say, that his warmth had definitely not come from any fire? Abigail tilted her head to one side and looked at him appraisingly.

"You shaved," she noted.

He nodded. "And had a wash outside," he added. "But I'm sure you still smell better than I do."

She laughed. "Thank you. I think."

Miles nudged a piece of slimy hay with his toe. "We could kiss." He looked at her from under his eyelashes.

"We could."

"I don't want to rush you, Abby."

She shook her head, with an amused smile. "You aren't. Garretts generally do it right after the ceremony. It comes from having to wait."

"I see—" Miles trailed off. Abby had stepped up to him and put her arms around him. What was she about?

"Don't worry," she whispered, still smiling. "I'm just going to lay one on you."

He realized, belatedly, that he wasn't prepared for her actions. He and Abigail had kissed often enough, but this kiss rocked him to the core. Perhaps it was because he knew it could definitely lead to other things. Miles threw his arms around her and held on.

Too soon, she allowed him to breathe. He blinked.

"I think," he managed, "I would like to have another of those laid on me."

She obliged him. Miles clung to her and hoped he wouldn't embarrass himself by having his knees buckle under him.

He'd planned to give her a goodly while to accustom herself fully to him, perhaps even a few days, but if she didn't stop kissing him thusly, he sincerely doubted he would be able to do much but hold onto the ragged edges of his wits. And, after all, Garretts did seem to have a schedule about these things. If Abigail wanted him now, who was he to say her nay?

He tore his mouth away. "I'm going to fall down soon, I think. Perhaps we could retire to the bed and go with the flow for a time."

Abigail laughed. "What is your family going to think when they hear you talking like a twentieth-century guy?"

"They'll think I've gone daft," he said, leading her to his bed and lying down beside her. "You should have seen the look the abbot cast my way at Seakirk when I told him to get the lead out."

"And where is the friar in question?"

"In the little room above the gatehouse," he said. He buried his hands in her hair and turned her face to his. He smiled. He'd been itching to get his hands in her hair for what seemed like years.

"Is he just a junior priest, then?" she asked.

"Nay. He's a powerful abbot."

She choked. "I see your nefarious reputation has its advantages."

He grinned at her. "Are you sorry you wed with such a one as I?"

"No, Dastardly Dan, I'm not," she said, tugging on his ear. "Come here and kiss me, you bad man."

How could he refuse? He kissed her as she wished, then he kissed her as he wished. Then he wished for less clothing between them.

"Oh, my," she said, when his hand trailed over her increasingly bare flesh.

"Indeed," he said with a shiver, as her cold fingers wandered over his chest. He would have to build better fireplaces. Perhaps he would raze the bloody keep to the ground and start over again. Abigail's hands found the warmth of his back and he yelped. Aye, more heat was surely a necessity he would see to as soon as possible.

When tunics had been discarded, he pulled her close to him and relished the feel of her bare skin against his.

"Oh, Abby," he whispered, closing his mouth over hers.

She was trembling. He hoped it was from passion and

not fear. He knew it couldn't be from the cold. He was hotter than if he'd been standing in the midst of a pile of kindling.

He kissed and caressed her until both their breaths were coming in gasps. Then Abigail tore her mouth from his.

"Did you hear something?"

"Nay," he said, trying to recapture her mouth.

"It's a thumping noise, Miles."

"That's the blood pounding in your ears. 'Tis passion, Abby."

She eluded his lips. "Those are fists pounding on your gates, bucko. It isn't passion, it's company."

Miles lifted his head and frowned. "Damn."

Abigail froze. "Bad guys?"

Miles looked down at her grimly. "Knocking? Doubtful, my love. Enemies generally prefer a sneak attack."

"Then who could it be?" she asked, reaching for her tunic.

"My bloody sire, most likely." Why Rhys had chosen this precise moment for a visit . . . Miles growled. "I'm going to kill him for the interruption."

Her smile started in her eyes. "I really like you a lot."

He kissed her again, for good measure, then tore himself away and rose. He donned his tunic and waited while Abigail did the same.

"We may as well go let him in," he grumbled. "He'll pound all day if we don't."

"What are you going to tell him about me?" she asked. She looked very worried.

He shrugged. "We'll tell them you're from Michigan."

"Don't I have to be some kind of royalty to marry you?" she asked. She was starting to wheeze again.

Miles gathered her close. "As I'm hardly royalty myself, nay, you needn't be. But we can make you such, if you like." He pulled back and grinned at her. "What shall you be? Princess of Freezing Bluff?"

"I don't know why you think this is so funny," she said, her teeth chattering.

Miles laughed and kissed her. "'Tis merely my sire, Abby. He will love you because you are you. We'll tell him you're from Michigan, which is a very long way away, and that you have no family nearby. You were out, lost your way, and wound up at my hall. That's truth enough for the moment. We'll worry about the rest later."

"If you say so."

"Trust me. Now, let's go let the irritating old man in."

He hadn't taken ten steps when the front door burst open and not only his father, but his father and all four of his brothers burst into the hall, swords drawn, looking for all the world as if they'd expected a battle.

Rhys pulled up short and gaped. Robin, Nicholas, Montgomery, and John all did the same, piling up behind their father and almost sending him sprawling. Once the armored group of five regained their collective balance, a hush descended.

"So, 'tis as the abbot said," Robin whispered, in disbelief. "He *did* find a wench daft enough to wed him."

Rhys silenced his eldest son with an elbow to the ribs, then looked at Miles assessingly.

"I assumed I would come and find you overrun by ruffians, since you sent back your guardsmen."

"Nay, I am well," Miles said, fighting his smile.

Rhys nodded. "I can see why you wanted the hall to yourself."

"Aye," Miles agreed, "I daresay you can."

"Saints, she's fetching," Montgomery and John said together.

Miles scowled. His younger brothers were twins, and randy ones at that. He put an arm possessively around his wife.

"Aye, she is," he growled. "And she wed *me.*"

"Poor girl," Robin said, with a regretful shake of his head. "Montgomery, go fetch Mother and the girls so they can offer Miles' bride some well-needed comfort. I've no doubt she's had a very *trying* day."

Miles growled at Robin. His eldest brother sent a nasty grin back his way. Miles turned his attention back to his sire. He watched his father chew on the facts for a moment or two and come to a decision. Rhys resheathed his sword and crossed the hall. He took Abigail's hand and raised it to his lips.

"Well met, daughter," he said, with a gentle smile. "My son smiles, so I must assume you have made him do so. Now, how does he sit with you? Tolerably well?"

"Oh," Abigail said faintly, "I think he's wonderful."

Miles beamed at his father. "She has excellent taste, Papa, don't you think?"

Rhys laughed. "Saints, Miles, here I thought I would find you shut up in this pile of stones like a hermit, and now I find I've interrupted the post-nuptial festivities."

"Aye," Miles said, remembering why he'd been irritated with his sire. "Your timing is, as usual, very poor."

He would have said quite a bit more, but he didn't have the chance, for his mother, sisters, sister-in law, and numerous nieces and nephews had entered the hall, along with the abbot, several people who weren't family but thought they were, and an army of servants. Miles groaned. Where was he going to put all these souls? And where was he going to find privacy with Abigail?

"Peachy," he muttered to Abigail, then threw his father a very disgruntled look. He received a wink and a hearty laugh in return. Miles scowled and turned to watch his mother come toward him. He had the feeling, much to his further disgruntlement, that once the introductions were made, it would be the last he would see of his wife for quite some time.

Abby staggered under the onslaught of people. Once Miles' mother had entered the room, chaos erupted. If her beauty hadn't been enough to do it, the way she herded the men into work parties certainly would have. She was followed by at least two dozen people who were dressed very nicely, and at least a dozen who Abby surmised must be servants. Miles' mother came to her immediately.

"I'm Gwen," she said, "and I can see why Miles kept you a secret, for he would have been fighting his brothers to have you."

"Oh," Abby said, clutching Miles' hand, "I think I would have liked him best anyway."

Miles laughed and gave Abby's hand a gentle squeeze. "I think she loves me, Mama."

"How on earth were you fortunate enough to find her, my son?"

"Abby chased her cat into my moat."

Abby willed Miles to look at her, and he did—finally. He winked, then leaned down to kiss her.

"I'm afraid the only privacy we may have is in the stables. When I can get you away from the women of my family, that is."

"Shucks, what's a little hay between friends?"

"My thoughts exactly—"

And that was the last she saw of him for quite some time. Gwen took her in hand. Abby found nothing but affection and acceptance in Gwen's aqua eyes, and soon felt completely at ease with the woman. Gwen formally introduced her to Miles' four brothers, his twin sister, and his elder sister. Then there were the in-laws, which was confusing in its own right; grandchildren, and then non-family members who seemed to feel just like family. Abby promptly forgot everyone's name. Oh, the hazards of too many in-laws!

"Greenery!" one older boy yelled. "Where does it go, Grandmother Gwen?"

Gwen linked arms with Abby. " 'Tis Abby's hall, Phillip. She'll tell you where she likes it."

"And we've things for you," said another in-law, a woman who looked like a younger version of Gwen. "I'm Amanda. Miles and I fight, but not as badly as I fight with

Robin. Oddly enough, I had the feeling Miles would marry soon. I think I must have brought these with you in mind." She held up a basket filled with, of all things, solid soap, clean linen towels, and a comb. Abby sniffed the soap cautiously, then smiled in relief.

"Oh, *thank* you."

"Aye, and I've things for you, too," another young woman said. She had long, blond hair and dusty green eyes. "I'm Anne, Robin's wife, and I never fight with Miles. I think he's wonderful, even when he's being moody. I daresay you've already begun to tame him. He seems very cheerful."

"Well, I—" Abby began, then she was distracted by clothes that didn't look like Miles' hand-me-downs.

Then it was off to a corner behind a makeshift screen. She was given hot water and no privacy for a sponge bath, but the clothes more than made up for that. No sooner had she been properly dressed and coiffed, than heavenly smells began to waft from the kitchen.

She came around the screen to find that the hall had been transformed. The floor had been freshened up, tables had been set up and covered with tablecloths, and food was starting to pour from the kitchen. Greenery had been scattered all over the hall and even a tapestry had been hung.

She looked for Miles. He was standing near the bonfire listening to his younger brothers, who seemed to be tumbling over each other trying to tell him some story. Then he caught sight of her. Abby blushed as Miles left his siblings talking to thin air and came directly across the room, pushing family and furniture out of his way to get to her. She smiled weakly.

"Like the dress?"

His mouth came down on hers. Well, that was answer enough. She clutched his arms as he finally lifted his head. Once she could focus again, she looked at him.

"I guess you do."

He smiled down at her. "Aye, I do." He stepped back a

pace, made her a low bow, then offered her his arm. "Shall we partake of the festivities?"

Abby took his arm and let him lead her to the table. Within minutes, the table was overflowing with food. A small handful of musicians produced instruments and began to play. The festivities were soon going full swing. Abby had barely started to eat before she found herself being paid more attention to than the medieval celebration going on around her.

Toddlers toddled over to her. Children wanted to touch her hair and listen to her talk with her strange accent. And once they'd done that to their satisfaction, they simply wanted to be near her. Miles' family hovered around her, telling her stories about her new husband, asking her questions about her own life. His older brothers repeatedly asked why she'd settled for such a clod of dirt when there were two perfectly good de Piaget brothers still looking for wives.

After quite a while spent at the table, the company adjourned to chairs encircling the fire. Abby leaned back against her chair and looked around her, hardly able to believe the twists and turns life had sent her along over the past few days. She shook her head, marveling. Her grandmother's favorite saying had been "All in due time." That, of course, had always been preceded by a bout of serious headshaking. Abby understood completely. Who would have thought she would find the man of her dreams and the Christmas she'd always wanted seven hundred years in the past? Maybe *due time* had a sense of humor—but what a wonderful sense of humor! So Miles' hall wasn't exactly something Currier and Ives would have put to canvas; this was so much better because it was real.

Food abounded. Family was gathered around her, a family that came with helpful hands, warm hearts, and teasing smiles. She had a tree in the form of the greenery Miles' family had lovingly brought to spruce up his castle. The fire sparkled enough for hundreds of twinkling lights. And her best gift sat next to her, running his thumb over the back of her hand and looking at her with love in his eyes. He had given her so much more than a roof over her head, his own clothes to wear, and inedible stew. Abby smiled at him through her tears.

"Thank you," she said simply.

He smiled in return. "For all these appropriately Christmassy items? For my family?"

She nodded. "And, most especially, for you."

"God bless my surly and moody self," he said, with a gentle smile. He put his arm around her and pulled her close. "I love you," he whispered into her ear.

"I love you, too."

He pulled back and looked at her. "I don't know what my life would have been like without you . . . ha . . . ha . . . . ha-hachoo!"

"Uncle Miles!" a young boy said, frothing at the mouth with excitement. "Look what I found outside!"

"Oh, kittens," Abby exclaimed. "How wonderful!"

"Won—wonder—hachoo!" Miles sneezed. "Dab cats!"

"Oh, Kendrick," Amanda exclaimed, following hard on the boy's heels, "put the kittens back outside!" She looked at Abby apologetically. "His father put him up to it, of course, the lout." She turned to the brother in question and glared. "Saints, Robin, you know Miles can't bear the smell of the beasties!"

Robin didn't appear to care. He was tipped back in his chair, laughing heartily. Or at least he was until Amanda marched over, put her foot on the front of his chair, and shoved.

"Out, now," Miles said, hauling Abby to her feet. "Before the war erupts."

"Where to?" she asked as he dragged her toward the door, away from his laughing family and bellowing brother.

"The stables. They'll never look for us there."

Abby fled with him outside and out to the stables. They

stopped finally in front of a stall. The hay was covered with a blanket and a candle had been left lit on a stool.

"My mother obviously thinks nothing of my horseflesh," Miles grumbled. "She could have burned the whole bloody place down."

"Your mother did this?"

He smiled down at her and drew her into his arms. "She was freshly wed once too. She likes you very much, else she wouldn't have bothered. Come to think of it, I like you very much too."

"How convenient," she said, smiling up at him.

"I thought so," he said, lowering his mouth to hers. "Now, where were we before my family overran our wedding bed?"

And as Miles made her his in that very chilly stable, Abby decided several things.

One, central heating just wasn't all it was cracked up to be.

Two, condemned heretics made mighty fine lovers.

And three, Sir Sweetums deserved a promotion!

Epilogue

Sir Maximillian Sweetums reclined on a most comfortable cloud, contemplating his well-deserved repast. He brought a particularly plump Tender Vittle to his aristocratic nose and sniffed critically. Ah, the bouquet was excellent! He partook with relish.

"So, Boss, you finished up de job?"

Sir Sweetums was in such a fine mood, he didn't begrudge the bulldog his interruption of afternoon tea. "Yes, dear Bruno, my task is finished. The Abigail is well settled."

"Yeah, Boss, but dose kids she's gonna get." The bulldog shuddered. "Yikes!"

"Never fear, Bruno. I'll be there to aid her when she needs it. And I'll have a care for her little ones. All part of the job, you know."

Bruno struggled to scratch behind his ear. Once he managed to get his foot within range, he scratched thoughtfully.

"Dese jobs, Boss. Uh, don't you need some help sometimes?"

"Indeed, Bruno, it is a most taxing venture," Sir Sweetums agreed. "Never a moment to sit idly by."

"Den, uh, Boss, I was wonderin', you know, when . . . uh—"

The bulldog was positively aquiver with nervousness. Sir Sweetums looked at his loyal companion and felt compassion stir within his feline breast.

"Perhaps the next assignment, dear boy. It looks to be quite a tangle to unravel."

"Golly, Boss, really? I really get to go dis time?"

Bruno leaped up in joy, lost his balance and fell through half a dozen clouds before he remembered how it all worked.

Sir Sweetums sighed. It would be a very long unraveling indeed, with Bruno aboard.

"More cream, Boss?" Bruno bellowed happily from quite a distance. "Anyting else I can get yous?"

"Perhaps something from a different galaxy, my friend," Sir Sweetums called.

Bruno bounded off enthusiastically. Sir Sweetums resettled himself to enjoy his peace and quiet. Yes, indeed, how happy The Abigail and The Miles were together. Sir Sweetums basked in the glow of a task well finished. The tranquillity was, of course, destined to last only as long as it took The Abigail to produce a child or two.

Bruno was, unfortunately, very correct about the offspring. Yikes! was the word indeed.

But never fear, dear reader, never fear! Sir Sweetums knew that The Abigail and her dashing Sir Miles would weather any storm together and love each other more for the surviving of it. In time he would, as a member of the Guardian Feline Association, have The Abigail's darkhaired, gray-eyed children to watch over. With any luck at all, they wouldn't inherit The Miles' propensity for sneezing at the slightest provocation. Sir Sweetums smiled.

It was indeed a wonderful afterlife!

TIMELESS

*Four breathtaking tales of hearts
that reach across time—for love...*

Linda Lael Miller, the *New York Times*
bestselling author, takes a vintage dress-shop
owner on a breathtaking adventure in medieval
England—where bewitching love awaits...

Diana Bane unlocks the secret love behind
Maggie's taunting dreams of a clan war from
centuries past...

Anna Jennet's heroine takes a plunge into
the sea from the cliffs of Cornwall—and falls
back in time, into the arms of a heroic knight...

Elaine Crawford finds time is of the
essence when an engaged workaholic inherits a
California ranch   a place she's seen somewhere
before...

____0-425-13701-5/$4.99